SELECTED STORIES OF BRET HARTE: THE OUTCASTS OF POKER FLAT AND 20 OTHER STORIES
BY
Bret Harte

SELECTED STORIES OF BRET HARTE: THE OUTCASTS OF POKER FLAT AND 20 OTHER STORIES

Published by Lasso Press

New York City, NY

First published 1900

Copyright © Lasso Press, 2015

All rights reserved

ABOUT LASSO PRESS

<u>Lasso Press</u> brings the Wild West back to life with the greatest Western classics ever put to paper.

Introduction

America has always had a fascination with the Wild West, and schoolchildren grow up learning about famous Westerners like Wyatt Earp, Buffalo Bill, Wild Bill Hicock, as well as the infamous shootout at O.K. Corral. Pioneering and cowboys and Indians have been just as popular in Hollywood, with Westerners helping turn John Wayne and Clint Eastwood into legends on the silver screen. HBO's Deadwood, about the historical 19th century mining town on the frontier was popular last decade.

Not surprisingly, a lot has been written about the west, and one of the best known writers about the west in the 19th century was Francis Bret Harte (1836-1902), who wrote poetry and short stories during his literary career. Harte was on the west coast by the 1860s, placing himself in perfect position to document and depict frontier life.

Selected Stories of Bret Harte

THE LUCK OF ROARING CAMP

There was commotion in Roaring Camp. It could not have been a fight, for in 1850 that was not novel enough to have called together the entire settlement. The ditches and claims were not only deserted, but "Tuttle's grocery" had contributed its gamblers, who, it will be remembered, calmly continued their game the day that French Pete and Kanaka Joe shot each other to death over the bar in the front room. The whole camp was collected before a rude cabin on the outer edge of the clearing. Conversation was carried on in a low tone, but the name of a woman was frequently repeated. It was a name familiar enough in the camp,—"Cherokee Sal."

Perhaps the less said of her the better. She was a coarse and, it is to be feared, a very sinful woman. But at that time she was the only woman in Roaring Camp, and was just then lying in sore extremity, when she most needed the ministration of her own sex. Dissolute, abandoned, and irreclaimable, she was yet suffering a martyrdom hard enough to bear even when veiled by sympathizing womanhood, but now terrible in her loneliness. The primal curse had come to her in that original isolation which must have made the punishment of the first transgression so dreadful. It was, perhaps, part of the expiation of her sin that, at a moment when she most lacked her sex's intuitive tenderness and care, she met only the half-contemptuous faces of her masculine associates. Yet a few of the spectators were, I think, touched by her sufferings. Sandy Tipton thought it was "rough on Sal," and, in the contemplation of her condition, for a moment rose superior to the fact that he had an ace and two bowers in his sleeve.

It will be seen also that the situation was novel. Deaths were by no means uncommon in Roaring Camp, but a birth was a new thing. People had been dismissed the camp effectively, finally, and with no possibility of return; but this was the first time that anybody had been introduced AB INITIO. Hence the excitement.

"You go in there, Stumpy," said a prominent citizen known as "Kentuck," addressing one of the loungers. "Go in there, and see what you kin do. You've had experience in them things."

Perhaps there was a fitness in the selection. Stumpy, in other climes, had been the putative head of two families; in fact, it was owing to some legal informality in these proceedings that Roaring Camp—a city of refuge—was indebted to his company. The crowd approved the choice, and Stumpy was wise enough to bow to the majority. The door closed on the extempore surgeon and midwife, and Roaring Camp sat down outside, smoked its pipe, and awaited the issue.

The assemblage numbered about a hundred men. One or two of these were actual fugitives from justice, some were criminal, and all were reckless. Physically they exhibited no indication of their past lives and character. The greatest scamp had a Raphael face, with a profusion of blonde hair; Oakhurst, a gambler, had the melancholy air and intellectual abstraction of a

Hamlet; the coolest and most courageous man was scarcely over five feet in height, with a soft voice and an embarrassed, timid manner. The term "roughs" applied to them was a distinction rather than a definition. Perhaps in the minor details of fingers, toes, ears, etc., the camp may have been deficient, but these slight omissions did not detract from their aggregate force. The strongest man had but three fingers on his right hand; the best shot had but one eye.

Such was the physical aspect of the men that were dispersed around the cabin. The camp lay in a triangular valley between two hills and a river. The only outlet was a steep trail over the summit of a hill that faced the cabin, now illuminated by the rising moon. The suffering woman might have seen it from the rude bunk whereon she lay,—seen it winding like a silver thread until it was lost in the stars above.

A fire of withered pine boughs added sociability to the gathering. By degrees the natural levity of Roaring Camp returned. Bets were freely offered and taken regarding the result. Three to five that "Sal would get through with it;" even that the child would survive; side bets as to the sex and complexion of the coming stranger. In the midst of an excited discussion an exclamation came from those nearest the door, and the camp stopped to listen. Above the swaying and moaning of the pines, the swift rush of the river, and the crackling of the fire rose a sharp, querulous cry,—a cry unlike anything heard before in the camp. The pines stopped moaning, the river ceased to rush, and the fire to crackle. It seemed as if Nature had stopped to listen too.

The camp rose to its feet as one man! It was proposed to explode a barrel of gunpowder; but in consideration of the situation of the mother, better counsels prevailed, and only a few revolvers were discharged; for whether owing to the rude surgery of the camp, or some other reason, Cherokee Sal was sinking fast. Within an hour she had climbed, as it were, that rugged road that led to the stars, and so passed out of Roaring Camp, its sin and shame, forever. I do not think that the announcement disturbed them much, except in speculation as to the fate of the child. "Can he live now?" was asked of Stumpy. The answer was doubtful. The only other being of Cherokee Sal's sex and maternal condition in the settlement was an ass. There was some conjecture as to fitness, but the experiment was tried. It was less problematical than the ancient treatment of Romulus and Remus, and apparently as successful.

When these details were completed, which exhausted another hour, the door was opened, and the anxious crowd of men, who had already formed themselves into a queue, entered in single file. Beside the low bunk or shelf, on which the figure of the mother was starkly outlined below the blankets, stood a pine table. On this a candle-box was placed, and within it, swathed in staring red flannel, lay the last arrival at Roaring Camp. Beside the candle-box was placed a hat. Its use was soon indicated. "Gentlemen," said Stumpy, with a singular mixture of authority and EX OFFICIO complacency,—"gentlemen will please pass in at the front door, round the table, and out at the back door. Them as wishes to contribute anything toward the orphan will find a hat handy." The first man entered with his hat on; he uncovered, however, as he looked about him, and so unconsciously set an example to the next. In such communities good and bad actions are catching. As the procession filed in comments were audible,—criticisms addressed perhaps rather to Stumpy in the character of showman; "Is that him?" "Mighty small specimen;" "Has n't more 'n got the color;" "Ain't bigger nor a derringer." The contributions were as characteristic: A silver tobacco box; a doubloon; a navy revolver, silver mounted; a gold specimen; a very beautifully embroidered lady's handkerchief (from Oakhurst the gambler); a diamond breastpin; a diamond ring (suggested by the pin, with the remark from the giver that he "saw that pin and went two diamonds better"); a slung-shot; a Bible (contributor not detected); a golden spur; a silver teaspoon (the initials, I regret to say, were not the giver's); a pair of surgeon's shears; a lancet; a Bank of England note for 5 pounds; and about $200 in loose gold and silver coin. During these proceedings Stumpy maintained a silence as impassive as the dead on his left, a gravity as inscrutable as that of the newly born on his right. Only one incident occurred to break the monotony of the curious procession. As Kentuck bent over the candle-box half curiously, the child turned, and, in a spasm of pain, caught at his groping finger, and held it fast for a moment. Kentuck looked foolish and embarrassed. Something like a blush tried to assert itself in his weather-beaten cheek. "The damned little cuss!" he said, as he extricated his finger, with perhaps more tenderness and care than he might have been deemed capable of showing. He held that finger a little apart from its fellows as he went out, and examined it curiously. The examination provoked the same original remark in regard to the child. In fact, he seemed to enjoy repeating it. "He rastled with my finger," he remarked to Tipton, holding up the member, "the damned little cuss!"

It was four o'clock before the camp sought repose. A light burnt in the cabin where the watchers sat, for Stumpy did not go to bed that night. Nor did Kentuck. He drank quite freely, and related with great gusto his experience, invariably ending with his characteristic condemnation of the newcomer. It seemed to relieve him of any unjust implication of sentiment, and Kentuck had the weaknesses of the nobler sex. When everybody else had gone to bed, he walked down to the river and whistled reflectingly. Then he walked up the gulch past the cabin, still whistling with demonstrative unconcern. At a large redwood-tree he paused and retraced his steps, and again passed the cabin. Halfway down to the river's bank he again paused, and then returned and knocked at the door. It was opened by Stumpy. "How goes it?" said Kentuck, looking past Stumpy toward the candle-box. "All serene!" replied Stumpy. "Anything up?" "Nothing." There was a pause—an embarrassing one—Stumpy still holding the door. Then Kentuck had recourse to his finger, which he held up to Stumpy. "Rastled with it,—the damned little cuss," he said, and retired.

The next day Cherokee Sal had such rude sepulture as Roaring Camp afforded. After her body had been committed to the hillside, there was a formal meeting of the camp to discuss what should be done with her infant. A resolution to adopt it was unanimous and enthusiastic. But an animated discussion in regard to the manner and feasibility of providing for its wants at once sprang up. It was remarkable that the argument partook of none of those fierce personalities with which discussions were usually conducted at Roaring Camp. Tipton proposed that they should send the child to Red Dog,—a distance of forty miles,—where female attention could be procured. But the unlucky suggestion met with fierce and unanimous opposition. It was evident that no plan which entailed parting from their new acquisition would for a moment be entertained. "Besides," said Tom Ryder, "them fellows at Red Dog would swap it, and ring in somebody else on us." A disbelief in the honesty of other camps prevailed at Roaring Camp, as in other places.

The introduction of a female nurse in the camp also met with objection. It was argued that no decent woman could be prevailed to accept Roaring Camp as her home, and the speaker urged that "they didn't want any more of the other kind." This unkind allusion to the defunct mother, harsh as it may seem, was the first spasm of propriety,—the first symptom of the camp's regeneration. Stumpy advanced nothing. Perhaps he felt a certain delicacy in interfering with the selection of a possible successor in office. But when questioned, he averred stoutly that he and "Jinny"—the mammal before alluded to—could manage to rear the child. There was something original, independent, and heroic about the plan that pleased the camp. Stumpy was retained. Certain articles were sent for to Sacramento. "Mind," said the treasurer, as he pressed a bag of gold-dust into the expressman's hand, "the best that can be got,—lace, you know, and filigree-work and frills,—damn the cost!"

Strange to say, the child thrived. Perhaps the invigorating climate of the mountain camp was compensation for material deficiencies. Nature took the foundling to her broader breast. In that rare atmosphere of the Sierra foothills,—that air pungent with balsamic odor, that ethereal cordial at once bracing and exhilarating,—he may have found food and nourishment, or a subtle chemistry that transmuted ass's milk to lime and phosphorus. Stumpy inclined to the belief that it was the latter and good nursing. "Me and that ass," he would say, "has been father and mother to him! Don't you," he would add, apostrophizing the helpless bundle before him, "never go back on us."

By the time he was a month old the necessity of giving him a name became apparent. He had generally been known as "The Kid," "Stumpy's Boy," "The Coyote" (an allusion to his vocal powers), and even by Kentuck's endearing diminutive of "The damned little cuss." But these were felt to be vague and unsatisfactory, and were at last dismissed under another influence. Gamblers and adventurers are generally superstitious, and Oakhurst one day declared that the baby had brought "the luck" to Roaring Camp. It was certain that of late they had been successful. "Luck" was the name agreed upon, with the prefix of Tommy for greater convenience. No allusion was made to the mother, and the father was unknown. "It's better," said the philosophical Oakhurst, "to take a fresh deal all round. Call him Luck, and start him fair." A day was accordingly set apart for the christening. What was meant by this ceremony the reader may imagine who has already gathered some idea of the reckless irreverence of Roaring Camp. The master of ceremonies was one "Boston," a noted wag, and the occasion seemed to promise the greatest facetiousness. This ingenious satirist had spent two days in preparing a burlesque of the Church service, with pointed local allusions. The choir was properly trained, and Sandy Tipton was to stand godfather. But after the procession had marched to the grove with music and banners, and the child had been deposited before a mock altar, Stumpy stepped before the expectant crowd. "It ain't my style to spoil fun, boys," said the little man, stoutly eyeing the faces around him, "but it strikes me that this thing ain't exactly on the squar. It's playing it pretty low down on this yer baby to ring in fun on him that he ain't goin' to understand. And ef there's goin' to be any godfathers round, I'd like to see who's got any better rights than me." A silence followed Stumpy's speech. To the credit of all humorists be it said that the first man to acknowledge its justice was the satirist thus stopped of his fun. "But," said Stumpy, quickly following up his advantage, "we're here for a christening, and we'll have it. I proclaim you Thomas Luck, according to the laws of the United States and the State of California, so help me God." It was the first time that the name of the Deity had been otherwise uttered than profanely in the camp. The form of christening was perhaps even more ludicrous than the satirist had conceived; but strangely enough, nobody saw it and nobody laughed. "Tommy" was christened as seriously as he would have been under a Christian roof and cried and was comforted in as orthodox fashion.

And so the work of regeneration began in Roaring Camp. Almost imperceptibly a change came over the settlement. The cabin assigned to "Tommy Luck"—or "The Luck," as he was more frequently called—first showed signs of improvement. It was kept scrupulously clean and whitewashed. Then it was boarded, clothed, and papered. The rose wood cradle, packed eighty miles by mule, had, in Stumpy's way of putting it, "sorter killed the rest of the furniture." So the rehabilitation of the cabin became a necessity. The men who were in the habit of lounging in at Stumpy's to see "how 'The Luck' got on" seemed to appreciate the change, and in self-defense the rival establishment of "Tuttle's grocery" bestirred itself and imported a carpet and mirrors. The reflections of the latter on the appearance of Roaring Camp tended to produce stricter habits of personal cleanliness. Again Stumpy imposed a kind of quarantine upon those who aspired to the honor and privilege of holding The Luck. It was a cruel mortification to Kentuck—who, in the carelessness of a large nature and the habits of frontier life, had begun to regard all garments as a second cuticle, which, like a snake's, only sloughed off through decay—to be debarred this privilege from certain prudential reasons. Yet such was the subtle influence of innovation that he thereafter appeared regularly every afternoon in a clean shirt and face still shining from his ablutions. Nor were moral and social sanitary laws neglected. "Tommy," who was supposed to spend his whole existence in a persistent attempt to repose, must not be disturbed by noise. The shouting and yelling, which had gained the camp its infelicitous title, were not permitted within hearing distance of Stumpy's. The men conversed in whispers or smoked with Indian gravity. Profanity was tacitly given up in these sacred precincts, and throughout the camp a popular form of expletive, known as "D—n the luck!" and "Curse the luck!" was abandoned, as having a new personal bearing. Vocal music was not interdicted, being supposed to have a soothing, tranquilizing quality; and one song, sung by "Man-o'-War Jack," an English sailor from her

Majesty's Australian colonies, was quite popular as a lullaby. It was a lugubrious recital of the exploits of "the Arethusa, Seventy-four," in a muffled minor, ending with a prolonged dying fall at the burden of each verse, "On b-oo-o-ard of the Arethusa." It was a fine sight to see Jack holding The Luck, rocking from side to side as if with the motion of a ship, and crooning forth this naval ditty. Either through the peculiar rocking of Jack or the length of his song,—it contained ninety stanzas, and was continued with conscientious deliberation to the bitter end,— the lullaby generally had the desired effect. At such times the men would lie at full length under the trees in the soft summer twilight, smoking their pipes and drinking in the melodious utterances. An indistinct idea that this was pastoral happiness pervaded the camp. "This 'ere kind o' think," said the Cockney Simmons, meditatively reclining on his elbow, "is 'evingly." It reminded him of Greenwich.

On the long summer days The Luck was usually carried to the gulch from whence the golden store of Roaring Camp was taken. There, on a blanket spread over pine boughs, he would lie while the men were working in the ditches below. Latterly there was a rude attempt to decorate this bower with flowers and sweet-smelling shrubs, and generally some one would bring him a cluster of wild honeysuckles, azaleas, or the painted blossoms of Las Mariposas. The men had suddenly awakened to the fact that there were beauty and significance in these trifles, which they had so long trodden carelessly beneath their feet. A flake of glittering mica, a fragment of variegated quartz, a bright pebble from the bed of the creek, became beautiful to eyes thus cleared and strengthened, and were invariably pat aside for The Luck. It was wonderful how many treasures the woods and hillsides yielded that "would do for Tommy." Surrounded by playthings such as never child out of fairyland had before, it is to be hoped that Tommy was content. He appeared to be serenely happy, albeit there was an infantine gravity about him, a contemplative light in his round gray eyes, that sometimes worried Stumpy. He was always tractable and quiet, and it is recorded that once, having crept beyond his "corral,"—a hedge of tessellated pine boughs, which surrounded his bed,—he dropped over the bank on his head in the soft earth, and remained with his mottled legs in the air in that position for at least five minutes with unflinching gravity. He was extricated without a murmur. I hesitate to record the many other instances of his sagacity, which rest, unfortunately, upon the statements of prejudiced friends. Some of them were not without a tinge of superstition. "I crep' up the bank just now," said Kentuck one day, in a breathless state of excitement "and dern my skin if he was a-talking to a jay bird as was a-sittin' on his lap. There they was, just as free and sociable as anything you please, a-jawin' at each other just like two cherrybums." Howbeit, whether creeping over the pine boughs or lying lazily on his back blinking at the leaves above him, to him the birds sang, the squirrels chattered, and the flowers bloomed. Nature was his nurse and playfellow. For him she would let slip between the leaves golden shafts of sunlight that fell just within his grasp; she would send wandering breezes to visit him with the balm of bay and resinous gum; to him the tall redwoods nodded familiarly and sleepily, the bumblebees buzzed, and the rooks cawed a slumbrous accompaniment.

Such was the golden summer of Roaring Camp. They were "flush times," and the luck was with them. The claims had yielded enormously. The camp was jealous of its privileges and looked suspiciously on strangers. No encouragement was given to immigration, and, to make their seclusion more perfect, the land on either side of the mountain wall that surrounded the camp they duly preempted. This, and a reputation for singular proficiency with the revolver, kept the reserve of Roaring Camp inviolate. The expressman—their only connecting link with the surrounding world—sometimes told wonderful stories of the camp. He would say, "They've a street up there in 'Roaring' that would lay over any street in Red Dog. They've got vines and flowers round their houses, and they wash themselves twice a day. But they're mighty rough on strangers, and they worship an Ingin baby."

With the prosperity of the camp came a desire for further improvement. It was proposed to build a hotel in the following spring, and to invite one or two decent families to reside there for the sake of The Luck, who might perhaps profit by female companionship. The sacrifice that this concession to the sex cost these men, who were fiercely skeptical in regard to its general virtue and usefulness, can only be accounted for by their affection for Tommy. A few still held out. But the resolve could not be carried into effect for three months, and the minority meekly yielded in the hope that something might turn up to prevent it. And it did.

The winter of 1851 will long be remembered in the foothills. The snow lay deep on the Sierras, and every mountain creek became a river, and every river a lake. Each gorge and gulch was transformed into a tumultuous watercourse that descended the hillsides, tearing down giant trees and scattering its drift and debris along the plain. Red Dog had been twice under water, and Roaring Camp had been forewarned. "Water put the gold into them gulches," said Stumpy. "It been here once and will be here again!" And that night the North Fork suddenly leaped over its banks and swept up the triangular valley of Roaring Camp.

In the confusion of rushing water, crashing trees, and crackling timber, and the darkness which seemed to flow with the water and blot out the fair valley, but little could be done to collect the scattered camp. When the morning broke, the cabin of Stumpy, nearest the river-bank, was gone. Higher up the gulch they found the body of its unlucky owner; but the pride, the hope, the joy, The Luck, of Roaring Camp had disappeared. They were returning with sad hearts when a shout from the bank recalled them.

It was a relief-boat from down the river. They had picked up, they said, a man and an infant, nearly exhausted, about two miles below. Did anybody know them, and did they belong here?

It needed but a glance to show them Kentuck lying there, cruelly crushed and bruised, but still holding The Luck of Roaring Camp in his arms. As they bent over the strangely assorted pair, they saw that the child was cold and pulseless. "He is dead," said one. Kentuck opened his eyes. "Dead?" he repeated feebly. "Yes, my man, and you are dying too." A smile lit the eyes of the expiring Kentuck. "Dying!" he repeated; "he's a-taking me with him. Tell the boys I've got The Luck with me now;" and the strong man, clinging to the frail babe as a drowning man is said to cling to a straw, drifted away into the shadowy river that flows forever to the unknown sea.

* * * * * * * * *

THE OUTCASTS OF POKER FLAT

As Mr. John Oakhurst, gambler, stepped into the main street of Poker Flat on the morning of the twenty-third of November, 1850, he was conscious of a change in its moral atmosphere since the preceding night. Two or three men, conversing earnestly together, ceased as he approached, and exchanged significant glances. There was a Sabbath lull in the air which, in a settlement unused to Sabbath influences, looked ominous.

Mr. Oakhurst's calm, handsome face betrayed small concern in these indications. Whether he was conscious of any predisposing cause was another question. "I reckon they're after somebody," he reflected; "likely it's me." He returned to his pocket the handkerchief with which he had been whipping away the red dust of Poker Flat from his neat boots, and quietly discharged his mind of any further conjecture.

In point of fact, Poker Flat was "after somebody." It had lately suffered the loss of several thousand dollars, two valuable horses, and a prominent citizen. It was experiencing a spasm of virtuous reaction, quite as lawless and ungovernable as any of the acts that had provoked it. A secret committee had determined to rid the town of all improper persons. This was done permanently in regard of two men who were then hanging from the boughs of a sycamore in the gulch, and temporarily in the banishment of certain other objectionable characters. I regret to say that some of these were ladies. It is but due to the sex, however, to state that their impropriety was professional, and it was only in such easily established standards of evil that Poker Flat ventured to sit in judgment.

Mr. Oakhurst was right in supposing that he was included in this category. A few of the committee had urged hanging him as a possible example, and a sure method of reimbursing themselves from his pockets of the sums he had won from them. "It's agin justice," said Jim Wheeler, "to let this yer young man from Roaring Camp—an entire stranger—carry away our money." But a crude sentiment of equity residing in the breasts of those who had been fortunate enough to win from Mr. Oakhurst overruled this narrower local prejudice.

Mr. Oakhurst received his sentence with philosophic calmness, none the less coolly that he was aware of the hesitation of his judges. He was too much of a gambler not to accept Fate. With him life was at best an uncertain game, and he recognized the usual percentage in favor of the dealer.

A body of armed men accompanied the deported wickedness of Poker Flat to the outskirts of the settlement. Besides Mr. Oakhurst, who was known to be a coolly desperate man, and for whose intimidation the armed escort was intended, the expatriated party consisted of a young woman familiarly known as the "Duchess"; another, who had won the title of "Mother Shipton"; and "Uncle Billy," a suspected sluice-robber and confirmed drunkard. The cavalcade provoked no comments from the spectators, nor was any word uttered by the escort. Only, when the gulch which marked the uttermost limit of Poker Flat was reached, the leader spoke briefly and to the point. The exiles were forbidden to return at the peril of their lives.

As the escort disappeared, their pent-up feelings found vent in a few hysterical tears from the Duchess, some bad language from Mother Shipton, and a Parthian volley of expletives from Uncle Billy. The philosophic Oakhurst alone remained silent. He listened calmly to Mother Shipton's desire to cut somebody's heart out, to the repeated statements of the Duchess that she would die in the road, and to the alarming oaths that seemed to be bumped out of Uncle Billy as he rode forward. With the easy good humor characteristic of his class, he insisted upon exchanging his own riding horse, "Five Spot," for the sorry mule which the Duchess rode. But even this act did not draw the party into any closer sympathy. The young woman readjusted her somewhat draggled plumes with a feeble, faded coquetry; Mother Shipton eyed the possessor of "Five Spot" with malevolence, and Uncle Billy included the whole party in one sweeping anathema.

The road to Sandy Bar—a camp that, not having as yet experienced the regenerating influences of Poker Flat, consequently seemed to offer some invitation to the emigrants—lay over a steep mountain range. It was distant a day's severe travel. In that advanced season, the party soon passed out of the moist, temperate regions of the foothills into the dry, cold, bracing air of the Sierras. The trail was narrow and difficult. At noon the Duchess, rolling out of her saddle upon the ground, declared her intention of going no farther, and the party halted.

The spot was singularly wild and impressive. A wooded amphitheater, surrounded on three sides by precipitous cliffs of naked granite, sloped gently toward the crest of another precipice that overlooked the valley. It was, undoubtedly, the most suitable spot for a camp, had camping been advisable. But Mr. Oakhurst knew that scarcely half the journey to Sandy Bar was accomplished, and the party were not equipped or provisioned for delay. This fact he pointed out to his companions curtly, with a philosophic commentary on the folly of "throwing up their hand before the game was played out." But they were furnished with liquor, which in this emergency stood them in place of food, fuel, rest, and prescience. In spite of his remonstrances, it was not long before they were more or less under its influence. Uncle Billy passed rapidly from a bellicose state into one of stupor, the Duchess became maudlin, and Mother Shipton snored. Mr. Oakhurst alone remained erect, leaning against a rock, calmly surveying them.

Mr. Oakhurst did not drink. It interfered with a profession which required coolness, impassiveness, and presence of mind, and, in his own language, he "couldn't afford it." As he gazed at his recumbent fellow exiles, the loneliness begotten of his pariah trade, his habits of life, his very vices, for the first time seriously oppressed him. He bestirred himself in dusting his black clothes, washing his hands and face, and other acts characteristic of his studiously neat habits, and for a moment forgot his annoyance. The thought of deserting his weaker and more pitiable companions never perhaps occurred to him. Yet he could not help feeling the want of that excitement which, singularly enough, was most conducive to that calm equanimity for which he was notorious. He looked at the gloomy walls that rose a thousand feet sheer above the circling pines around him; at the sky, ominously clouded; at the valley below, already deepening into shadow. And, doing so, suddenly he heard his own name called.

A horseman slowly ascended the trail. In the fresh, open face of the newcomer Mr. Oakhurst recognized Tom Simson, otherwise known as the "Innocent" of Sandy Bar. He had met him some months before over a "little game," and had, with perfect equanimity, won the entire fortune—amounting to some forty dollars—of that guileless youth. After the game was finished, Mr. Oakhurst drew the youthful speculator behind the door and thus addressed him: "Tommy, you're a good little man, but you can't gamble worth a cent. Don't try it over again." He then handed him his money back, pushed him gently from the room, and so made a devoted slave of Tom Simson.

There was a remembrance of this in his boyish and enthusiastic greeting of Mr. Oakhurst. He had started, he said, to go to Poker Flat to seek his fortune. "Alone?" No, not exactly alone; in fact (a giggle), he had run away with Piney Woods. Didn't Mr. Oakhurst remember Piney? She that used to wait on the table at the Temperance House? They had been engaged a long time, but old Jake Woods had objected, and so they had run away, and were going to Poker Flat to be married, and here they were. And they were tired out, and how lucky it was they had found a place to camp and company. All this the Innocent delivered rapidly, while Piney, a stout, comely damsel of fifteen, emerged from behind the pine tree, where she had been blushing unseen, and rode to the side of her lover.

Mr. Oakhurst seldom troubled himself with sentiment, still less with propriety; but he had a vague idea that the situation was not fortunate. He retained, however, his presence of mind sufficiently to kick Uncle Billy, who was about to say something, and Uncle Billy was sober enough to recognize in Mr. Oakhurst's kick a superior power that would not bear trifling. He then endeavored to dissuade Tom Simson from delaying further, but in vain. He even pointed out the fact that there was no provision, nor means of making a camp. But, unluckily, the Innocent met this objection by assuring the party that he was provided with an extra mule loaded with provisions and by the discovery of a rude attempt at a log house near the trail. "Piney can stay with Mrs. Oakhurst," said the Innocent, pointing to the Duchess, "and I can shift for myself."

Nothing but Mr. Oakhurst's admonishing foot saved Uncle Billy from bursting into a roar of laughter. As it was, he felt compelled to retire up the canyon until he could recover his gravity. There he confided the joke to the tall pine trees, with many slaps of his leg, contortions of his face, and the usual profanity. But when he returned to the party, he found them seated by a fire— for the air had grown strangely chill and the sky overcast—in apparently amicable conversation. Piney was actually talking in an impulsive, girlish fashion to the Duchess, who was listening with an interest and animation she had not shown for many days. The Innocent was holding forth, apparently with equal effect, to Mr. Oakhurst and Mother Shipton, who was actually relaxing into amiability. "Is this yer a damned picnic?" said Uncle Billy with inward scorn as he surveyed the sylvan group, the glancing firelight, and the tethered animals in the foreground. Suddenly an idea mingled with the alcoholic fumes that disturbed his brain. It was apparently of a jocular nature, for he felt impelled to slap his leg again and cram his fist into his mouth.

As the shadows crept slowly up the mountain, a slight breeze rocked the tops of the pine trees, and moaned through their long and gloomy aisles. The ruined cabin, patched and covered with pine boughs, was set apart for the ladies. As the lovers parted, they unaffectedly exchanged a kiss, so honest and sincere that it might have been heard above the swaying pines. The frail Duchess and the malevolent Mother Shipton were probably too stunned to remark upon this last evidence of simplicity, and so turned without a word to the hut. The fire was replenished, the men lay down before the door, and in a few minutes were asleep.

Mr. Oakhurst was a light sleeper. Toward morning he awoke benumbed and cold. As he stirred the dying fire, the wind, which was now blowing strongly, brought to his cheek that which caused the blood to leave it—snow!

He started to his feet with the intention of awakening the sleepers, for there was no time to lose. But turning to where Uncle Billy had been lying, he found him gone. A suspicion leaped to his brain and a curse to his lips. He ran to the spot where the mules had been tethered; they were no longer there. The tracks were already rapidly disappearing in the snow.

The momentary excitement brought Mr. Oakhurst back to the fire with his usual calm. He did not waken the sleepers. The Innocent slumbered peacefully, with a smile on his good-humored, freckled face; the virgin Piney slept beside her frailer sisters as sweetly as though attended by celestial guardians; and Mr. Oakhurst, drawing his blanket over his shoulders, stroked his mustaches and waited for the dawn. It came slowly in a whirling mist of snowflakes that dazzled and confused the eye. What could be seen of the landscape appeared magically changed. He looked over the valley, and summed up the present and future in two words—"snowed in!"

A careful inventory of the provisions, which, fortunately for the party, had been stored within the hut and so escaped the felonious fingers of Uncle Billy, disclosed the fact that with care and prudence they might last ten days longer. "That is," said Mr. Oakhurst, sotto voce to the Innocent, "if you're willing to board us. If you ain't—and perhaps you'd better not—you can wait till Uncle Billy gets back with provisions." For some occult reason, Mr. Oakhurst could not bring himself to disclose Uncle Billy's rascality, and so offered the hypothesis that he had wandered from the camp and had accidentally stampeded the animals. He dropped a warning to the Duchess and Mother Shipton, who of course knew the facts of their associate's defection.

"They'll find out the truth about us all when they find out anything," he added, significantly, "and there's no good frightening them now."

Tom Simson not only put all his worldly store at the disposal of Mr. Oakhurst, but seemed to enjoy the prospect of their enforced seclusion. "We'll have a good camp for a week, and then the snow'll melt, and we'll all go back together." The cheerful gaiety of the young man, and Mr. Oakhurst's calm, infected the others. The Innocent with the aid of pine boughs extemporized a thatch for the roofless cabin, and the Duchess directed Piney in the rearrangement of the interior with a taste and tact that opened the blue eyes of that provincial maiden to their fullest extent. "I reckon now you're used to fine things at Poker Flat," said Piney. The Duchess turned away sharply to conceal something that reddened her cheeks through its professional tint, and Mother Shipton requested Piney not to "chatter." But when Mr. Oakhurst returned from a weary search for the trail, he heard the sound of happy laughter echoed from the rocks. He stopped in some alarm, and his thoughts first naturally reverted to the whisky, which he had prudently cached. "And yet it don't somehow sound like whisky," said the gambler. It was not until he caught sight of the blazing fire through the still-blinding storm and the group around it that he settled to the conviction that it was "square fun."

Whether Mr. Oakhurst had cached his cards with the whisky as something debarred the free access of the community, I cannot say. It was certain that, in Mother Shipton's words, he "didn't say cards once" during that evening. Haply the time was beguiled by an accordion, produced somewhat ostentatiously by Tom Simson from his pack. Notwithstanding some difficulties attending the manipulation of this instrument, Piney Woods managed to pluck several reluctant melodies from its keys, to an accompaniment by the Innocent on a pair of bone castanets. But the crowning festivity of the evening was reached in a rude camp-meeting hymn, which the lovers, joining hands, sang with great earnestness and vociferation. I fear that a certain defiant tone and Covenanter's swing to its chorus, rather than any devotional quality, caused it speedily to infect the others, who at last joined in the refrain:

"I'm proud to live in the service of the Lord,

And I'm bound to die in His army."

The pines rocked, the storm eddied and whirled above the miserable group, and the flames of their altar leaped heavenward as if in token of the vow.

At midnight the storm abated, the rolling clouds parted, and the stars glittered keenly above the sleeping camp. Mr. Oakhurst, whose professional habits had enabled him to live on the smallest possible amount of sleep, in dividing the watch with Tom Simson somehow managed to take upon himself the greater part of that duty. He excused himself to the Innocent by saying that he had "often been a week without sleep." "Doing what?" asked Tom. "Poker!" replied Oakhurst, sententiously; "when a man gets a streak of luck,—nigger luck—he don't get tired. The luck gives in first. Luck," continued the gambler, reflectively, "is a mighty queer thing. All you know about it for certain is that it's bound to change. And it's finding out when it's going to change that makes you. We've had a streak of bad luck since we left Poker Flat—you come along, and slap you get into it, too. If you can hold your cards right along you're all right. For," added the gambler, with cheerful irrelevance,

"'I'm proud to live in the service of the Lord,

And I'm bound to die in His army.'"

The third day came, and the sun, looking through the white-curtained valley, saw the outcasts divide their slowly decreasing store of provisions for the morning meal. It was one of the peculiarities of that mountain climate that its rays diffused a kindly warmth over the wintry landscape, as if in regretful commiseration of the past. But it revealed drift on drift of snow piled high around the hut—a hopeless, uncharted, trackless sea of white lying below the rocky shores to which the castaways still clung. Through the marvelously clear air the smoke of the pastoral village of Poker Flat rose miles away. Mother Shipton saw it, and from a remote pinnacle of her rocky fastness hurled in that direction a final malediction. It was her last vituperative attempt, and perhaps for that reason was invested with a certain degree of sublimity. It did her good, she privately informed the Duchess. "Just you go out there and cuss, and see." She then set herself to the task of amusing "the child," as she and the Duchess were pleased to call Piney. Piney was no chicken, but it was a soothing and original theory of the pair thus to account for the fact that she didn't swear and wasn't improper.

When night crept up again through the gorges, the reedy notes of the accordion rose and fell in fitful spasms and long-drawn gasps by the flickering campfire. But music failed to fill entirely the aching void left by insufficient food, and a new diversion was proposed by Piney— storytelling. Neither Mr. Oakhurst nor his female companions caring to relate their personal experiences, this plan would have failed too but for the Innocent. Some months before he had chanced upon a stray copy of Mr. Pope's ingenious translation of the ILIAD. He now proposed to narrate the principal incidents of that poem—having thoroughly mastered the argument and fairly forgotten the words—in the current vernacular of Sandy Bar. And so for the rest of that night the Homeric demigods again walked the earth. Trojan bully and wily Greek wrestled in the winds, and the great pines in the canyon seemed to bow to the wrath of the son of Peleus. Mr. Oakhurst listened with quiet satisfaction. Most especially was he interested in the fate of "Ash-heels," as the Innocent persisted in denominating the "swift-footed Achilles."

So with small food and much of Homer and the accordion, a week passed over the heads of the outcasts. The sun again forsook them, and again from leaden skies the snowflakes were sifted over the land. Day by day closer around them drew the snowy circle, until at last they looked from their prison over drifted walls of dazzling white that towered twenty feet above their heads. It became more and more difficult to replenish their fires, even from the fallen trees beside them, now half-hidden in the drifts. And yet no one complained. The lovers turned from the dreary prospect and looked into each other's eyes, and were happy. Mr. Oakhurst settled himself coolly to the losing game before him. The Duchess, more cheerful than she had been, assumed the care of Piney. Only Mother Shipton—once the strongest of the party—seemed to sicken and fade. At midnight on the tenth day she called Oakhurst to her side. "I'm going," she said, in a voice of querulous weakness, "but don't say anything about it. Don't waken the kids. Take the bundle from under my head and open it." Mr. Oakhurst did so. It contained Mother Shipton's rations for the last week, untouched. "Give 'em to the child," she said, pointing to the sleeping Piney. "You've starved yourself," said the gambler. "That's what they call it," said the woman, querulously, as she lay down again and, turning her face to the wall, passed quietly away.

The accordion and the bones were put aside that day, and Homer was forgotten. When the body of Mother Shipton had been committed to the snow, Mr. Oakhurst took the Innocent aside, and showed him a pair of snowshoes, which he had fashioned from the old pack saddle. "There's one chance in a hundred to save her yet," he said, pointing to Piney; "but it's there," he added, pointing toward Poker Flat. "If you can reach there in two days she's safe." "And you?" asked Tom Simson. "I'll stay here," was the curt reply.

The lovers parted with a long embrace. "You are not going, too?" said the Duchess as she saw Mr. Oakhurst apparently waiting to accompany him. "As far as the canyon," he replied. He turned suddenly, and kissed the Duchess, leaving her pallid face aflame and her trembling limbs rigid with amazement.

Night came, but not Mr. Oakhurst. It brought the storm again and the whirling snow. Then the Duchess, feeding the fire, found that someone had quietly piled beside the hut enough fuel to last a few days longer. The tears rose to her eyes, but she hid them from Piney.

The women slept but little. In the morning, looking into each other's faces, they read their fate. Neither spoke; but Piney, accepting the position of the stronger, drew near and placed her arm around the Duchess's waist. They kept this attitude for the rest of the day. That night the storm reached its greatest fury, and, rending asunder the protecting pines, invaded the very hut.

Toward morning they found themselves unable to feed the fire, which gradually died away. As the embers slowly blackened, the Duchess crept closer to Piney, and broke the silence of many hours: "Piney, can you pray?" "No, dear," said Piney, simply. The Duchess, without knowing exactly why, felt relieved, and, putting her head upon Piney's shoulder, spoke no more. And so reclining, the younger and purer pillowing the head of her soiled sister upon her virgin breast, they fell asleep.

The wind lulled as if it feared to waken them. Feathery drifts of snow, shaken from the long pine boughs, flew like white-winged birds, and settled about them as they slept. The moon through the rifted clouds looked down upon what had been the camp. But all human stain, all trace of earthly travail, was hidden beneath the spotless mantle mercifully flung from above.

They slept all that day and the next, nor did they waken when voices and footsteps broke the silence of the camp. And when pitying fingers brushed the snow from their wan faces, you could scarcely have told from the equal peace that dwelt upon them which was she that had sinned. Even the law of Poker Flat recognized this, and turned away, leaving them still locked in each other's arms.

But at the head of the gulch, on one of the largest pine trees, they found the deuce of clubs pinned to the bark with a bowie knife. It bore the following, written in pencil, in a firm hand:

```
            BENEATH THIS TREE
            LIES THE BODY
                 OF
            JOHN OAKHURST,
    WHO STRUCK A STREAK OF BAD LUCK
    ON THE 23D OF NOVEMBER, 1850,
                AND
            HANDED IN HIS CHECKS
    ON THE 7TH DECEMBER, 1850.
```

And pulseless and cold, with a Derringer by his side and a bullet in his heart, though still calm as in life, beneath the snow lay he who was at once the strongest and yet the weakest of the outcasts of Poker Flat.

* * * * * * * * * *

MIGGLES

We were eight, including the driver. We had not spoken during the passage of the last six miles, since the jolting of the heavy vehicle over the roughening road had spoiled the Judge's last poetical quotation. The tall man beside the Judge was asleep, his arm passed through the swaying strap and his head resting upon it—altogether a limp, helpless-looking object, as if he had hanged himself and been cut down too late. The French lady on the back seat was asleep, too, yet in a half-conscious propriety of attitude, shown even in the disposition of the handkerchief which she held to her forehead and which partially veiled her face. The lady from Virginia City, traveling with her husband, had long since lost all individuality in a wild confusion of ribbons, veils, furs, and shawls. There was no sound but the rattling of wheels and the dash of rain upon the roof. Suddenly the stage stopped and we became dimly aware of voices. The driver was evidently in the midst of an exciting colloquy with someone in the road—a colloquy of which such fragments as "bridge gone," "twenty feet of water," "can't pass," were occasionally distinguishable above the storm. Then came a lull, and a mysterious voice from the road shouted the parting adjuration:

"Try Miggles's."

We caught a glimpse of our leaders as the vehicle slowly turned, of a horseman vanishing through the rain, and we were evidently on our way to Miggles's.

Who and where was Miggles? The Judge, our authority, did not remember the name, and he knew the country thoroughly. The Washoe traveler thought Miggles must keep a hotel. We only knew that we were stopped by high water in front and rear, and that Miggles was our rock of refuge. A ten minutes splashing through a tangled by-road, scarcely wide enough for the stage, and we drew up before a barred and boarded gate in a wide stone wall or fence about eight feet high. Evidently Miggles's, and evidently Miggles did not keep a hotel.

The driver got down and tried the gate. It was securely locked. "Miggles! O Miggles!"

No answer.

"Migg-ells! You Miggles!" continued the driver, with rising wrath.

"Migglesy!" joined the expressman, persuasively. "O Miggy! Mig!"

But no reply came from the apparently insensate Miggles. The Judge, who had finally got the window down, put his head out and propounded a series of questions, which if answered categorically would have undoubtedly elucidated the whole mystery, but which the driver evaded by replying that "if we didn't want to sit in the coach all night, we had better rise up and sing out for Miggles."

So we rose up and called on Miggles in chorus; then separately. And when we had finished, a Hibernian fellow-passenger from the roof called for "Maygells!" whereat we all laughed. While we were laughing, the driver cried "Shoo!"

We listened. To our infinite amazement the chorus of "Miggles" was repeated from the other side of the wall, even to the final and supplemental "Maygells."

"Extraordinary echo," said the Judge.

"Extraordinary damned skunk!" roared the driver, contemptuously. "Come out of that, Miggles, and show yourself! Be a man, Miggles! Don't hide in the dark; I wouldn't if I were you, Miggles," continued Yuba Bill, now dancing about in an excess of fury.

"Miggles!" continued the voice. "O Miggles!"

"My good man! Mr. Myghail!" said the Judge, softening the asperities of the name as much as possible. "Consider the inhospitality of refusing shelter from the inclemency of the weather to helpless females. Really, my dear sir—" But a succession of "Miggles," ending in a burst of laughter, drowned his voice.

Yuba Bill hesitated no longer. Taking a heavy stone from the road, he battered down the gate, and with the expressman entered the enclosure. We followed. Nobody was to be seen. In the gathering darkness all that we could distinguish was that we were in a garden—from the rosebushes that scattered over us a minute spray from their dripping leaves—and before a long, rambling wooden building.

"Do you know this Miggles?" asked the Judge of Yuba Bill.

"No, nor, don't want to," said Bill, shortly, who felt the Pioneer Stage Company insulted in his person by the contumacious Miggles.

"But, my dear sir," expostulated the Judge as he thought of the barred gate.

"Lookee here," said Yuba Bill, with fine irony, "hadn't you better go back and sit in the coach till yer introduced? I'm going in," and he pushed open the door of the building.

A long room lighted only by the embers of a fire that was dying on the large hearth at its farther extremity; the walls curiously papered, and the flickering firelight bringing out its grotesque pattern; somebody sitting in a large armchair by the fireplace. All this we saw as we crowded together into the room, after the driver and expressman.

"Hello, be you Miggles?" said Yuba Bill to the solitary occupant.

The figure neither spoke nor stirred. Yuba Bill walked wrathfully toward it, and turned the eye of his coach lantern upon its face. It was a man's face, prematurely old and wrinkled, with very large eyes, in which there was that expression of perfectly gratuitous solemnity which I had sometimes seen in an owl's. The large eyes wandered from Bill's face to the lantern, and finally fixed their gaze on that luminous object, without further recognition.

Bill restrained himself with an effort.

"Miggles! Be you deaf? You ain't dumb anyhow, you know"; and Yuba Bill shook the insensate figure by the shoulder.

To our great dismay, as Bill removed his hand, the venerable stranger apparently collapsed— sinking into half his size and an undistinguishable heap of clothing.

"Well, dern my skin," said Bill, looking appealingly at us, and hopelessly retiring from the contest.

The Judge now stepped forward, and we lifted the mysterious invertebrate back into his original position. Bill was dismissed with the lantern to reconnoiter outside, for it was evident that from the helplessness of this solitary man there must be attendants near at hand, and we all drew around the fire. The Judge, who had regained his authority, and had never lost his conversational amiability—standing before us with his back to the hearth—charged us, as an imaginary jury, as follows:

"It is evident that either our distinguished friend here has reached that condition described by Shakespeare as 'the sere and yellow leaf,' or has suffered some premature abatement of his mental and physical faculties. Whether he is really the Miggles—"

Here he was interrupted by "Miggles! O Miggles! Migglesy! Mig!" and, in fact, the whole chorus of Miggles in very much the same key as it had once before been delivered unto us.

We gazed at each other for a moment in some alarm. The Judge, in particular, vacated his position quickly, as the voice seemed to come directly over his shoulder. The cause, however, was soon discovered in a large magpie who was perched upon a shelf over the fireplace, and who immediately relapsed into a sepulchral silence which contrasted singularly with his previous volubility. It was, undoubtedly, his voice which we had heard in the road, and our friend in the chair was not responsible for the discourtesy. Yuba Bill, who re-entered the room after an unsuccessful search, was loath to accept the explanation, and still eyed the helpless sitter with suspicion. He had found a shed in which he had put up his horses, but he came back dripping and skeptical. "Thar ain't nobody but him within ten mile of the shanty, and that 'ar damned old skeesicks knows it."

But the faith of the majority proved to be securely based. Bill had scarcely ceased growling before we heard a quick step upon the porch, the trailing of a wet skirt, the door was flung open, and with flash of white teeth, a sparkle of dark eyes, and an utter absence of ceremony or diffidence, a young woman entered, shut the door, and, panting, leaned back against it.

"Oh, if you please, I'm Miggles!"

And this was Miggles! this bright-eyed, full-throated young woman, whose wet gown of coarse blue stuff could not hide the beauty of the feminine curves to which it clung; from the chestnut crown of whose head, topped by a man's oilskin sou'wester, to the little feet and ankles, hidden somewhere in the recesses of her boy's brogans, all was grace—this was Miggles, laughing at us, too, in the most airy, frank, offhand manner imaginable.

"You see, boys," said she, quite out of breath, and holding one little hand against her side, quite unheeding the speechless discomfiture of our party, or the complete demoralization of Yuba Bill, whose features had relaxed into an expression of gratuitous and imbecile cheerfulness—"you see, boys, I was mor'n two miles away when you passed down the road. I thought you might pull up here, and so I ran the whole way, knowing nobody was home but Jim,—and—and—I'm out of breath—and—that lets me out."

And here Miggles caught her dripping oilskin hat from her head, with a mischievous swirl that scattered a shower of raindrops over us; attempted to put back her hair; dropped two hairpins in the attempt; laughed and sat down beside Yuba Bill, with her hands crossed lightly on her lap.

The Judge recovered himself first, and essayed an extravagant compliment.

"I'll trouble you for that thar harpin," said Miggles, gravely. Half a dozen hands were eagerly stretched forward; the missing hairpin was restored to its fair owner; and Miggles, crossing the room, looked keenly in the face of the invalid. The solemn eyes looked back at hers with an expression we had never seen before. Life and intelligence seemed to struggle back into the rugged face. Miggles laughed again—it was a singularly eloquent laugh—and turned her black eyes and white teeth once more toward us.

"This afflicted person is—" hesitated the Judge.

"Jim," said Miggles.

"Your father?"

"No."

"Brother?"

"No."

"Husband?"

Miggles darted a quick, half-defiant glance at the two lady passengers who I had noticed did not participate in the general masculine admiration of Miggles, and said gravely, "No; it's Jim."

There was an awkward pause. The lady passengers moved closer to each other; the Washoe husband looked abstractedly at the fire; and the tall man apparently turned his eyes inward for self-support at this emergency. But Miggles's laugh, which was very infectious, broke the silence. "Come," she said briskly, "you must be hungry. Who'll bear a hand to help me get tea?"

She had no lack of volunteers. In a few moments Yuba Bill was engaged like Caliban in bearing logs for this Miranda; the expressman was grinding coffee on the veranda; to myself the arduous duty of slicing bacon was assigned; and the Judge lent each man his good-humored and voluble counsel. And when Miggles, assisted by the Judge and our Hibernian "deck passenger," set the table with all the available crockery, we had become quite joyous, in spite of the rain that beat against windows, the wind that whirled down the chimney, the two ladies who whispered together in the corner, or the magpie who uttered a satirical and croaking commentary on their conversation from his perch above. In the now bright, blazing fire we could see that the walls were papered with illustrated journals, arranged with feminine taste and discrimination. The furniture was extemporized, and adapted from candle boxes and packing-cases, and covered with gay calico, or the skin of some animal. The armchair of the helpless Jim was an ingenious variation of a flour barrel. There was neatness, and even a taste for the picturesque, to be seen in the few details of the long low room.

The meal was a culinary success. But more, it was a social triumph—chiefly, I think, owing to the rare tact of Miggles in guiding the conversation, asking all the questions herself, yet bearing throughout a frankness that rejected the idea of any concealment on her own part, so that we talked of ourselves, of our prospects, of the journey, of the weather, of each other—of everything but our host and hostess. It must be confessed that Miggles's conversation was never elegant, rarely grammatical, and that at times she employed expletives the use of which had generally been yielded to our sex. But they were delivered with such a lighting-up of teeth and eyes, and were usually followed by a laugh—a laugh peculiar to Miggles—so frank and honest that it seemed to clear the moral atmosphere.

Once during the meal we heard a noise like the rubbing of a heavy body against the outer walls of the house. This was shortly followed by a scratching and sniffling at the door. "That's Joaquin," said Miggles, in reply to our questioning glances; "would you like to see him?" Before we could answer she had opened the door, and disclosed a half-grown grizzly, who instantly raised himself on his haunches, with his forepaws hanging down in the popular attitude of mendicancy, and looked admiringly at Miggles, with a very singular resemblance in his manner to Yuba Bill. "That's my watch dog," said Miggles, in explanation. "Oh, he don't bite," she added, as the two lady passengers fluttered into a corner. "Does he, old Toppy?" (the latter remark being addressed directly to the sagacious Joaquin). "I tell you what, boys," continued Miggles after she had fed and closed the door on URSA MINOR, "you were in big luck that Joaquin wasn't hanging round when you dropped in tonight." "Where was he?" asked the Judge. "With me," said Miggles. "Lord love you; he trots round with me nights like as if he was a man."

We were silent for a few moments, and listened to the wind. Perhaps we all had the same picture before us—of Miggles walking through the rainy woods, with her savage guardian at her side. The Judge, I remember, said something about Una and her lion; but Miggles received it as she did other compliments, with quiet gravity. Whether she was altogether unconscious of the admiration she excited—she could hardly have been oblivious of Yuba Bill's adoration—I know not; but her very frankness suggested a perfect sexual equality that was cruelly humiliating to the younger members of our party.

The incident of the bear did not add anything in Miggles's favor to the opinions of those of her own sex who were present. In fact, the repast over, a chillness radiated from the two lady passengers that no pine boughs brought in by Yuba Bill and cast as a sacrifice upon the hearth could wholly overcome. Miggles felt it; and, suddenly declaring that it was time to "turn in," offered to show the ladies to their bed in an adjoining room. "You boys will have to camp out here by the fire as well as you can," she added, "for thar ain't but the one room."

Our sex—by which, my dear sir, I allude of course to the stronger portion of humanity—has been generally relieved from the imputation of curiosity, or a fondness for gossip. Yet I am constrained to say that hardly had the door closed on Miggles than we crowded together, whispering, snickering, smiling, and exchanging suspicions, surmises, and a thousand speculations in regard to our pretty hostess and her singular companion. I fear that we even hustled that imbecile paralytic, who sat like a voiceless Memnon in our midst, gazing with the serene indifference of the Past in his passionate eyes upon our wordy counsels. In the midst of an exciting discussion the door opened again, and Miggles re-entered.

But not, apparently, the same Miggles who a few hours before had flashed upon us. Her eyes were downcast, and as she hesitated for a moment on the threshold, with a blanket on her arm, she seemed to have left behind her the frank fearlessness which had charmed us a moment before. Coming into the room, she drew a low stool beside the paralytic's chair, sat down, drew the blanket over her shoulders, and saying, "If it's all the same to you, boys, as we're rather crowded, I'll stop here tonight," took the invalid's withered hand in her own, and turned her eyes upon the dying fire. An instinctive feeling that this was only premonitory to more confidential relations, and perhaps some shame at our previous curiosity, kept us silent. The rain still beat upon the roof, wandering gusts of wind stirred the embers into momentary brightness, until, in a lull of the elements, Miggles suddenly lifted up her head, and, throwing her hair over her shoulder, turned her face upon the group and asked:

"Is there any of you that knows me?"

There was no reply.

"Think again! I lived at Marysville in '53. Everybody knew me there, and everybody had the right to know me. I kept the Polka saloon until I came to live with Jim. That's six years ago. Perhaps I've changed some."

The absence of recognition may have disconcerted her. She turned her head to the fire again, and it was some seconds before she again spoke, and then more rapidly:

"Well, you see I thought some of you must have known me. There's no great harm done, anyway. What I was going to say was this: Jim here"—she took his hand in both of hers as she spoke—"used to know me, if you didn't, and spent a heap of money upon me. I reckon he spent all he had. And one day—it's six years ago this winter—Jim came into my back room, sat down on my sofy, like as you see him in that chair, and never moved again without help. He was struck all of a heap, and never seemed to know what ailed him. The doctors came and said as how it was caused all along of his way of life—for Jim was mighty free and wild-like—and that he would never get better, and couldn't last long anyway. They advised me to send him to Frisco to the hospital, for he was no good to anyone and would be a baby all his life. Perhaps it was something in Jim's eye, perhaps it was that I never had a baby, but I said 'No.' I was rich then, for I was popular with everybody—gentlemen like yourself, sir, came to see me—and I sold out my business and bought this yer place, because it was sort of out of the way of travel, you see, and I brought my baby here."

With a woman's intuitive tact and poetry, she had, as she spoke, slowly shifted her position so as to bring the mute figure of the ruined man between her and her audience, hiding in the shadow behind it, as if she offered it as a tacit apology for her actions. Silent and expressionless, it yet spoke for her; helpless, crushed, and smitten with the Divine thunderbolt, it still stretched an invisible arm around her.

Hidden in the darkness, but still holding his hand, she went on:

"It was a long time before I could get the hang of things about yer, for I was used to company and excitement. I couldn't get any woman to help me, and a man I dursen't trust; but what with the Indians hereabout, who'd do odd jobs for me, and having everything sent from the North Fork, Jim and I managed to worry through. The Doctor would run up from Sacramento once in a while. He'd ask to see 'Miggles's baby,' as he called Jim, and when he'd go away, he'd say, 'Miggles; you're a trump—God bless you'; and it didn't seem so lonely after that. But the last time he was here he said, as he opened the door to go, 'Do you know, Miggles, your baby will grow up to be a man yet and an honor to his mother; but not here, Miggles, not here!' And I thought he went away sad—and—and—" and here Miggles's voice and head were somehow both lost completely in the shadow.

"The folks about here are very kind," said Miggles, after a pause, coming a little into the light again. "The men from the fork used to hang around here, until they found they wasn't wanted, and the women are kind—and don't call. I was pretty lonely until I picked up Joaquin in the woods yonder one day, when he wasn't so high, and taught him to beg for his dinner; and then thar's Polly—that's the magpie—she knows no end of tricks, and makes it quite sociable of evenings with her talk, and so I don't feel like as I was the only living being about the ranch. And Jim here," said Miggles, with her old laugh again, and coming out quite into the firelight, "Jim—why, boys, you would admire to see how much he knows for a man like him. Sometimes I bring him flowers, and he looks at 'em just as natural as if he knew 'em; and times, when we're sitting alone, I read him those things on the wall. Why, Lord!" said Miggles, with her frank laugh, "I've read him that whole side of the house this winter. There never was such a man for reading as Jim."

"Why," asked the Judge, "do you not marry this man to whom you have devoted your youthful life?"

"Well, you see," said Miggles, "it would be playing it rather low down on Jim, to take advantage of his being so helpless. And then, too, if we were man and wife, now, we'd both know that I was bound to do what I do now of my own accord."

"But you are young yet and attractive—"

"It's getting late," said Miggles, gravely, "and you'd better all turn in. Good night, boys"; and, throwing the blanket over her head, Miggles laid herself down beside Jim's chair, her head pillowed on the low stool that held his feet, and spoke no more. The fire slowly faded from the hearth; we each sought our blankets in silence; and presently there was no sound in the long room but the pattering of the rain upon the roof and the heavy breathing of the sleepers.

It was nearly morning when I awoke from a troubled dream. The storm had passed, the stars were shining, and through the shutterless window the full moon, lifting itself over the solemn pines without, looked into the room. It touched the lonely figure in the chair with an infinite compassion, and seemed to baptize with a shining flood the lowly head of the woman whose hair, as in the sweet old story, bathed the feet of him she loved. It even lent a kindly poetry to the rugged outline of Yuba Bill, half-reclining on his elbow between them and his passengers, with savagely patient eyes keeping watch and ward. And then I fell asleep and only woke at broad day, with Yuba Bill standing over me, and "All aboard" ringing in my ears.

Coffee was waiting for us on the table, but Miggles was gone. We wandered about the house and lingered long after the horses were harnessed, but she did not return. It was evident that she wished to avoid a formal leave-taking, and had so left us to depart as we had come. After we had helped the ladies into the coach, we returned to the house and solemnly shook hands with the paralytic Jim, as solemnly settling him back into position after each handshake. Then we looked for the last time around the long low room, at the stool where Miggles had sat, and slowly took our seats in the waiting coach. The whip cracked, and we were off!

But as we reached the highroad, Bill's dexterous hand laid the six horses back on their haunches, and the stage stopped with a jerk. For there, on a little eminence beside the road, stood Miggles, her hair flying, her eyes sparkling, her white handkerchief waving, and her white teeth flashing a last "good-by." We waved our hats in return. And then Yuba Bill, as if fearful of further fascination, madly lashed his horses forward, and we sank back in our seats. We exchanged not a word until we reached the North Fork, and the stage drew up at the Independence House. Then, the Judge leading, we walked into the barroom and took our places gravely at the bar.

"Are your glasses charged, gentlemen?" said the Judge, solemnly taking off his white hat.

They were.

"Well, then, here's to MIGGLES. GOD BLESS HER!"

Perhaps He had. Who knows?

* * * * * * * * *

TENNESSEE'S PARTNER

I do not think that we ever knew his real name. Our ignorance of it certainly never gave us any social inconvenience, for at Sandy Bar in 1854 most men were christened anew. Sometimes these appellatives were derived from some distinctiveness of dress, as in the case of "Dungaree Jack"; or from some peculiarity of habit, as shown in "Saleratus Bill," so called from an undue proportion of that chemical in his daily bread; or for some unlucky slip, as exhibited in "The Iron Pirate," a mild, inoffensive man, who earned that baleful title by his unfortunate mispronunciation of the term "iron pyrites." Perhaps this may have been the beginning of a rude heraldry; but I am constrained to think that it was because a man's real name in that day rested solely upon his own unsupported statement. "Call yourself Clifford, do you?" said Boston, addressing a timid newcomer with infinite scorn; "hell is full of such Cliffords!" He then introduced the unfortunate man, whose name happened to be really Clifford, as "Jay-bird Charley"—an unhallowed inspiration of the moment that clung to him ever after.

But to return to Tennessee's Partner, whom we never knew by any other than this relative title; that he had ever existed as a separate and distinct individuality we only learned later. It seems that in 1853 he left Poker Flat to go to San Francisco, ostensibly to procure a wife. He never got any farther than Stockton. At that place he was attracted by a young person who waited upon the table at the hotel where he took his meals. One morning he said something to her which caused her to smile not unkindly, to somewhat coquettishly break a plate of toast over his upturned, serious, simple face, and to retreat to the kitchen. He followed her, and emerged a few moments later, covered with more toast and victory. That day week they were married by a justice of the peace, and returned to Poker Flat. I am aware that something more might be made of this episode, but I prefer to tell it as it was current at Sandy Bar—in the gulches and barrooms—where all sentiment was modified by a strong sense of humor.

Of their married felicity but little is known, perhaps for the reason that Tennessee, then living with his Partner, one day took occasion to say something to the bride on his own account, at which, it is said, she smiled not unkindly and chastely retreated—this time as far as Marysville, where Tennessee followed her, and where they went to housekeeping without the aid of a justice of the peace. Tennessee's Partner took the loss of his wife simply and seriously, as was his fashion. But to everybody's surprise, when Tennessee one day returned from Marysville, without his Partner's wife—she having smiled and retreated with somebody else—Tennessee's Partner was the first man to shake his hand and greet him with affection. The boys who had gathered in the canyon to see the shooting were naturally indignant. Their indignation might have found vent in sarcasm but for a certain look in Tennessee's Partner's eye that indicated a lack of humorous appreciation. In fact, he was a grave man, with a steady application to practical detail which was unpleasant in a difficulty.

Meanwhile a popular feeling against Tennessee had grown up on the Bar. He was known to be a gambler; he was suspected to be a thief. In these suspicions Tennessee's Partner was equally compromised; his continued intimacy with Tennessee after the affair above quoted could only be accounted for on the hypothesis of a copartnership of crime. At last Tennessee's guilt became flagrant. One day he overtook a stranger on his way to Red Dog. The stranger afterward related that Tennessee beguiled the time with interesting anecdote and reminiscence, but illogically concluded the interview in the following words: "And now, young man, I'll trouble you for your knife, your pistols, and your money. You see your weppings might get you into trouble at Red Dog, and your money's a temptation to the evilly disposed. I think you said your address was San Francisco. I shall endeavor to call." It may be stated here that Tennessee had a fine flow of humor, which no business preoccupation could wholly subdue.

This exploit was his last. Red Dog and Sandy Bar made common cause against the highwayman. Tennessee was hunted in very much the same fashion as his prototype, the grizzly. As the toils closed around him, he made a desperate dash through the Bar, emptying his revolver at the crowd before the Arcade Saloon, and so on up Grizzly Canyon; but at its farther extremity he was stopped by a small man on a gray horse. The men looked at each other a moment in silence. Both were fearless, both self-possessed and independent; and both types of a civilization that in the seventeenth century would have been called heroic, but, in the nineteenth, simply "reckless." "What have you got there?—I call," said Tennessee, quietly. "Two bowers and an ace," said the stranger, as quietly, showing two revolvers and a bowie knife. "That takes me," returned Tennessee; and with this gamblers' epigram, he threw away his useless pistol, and rode back with his captor.

It was a warm night. The cool breeze which usually sprang up with the going down of the sun behind the chaparral-crested mountain was that evening withheld from Sandy Bar. The little canyon was stifling with heated resinous odors, and the decaying driftwood on the Bar sent forth faint, sickening exhalations. The feverishness of day, and its fierce passions, still filled the camp. Lights moved restlessly along the bank of the river, striking no answering reflection from its tawny current. Against the blackness of the pines the windows of the old loft above the express office stood out staringly bright; and through their curtainless panes the loungers below could see the forms of those who were even then deciding the fate of Tennessee. And above all this, etched on the dark firmament, rose the Sierra, remote and passionless, crowned with remoter passionless stars.

The trial of Tennessee was conducted as fairly as was consistent with a judge and jury who felt themselves to some extent obliged to justify, in their verdict, the previous irregularities of arrest and indictment. The law of Sandy Bar was implacable, but not vengeful. The excitement and personal feeling of the chase were over; with Tennessee safe in their hands they were ready to listen patiently to any defense, which they were already satisfied was insufficient. There being no doubt in their own minds, they were willing to give the prisoner the benefit of any that might exist. Secure in the hypothesis that he ought to be hanged, on general principles, they indulged him with more latitude of defense than his reckless hardihood seemed to ask. The Judge appeared to be more anxious than the prisoner, who, otherwise unconcerned, evidently took a grim pleasure in the responsibility he had created. "I don't take any hand in this yer game," had been his invariable but good-humored reply to all questions. The Judge—who was also his captor—for a moment vaguely regretted that he had not shot him "on sight" that morning, but presently dismissed this human weakness as unworthy of the judicial mind. Nevertheless, when there was a tap at the door, and it was said that Tennessee's Partner was there on behalf of the prisoner, he was admitted at once without question. Perhaps the younger members of the jury, to whom the proceedings were becoming irksomely thoughtful, hailed him as a relief.

For he was not, certainly, an imposing figure. Short and stout, with a square face sunburned into a preternatural redness, clad in a loose duck "jumper" and trousers streaked and splashed with red soil, his aspect under any circumstances would have been quaint, and was now even ridiculous. As he stooped to deposit at his feet a heavy carpetbag he was carrying, it became obvious, from partially developed legends and inscriptions, that the material with which his trousers had been patched had been originally intended for a less ambitious covering. Yet he advanced with great gravity, and after having shaken the hand of each person in the room with labored cordiality, he wiped his serious, perplexed face on a red bandanna handkerchief, a shade lighter than his complexion, laid his powerful hand upon the table to steady himself, and thus addressed the Judge:

"I was passin' by," he began, by way of apology, "and I thought I'd just step in and see how things was gittin' on with Tennessee thar—my pardner. It's a hot night. I disremember any sich weather before on the Bar."

He paused a moment, but nobody volunteering any other meteorological recollection, he again had recourse to his pocket handkerchief, and for some moments mopped his face diligently.

"Have you anything to say in behalf of the prisoner?" said the Judge, finally.

"Thet's it," said Tennessee's Partner, in a tone of relief. "I come yar as Tennessee's pardner—knowing him nigh on four year, off and on, wet and dry, in luck and out o' luck. His ways ain't allers my ways, but thar ain't any p'ints in that young man, thar ain't any liveliness as he's been up to, as I don't know. And you sez to me, sez you—confidential-like, and between man and man—sez you, 'Do you know anything in his behalf?' and I sez to you, sez I—confidential-like, as between man and man—'What should a man know of his pardner?'"

"Is this all you have to say?" asked the Judge impatiently, feeling, perhaps, that a dangerous sympathy of humor was beginning to humanize the Court.

"Thet's so," continued Tennessee's Partner. "It ain't for me to say anything agin' him. And now, what's the case? Here's Tennessee wants money, wants it bad, and doesn't like to ask it of his old pardner. Well, what does Tennessee do? He lays for a stranger, and he fetches that stranger. And you lays for HIM, and you fetches HIM; and the honors is easy. And I put it to you, bein' a far-minded man, and to you, gentlemen, all, as far-minded men, ef this isn't so."

"Prisoner," said the Judge, interrupting, "have you any questions to ask this man?"

"No! no!" continued Tennessee's Partner, hastily. "I play this yer hand alone. To come down to the bedrock, it's just this: Tennessee, thar, has played it pretty rough and expensive-like on a stranger, and on this yer camp. And now, what's the fair thing? Some would say more; some would say less. Here's seventeen hundred dollars in coarse gold and a watch—it's about all my pile—and call it square!" And before a hand could be raised to prevent him, he had emptied the contents of the carpetbag upon the table.

For a moment his life was in jeopardy. One or two men sprang to their feet, several hands groped for hidden weapons, and a suggestion to "throw him from the window" was only overridden by a gesture from the Judge. Tennessee laughed. And apparently oblivious of the excitement, Tennessee's Partner improved the opportunity to mop his face again with his handkerchief.

When order was restored, and the man was made to understand, by the use of forcible figures and rhetoric, that Tennessee's offense could not be condoned by money, his face took a more serious and sanguinary hue, and those who were nearest to him noticed that his rough hand trembled slightly on the table. He hesitated a moment as he slowly returned the gold to the carpetbag, as if he had not yet entirely caught the elevated sense of justice which swayed the tribunal, and was perplexed with the belief that he had not offered enough. Then he turned to the Judge, and saying, "This yer is a lone hand, played alone, and without my pardner," he bowed to the jury and was about to withdraw when the Judge called him back. "If you have anything to say to Tennessee, you had better say it now." For the first time that evening the eyes of the prisoner and his strange advocate met. Tennessee smiled, showed his white teeth, and, saying, "Euchred, old man!" held out his hand. Tennessee's Partner took it in his own, and saying, "I just dropped in as I was passin' to see how things was gettin' on," let the hand passively fall, and adding that it was a warm night, again mopped his face with his handkerchief, and without another word withdrew.

The two men never again met each other alive. For the unparalleled insult of a bribe offered to Judge Lynch—who, whether bigoted, weak, or narrow, was at least incorruptible—firmly fixed in the mind of that mythical personage any wavering determination of Tennessee's fate; and at the break of day he was marched, closely guarded, to meet it at the top of Marley's Hill.

How he met it, how cool he was, how he refused to say anything, how perfect were the arrangements of the committee, were all duly reported, with the addition of a warning moral and example to all future evildoers, in the RED DOG CLARION, by its editor, who was present, and to whose vigorous English I cheerfully refer the reader. But the beauty of that midsummer morning, the blessed amity of earth and air and sky, the awakened life of the free woods and hills, the joyous renewal and promise of Nature, and above all, the infinite Serenity that thrilled through each, was not reported, as not being a part of the social lesson. And yet, when the weak and foolish deed was done, and a life, with its possibilities and responsibilities, had passed out of the misshapen thing that dangled between earth and sky, the birds sang, the flowers bloomed, the sun shone, as cheerily as before; and possibly the RED DOG CLARION was right.

Tennessee's Partner was not in the group that surrounded the ominous tree. But as they turned to disperse attention was drawn to the singular appearance of a motionless donkey cart halted at the side of the road. As they approached, they at once recognized the venerable "Jenny" and the two-wheeled cart as the property of Tennessee's Partner—used by him in carrying dirt from his claim; and a few paces distant the owner of the equipage himself, sitting under a buckeye tree, wiping the perspiration from his glowing face. In answer to an inquiry, he said he had come for the body of the "diseased," "if it was all the same to the committee." He didn't wish to "hurry anything"; he could "wait." He was not working that day; and when the gentlemen were done with the "diseased," he would take him. "Ef thar is any present," he added, in his simple, serious way, "as would care to jine in the fun'l, they kin come." Perhaps it was from a sense of humor, which I have already intimated was a feature of Sandy Bar—perhaps it was from something even better than that; but two-thirds of the loungers accepted the invitation at once.

It was noon when the body of Tennessee was delivered into the hands of his Partner. As the cart drew up to the fatal tree, we noticed that it contained a rough, oblong box—apparently made from a section of sluicing and half-filled with bark and the tassels of pine. The cart was further decorated with slips of willow, and made fragrant with buckeye blossoms. When the body was deposited in the box, Tennessee's Partner drew over it a piece of tarred canvas, and gravely mounting the narrow seat in front, with his feet upon the shafts, urged the little donkey forward. The equipage moved slowly on, at that decorous pace which was habitual with "Jenny" even under less solemn circumstances. The men—half curiously, half jestingly, but all good-humoredly—strolled along beside the cart; some in advance, some a little in the rear of the homely catafalque. But, whether from the narrowing of the road or some present sense of decorum, as the cart passed on, the company fell to the rear in couples, keeping step, and otherwise assuming the external show of a formal procession. Jack Folinsbee, who had at the outset played a funeral march in dumb show upon an imaginary trombone, desisted, from a lack of sympathy and appreciation—not having, perhaps, your true humorist's capacity to be content with the enjoyment of his own fun.

The way led through Grizzly Canyon—by this time clothed in funereal drapery and shadows. The redwoods, burying their moccasined feet in the red soil, stood in Indian file along the track, trailing an uncouth benediction from their bending boughs upon the passing bier. A hare, surprised into helpless inactivity, sat upright and pulsating in the ferns by the roadside as the cortege went by. Squirrels hastened to gain a secure outlook from higher boughs; and the bluejays, spreading their wings, fluttered before them like outriders, until the outskirts of Sandy Bar were reached, and the solitary cabin of Tennessee's Partner.

Viewed under more favorable circumstances, it would not have been a cheerful place. The unpicturesque site, the rude and unlovely outlines, the unsavory details, which distinguish the nest-building of the California miner, were all here, with the dreariness of decay superadded. A few paces from the cabin there was a rough enclosure, which in the brief days of Tennessee's Partner's matrimonial felicity had been used as a garden, but was now overgrown with fern. As we approached it we were surprised to find that what we had taken for a recent attempt at cultivation was the broken soil about an open grave.

The cart was halted before the enclosure; and rejecting the offers of assistance with the same air of simple self-reliance he had displayed throughout, Tennessee's Partner lifted the rough coffin on his back and deposited it, unaided, within the shallow grave. He then nailed down the board which served as a lid; and mounting the little mound of earth beside it, took off his hat, and slowly mopped his face with his handkerchief. This the crowd felt was a preliminary to speech; and they disposed themselves variously on stumps and boulders, and sat expectant.

"When a man," began Tennessee's Partner, slowly, "has been running free all day, what's the natural thing for him to do? Why, to come home. And if he ain't in a condition to go home, what can his best friend do? Why, bring him home! And here's Tennessee has been running free, and we brings him home from his wandering." He paused, and picked up a fragment of quartz, rubbed it thoughtfully on his sleeve, and went on: "It ain't the first time that I've packed him on my back, as you see'd me now. It ain't the first time that I brought him to this yer cabin when he couldn't help himself; it ain't the first time that I and 'Jinny' have waited for him on yon hill, and picked him up and so fetched him home, when he couldn't speak, and didn't know me. And now that it's the last time, why"—he paused and rubbed the quartz gently on his sleeve—"you see it's sort of rough on his pardner. And now, gentlemen," he added, abruptly, picking up his long-handled shovel, "the fun'l's over; and my thanks, and Tennessee's thanks, to you for your trouble."

Resisting any proffers of assistance, he began to fill in the grave, turning his back upon the crowd that after a few moments' hesitation gradually withdrew. As they crossed the little ridge that hid Sandy Bar from view, some, looking back, thought they could see Tennessee's Partner, his work done, sitting upon the grave, his shovel between his knees, and his face buried in his red bandanna handkerchief. But it was argued by others that you couldn't tell his face from his handkerchief at that distance; and this point remained undecided.

In the reaction that followed the feverish excitement of that day, Tennessee's Partner was not forgotten. A secret investigation had cleared him of any complicity in Tennessee's guilt, and left only a suspicion of his general sanity. Sandy Bar made a point of calling on him, and proffering various uncouth, but well-meant kindnesses. But from that day his rude health and great strength seemed visibly to decline; and when the rainy season fairly set in, and the tiny grass-blades were beginning to peep from the rocky mound above Tennessee's grave, he took to his bed. One night, when the pines beside the cabin were swaying in the storm, and trailing their slender fingers over the roof, and the roar and rush of the swollen river were heard below, Tennessee's Partner lifted his head from the pillow, saying, "It is time to go for Tennessee; I must put 'Jinny' in the cart"; and would have risen from his bed but for the restraint of his attendant. Struggling, he still pursued his singular fancy: "There, now, steady, 'Jinny'—steady, old girl. How dark it is! Look out for the ruts—and look out for him, too, old gal. Sometimes, you know, when he's blind-drunk, he drops down right in the trail. Keep on straight up to the pine on the top of the hill. Thar—I told you so!—thar he is—coming this way, too—all by himself, sober, and his face a-shining. Tennessee! Pardner!"

And so they met.

* * * * * * * * *

THE IDYL OF RED GULCH

Sandy was very drunk. He was lying under an azalea bush, in pretty much the same attitude in which he had fallen some hours before. How long he had been lying there he could not tell, and didn't care; how long he should lie there was a matter equally indefinite and unconsidered. A tranquil philosophy, born of his physical condition, suffused and saturated his moral being.

The spectacle of a drunken man, and of this drunken man in particular, was not, I grieve to say, of sufficient novelty in Red Gulch to attract attention. Earlier in the day some local satirist had erected a temporary tombstone at Sandy's head, bearing the inscription, "Effects of McCorkle's whisky—kills at forty rods," with a hand pointing to McCorkle's saloon. But this, I imagine, was, like most local satire, personal; and was a reflection upon the unfairness of the process rather than a commentary upon the impropriety of the result. With this facetious exception, Sandy had been undisturbed. A wandering mule, released from his pack, had cropped the scant herbage beside him, and sniffed curiously at the prostrate man; a vagabond dog, with that deep sympathy which the species have for drunken men, had licked his dusty boots, and curled himself up at his feet, and lay there, blinking one eye in the sunlight, with a simulation of dissipation that was ingenious and doglike in its implied flattery of the unconscious man beside him.

Meanwhile the shadows of the pine trees had slowly swung around until they crossed the road, and their trunks barred the open meadow with gigantic parallels of black and yellow. Little puffs of red dust, lifted by the plunging hoofs of passing teams, dispersed in a grimy shower upon the recumbent man. The sun sank lower and lower; and still Sandy stirred not. And then the repose of this philosopher was disturbed, as other philosophers have been, by the intrusion of an unphilosophical sex.

"Miss Mary," as she was known to the little flock that she had just dismissed from the log schoolhouse beyond the pines, was taking her afternoon walk. Observing an unusually fine cluster of blossoms on the azalea bush opposite, she crossed the road to pluck it—picking her way through the red dust, not without certain fierce little shivers of disgust and some feline circumlocution. And then she came suddenly upon Sandy!

Of course she uttered the little staccato cry of her sex. But when she had paid that tribute to her physical weakness she became overbold, and halted for a moment—at least six feet from this prostrate monster—with her white skirts gathered in her hand, ready for flight. But neither sound nor motion came from the bush. With one little foot she then overturned the satirical headboard, and muttered "Beasts!"—an epithet which probably, at that moment, conveniently classified in her mind the entire male population of Red Gulch. For Miss Mary, being possessed of certain rigid notions of her own, had not, perhaps, properly appreciated the demonstrative gallantry for which the Californian has been so justly celebrated by his brother Californians, and had, as a newcomer, perhaps fairly earned the reputation of being "stuck-up."

As she stood there she noticed, also, that the slant sunbeams were heating Sandy's head to what she judged to be an unhealthy temperature, and that his hat was lying uselessly at his side. To pick it up and to place it over his face was a work requiring some courage, particularly as his eyes were open. Yet she did it, and made good her retreat. But she was somewhat concerned, on looking back, to see that the hat was removed, and that Sandy was sitting up and saying something.

The truth was, that in the calm depths of Sandy's mind he was satisfied that the rays of the sun were beneficial and healthful; that from childhood he had objected to lying down in a hat; that no people but condemned fools, past redemption, ever wore hats; and that his right to dispense with them when he pleased was inalienable. This was the statement of his inner consciousness. Unfortunately, its outward expression was vague, being limited to a repetition of the following formula—"Su'shine all ri'! Wasser maar, eh? Wass up, su'shine?"

Miss Mary stopped, and, taking fresh courage from her vantage of distance, asked him if there was anything that he wanted.

"Wass up? Wasser maar?" continued Sandy, in a very high key.

"Get up, you horrid man!" said Miss Mary, now thoroughly incensed; "get up, and go home."

Sandy staggered to his feet. He was six feet high, and Miss Mary trembled. He started forward a few paces and then stopped.

"Wass I go home for?" he suddenly asked, with great gravity.

"Go and take a bath," replied Miss Mary, eying his grimy person with great disfavor.

To her infinite dismay, Sandy suddenly pulled off his coat and vest, threw them on the ground, kicked off his boots, and, plunging wildly forward, darted headlong over the hill, in the direction of the river.

"Goodness heavens!—the man will be drowned!" said Miss Mary; and then, with feminine inconsistency, she ran back to the schoolhouse and locked herself in.

That night, while seated at supper with her hostess, the blacksmith's wife, it came to Miss Mary to ask, demurely, if her husband ever got drunk. "Abner," responded Mrs. Stidger, reflectively, "let's see: Abner hasn't been tight since last 'lection." Miss Mary would have liked to ask if he preferred lying in the sun on these occasions, and if a cold bath would have hurt him; but this would have involved an explanation, which she did not then care to give. So she contented herself with opening her gray eyes widely at the red-cheeked Mrs. Stidger—a fine specimen of Southwestern efflorescence—and then dismissed the subject altogether. The next day she wrote to her dearest friend, in Boston: "I think I find the intoxicated portion of this community the least objectionable. I refer, my dear, to the men, of course. I do not know anything that could make the women tolerable."

In less than a week Miss Mary had forgotten this episode, except that her afternoon walks took thereafter, almost unconsciously, another direction. She noticed, however, that every morning a fresh cluster of azalea blossoms appeared among the flowers on her desk. This was not strange, as her little flock were aware of her fondness for flowers, and invariably kept her desk bright with anemones, syringas, and lupines; but, on questioning them, they one and all professed ignorance of the azaleas. A few days later, Master Johnny Stidger, whose desk was nearest to the window, was suddenly taken with spasms of apparently gratuitous laughter that threatened the discipline of the school. All that Miss Mary could get from him was, that someone had been "looking in the winder." Irate and indignant, she sallied from her hive to do battle with the intruder. As she turned the corner of the schoolhouse she came plump upon the quondam drunkard—now perfectly sober, and inexpressibly sheepish and guilty-looking.

These facts Miss Mary was not slow to take a feminine advantage of, in her present humor. But it was somewhat confusing to observe, also, that the beast, despite some faint signs of past dissipation, was amiable-looking—in fact, a kind of blond Samson whose corn-colored, silken beard apparently had never yet known the touch of barber's razor or Delilah's shears. So that the cutting speech which quivered on her ready tongue died upon her lips, and she contented herself with receiving his stammering apology with supercilious eyelids and the gathered skirts of uncontamination. When she re-entered the schoolroom, her eyes fell upon the azaleas with a new sense of revelation. And then she laughed, and the little people all laughed, and they were all unconsciously very happy.

It was on a hot day—and not long after this—that two short-legged boys came to grief on the threshold of the school with a pail of water, which they had laboriously brought from the spring, and that Miss Mary compassionately seized the pail and started for the spring herself. At the foot of the hill a shadow crossed her path, and a blue-shirted arm dexterously but gently relieved her of her burden. Miss Mary was both embarrassed and angry. "If you carried more of that for yourself," she said, spitefully, to the blue arm, without deigning to raise her lashes to its owner, "you'd do better." In the submissive silence that followed she regretted the speech, and thanked him so sweetly at the door that he stumbled. Which caused the children to laugh again—a laugh in which Miss Mary joined, until the color came faintly into her pale cheek. The next day a barrel was mysteriously placed beside the door, and as mysteriously filled with fresh spring water every morning.

Nor was this superior young person without other quiet attentions. "Profane Bill," driver of the Slumgullion Stage, widely known in the newspapers for his "gallantry" in invariably offering the box seat to the fair sex, had excepted Miss Mary from this attention, on the ground that he had a habit of "cussin' on upgrades," and gave her half the coach to herself. Jack Hamlin, a gambler, having once silently ridden with her in the same coach, afterward threw a decanter at the head of a confederate for mentioning her name in a barroom. The overdressed mother of a pupil whose paternity was doubtful had often lingered near this astute Vestal's temple, never daring to enter its sacred precincts, but content to worship the priestess from afar.

With such unconscious intervals the monotonous procession of blue skies, glittering sunshine, brief twilights, and starlit nights passed over Red Gulch. Miss Mary grew fond of walking in the sedate and proper woods. Perhaps she believed, with Mrs. Stidger, that the balsamic odors of the firs "did her chest good," for certainly her slight cough was less frequent and her step was firmer; perhaps she had learned the unending lesson which the patient pines are never weary of repeating to heedful or listless ears. And so, one day, she planned a picnic on Buckeye Hill, and took the children with her. Away from the dusty road, the straggling shanties, the yellow ditches, the clamor of restless engines, the cheap finery of shop windows, the deeper glitter of paint and colored glass, and the thin veneering which barbarism takes upon itself in such localities—what infinite relief was theirs! The last heap of ragged rock and clay passed, the last unsightly chasm crossed—how the waiting woods opened their long files to receive them! How the children—perhaps because they had not yet grown quite away from the breast of the bounteous Mother—threw themselves face downward on her brown bosom with uncouth caresses, filling the air with their laughter; and how Miss Mary herself—felinely fastidious and intrenched as she was in the purity of spotless skirts, collar, and cuffs—forgot all, and ran like a crested quail at the head of her brood until, romping, laughing, and panting, with a loosened braid of brown hair, a hat hanging by a knotted ribbon from her throat, she came suddenly and violently, in the heart of the forest, upon—the luckless Sandy!

The explanations, apologies, and not overwise conversation that ensued need not be indicated here. It would seem, however, that Miss Mary had already established some acquaintance with this ex-drunkard. Enough that he was soon accepted as one of the party; that the children, with that quick intelligence which Providence gives the helpless, recognized a friend, and played with his blond beard and long silken mustache, and took other liberties—as the helpless are apt to do. And when he had built a fire against a tree, and had shown them other mysteries of woodcraft, their admiration knew no bounds. At the close of two such foolish, idle, happy hours he found himself lying at the feet of the schoolmistress, gazing dreamily in her face, as she sat upon the sloping hillside weaving wreaths of laurel and syringa, in very much the same attitude as he had lain when first they met. Nor was the similitude greatly forced. The weakness of an easy, sensuous nature that had found a dreamy exaltation in liquor, it is to be feared was now finding an equal intoxication in love.

I think that Sandy was dimly conscious of this himself. I know that he longed to be doing something—slaying a grizzly, scalping a savage, or sacrificing himself in some way for the sake of this sallow-faced, gray-eyed schoolmistress. As I should like to present him in a heroic attitude, I stay my hand with great difficulty at this moment, being only withheld from introducing such an episode by a strong conviction that it does not usually occur at such times. And I trust that my fairest reader, who remembers that, in a real crisis, it is always some uninteresting stranger or unromantic policeman, and not Adolphus, who rescues, will forgive the omission.

So they sat there, undisturbed—the woodpeckers chattering overhead and the voices of the children coming pleasantly from the hollow below. What they said matters little. What they thought—which might have been interesting—did not transpire. The woodpeckers only learned how Miss Mary was an orphan; how she left her uncle's house, to come to California, for the sake of health and independence; how Sandy was an orphan, too; how he came to California for excitement; how he had lived a wild life, and how he was trying to reform; and other details, which, from a woodpecker's viewpoint, undoubtedly must have seemed stupid, and a waste of time. But even in such trifles was the afternoon spent; and when the children were again gathered, and Sandy, with a delicacy which the schoolmistress well understood, took leave of them quietly at the outskirts of the settlement, it had seemed the shortest day of her weary life.

As the long, dry summer withered to its roots, the school term of Red Gulch—to use a local euphuism—"dried up" also. In another day Miss Mary would be free; and for a season, at least, Red Gulch would know her no more. She was seated alone in the schoolhouse, her cheek resting on her hand, her eyes half-closed in one of those daydreams in which Miss Mary—I fear to the danger of school discipline—was lately in the habit of indulging. Her lap was full of mosses, ferns, and other woodland memories. She was so preoccupied with these and her own thoughts that a gentle tapping at the door passed unheard, or translated itself into the remembrance of far-off woodpeckers. When at last it asserted itself more distinctly, she started up with a flushed cheek and opened the door. On the threshold stood a woman the self-assertion and audacity of whose dress were in singular contrast to her timid, irresolute bearing.

Miss Mary recognized at a glance the dubious mother of her anonymous pupil. Perhaps she was disappointed, perhaps she was only fastidious; but as she coldly invited her to enter, she half-unconsciously settled her white cuffs and collar, and gathered closer her own chaste skirts. It was, perhaps, for this reason that the embarrassed stranger, after a moment's hesitation, left her gorgeous parasol open and sticking in the dust beside the door, and then sat down at the farther end of a long bench. Her voice was husky as she began:

"I heerd tell that you were goin' down to the Bay tomorrow, and I couldn't let you go until I came to thank you for your kindness to my Tommy."

Tommy, Miss Mary said, was a good boy, and deserved more than the poor attention she could give him.

"Thank you, miss; thank ye!" cried the stranger, brightening even through the color which Red Gulch knew facetiously as her "war paint," and striving, in her embarrassment, to drag the long bench nearer the schoolmistress. "I thank you, miss, for that! and if I am his mother, there ain't a sweeter, dearer, better boy lives than him. And if I ain't much as says it, thar ain't a sweeter, dearer, angeler teacher lives than he's got."

Miss Mary, sitting primly behind her desk, with a ruler over her shoulder, opened her gray eyes widely at this, but said nothing.

"It ain't for you to be complimented by the like of me, I know," she went on, hurriedly. "It ain't for me to be comin' here, in broad day, to do it, either; but I come to ask a favor—not for me, miss—not for me, but for the darling boy."

Encouraged by a look in the young schoolmistress's eye, and putting her lilac-gloved hands together, the fingers downward, between her knees, she went on, in a low voice:

"You see, miss, there's no one the boy has any claim on but me, and I ain't the proper person to bring him up. I thought some, last year, of sending him away to Frisco to school, but when they talked of bringing a schoolma'am here, I waited till I saw you, and then I knew it was all right, and I could keep my boy a little longer. And O, miss, he loves you so much; and if you could hear him talk about you, in his pretty way, and if he could ask you what I ask you now, you couldn't refuse him.

"It is natural," she went on, rapidly, in a voice that trembled strangely between pride and humility—"it's natural that he should take to you, miss, for his father, when I first knew him, was a gentleman—and the boy must forget me, sooner or later—and so I ain't goin' to cry about that. For I come to ask you to take my Tommy—God bless him for the bestest, sweetest boy that lives—to—to—take him with you."

She had risen and caught the young girl's hand in her own, and had fallen on her knees beside her.

"I've money plenty, and it's all yours and his. Put him in some good school, where you can go and see him, and help him to—to—to forget his mother. Do with him what you like. The worst you can do will be kindness to what he will learn with me. Only take him out of this wicked life, this cruel place, this home of shame and sorrow. You will; I know you will—won't you? You will—you must not, you cannot say no! You will make him as pure, as gentle as yourself; and when he has grown up, you will tell him his father's name—the name that hasn't passed my lips for years—the name of Alexander Morton, whom they call here Sandy! Miss Mary!—do not take your hand away! Miss Mary, speak to me! You will take my boy? Do not put your face from me. I know it ought not to look on such as me. Miss Mary!—my God, be merciful!—she is leaving me!"

Miss Mary had risen and, in the gathering twilight, had felt her way to the open window. She stood there, leaning against the casement, her eyes fixed on the last rosy tints that were fading from the western sky. There was still some of its light on her pure young forehead, on her white collar, on her clasped white hands, but all fading slowly away. The suppliant had dragged herself, still on her knees, beside her.

"I know it takes time to consider. I will wait here all night; but I cannot go until you speak. Do not deny me now. You will!—I see it in your sweet face—such a face as I have seen in my dreams. I see it in your eyes, Miss Mary!—you will take my boy!"

The last red beam crept higher, suffused Miss Mary's eyes with something of its glory, flickered, and faded, and went out. The sun had set on Red Gulch. In the twilight and silence Miss Mary's voice sounded pleasantly.

"I will take the boy. Send him to me tonight."

The happy mother raised the hem of Miss Mary's skirts to her lips. She would have buried her hot face in its virgin folds, but she dared not. She rose to her feet.

"Does—this man—know of your intention?" asked Miss Mary, suddenly.

"No, nor cares. He has never even seen the child to know it."

"Go to him at once—tonight—now! Tell him what you have done. Tell him I have taken his child, and tell him—he must never see—see—the child again. Wherever it may be, he must not come; wherever I may take it, he must not follow! There, go now, please—I'm weary, and—have much yet to do!"

They walked together to the door. On the threshold the woman turned.

"Good night."

She would have fallen at Miss Mary's feet. But at the same moment the young girl reached out her arms, caught the sinful woman to her own pure breast for one brief moment, and then closed and locked the door.

It was with a sudden sense of great responsibility that Profane Bill took the reins of the Slumgullion Stage the next morning, for the schoolmistress was one of his passengers. As he entered the highroad, in obedience to a pleasant voice from the "inside," he suddenly reined up his horses and respectfully waited as Tommy hopped out at the command of Miss Mary. "Not that bush, Tommy—the next."

Tommy whipped out his new pocketknife, and, cutting a branch from a tall azalea bush, returned with it to Miss Mary.

"All right now?"

"All right."

And the stage door closed on the Idyl of Red Gulch.

* * * * * * * * * *

BROWN OF CALAVERAS

A subdued tone of conversation, and the absence of cigar smoke and boot heels at the windows of the Wingdam stagecoach, made it evident that one of the inside passengers was a woman. A disposition on the part of loungers at the stations to congregate before the window, and some concern in regard to the appearance of coats, hats, and collars, further indicated that she was lovely. All of which Mr. Jack Hamlin, on the box seat, noted with the smile of cynical philosophy. Not that he depreciated the sex, but that he recognized therein a deceitful element, the pursuit of which sometimes drew mankind away from the equally uncertain blandishments of poker—of which it may be remarked that Mr. Hamlin was a professional exponent.

So that when he placed his narrow boot on the wheel and leaped down, he did not even glance at the window from which a green veil was fluttering, but lounged up and down with that listless and grave indifference of his class, which was, perhaps, the next thing to good breeding. With his closely buttoned figure and self-contained air he was a marked contrast to the other passengers, with their feverish restlessness and boisterous emotion; and even Bill Masters, a graduate of Harvard, with his slovenly dress, his overflowing vitality, his intense appreciation of lawlessness and barbarism, and his mouth filled with crackers and cheese, I fear cut but an unromantic figure beside this lonely calculator of chances, with his pale Greek face and Homeric gravity.

The driver called "All aboard!" and Mr. Hamlin returned to the coach. His foot was upon the wheel, and his face raised to the level of the open window, when, at the same moment, what appeared to him to be the finest eyes in the world suddenly met his. He quietly dropped down again, addressed a few words to one of the inside passengers, effected an exchange of seats, and as quietly took his place inside. Mr. Hamlin never allowed his philosophy to interfere with decisive and prompt action.

I fear that this irruption of Jack cast some restraint upon the other passengers—particularly those who were making themselves most agreeable to the lady. One of them leaned forward, and apparently conveyed to her information regarding Mr. Hamlin's profession in a single epithet. Whether Mr. Hamlin heard it, or whether he recognized in the informant a distinguished jurist from whom, but a few evenings before, he had won several thousand dollars, I cannot say. His colorless face betrayed no sign; his black eyes, quietly observant, glanced indifferently past the legal gentleman, and rested on the much more pleasing features of his neighbor. An Indian stoicism—said to be an inheritance from his maternal ancestor—stood him in good service, until the rolling wheels rattled upon the river gravel at Scott's Ferry, and the stage drew up at the International Hotel for dinner. The legal gentleman and a member of Congress leaped out, and stood ready to assist the descending goddess, while Colonel Starbottle, of Siskiyou, took charge of her parasol and shawl. In this multiplicity of attention there was a momentary confusion and delay. Jack Hamlin quietly opened the OPPOSITE door of the coach, took the lady's hand—with that decision and positiveness which a hesitating and undecided sex know how to admire—and in an instant had dexterously and gracefully swung her to the ground, and again lifted her to the platform. An audible chuckle on the box, I fear, came from that other cynic, "Yuba Bill," the driver. "Look keerfully arter that baggage, Kernel," said the expressman, with affected concern, as he looked after Colonel Starbottle, gloomily bringing up the rear of the triumphant procession to the waiting-room.

Mr. Hamlin did not stay for dinner. His horse was already saddled, and awaiting him. He dashed over the ford, up the gravelly hill, and out into the dusty perspective of the Wingdam road, like one leaving pleasant fancy behind him. The inmates of dusty cabins by the roadside shaded their eyes with their hands and looked after him, recognizing the man by his horse, and speculating what "was up with Comanche Jack." Yet much of this interest centered in the horse, in a community where the time made by "French Pete's" mare in his run from the Sheriff of Calaveras eclipsed all concern in the ultimate fate of that worthy.

The sweating flanks of his gray at length recalled him to himself. He checked his speed, and, turning into a by-road, sometimes used as a cutoff, trotted leisurely along, the reins hanging listlessly from his fingers. As he rode on, the character of the landscape changed and became more pastoral. Openings in groves of pine and sycamore disclosed some rude attempts at cultivation—a flowering vine trailed over the porch of one cabin, and a woman rocked her cradled babe under the roses of another. A little farther on Mr. Hamlin came upon some barelegged children wading in the willowy creek, and so wrought upon them with a badinage peculiar to himself that they were emboldened to climb up his horse's legs and over his saddle, until he was fain to develop an exaggerated ferocity of demeanor, and to escape, leaving behind some kisses and coin. And then, advancing deeper into the woods, where all signs of habitation failed, he began to sing—uplifting a tenor so singularly sweet, and shaded by a pathos so subduing and tender, that I wot the robins and linnets stopped to listen. Mr. Hamlin's voice was not cultivated; the subject of his song was some sentimental lunacy borrowed from the Negro minstrels; but there thrilled through all some occult quality of tone and expression that was unspeakably touching. Indeed, it was a wonderful sight to see this sentimental blackleg, with a pack of cards in his pocket and a revolver at his back, sending his voice before him through the dim woods with a plaint about his "Nelly's grave" in a way that overflowed the eyes of the listener. A sparrow hawk, fresh from his sixth victim, possibly recognizing in Mr. Hamlin a kindred spirit, stared at him in surprise, and was fain to confess the superiority of man. With a superior predatory capacity, HE couldn't sing.

But Mr. Hamlin presently found himself again on the highroad, and at his former pace. Ditches and banks of gravel, denuded hillsides, stumps, and decayed trunks of trees, took the place of woodland and ravine, and indicated his approach to civilization. Then a church steeple came in sight, and he knew that he had reached home. In a few moments he was clattering down the single narrow street that lost itself in a chaotic ruin of races, ditches, and tailings at the foot of the hill, and dismounted before the gilded windows of the "Magnolia" saloon. Passing through the long barroom, he pushed open a green-baize door, entered a dark passage, opened another door with a passkey, and found himself in a dimly lighted room whose furniture, though elegant and costly for the locality, showed signs of abuse. The inlaid center table was overlaid with stained disks that were not contemplated in the original design. The embroidered armchairs were discolored, and the green velvet lounge, on which Mr. Hamlin threw himself, was soiled at the foot with the red soil of Wingdam.

Mr. Hamlin did not sing in his cage. He lay still, looking at a highly colored painting above him representing a young creature of opulent charms. It occurred to him then, for the first time, that he had never seen exactly that kind of a woman, and that if he should, he would not, probably, fall in love with her. Perhaps he was thinking of another style of beauty. But just then someone knocked at the door. Without rising, he pulled a cord that apparently shot back a bolt, for the door swung open, and a man entered.

The newcomer was broad-shouldered and robust—a vigor not borne out in the face, which, though handsome, was singularly weak, and disfigured by dissipation. He appeared to be also under the influence of liquor, for he started on seeing Mr. Hamlin, and said, "I thought Kate was here," stammered, and seemed confused and embarrassed.

Mr. Hamlin smiled the smile which he had before worn on the Wingdam coach, and sat up, quite refreshed and ready for business.

"You didn't come up on the stage," continued the newcomer, "did you?"

"No," replied Hamlin; "I left it at Scott's Ferry. It isn't due for half an hour yet. But how's luck, Brown?"

"Damn bad," said Brown, his face suddenly assuming an expression of weak despair; "I'm cleaned out again, Jack," he continued, in a whining tone that formed a pitiable contrast to his bulky figure, "can't you help me with a hundred till tomorrow's cleanup? You see I've got to send money home to the old woman, and—you've won twenty times that amount from me."

The conclusion was, perhaps, not entirely logical, but Jack overlooked it, and handed the sum to his visitor. "The old-woman business is about played out, Brown," he added, by way of commentary; "why don't you say you want to buck agin' faro? You know you ain't married!"

"Fact, sir," said Brown, with a sudden gravity, as if the mere contact of the gold with the palm of the hand had imparted some dignity to his frame. "I've got a wife—a damned good one, too, if I do say it—in the States. It's three year since I've seen her, and a year since I've writ to her. When things is about straight, and we get down to the lead, I'm going to send for her."

"And Kate?" queried Mr. Hamlin, with his previous smile.

Mr. Brown of Calaveras essayed an archness of glance, to cover his confusion, which his weak face and whisky-muddled intellect but poorly carried out, and said:

"Damn it, Jack, a man must have a little liberty, you know. But come, what do you say to a little game? Give us a show to double this hundred."

Jack Hamlin looked curiously at his fatuous friend. Perhaps he knew that the man was predestined to lose the money, and preferred that it should flow back into his own coffers rather than any other. He nodded his head, and drew his chair toward the table. At the same moment there came a rap upon the door.

"It's Kate," said Mr. Brown.

Mr. Hamlin shot back the bolt, and the door opened. But, for the first time in his life, he staggered to his feet, utterly unnerved and abashed, and for the first time in his life the hot blood crimsoned his colorless cheeks to his forehead. For before him stood the lady he had lifted from the Wingdam coach, whom Brown—dropping his cards with a hysterical laugh—greeted as:

"My old woman, by thunder!"

They say that Mrs. Brown burst into tears, and reproaches of her husband. I saw her, in 1857, at Marysville, and disbelieve the story. And the WINGDAM CHRONICLE, of the next week, under the head of "Touching Reunion," said: "One of those beautiful and touching incidents, peculiar to California life, occurred last week in our city. The wife of one of Wingdam's eminent pioneers, tired of the effete civilization of the East and its inhospitable climate, resolved to join her noble husband upon these golden shores. Without informing him of her intention, she undertook the long journey, and arrived last week. The joy of the husband may be easier imagined than described. The meeting is said to have been indescribably affecting. We trust her example may be followed."

Whether owing to Mrs. Brown's influence, or to some more successful speculations, Mr. Brown's financial fortune from that day steadily improved. He bought out his partners in the "Nip and Tuck" lead, with money which was said to have been won at poker, a week or two after his wife's arrival, but which rumor, adopting Mrs. Brown's theory that Brown had forsworn the gaming-table, declared to have been furnished by Mr. Jack Hamlin. He built and furnished the "Wingdam House," which pretty Mrs. Brown's great popularity kept overflowing with guests. He was elected to the Assembly, and gave largess to churches. A street in Wingdam was named in his honor.

Yet it was noted that in proportion as he waxed wealthy and fortunate, he grew pale, thin, and anxious. As his wife's popularity increased, he became fretful and impatient. The most uxorious of husbands, he was absurdly jealous. If he did not interfere with his wife's social liberty, it was because it was maliciously whispered that his first and only attempt was met by an outburst from Mrs. Brown that terrified him into silence. Much of this kind of gossip came from those of her own sex whom she had supplanted in the chivalrous attentions of Wingdam, which, like most popular chivalry, was devoted to an admiration of power, whether of masculine force or feminine beauty. It should be remembered, too, in her extenuation that since her arrival, she had been the unconscious priestess of a mythological worship, perhaps not more ennobling to her womanhood than that which distinguished an older Greek democracy. I think that Brown was dimly conscious of this. But his only confidant was Jack Hamlin, whose INFELIX reputation naturally precluded any open intimacy with the family, and whose visits were infrequent.

It was midsummer, and a moonlit night; and Mrs. Brown, very rosy, large-eyed, and pretty, sat upon the piazza, enjoying the fresh incense of the mountain breeze, and, it is to be feared, another incense which was not so fresh, nor quite as innocent. Beside her sat Colonel Starbottle and Judge Boompointer, and a later addition to her court in the shape of a foreign tourist. She was in good spirits.

"What do you see down the road?" inquired the gallant Colonel, who had been conscious, for the last few minutes, that Mrs. Brown's attention was diverted.

"Dust," said Mrs. Brown, with a sigh. "Only Sister Anne's 'flock of sheep.'"

The Colonel, whose literary recollections did not extend farther back than last week's paper, took a more practical view. "It ain't sheep," he continued; "it's a horseman. Judge, ain't that Jack Hamlin's gray?"

But the Judge didn't know; and as Mrs. Brown suggested the air was growing too cold for further investigations, they retired to the parlor.

Mr. Brown was in the stable, where he generally retired after dinner. Perhaps it was to show his contempt for his wife's companions; perhaps, like other weak natures, he found pleasure in the exercise of absolute power over inferior animals. He had a certain gratification in the training of a chestnut mare, whom he could beat or caress as pleased him, which he couldn't do with Mrs. Brown. It was here that he recognized a certain gray horse which had just come in, and, looking a little farther on, found his rider. Brown's greeting was cordial and hearty, Mr. Hamlin's somewhat restrained. But at Brown's urgent request, he followed him up the back stairs to a narrow corridor, and thence to a small room looking out upon the stable yard. It was plainly furnished with a bed, a table, a few chairs, and a rack for guns and whips.

"This yer's my home, Jack," said Brown, with a sigh, as he threw himself upon the bed, and motioned his companion to a chair. "Her room's t'other end of the hall. It's more'n six months since we've lived together, or met, except at meals. It's mighty rough papers on the head of the house, ain't it?" he said, with a forced laugh. "But I'm glad to see you, Jack, damn glad," and he reached from the bed, and again shook the unresponsive hand of Jack Hamlin.

"I brought ye up here, for I didn't want to talk in the stable; though, for the matter of that, it's all round town. Don't strike a light. We can talk here in the moonshine. Put up your feet on that winder, and sit here beside me. Thar's whisky in that jug."

Mr. Hamlin did not avail himself of the information. Brown of Calaveras turned his face to the wall and continued:

"If I didn't love the woman, Jack, I wouldn't mind. But it's loving her, and seeing her, day arter day, goin' on at this rate, and no one to put down the brake; that's what gits me! But I'm glad to see ye, Jack, damn glad."

In the darkness he groped about until he had found and wrung his companion's hand again. He would have detained it, but Jack slipped it into the buttoned breast of his coat, and asked, listlessly, "How long has this been going on?"

"Ever since she came here; ever since the day she walked into the Magnolia. I was a fool then; Jack, I'm a fool now; but I didn't know how much I loved her till then. And she hasn't been the same woman since.

"But that ain't all, Jack; and it's what I wanted to see you about, and I'm glad you've come. It ain't that she doesn't love me any more; it ain't that she fools with every chap that comes along, for, perhaps, I staked her love and lost it, as I did everything else at the Magnolia; and, perhaps, foolin' is nateral to some women, and thar ain't no great harm done, 'cept to the fools. But, Jack, I think—I think she loves somebody else. Don't move, Jack; don't move; if your pistol hurts ye, take it off.

"It's been more'n six months now that she's seemed unhappy and lonesome, and kinder nervous and scared-like. And sometimes I've ketched her lookin' at me sort of timid and pitying. And she writes to somebody. And for the last week she's been gathering her own things—trinkets, and furbelows, and jew'lry—and, Jack, I think she's goin' off. I could stand all but that. To have her steal away like a thief—" He put his face downward to the pillow, and for a few moments there was no sound but the ticking of a clock on the mantel. Mr. Hamlin lit a cigar, and moved to the open window. The moon no longer shone into the room, and the bed and its occupant were in shadow. "What shall I do, Jack?" said the voice from the darkness.

The answer came promptly and clearly from the window-side: "Spot the man, and kill him on sight."

"But, Jack?"

"He's took the risk!"

"But will that bring HER back?"

Jack did not reply, but moved from the window toward the door.

"Don't go yet, Jack; light the candle, and sit by the table. It's a comfort to see ye, if nothin' else."

Jack hesitated, and then complied. He drew a pack of cards from his pocket and shuffled them, glancing at the bed. But Brown's face was turned to the wall. When Mr. Hamlin had shuffled the cards, he cut them, and dealt one card on the opposite side of the table and toward the bed, and another on his side of the table for himself. The first was a deuce, his own card, a king. He then shuffled and cut again. This time "dummy" had a queen, and himself a four-spot. Jack brightened up for the third deal. It brought his adversary a deuce, and himself a king again. "Two out of three," said Jack, audibly.

"What's that, Jack?" said Brown.

"Nothing."

Then Jack tried his hand with dice; but he always threw sixes, and his imaginary opponent aces. The force of habit is sometimes confusing.

Meanwhile, some magnetic influence in Mr. Hamlin's presence, or the anodyne of liquor, or both, brought surcease of sorrow, and Brown slept. Mr. Hamlin moved his chair to the window, and looked out on the town of Wingdam, now sleeping peacefully—its harsh outlines softened and subdued, its glaring colors mellowed and sobered in the moonlight that flowed over all. In the hush he could hear the gurgling of water in the ditches, and the sighing of the pines beyond the hill. Then he looked up at the firmament, and as he did so a star shot across the twinkling field. Presently another, and then another. The phenomenon suggested to Mr. Hamlin a fresh augury. If in another fifteen minutes another star should fall—He sat there, watch in hand, for twice that time, but the phenomenon was not repeated.

The clock struck two, and Brown still slept. Mr. Hamlin approached the table and took from his pocket a letter, which he read by the flickering candlelight. It contained only a single line, written in pencil, in a woman's hand:

"Be at the corral, with the buggy, at three."

The sleeper moved uneasily, and then awoke. "Are you there Jack?"

"Yes."

"Don't go yet. I dreamed just now, Jack—dreamed of old times. I thought that Sue and me was being married agin, and that the parson, Jack, was—who do you think?—you!"

The gambler laughed, and seated himself on the bed—the paper still in his hand.

"It's a good sign, ain't it?" queried Brown.

"I reckon. Say, old man, hadn't you better get up?"

The "old man," thus affectionately appealed to, rose, with the assistance of Hamlin's outstretched hand.

"Smoke?"

Brown mechanically took the proffered cigar.

"Light?"

Jack had twisted the letter into a spiral, lit it, and held it for his companion. He continued to hold it until it was consumed, and dropped the fragment—a fiery star—from the open window. He watched it as it fell, and then returned to his friend.

"Old man," he said, placing his hands upon Brown's shoulders, "in ten minutes I'll be on the road, and gone like that spark. We won't see each other agin; but, before I go, take a fool's advice: sell out all you've got, take your wife with you, and quit the country. It ain't no place for you, nor her. Tell her she must go; make her go, if she won't. Don't whine because you can't be a saint, and she ain't an angel. Be a man—and treat her like a woman. Don't be a damn fool. Good-by."

He tore himself from Brown's grasp, and leaped down the stairs like a deer. At the stable door he collared the half-sleeping hostler and backed him against the wall. "Saddle my horse in two minutes, or I'll—" The ellipsis was frightfully suggestive.

"The missis said you was to have the buggy," stammered the man.

"Damn the buggy!"

The horse was saddled as fast as the nervous hands of the astounded hostler could manipulate buckle and strap.

"Is anything up, Mr. Hamlin?" said the man, who, like all his class, admired the elan of his fiery patron, and was really concerned in his welfare.

"Stand aside!"

The man fell back. With an oath, a bound, and clatter, Jack was into the road. In another moment, to the man's half-awakened eyes, he was but a moving cloud of dust in the distance, toward which a star just loosed from its brethren was trailing a stream of fire.

But early that morning the dwellers by the Wingdam turnpike, miles away, heard a voice, pure as a skylark's, singing afield. They who were asleep turned over on their rude couches to dream of youth and love and olden days. Hard-faced men and anxious gold-seekers, already at work, ceased their labors and leaned upon their picks, to listen to a romantic vagabond ambling away against the rosy sunrise.

* * * * * * * * *

HIGH-WATER MARK

When the tide was out on the Dedlow Marsh, its extended dreariness was patent. Its spongy, low-lying surface, sluggish, inky pools, and tortuous sloughs, twisting their slimy way, eel-like, toward the open bay, were all hard facts. So were the few green tussocks, with their scant blades, their amphibious flavor and unpleasant dampness. And if you choose to indulge your fancy—although the flat monotony of the Dedlow Marsh was not inspiring—the wavy line of scattered drift gave an unpleasant consciousness of the spent waters, and made the dead certainty of the returning tide a gloomy reflection which no present sunshine could dissipate. The greener meadowland seemed oppressed with this idea, and made no positive attempt at vegetation until the work of reclamation should be complete. In the bitter fruit of the low cranberry bushes one might fancy he detected a naturally sweet disposition curdled and soured by an injudicious course of too much regular cold water.

The vocal expression of the Dedlow Marsh was also melancholy and depressing. The sepulchral boom of the bittern, the shriek of the curlew, the scream of passing brent, the wrangling of quarrelsome teal, the sharp, querulous protest of the startled crane, and syllabled complaint of the "killdeer" plover, were beyond the power of written expression. Nor was the aspect of these mournful fowls at all cheerful and inspiring. Certainly not the blue heron standing mid-leg deep in the water, obviously catching cold in a reckless disregard of wet feet and consequences; nor the mournful curlew, the dejected plover, or the low-spirited snipe, who saw fit to join him in his suicidal contemplation; nor the impassive kingfisher—an ornithological Marius—reviewing the desolate expanse; nor the black raven that went to and fro over the face of the marsh continually, but evidently couldn't make up his mind whether the waters had subsided, and felt low-spirited in the reflection that, after all this trouble, he wouldn't be able to give a definite answer. On the contrary, it was evident at a glance that the dreary expanse of Dedlow Marsh told unpleasantly on the birds, and that the season of migration was looked forward to with a feeling of relief and satisfaction by the full-grown, and of extravagant anticipation by the callow, brood. But if Dedlow Marsh was cheerless at the slack of the low tide, you should have seen it when the tide was strong and full. When the damp air blew chilly over the cold, glittering expanse, and came to the faces of those who looked seaward like another tide; when a steel-like glint marked the low hollows and the sinuous line of slough; when the great shell-incrusted trunks of fallen trees arose again, and went forth on their dreary, purposeless wanderings, drifting hither and thither, but getting no farther toward any goal at the falling tide or the day's decline than the cursed Hebrew in the legend; when the glossy ducks swung silently, making neither ripple nor furrow on the shimmering surface; when the fog came in with the tide and shut out the blue above, even as the green below had been obliterated; when boatmen lost in that fog, paddling about in a hopeless way, started at what seemed the brushing of mermen's fingers on the boat's keel, or shrank from the tufts of grass spreading around like the floating hair of a corpse, and knew by these signs that they were lost upon Dedlow Marsh and must make a night of it, and a gloomy one at that—then you might know something of Dedlow Marsh at high water.

Let me recall a story connected with this latter view which never failed to recur to my mind in my long gunning excursions upon Dedlow Marsh. Although the event was briefly recorded in the county paper, I had the story, in all its eloquent detail, from the lips of the principal actor. I cannot hope to catch the varying emphasis and peculiar coloring of feminine delineation, for my narrator was a woman; but I'll try to give at least its substance.

She lived midway of the great slough of Dedlow Marsh and a good-sized river, which debouched four miles beyond into an estuary formed by the Pacific Ocean, on the long sandy peninsula which constituted the southwestern boundary of a noble bay. The house in which she lived was a small frame cabin raised from the marsh a few feet by stout piles, and was three miles distant from the settlements upon the river. Her husband was a logger—a profitable business in a county where the principal occupation was the manufacture of lumber.

It was the season of early spring when her husband left on the ebb of a high tide, with a raft of logs for the usual transportation to the lower end of the bay. As she stood by the door of the little cabin when the voyagers departed she noticed a cold look in the southeastern sky, and she remembered hearing her husband say to his companions that they must endeavor to complete their voyage before the coming of the southwesterly gale which he saw brewing. And that night it began to storm and blow harder than she had ever before experienced, and some great trees fell in the forest by the river, and the house rocked like her baby's cradle.

But however the storm might roar about the little cabin, she knew that one she trusted had driven bolt and bar with his own strong hand, and that had he feared for her he would not have left her. This, and her domestic duties, and the care of her little sickly baby, helped to keep her mind from dwelling on the weather, except, of course, to hope that he was safely harbored with the logs at Utopia in the dreary distance. But she noticed that day, when she went out to feed the chickens and look after the cow, that the tide was up to the little fence of their garden-patch, and the roar of the surf on the south beach, though miles away, she could hear distinctly. And she began to think that she would like to have someone to talk with about matters, and she believed that if it had not been so far and so stormy, and the trail so impassable, she would have taken the baby and have gone over to Ryckman's, her nearest neighbor. But then, you see, he might have returned in the storm, all wet, with no one to see to him; and it was a long exposure for baby, who was croupy and ailing.

But that night, she never could tell why, she didn't feel like sleeping or even lying down. The storm had somewhat abated, but she still "sat and sat," and even tried to read. I don't know whether it was a Bible or some profane magazine that this poor woman read, but most probably the latter, for the words all ran together and made such sad nonsense that she was forced at last to put the book down and turn to that dearer volume which lay before her in the cradle, with its white initial leaf as yet unsoiled, and try to look forward to its mysterious future. And, rocking the cradle, she thought of everything and everybody, but still was wide-awake as ever.

It was nearly twelve o'clock when she at last lay down in her clothes. How long she slept she could not remember, but she awoke with a dreadful choking in her throat, and found herself standing, trembling all over, in the middle of the room, with her baby clasped to her breast, and she was "saying something." The baby cried and sobbed, and she walked up and down trying to hush it when she heard a scratching at the door. She opened it fearfully, and was glad to see it was only old Pete, their dog, who crawled, dripping with water, into the room. She would like to have looked out, not in the faint hope of her husband's coming, but to see how things looked; but the wind shook the door so savagely that she could hardly hold it. Then she sat down a little while, and then walked up and down a little while, and then she lay down again a little while. Lying close by the wall of the little cabin, she thought she heard once or twice something scrape slowly against the clapboards, like the scraping of branches. Then there was a little gurgling sound, "like the baby made when it was swallowing"; then something went "click-click" and "cluck-cluck," so that she sat up in bed. When she did so she was attracted by something else that seemed creeping from the back door toward the center of the room. It wasn't much wider than her little finger, but soon it swelled to the width of her hand, and began spreading all over the floor. It was water.

She ran to the front door and threw it wide open, and saw nothing but water. She ran to the back door and threw it open, and saw nothing but water. She ran to the side window, and throwing that open, she saw nothing but water. Then she remembered hearing her husband once say that there was no danger in the tide, for that fell regularly, and people could calculate on it, and that he would rather live near the bay than the river, whose banks might overflow at any time. But was it the tide? So she ran again to the back door, and threw out a stick of wood. It drifted away toward the bay. She scooped up some of the water and put it eagerly to her lips. It was fresh and sweet. It was the river, and not the tide!

It was then—O God be praised for his goodness! she did neither faint nor fall; it was then— blessed be the Saviour, for it was his merciful hand that touched and strengthened her in this awful moment—that fear dropped from her like a garment, and her trembling ceased. It was then and thereafter that she never lost her self-command, through all the trials of that gloomy night.

She drew the bedstead toward the middle of the room, and placed a table upon it and on that she put the cradle. The water on the floor was already over her ankles, and the house once or twice moved so perceptibly, and seemed to be racked so, that the closet doors all flew open. Then she heard the same rasping and thumping against the wall, and, looking out, saw that a large uprooted tree, which had lain near the road at the upper end of the pasture, had floated down to the house. Luckily its long roots dragged in the soil and kept it from moving as rapidly as the current, for had it struck the house in its full career, even the strong nails and bolts in the piles could not have withstood the shock. The hound had leaped upon its knotty surface, and crouched near the roots shivering and whining. A ray of hope flashed across her mind. She drew a heavy blanket from the bed, and, wrapping it about the babe, waded in the deepening waters to the door. As the tree swung again, broadside on, making the little cabin creak and tremble, she leaped on to its trunk. By God's mercy she succeeded in obtaining a footing on its slippery surface, and, twining an arm about its roots, she held in the other her moaning child. Then something cracked near the front porch, and the whole front of the house she had just quitted fell forward—just as cattle fall on their knees before they lie down—and at the same moment the great redwood tree swung round and drifted away with its living cargo into the black night.

For all the excitement and danger, for all her soothing of her crying babe, for all the whistling of the wind, for all the uncertainty of her situation, she still turned to look at the deserted and water-swept cabin. She remembered even then, and she wonders how foolish she was to think of it at that time, that she wished she had put on another dress and the baby's best clothes; and she kept praying that the house would be spared so that he, when he returned, would have something to come to, and it wouldn't be quite so desolate, and—how could he ever know what had become of her and baby? And at the thought she grew sick and faint. But she had something else to do besides worrying, for whenever the long roots of her ark struck an obstacle, the whole trunk made half a revolution, and twice dipped her in the black water. The hound, who kept distracting her by running up and down the tree and howling, at last fell off at one of these collisions. He swam for some time beside her, and she tried to get the poor beast up on the tree, but he "acted silly" and wild, and at last she lost sight of him forever. Then she and her baby were left alone. The light which had burned for a few minutes in the deserted cabin was quenched suddenly. She could not then tell whither she was drifting. The outline of the white dunes on the peninsula showed dimly ahead, and she judged the tree was moving in a line with the river. It must be about slack water, and she had probably reached the eddy formed by the confluence of the tide and the overflowing waters of the river. Unless the tide fell soon, there was present danger of her drifting to its channel, and being carried out to sea or crushed in the floating drift. That peril averted, if she were carried out on the ebb toward the bay, she might hope to strike one of the wooded promontories of the peninsula, and rest till daylight. Sometimes she thought she heard voices and shouts from the river, and the bellowing of cattle and bleating of sheep. Then again it was only the ringing in her ears and throbbing of her heart. She found at about this time that she was so chilled and stiffened in her cramped position that she could scarcely move, and the baby cried so when she put it to her breast that she noticed the milk refused to flow; and she was so frightened at that, that she put her head under her shawl, and for the first time cried bitterly.

When she raised her head again, the boom of the surf was behind her, and she knew that her ark had again swung round. She dipped up the water to cool her parched throat, and found that it was salt as her tears. There was a relief, though, for by this sign she knew that she was drifting with the tide. It was then the wind went down, and the great and awful silence oppressed her.

There was scarcely a ripple against the furrowed sides of the great trunk on which she rested, and around her all was black gloom and quiet. She spoke to the baby just to hear herself speak, and to know that she had not lost her voice. She thought then—it was queer, but she could not help thinking it—how awful must have been the night when the great ship swung over the Asiatic peak, and the sounds of creation were blotted out from the world. She thought, too, of mariners clinging to spars, and of poor women who were lashed to rafts, and beaten to death by the cruel sea. She tried to thank God that she was thus spared, and lifted her eyes from the baby, who had fallen into a fretful sleep. Suddenly, away to the southward, a great light lifted itself out of the gloom, and flashed and flickered, and flickered and flashed again. Her heart fluttered quickly against the baby's cold cheek. It was the lighthouse at the entrance of the bay. As she was yet wondering, the tree suddenly rolled a little, dragged a little, and then seemed to lie quiet and still. She put out her hand and the current gurgled against it. The tree was aground, and, by the position of the light and the noise of the surf, aground upon the Dedlow Marsh.

Had it not been for her baby, who was ailing and croupy, had it not been for the sudden drying up of that sensitive fountain, she would have felt safe and relieved. Perhaps it was this which tended to make all her impressions mournful and gloomy. As the tide rapidly fell, a great flock of black brent fluttered by her, screaming and crying. Then the plover flew up and piped mournfully as they wheeled around the trunk, and at last fearlessly lit upon it like a gray cloud. Then the heron flew over and around her, shrieking and protesting, and at last dropped its gaunt legs only a few yards from her. But, strangest of all, a pretty white bird, larger than a dove—like a pelican, but not a pelican—circled around and around her. At last it lit upon a rootlet of the tree, quite over her shoulder. She put out her hand and stroked its beautiful white neck, and it never appeared to move. It stayed there so long that she thought she would lift up the baby to see it, and try to attract her attention. But when she did so, the child was so chilled and cold, and had such a blue look under the little lashes which it didn't raise at all, that she screamed aloud, and the bird flew away, and she fainted.

Well, that was the worst of it, and perhaps it was not so much, after all, to any but herself. For when she recovered her senses it was bright sunlight, and dead low water. There was a confused noise of guttural voices about her, and an old squaw, singing an Indian "hushaby," and rocking herself from side to side before a fire built on the marsh, before which she, the recovered wife and mother, lay weak and weary. Her first thought was for her baby, and she was about to speak, when a young squaw, who must have been a mother herself, fathomed her thought and brought her the "mowitch," pale but living, in such a queer little willow cradle all bound up, just like the squaw's own young one, that she laughed and cried together, and the young squaw and the old squaw showed their big white teeth and glinted their black eyes and said, "Plenty get well, skeena mowitch," "wagee man come plenty soon," and she could have kissed their brown faces in her joy. And then she found that they had been gathering berries on the marsh in their queer, comical baskets, and saw the skirt of her gown fluttering on the tree from afar, and the old squaw couldn't resist the temptation of procuring a new garment, and came down and discovered the "wagee" woman and child. And of course she gave the garment to the old squaw, as you may imagine, and when HE came at last and rushed up to her, looking about ten years older in his anxiety, she felt so faint again that they had to carry her to the canoe. For, you see, he knew nothing about the flood until he met the Indians at Utopia, and knew by the signs that the poor woman was his wife. And at the next high tide he towed the tree away back home, although it wasn't worth the trouble, and built another house, using the old tree for the foundation and props, and called it after her, "Mary's Ark!" But you may guess the next house was built above high-water mark. And that's all.

Not much, perhaps, considering the malevolent capacity of the Dedlow Marsh. But you must tramp over it at low water, or paddle over it at high tide, or get lost upon it once or twice in the fog, as I have, to understand properly Mary's adventure, or to appreciate duly the blessings of living beyond High-Water Mark.

* * * * * * * * * *

A LONELY RIDE

As I stepped into the Slumgullion stage I saw that it was a dark night, a lonely road, and that I was the only passenger. Let me assure the reader that I have no ulterior design in making this assertion. A long course of light reading has forewarned me what every experienced intelligence must confidently look for from such a statement. The storyteller who willfully tempts Fate by such obvious beginnings; who is to the expectant reader in danger of being robbed or half-murdered, or frightened by an escaped lunatic, or introduced to his ladylove for the first time, deserves to be detected. I am relieved to say that none of these things occurred to me. The road from Wingdam to Slumgullion knew no other banditti than the regularly licensed hotelkeepers; lunatics had not yet reached such depth of imbecility as to ride of their own free will in California stages; and my Laura, amiable and long-suffering as she always is, could not, I fear, have borne up against these depressing circumstances long enough to have made the slightest impression on me.

I stood with my shawl and carpetbag in hand, gazing doubtingly on the vehicle. Even in the darkness the red dust of Wingdam was visible on its roof and sides, and the red slime of Slumgullion clung tenaciously to its wheels. I opened the door; the stage creaked easily, and in the gloomy abyss the swaying straps beckoned me, like ghostly hands, to come in now and have my sufferings out at once.

I must not omit to mention the occurrence of a circumstance which struck me as appalling and mysterious. A lounger on the steps of the hotel, who I had reason to suppose was not in any way connected with the stage company, gravely descended, and walking toward the conveyance, tried the handle of the door, opened it, expectorated in the carriage, and returned to the hotel with a serious demeanor. Hardly had he resumed his position when another individual, equally disinterested, impassively walked down the steps, proceeded to the back of the stage, lifted it, expectorated carefully on the axle, and returned slowly and pensively to the hotel. A third spectator wearily disengaged himself from one of the Ionic columns of the portico and walked to the box, remained for a moment in serious and expectorative contemplation of the boot, and then returned to his column. There was something so weird in this baptism that I grew quite nervous.

Perhaps I was out of spirits. A number of infinitesimal annoyances, winding up with the resolute persistency of the clerk at the stage office to enter my name misspelt on the waybill, had not predisposed me to cheerfulness. The inmates of the Eureka House, from a social viewpoint, were not attractive. There was the prevailing opinion—so common to many honest people—that a serious style of deportment and conduct toward a stranger indicates high gentility and elevated station. Obeying this principle, all hilarity ceased on my entrance to supper, and general remark merged into the safer and uncompromising chronicle of several bad cases of diphtheria, then epidemic at Wingdam. When I left the dining-room, with an odd feeling that I had been supping exclusively on mustard and tea leaves, I stopped a moment at the parlor door. A piano, harmoniously related to the dinner bell, tinkled responsive to a diffident and uncertain touch. On the white wall the shadow of an old and sharp profile was bending over several symmetrical and shadowy curls. "I sez to Mariar, Mariar, sez I, 'Praise to the face is open disgrace.'" I heard no more. Dreading some susceptibility to sincere expression on the subject of female loveliness, I walked away, checking the compliment that otherwise might have risen unbidden to my lips, and have brought shame and sorrow to the household.

It was with the memory of these experiences resting heavily upon me that I stood hesitatingly before the stage door. The driver, about to mount, was for a moment illuminated by the open door of the hotel. He had the wearied look which was the distinguishing expression of Wingdam. Satisfied that I was properly waybilled and receipted for, he took no further notice of me. I looked longingly at the box seat, but he did not respond to the appeal. I flung my carpetbag into the chasm, dived recklessly after it, and—before I was fairly seated—with a great sigh, a creaking of unwilling springs, complaining bolts, and harshly expostulating axle, we moved away. Rather the hotel door slipped behind, the sound of the piano sank to rest, and the night and its shadows moved solemnly upon us.

To say it was dark expressed but faintly the pitchy obscurity that encompassed the vehicle. The roadside trees were scarcely distinguishable as deeper masses of shadow; I knew them only by the peculiar sodden odor that from time to time sluggishly flowed in at the open window as we rolled by. We proceeded slowly; so leisurely that, leaning from the carriage, I more than once detected the fragrant sigh of some astonished cow, whose ruminating repose upon the highway we had ruthlessly disturbed. But in the darkness our progress, more the guidance of some mysterious instinct than any apparent volition of our own, gave an indefinable charm of security to our journey that a moment's hesitation or indecision on the part of the driver would have destroyed.

I had indulged a hope that in the empty vehicle I might obtain that rest so often denied me in its crowded condition. It was a weak delusion. When I stretched out my limbs it was only to find that the ordinary conveniences for making several people distinctly uncomfortable were distributed throughout my individual frame. At last, resting my arms on the straps, by dint of much gymnastic effort I became sufficiently composed to be aware of a more refined species of torture. The springs of the stage, rising and falling regularly, produced a rhythmical beat which began to absorb my attention painfully. Slowly this thumping merged into a senseless echo of the mysterious female of the hotel parlor, and shaped itself into this awful and benumbing axiom— "Praise-to-the-face-is-open-disgrace. Praise-to-the-face-is-open-disgrace." Inequalities of the road only quickened its utterance or drawled it to an exasperating length.

It was of no use to consider the statement seriously. It was of no use to except to it indignantly. It was of no use to recall the many instances where praise to the face had redounded to the everlasting honor of praiser and bepraised; of no use to dwell sentimentally on modest genius and courage lifted up and strengthened by open commendation; of no use to except to the mysterious female, to picture her as rearing a thin-blooded generation on selfish and mechanically repeated axioms—all this failed to counteract the monotonous repetition of this sentence. There was nothing to do but to give in—and I was about to accept it weakly, as we too often treat other illusions of darkness and necessity, for the time being, when I became aware of some other annoyance that had been forcing itself upon me for the last few moments. How quiet the driver was!

Was there any driver? Had I any reason to suppose that he was not lying gagged and bound on the roadside, and the highwayman with blackened face who did the thing so quietly driving me— whither? The thing is perfectly feasible. And what is this fancy now being jolted out of me? A story? It's of no use to keep it back—particularly in this abysmal vehicle, and here it comes: I am a Marquis—a French Marquis; French, because the peerage is not so well known, and the country is better adapted to romantic incident—a Marquis, because the democratic reader delights in the nobility. My name is something LIGNY. I am coming from Paris to my country seat at St. Germain. It is a dark night, and I fall asleep and tell my honest coachman, Andre, not to disturb me, and dream of an angel. The carriage at last stops at the chateau. It is so dark that when I alight I do not recognize the face of the footman who holds the carriage door. But what of that?—PESTE! I am heavy with sleep. The same obscurity also hides the old familiar indecencies of the statues on the terrace; but there is a door, and it opens and shuts behind me smartly. Then I find myself in a trap, in the presence of the brigand who has quietly gagged poor Andre and conducted the carriage thither. There is nothing for me to do, as a gallant French Marquis, but to say, "PARBLEU!" draw my rapier, and die valorously! I am found a week or two after outside a deserted cabaret near the barrier, with a hole through my ruffled linen and my pockets stripped. No; on second thoughts, I am rescued—rescued by the angel I have been dreaming of, who is the assumed daughter of the brigand but the real daughter of an intimate friend.

Looking from the window again, in the vain hope of distinguishing the driver, I found my eyes were growing accustomed to the darkness. I could see the distant horizon, defined by India-inky woods, relieving a lighter sky. A few stars widely spaced in this picture glimmered sadly. I noticed again the infinite depth of patient sorrow in their serene faces; and I hope that the vandal who first applied the flippant "twinkle" to them may not be driven melancholy-mad by their reproachful eyes. I noticed again the mystic charm of space that imparts a sense of individual solitude to each integer of the densest constellation, involving the smallest star with immeasurable loneliness. Something of this calm and solitude crept over me, and I dozed in my gloomy cavern. When I awoke the full moon was rising. Seen from my window, it had an indescribably unreal and theatrical effect. It was the full moon of NORMA—that remarkable celestial phenomenon which rises so palpably to a hushed audience and a sublime andante chorus, until the CASTA DIVA is sung—the "inconstant moon" that then and thereafter remains fixed in the heavens as though it were a part of the solar system inaugurated by Joshua. Again the white-robed Druids filed past me, again I saw that improbable mistletoe cut from that impossible oak, and again cold chills ran down my back with the first strain of the recitative. The thumping springs essayed to beat time, and the private-box-like obscurity of the vehicle lent a cheap enchantment to the view. But it was a vast improvement upon my past experience, and I hugged the fond delusion.

My fears for the driver were dissipated with the rising moon. A familiar sound had assured me of his presence in the full possession of at least one of his most important functions. Frequent and full expectoration convinced me that his lips were as yet not sealed by the gag of highwaymen, and soothed my anxious ear. With this load lifted from my mind, and assisted by the mild presence of Diana, who left, as when she visited Endymion, much of her splendor outside my cavern—I looked around the empty vehicle. On the forward seat lay a woman's hairpin. I picked it up with an interest that, however, soon abated. There was no scent of the roses to cling to it still, not even of hair oil. No bend or twist in its rigid angles betrayed any trait of its wearer's character. I tried to think that it might have been "Mariar's." I tried to imagine that, confining the symmetrical curls of that girl, it might have heard the soft compliments whispered in her ears which provoked the wrath of the aged female. But in vain. It was reticent and unswerving in its upright fidelity, and at last slipped listlessly through my fingers.

I had dozed repeatedly—waked on the threshold of oblivion by contact with some of the angles of the coach, and feeling that I was unconsciously assuming, in imitation of a humble insect of my childish recollection, that spherical shape which could best resist those impressions, when I perceived that the moon, riding high in the heavens, had begun to separate the formless masses of the shadowy landscape. Trees isolated, in clumps and assemblages, changed places before my window. The sharp outlines of the distant hills came back, as in daylight, but little softened in the dry, cold, dewless air of a California summer night. I was wondering how late it was, and thinking that if the horses of the night traveled as slowly as the team before us, Faustus might have been spared his agonizing prayer, when a sudden spasm of activity attacked my driver. A succession of whip-snappings, like a pack of Chinese crackers, broke from the box before me. The stage leaped forward, and when I could pick myself from under the seat, a long white building had in some mysterious way rolled before my window. It must be Slumgullion! As I descended from the stage I addressed the driver:

"I thought you changed horses on the road?"

"So we did. Two hours ago."

"That's odd. I didn't notice it."

"Must have been asleep, sir. Hope you had a pleasant nap. Bully place for a nice quiet snooze—empty stage, sir!"

* * * * * * * * * *

THE MAN OF NO ACCOUNT

His name was Fagg—David Fagg. He came to California in '52 with us, in the SKYSCRAPER. I don't think he did it in an adventurous way. He probably had no other place to go to. When a knot of us young fellows would recite what splendid opportunities we resigned to go, and how sorry our friends were to have us leave, and show daguerreotypes and locks of hair, and talk of Mary and Susan, the man of no account used to sit by and listen with a pained, mortified expression on his plain face, and say nothing. I think he had nothing to say. He had no associates except when we patronized him; and, in point of fact, he was a good deal of sport to us. He was always seasick whenever we had a capful of wind. He never got his sea legs on, either. And I never shall forget how we all laughed when Rattler took him the piece of pork on a string, and— But you know that time-honored joke. And then we had such a splendid lark with him. Miss Fanny Twinkler couldn't bear the sight of him, and we used to make Fagg think that she had taken a fancy to him, and send him little delicacies and books from the cabin. You ought to have witnessed the rich scene that took place when he came up, stammering and very sick, to thank her! Didn't she flash up grandly and beautifully and scornfully? So like "Medora," Rattler said— Rattler knew Byron by heart—and wasn't old Fagg awfully cut up? But he got over it, and when Rattler fell sick at Valparaiso, old Fagg used to nurse him. You see he was a good sort of fellow, but he lacked manliness and spirit.

He had absolutely no idea of poetry. I've seen him sit stolidly by, mending his old clothes, when Rattler delivered that stirring apostrophe of Byron's to the ocean. He asked Rattler once, quite seriously, if he thought Byron was ever seasick. I don't remember Rattler's reply, but I know we all laughed very much, and I have no doubt it was something good for Rattler was smart.

When the SKYSCRAPER arrived at San Francisco we had a grand "feed." We agreed to meet every year and perpetuate the occasion. Of course we didn't invite Fagg. Fagg was a steerage passenger, and it was necessary, you see, now we were ashore, to exercise a little discretion. But Old Fagg, as we called him—he was only about twenty-five years old, by the way—was the source of immense amusement to us that day. It appeared that he had conceived the idea that he could walk to Sacramento, and actually started off afoot. We had a good time, and shook hands with one another all around, and so parted. Ah me! only eight years ago, and yet some of those hands then clasped in amity have been clenched at each other, or have dipped furtively in one another's pockets. I know that we didn't dine together the next year, because young Barker swore he wouldn't put his feet under the same mahogany with such a very contemptible scoundrel as that Mixer; and Nibbles, who borrowed money at Valparaiso of young Stubbs, who was then a waiter in a restaurant, didn't like to meet such people.

When I bought a number of shares in the Coyote Tunnel at Mugginsville, in '54, I thought I'd take a run up there and see it. I stopped at the Empire Hotel, and after dinner I got a horse and rode round the town and out to the claim. One of those individuals whom newspaper correspondents call "our intelligent informant," and to whom in all small communities the right of answering questions is tacitly yielded, was quietly pointed out to me. Habit had enabled him to work and talk at the same time, and he never pretermitted either. He gave me a history of the claim, and added: "You see, stranger," (he addressed the bank before him) "gold is sure to come out'er that theer claim, (he put in a comma with his pick) but the old pro-pri-e-tor (he wriggled out the word and the point of his pick) warn't of much account (a long stroke of the pick for a period). He was green, and let the boys about here jump him"—and the rest of his sentence was confided to his hat, which he had removed to wipe his manly brow with his red bandanna.

I asked him who was the original proprietor.

"His name war Fagg."

I went to see him. He looked a little older and plainer. He had worked hard, he said, and was getting on "so-so." I took quite a liking to him and patronized him to some extent. Whether I did so because I was beginning to have a distrust for such fellows as Rattler and Mixer is not necessary for me to state.

You remember how the Coyote Tunnel went in, and how awfully we shareholders were done! Well, the next thing I heard was that Rattler, who was one of the heaviest shareholders, was up at Mugginsville keeping bar for the proprietor of the Mugginsville Hotel, and that old Fagg had struck it rich, and didn't know what to do with his money. All this was told me by Mixer, who had been there, settling up matters, and likewise that Fagg was sweet upon the daughter of the proprietor of the aforesaid hotel. And so by hearsay and letter I eventually gathered that old Robins, the hotel man, was trying to get up a match between Nellie Robins and Fagg. Nellie was a pretty, plump, and foolish little thing, and would do just as her father wished. I thought it would be a good thing for Fagg if he should marry and settle down; that as a married man he might be of some account. So I ran up to Mugginsville one day to look after things.

It did me an immense deal of good to make Rattler mix my drinks for me—Rattler! the gay, brilliant, and unconquerable Rattler, who had tried to snub me two years ago. I talked to him about old Fagg and Nellie, particularly as I thought the subject was distasteful. He never liked Fagg, and he was sure, he said, that Nellie didn't. Did Nellie like anybody else? He turned around to the mirror behind the bar and brushed up his hair! I understood the conceited wretch. I thought I'd put Fagg on his guard and get him to hurry up matters. I had a long talk with him. You could see by the way the poor fellow acted that he was badly stuck. He sighed, and promised to pluck up courage to hurry matters to a crisis. Nellie was a good girl, and I think had a sort of quiet respect for old Fagg's unobtrusiveness. But her fancy was already taken captive by Rattler's superficial qualities, which were obvious and pleasing. I don't think Nellie was any worse than you or I. We are more apt to take acquaintances at their apparent value than their intrinsic worth. It's less trouble, and, except when we want to trust them, quite as convenient. The difficulty with women is that their feelings are apt to get interested sooner than ours, and then, you know, reasoning is out of the question. This is what old Fagg would have known had he been of any account. But he wasn't. So much the worse for him.

It was a few months afterward and I was sitting in my office when in walked old Fagg. I was surprised to see him down, but we talked over the current topics in that mechanical manner of people who know that they have something else to say, but are obliged to get at it in that formal way. After an interval Fagg in his natural manner said:

"I'm going home!"

"Going home?"

"Yes—that is, I think I'll take a trip to the Atlantic States. I came to see you, as you know I have some little property, and I have executed a power of attorney for you to manage my affairs. I have some papers I'd like to leave with you. Will you take charge of them?"

"Yes," I said. "But what of Nellie?"

His face fell. He tried to smile, and the combination resulted in one of the most startling and grotesque effects I ever beheld. At length he said:

"I shall not marry Nellie—that is"—he seemed to apologize internally for the positive form of expression—"I think that I had better not."

"David Fagg," I said with sudden severity, "you're of no account!"

To my astonishment his face brightened. "Yes," said he, "that's it!—I'm of no account! But I always knew it. You see I thought Rattler loved that girl as well as I did, and I knew she liked him better than she did me, and would be happier I dare say with him. But then I knew that old Robins would have preferred me to him, as I was better off—and the girl would do as he said—and, you see, I thought I was kinder in the way—and so I left. But," he continued, as I was about to interrupt him, "for fear the old man might object to Rattler, I've lent him enough to set him up in business for himself in Dogtown. A pushing, active, brilliant fellow, you know, like Rattler can get along, and will soon be in his old position again—and you needn't be hard on him, you know, if he doesn't. Good-by."

I was too much disgusted with his treatment of that Rattler to be at all amiable, but as his business was profitable, I promised to attend to it, and he left. A few weeks passed. The return steamer arrived, and a terrible incident occupied the papers for days afterward. People in all parts of the State conned eagerly the details of an awful shipwreck, and those who had friends aboard went away by themselves, and read the long list of the lost under their breath. I read of the gifted, the gallant, the noble, and loved ones who had perished, and among them I think I was the first to read the name of David Fagg. For the "man of no account" had "gone home!"

* * * * * * * * * *

MLISS

CHAPTER I

Just where the Sierra Nevada begins to subside in gentler undulations, and the rivers grow less rapid and yellow, on the side of a great red mountain, stands "Smith's Pocket." Seen from the red road at sunset, in the red light and the red dust, its white houses look like the outcroppings of quartz on the mountainside. The red stage topped with red-shirted passengers is lost to view half a dozen times in the tortuous descent, turning up unexpectedly in out-of-the-way places, and vanishing altogether within a hundred yards of the town. It is probably owing to this sudden twist in the road that the advent of a stranger at Smith's Pocket is usually attended with a peculiar circumstance. Dismounting from the vehicle at the stage office, the too-confident traveler is apt to walk straight out of town under the impression that it lies in quite another direction. It is related that one of the tunnel men, two miles from town, met one of these self-reliant passengers with a carpetbag, umbrella, Harper's Magazine, and other evidences of "Civilization and Refinement," plodding along over the road he had just ridden, vainly endeavoring to find the settlement of Smith's Pocket.

An observant traveler might have found some compensation for his disappointment in the weird aspect of that vicinity. There were huge fissures on the hillside, and displacements of the red soil, resembling more the chaos of some primary elemental upheaval than the work of man; while halfway down, a long flume straddled its narrow body and disproportionate legs over the chasm, like an enormous fossil of some forgotten antediluvian. At every step smaller ditches crossed the road, hiding in their sallow depths unlovely streams that crept away to a clandestine union with the great yellow torrent below, and here and there were the ruins of some cabin with the chimney alone left intact and the hearthstone open to the skies.

The settlement of Smith's Pocket owed its origin to the finding of a "pocket" on its site by a veritable Smith. Five thousand dollars were taken out of it in one half-hour by Smith. Three thousand dollars were expended by Smith and others in erecting a flume and in tunneling. And then Smith's Pocket was found to be only a pocket, and subject like other pockets to depletion. Although Smith pierced the bowels of the great red mountain, that five thousand dollars was the first and last return of his labor. The mountain grew reticent of its golden secrets, and the flume steadily ebbed away the remainder of Smith's fortune. Then Smith went into quartz-mining; then into quartz-milling; then into hydraulics and ditching, and then by easy degrees into saloonkeeping. Presently it was whispered that Smith was drinking a great deal; then it was known that Smith was a habitual drunkard, and then people began to think, as they are apt to, that he had never been anything else. But the settlement of Smith's Pocket, like that of most discoveries, was happily not dependent on the fortune of its pioneer, and other parties projected tunnels and found pockets. So Smith's Pocket became a settlement, with its two fancy stores, its two hotels, its one express office, and its two first families. Occasionally its one long straggling street was overawed by the assumption of the latest San Francisco fashions, imported per express, exclusively to the first families; making outraged Nature, in the ragged outline of her furrowed surface, look still more homely, and putting personal insult on that greater portion of the population to whom the Sabbath, with a change of linen, brought merely the necessity of cleanliness without the luxury of adornment. Then there was a Methodist Church, and hard by a Monte Bank, and a little beyond, on the mountainside, a graveyard; and then a little schoolhouse.

"The Master," as he was known to his little flock, sat alone one night in the schoolhouse, with some open copybooks before him, carefully making those bold and full characters which are supposed to combine the extremes of chirographical and moral excellence, and had got as far as "Riches are deceitful," and was elaborating the noun with an insincerity of flourish that was quite in the spirit of his text, when he heard a gentle tapping. The woodpeckers had been busy about the roof during the day, and the noise did not disturb his work. But the opening of the door, and the tapping continuing from the inside, caused him to look up. He was slightly startled by the figure of a young girl, dirty and shabbily clad. Still, her great black eyes, her coarse, uncombed, lusterless black hair falling over her sunburned face, her red arms and feet streaked with the red soil, were all familiar to him. It was Melissa Smith—Smith's motherless child.

"What can she want here?" thought the master. Everybody knew "Mliss," as she was called, throughout the length and height of Red Mountain. Everybody knew her as an incorrigible girl. Her fierce, ungovernable disposition, her mad freaks and lawless character, were in their way as proverbial as the story of her father's weaknesses, and as philosophically accepted by the townsfolk. She wrangled with and fought the schoolboys with keener invective and quite as powerful arm. She followed the trails with a woodman's craft, and the master had met her before, miles away, shoeless, stockingless, and bareheaded on the mountain road. The miners' camps along the stream supplied her with subsistence during these voluntary pilgrimages, in freely offered alms. Not but that a larger protection had been previously extended to Mliss. The Rev. Joshua McSnagley, "stated" preacher, had placed her in the hotel as servant, by way of preliminary refinement, and had introduced her to his scholars at Sunday school. But she threw plates occasionally at the landlord, and quickly retorted to the cheap witticisms of the guests, and created in the Sabbath school a sensation that was so inimical to the orthodox dullness and placidity of that institution that, with a decent regard for the starched frocks and unblemished morals of the two pink-and-white-faced children of the first families, the reverend gentleman had her ignominiously expelled. Such were the antecedents, and such the character of Mliss as she stood before the master. It was shown in the ragged dress, the unkempt hair, and bleeding feet, and asked his pity. It flashed from her black, fearless eyes, and commanded his respect.

"I come here tonight," she said rapidly and boldly, keeping her hard glance on his, "because I knew you was alone. I wouldn't come here when them gals was here. I hate 'em and they hates me. That's why. You keep school, don't you? I want to be teached!"

If to the shabbiness of her apparel and uncomeliness of her tangled hair and dirty face she had added the humility of tears, the master would have extended to her the usual moiety of pity, and nothing more. But with the natural, though illogical, instincts of his species, her boldness awakened in him something of that respect which all original natures pay unconsciously to one another in any grade. And he gazed at her the more fixedly as she went on still rapidly, her hand on that door latch and her eyes on his:

"My name's Mliss—Mliss Smith! You can bet your life on that. My father's Old Smith—Old Bummer Smith—that's what's the matter with him. Mliss Smith—and I'm coming to school!"

"Well?" said the master.

Accustomed to be thwarted and opposed, often wantonly and cruelly, for no other purpose than to excite the violent impulses of her nature, the master's phlegm evidently took her by surprise. She stopped; she began to twist a lock of her hair between her fingers; and the rigid line of upper lip, drawn over the wicked little teeth, relaxed and quivered slightly. Then her eyes dropped, and something like a blush struggled up to her cheek and tried to assert itself through the splashes of redder soil, and the sunburn of years. Suddenly she threw herself forward, calling on God to strike her dead, and fell quite weak and helpless, with her face on the master's desk, crying and sobbing as if her heart would break.

The master lifted her gently and waited for the paroxysm to pass. When, with face still averted, she was repeating between her sobs the MEA CULPA of childish penitence—that "she'd be good, she didn't mean to," etc., it came to him to ask her why she had left Sabbath school.

Why had she left the Sabbath school?—why? Oh, yes. What did he (McSnagley) want to tell her she was wicked for? What did he tell her that God hated her for? If God hated her, what did she want to go to Sabbath school for? SHE didn't want to be "beholden" to anybody who hated her.

Had she told McSnagley this?

Yes, she had.

The master laughed. It was a hearty laugh, and echoed so oddly in the little schoolhouse, and seemed so inconsistent and discordant with the sighing of the pines without, that he shortly corrected himself with a sigh. The sigh was quite as sincere in its way, however, and after a moment of serious silence he asked about her father.

Her father? What father? Whose father? What had he ever done for her? Why did the girls hate her? Come now! what made the folks say, "Old Bummer Smith's Mliss!" when she passed? Yes;

oh yes. She wished he was dead—she was dead—everybody was dead; and her sobs broke forth anew.

The master then, leaning over her, told her as well as he could what you or I might have said after hearing such unnatural theories from childish lips; only bearing in mind perhaps better than you or I the unnatural facts of her ragged dress, her bleeding feet, and the omnipresent shadow of her drunken father. Then, raising her to her feet, he wrapped his shawl around her, and, bidding her come early in the morning, he walked with her down the road. There he bade her "good night." The moon shone brightly on the narrow path before them. He stood and watched the bent little figure as it staggered down the road, and waited until it had passed the little graveyard and reached the curve of the hill, where it turned and stood for a moment, a mere atom of suffering outlined against the far-off patient stars. Then he went back to his work. But the lines of the copybook thereafter faded into long parallels of never-ending road, over which childish figures seemed to pass sobbing and crying into the night. Then, the little schoolhouse seeming lonelier than before, he shut the door and went home.

The next morning Mliss came to school. Her face had been washed, and her coarse black hair bore evidence of recent struggles with the comb, in which both had evidently suffered. The old defiant look shone occasionally in her eyes, but her manner was tamer and more subdued. Then began a series of little trials and self-sacrifices, in which master and pupil bore an equal part, and which increased the confidence and sympathy between them. Although obedient under the master's eye, at times during recess, if thwarted or stung by a fancied slight, Mliss would rage in ungovernable fury, and many a palpitating young savage, finding himself matched with his own weapons of torment, would seek the master with torn jacket and scratched face and complaints of the dreadful Mliss. There was a serious division among the townspeople on the subject, some threatening to withdraw their children from such evil companionship, and others as warmly upholding the course of the master in his work of reclamation. Meanwhile, with a steady persistence that seemed quite astonishing to him on looking back afterward, the master drew Mliss gradually out of the shadow of her past life, as though it were but her natural progress down the narrow path on which he had set her feet the moonlit night of their first meeting. Remembering the experience of the evangelical McSnagley, he carefully avoided that Rock of Ages on which that unskillful pilot had shipwrecked her young faith. But if, in the course of her reading, she chanced to stumble upon those few words which have lifted such as she above the level of the older, the wiser, and the more prudent—if she learned something of a faith that is symbolized by suffering, and the old light softened in her eyes, it did not take the shape of a lesson. A few of the plainer people had made up a little sum by which the ragged Mliss was enabled to assume the garments of respect and civilization; and often a rough shake of the hand, and words of homely commendation from a red-shirted and burly figure, sent a glow to the cheek of the young master, and set him to thinking if it was altogether deserved.

Three months had passed from the time of their first meeting, and the master was sitting late one evening over the moral and sententious copies, when there came a tap at the door and again Mliss stood before him. She was neatly clad and clean-faced, and there was nothing perhaps but the long black hair and bright black eyes to remind him of his former apparition. "Are you busy?" she asked. "Can you come with me?"—and on his signifying his readiness, in her old willful way she said, "Come, then, quick!"

They passed out of the door together and into the dark road. As they entered the town the master asked her whither she was going. She replied, "To see my father."

It was the first time he had heard her call him by that filial title, or indeed anything more than "Old Smith" or the "Old Man." It was the first time in three months that she had spoken of him at all, and the master knew she had kept resolutely aloof from him since her great change. Satisfied from her manner that it was fruitless to question her purpose, he passively followed. In out-of-the-way places, low groggeries, restaurants, and saloons; in gambling hells and dance houses, the master, preceded by Mliss, came and went. In the reeking smoke and blasphemous outcries of low dens, the child, holding the master's hand, stood and anxiously gazed, seemingly unconscious of all in the one absorbing nature of her pursuit. Some of the revelers, recognizing Mliss, called to the child to sing and dance for them, and would have forced liquor upon her but for the interference of the master. Others, recognizing him mutely, made way for them to pass. So an hour slipped by. Then the child whispered in his ear that there was a cabin on the other side of the creek crossed by the long flume, where she thought he still might be. Thither they crossed—a toilsome half-hour's walk—but in vain. They were returning by the ditch at the abutment of the flume, gazing at the lights of the town on the opposite bank, when, suddenly, sharply, a quick report rang out on the clear night air. The echoes caught it, and carried it round and round Red Mountain, and set the dogs to barking all along the streams. Lights seemed to dance and move quickly on the outskirts of the town for a few moments, the stream rippled quite audibly beside them, a few stones loosened themselves from the hillside and splashed into the stream, a heavy wind seemed to surge the branches of the funereal pines, and then the silence seemed to fall thicker, heavier, and deadlier. The master turned toward Mliss with an unconscious gesture of protection, but the child had gone. Oppressed by a strange fear, he ran quickly down the trail to the river's bed, and, jumping from boulder to boulder, reached the base of Red Mountain and the outskirts of the village. Midway of the crossing he looked up and held his breath in awe. For high above him on the narrow flume he saw the fluttering little figure of his late companion crossing swiftly in the darkness.

He climbed the bank, and, guided by a few lights moving about a central point on the mountain, soon found himself breathless among a crowd of awe-stricken and sorrowful men. Out from among them the child appeared, and, taking the master's hand, led him silently before what seemed a ragged hole in the mountain. Her face was quite white, but her excited manner gone, and her look that of one to whom some long-expected event had at last happened—an expression that to the master in his bewilderment seemed almost like relief. The walls of the cavern were partly propped by decaying timbers. The child pointed to what appeared to be some ragged, castoff clothes left in the hole by the late occupant. The master approached nearer with his flaming dip, and bent over them. It was Smith, already cold, with a pistol in his hand and a bullet in his heart, lying beside his empty pocket.

CHAPTER II

The opinion which McSnagley expressed in reference to a "change of heart" supposed to be experienced by Mliss was more forcibly described in the gulches and tunnels. It was thought there that Mliss had "struck a good lead." So when there was a new grave added to the little enclosure, and at the expense of the master a little board and inscription put above it, the RED MOUNTAIN BANNER came out quite handsomely, and did the fair thing to the memory of one of "our oldest Pioneers," alluding gracefully to that "bane of noble intellects," and otherwise genteelly shelving our dear brother with the past. "He leaves an only child to mourn his loss," says the BANNER, "who is now an exemplary scholar, thanks to the efforts of the Rev. Mr. McSnagley." The Rev. McSnagley, in fact, made a strong point of Mliss's conversion, and, indirectly attributing to the unfortunate child the suicide of her father, made affecting allusions in Sunday school to the beneficial effects of the "silent tomb," and in this cheerful contemplation drove most of the children into speechless horror, and caused the pink-and-white scions of the first families to howl dismally and refuse to be comforted.

The long dry summer came. As each fierce day burned itself out in little whiffs of pearl-gray smoke on the mountain summits, and the upspringing breeze scattered its red embers over the landscape, the green wave which in early spring upheaved above Smith's grave grew sere and dry and hard. In those days the master, strolling in the little churchyard of a Sabbath afternoon, was sometimes surprised to find a few wild flowers plucked from the damp pine forests scattered there, and oftener rude wreaths hung upon the little pine cross. Most of these wreaths were formed of a sweet-scented grass, which the children loved to keep in their desks, intertwined with the plumes of the buckeye, the syringa, and the wood anemone, and here and there the master noticed the dark-blue cowl of the monkshood, or deadly aconite. There was something in the odd association of this noxious plant with these memorials which occasioned a painful sensation to the master deeper than his esthetic sense. One day, during a long walk, in crossing a wooded ridge he came upon Mliss in the heart of the forest, perched upon a prostrate pine on a fantastic throne formed by the hanging plumes of lifeless branches, her lap full of grasses and pine burrs, and crooning to herself one of the Negro melodies of her younger life. Recognizing him at a distance, she made room for him on her elevated throne, and with a grave assumption of hospitality and patronage that would have been ridiculous had it not been so terribly earnest, she fed him with pine nuts and crab apples. The master took that opportunity to point out to her the noxious and deadly qualities of the monkshood, whose dark blossoms he saw in her lap, and extorted from her a promise not to meddle with it as long as she remained his pupil. This done— as the master had tested her integrity before—he rested satisfied, and the strange feeling which had overcome him on seeing them died away.

Of the homes that were offered Mliss when her conversion became known, the master preferred that of Mrs. Morpher, a womanly and kindhearted specimen of Southwestern efflorescence, known in her maidenhood as the "Per-rairie Rose." Being one of those who contend resolutely against their own natures, Mrs. Morpher, by a long series of self-sacrifices and struggles, had at last subjugated her naturally careless disposition to principles of "order," which she considered, in common with Mr. Pope, as "Heaven's first law." But she could not entirely govern the orbits of her satellites, however regular her own movements, and even her own "Jeemes" sometimes collided with her. Again her old nature asserted itself in her children. Lycurgus dipped into the cupboard "between meals," and Aristides came home from school without shoes, leaving those important articles on the threshold, for the delight of a barefooted walk down the ditches. Octavia and Cassandra were "keerless" of their clothes. So with but one exception, however much the "Prairie Rose" might have trimmed and pruned and trained her own matured luxuriance, the little shoots came up defiantly wild and straggling. That one exception was Clytemnestra Morpher, aged fifteen. She was the realization of her mother's immaculate conception—neat, orderly, and dull.

It was an amiable weakness of Mrs. Morpher to imagine that "Clytie" was a consolation and model for Mliss. Following this fallacy, Mrs. Morpher threw Clytie at the head of Mliss when she was "bad," and set her up before the child for adoration in her penitential moments. It was not, therefore, surprising to the master to hear that Clytie was coming to school, obviously as a favor to the master and as an example for Mliss and others. For "Clytie" was quite a young lady. Inheriting her mother's physical peculiarities, and in obedience to the climatic laws of the Red Mountain region, she was an early bloomer. The youth of Smith's Pocket, to whom this kind of flower was rare, sighed for her in April and languished in May. Enamored swains haunted the schoolhouse at the hour of dismissal. A few were jealous of the master.

Perhaps it was this latter circumstance that opened the master's eyes to another. He could not help noticing that Clytie was romantic; that in school she required a great deal of attention; that her pens were uniformly bad and wanted fixing; that she usually accompanied the request with a certain expectation in her eye that was somewhat disproportionate to the quality of service she verbally required; that she sometimes allowed the curves of a round, plump white arm to rest on his when he was writing her copies; that she always blushed and flung back her blond curls when she did so. I don't remember whether I have stated that the master was a young man—it's of little consequence, however; he had been severely educated in the school in which Clytie was taking her first lesson, and, on the whole, withstood the flexible curves and factitious glance like the fine young Spartan that he was. Perhaps an insufficient quality of food may have tended to this asceticism. He generally avoided Clytie; but one evening, when she returned to the schoolhouse after something she had forgotten, and did not find it until the master walked home with her, I hear that he endeavored to make himself particularly agreeable—partly from the fact, I imagine, that his conduct was adding gall and bitterness to the already overcharged hearts of Clytemnestra's admirers.

The morning after this affecting episode Mliss did not come to school. Noon came, but not Mliss. Questioning Clytie on the subject, it appeared that they had left the school together, but the willful Mliss had taken another road. The afternoon brought her not. In the evening he called on Mrs. Morpher, whose motherly heart was really alarmed. Mr. Morpher had spent all day in search of her, without discovering a trace that might lead to her discovery. Aristides was summoned as a probable accomplice, but that equitable infant succeeded in impressing the household with his innocence. Mrs. Morpher entertained a vivid impression that the child would yet be found drowned in a ditch, or, what was almost as terrible, muddied and soiled beyond the redemption of soap and water. Sick at heart, the master returned to the schoolhouse. As he lit his lamp and seated himself at his desk, he found a note lying before him addressed to himself, in Mliss's handwriting. It seemed to be written on a leaf torn from some old memorandum book, and, to prevent sacrilegious trifling, had been sealed with six broken wafers. Opening it almost tenderly, the master read as follows:

RESPECTED SIR—When you read this, I am run away. Never to come back. NEVER, NEVER, NEVER. You can give my beeds to Mary Jennings, and my Amerika's Pride [a highly colored lithograph from a tobacco-box] to Sally Flanders. But don't you give anything to Clytie Morpher. Don't you dare to. Do you know what my opinion is of her, it is this, she is perfekly disgustin. That is all and no more at present from

Yours respectfully,

MELISSA SMITH.

The master sat pondering on this strange epistle till the moon lifted its bright face above the distant hills, and illuminated the trail that led to the schoolhouse, beaten quite hard with the coming and going of little feet. Then, more satisfied in mind, he tore the missive into fragments and scattered them along the road.

At sunrise the next morning he was picking his way through the palmlike fern and thick underbrush of the pine forest, starting the hare from its form, and awakening a querulous protest from a few dissipated crows, who had evidently been making a night of it, and so came to the wooded ridge where he had once found Mliss. There he found the prostrate pine and tasseled branches, but the throne was vacant. As he drew nearer, what might have been some frightened animal started through the crackling limbs. It ran up the tossed arms of the fallen monarch and sheltered itself in some friendly foliage. The master, reaching the old seat, found the nest still warm; looking up in the intertwining branches, he met the black eyes of the errant Mliss. They gazed at each other without speaking. She was first to break the silence.

"What do you want?" she asked curtly.

The master had decided on a course of action. "I want some crab apples," he said humbly.

"Sha'n't have 'em! go away. Why don't you get 'em of Clytemnerestera?" (It seemed to be a relief to Mliss to express her contempt in additional syllables to that classical young woman's already long-drawn title.) "O you wicked thing!"

"I am hungry, Lissy. I have eaten nothing since dinner yesterday. I am famished!" and the young man in a state of remarkable exhaustion leaned against the tree.

Melissa's heart was touched. In the bitter days of her gypsy life she had known the sensation he so artfully simulated. Overcome by his heartbroken tone, but not entirely divested of suspicion, she said:

"Dig under the tree near the roots, and you'll find lots; but mind you don't tell," for Mliss had HER hoards as well as the rats and squirrels.

But the master, of course, was unable to find them; the effects of hunger probably blinding his senses. Mliss grew uneasy. At length she peered at him through the leaves in an elfish way, and questioned:

"If I come down and give you some, you'll promise you won't touch me?"

The master promised.

"Hope you'll die if you do!"

The master accepted instant dissolution as a forfeit. Mliss slid down the tree. For a few moments nothing transpired but the munching of the pine nuts. "Do you feel better?" she asked, with some solicitude. The master confessed to a recuperated feeling, and then, gravely thanking her, proceeded to retrace his steps. As he expected, he had not gone far before she called him. He turned. She was standing there quite white, with tears in her widely opened orbs. The master felt that the right moment had come. Going up to her, he took both her hands, and looking in her tearful eyes, said, gravely, "Lissy, do you remember the first evening you came to see me?"

Lissy remembered.

"You asked me if you might come to school, for you wanted to learn something and be better, and I said—"

"Come," responded the child, promptly.

"What would YOU say if the master now came to you and said that he was lonely without his little scholar, and that he wanted her to come and teach him to be better?"

The child hung her head for a few moments in silence. The master waited patiently. Tempted by the quiet, a hare ran close to the couple, and raising her bright eyes and velvet forepaws, sat and gazed at them. A squirrel ran halfway down the furrowed bark of the fallen tree, and there stopped.

"We are waiting, Lissy," said the master, in a whisper, and the child smiled. Stirred by a passing breeze, the treetops rocked, and a long pencil of light stole through their interlaced boughs full on the doubting face and irresolute little figure. Suddenly she took the master's hand in her quick way. What she said was scarcely audible, but the master, putting the black hair back from her forehead, kissed her; and so, hand in hand, they passed out of the damp aisles and forest odors into the open sunlit road.

CHAPTER III

Somewhat less spiteful in her intercourse with other scholars, Mliss still retained an offensive attitude in regard to Clytemnestra. Perhaps the jealous element was not entirely lulled in her passionate little breast. Perhaps it was only that the round curves and plump outline offered more extended pinching surface. But while such ebullitions were under the master's control, her enmity occasionally took a new and irrepressible form.

The master in his first estimate of the child's character could not conceive that she had ever possessed a doll. But the master, like many other professed readers of character, was safer in a posteriori than a priori reasoning. Mliss had a doll, but then it was emphatically Mliss's doll—a smaller copy of herself. Its unhappy existence had been a secret discovered accidentally by Mrs. Morpher. It had been the old-time companion of Mliss's wanderings, and bore evident marks of suffering. Its original complexion was long since washed away by the weather and anointed by the slime of ditches. It looked very much as Mliss had in days past. Its one gown of faded stuff was dirty and ragged, as hers had been. Mliss had never been known to apply to it any childish term of endearment. She never exhibited it in the presence of other children. It was put severely to bed in a hollow tree near the schoolhouse, and only allowed exercise during Mliss's rambles. Fulfilling a stern duty to her doll, as she would to herself, it knew no luxuries.

Now Mrs. Morpher, obeying a commendable impulse, bought another doll and gave it to Mliss. The child received it gravely and curiously. The master on looking at it one day fancied he saw a slight resemblance in its round red cheeks and mild blue eyes to Clytemnestra. It became evident before long that Mliss had also noticed the same resemblance. Accordingly she hammered its waxen head on the rocks when she was alone, and sometimes dragged it with a string round its neck to and from school. At other times, setting it up on her desk, she made a pincushion of its patient and inoffensive body. Whether this was done in revenge of what she considered a second figurative obtrusion of Clytie's excellences upon her, or whether she had an intuitive appreciation of the rites of certain other heathens, and, indulging in that "fetish" ceremony, imagined that the original of her wax model would pine away and finally die, is a metaphysical question I shall not now consider.

In spite of these moral vagaries, the master could not help noticing in her different tasks the working of a quick, restless, and vigorous perception. She knew neither the hesitancy nor the doubts of childhood. Her answers in class were always slightly dashed with audacity. Of course she was not infallible. But her courage and daring in passing beyond her own depth and that of the floundering little swimmers around her, in their minds outweighed all errors of judgment. Children are not better than grown people in this respect, I fancy; and whenever the little red hand flashed above her desk, there was a wondering silence, and even the master was sometimes oppressed with a doubt of his own experience and judgment.

Nevertheless, certain attributes which at first amused and entertained his fancy began to afflict him with grave doubts. He could not but see that Mliss was revengeful, irreverent, and willful. That there was but one better quality which pertained to her semisavage disposition—the faculty of physical fortitude and self-sacrifice, and another, though not always an attribute of the noble savage—Truth. Mliss was both fearless and sincere; perhaps in such a character the adjectives were synonymous.

The master had been doing some hard thinking on this subject, and had arrived at that conclusion quite common to all who think sincerely, that he was generally the slave of his own prejudices, when he determined to call on the Rev. McSnagley for advice. This decision was somewhat humiliating to his pride, as he and McSnagley were not friends. But he thought of Mliss, and the evening of their first meeting; and perhaps with a pardonable superstition that it was not chance alone that had guided her willful feet to the schoolhouse, and perhaps with a complacent consciousness of the rare magnanimity of the act, he choked back his dislike and went to McSnagley.

The reverend gentleman was glad to see him. Moreover, he observed that the master was looking "peartish," and hoped he had got over the "neuralgy" and "rheumatiz." He himself had been troubled with a dumb "ager" since last conference. But he had learned to "rastle and pray."

Pausing a moment to enable the master to write his certain method of curing the dumb "ager" upon the book and volume of his brain, Mr. McSnagley proceeded to inquire after Sister Morpher. "She is an adornment to ChrisTEWanity, and has a likely growin' young family," added Mr. McSnagley; "and there's that mannerly young gal—so well behaved—Miss Clytie." In fact, Clytie's perfections seemed to affect him to such an extent that he dwelt for several minutes upon them. The master was doubly embarrassed. In the first place, there was an enforced contrast with poor Mliss in all this praise of Clytie. Secondly, there was something unpleasantly confidential in his tone of speaking of Mrs. Morpher's earliest born. So that the master, after a few futile efforts to say something natural, found it convenient to recall another engagement, and left without asking the information required, but in his after reflections somewhat unjustly giving the Rev. Mr. McSnagley the full benefit of having refused it.

Perhaps this rebuff placed the master and pupil once more in the close communion of old. The child seemed to notice the change in the master's manner, which had of late been constrained, and in one of their long postprandial walks she stopped suddenly, and mounting a stump, looked full in his face with big, searching eyes. "You ain't mad?" said she, with an interrogative shake of the black braids. "No." "Nor bothered?" "No." "Nor hungry?" (Hunger was to Mliss a sickness that might attack a person at any moment.) "No." "Nor thinking of her?" "Of whom, Lissy?" "That white girl." (This was the latest epithet invented by Mliss, who was a very dark brunette, to express Clytemnestra.) "No." "Upon your word?" (A substitute for "Hope you'll die!" proposed by the master.) "Yes." "And sacred honor?" "Yes." Then Mliss gave him a fierce little kiss, and, hopping down, fluttered off. For two or three days after that she condescended to appear more like other children, and be, as she expressed it, "good."

Two years had passed since the master's advent at Smith's Pocket, and as his salary was not large, and the prospects of Smith's Pocket eventually becoming the capital of the State not entirely definite, he contemplated a change. He had informed the school trustees privately of his intentions, but educated young men of unblemished moral character being scarce at that time, he consented to continue his school term through the winter to early spring. None else knew of his intention except his one friend, a Dr. Duchesne, a young Creole physician known to the people of Wingdam as "Duchesny." He never mentioned it to Mrs. Morpher, Clytie, or any of his scholars. His reticence was partly the result of a constitutional indisposition to fuss, partly a desire to be spared the questions and surmises of vulgar curiosity, and partly that he never really believed he was going to do anything before it was done.

He did not like to think of Mliss. It was a selfish instinct, perhaps, which made him try to fancy his feeling for the child was foolish, romantic, and unpractical. He even tried to imagine that she would do better under the control of an older and sterner teacher. Then she was nearly eleven, and in a few years, by the rules of Red Mountain, would be a woman. He had done his duty. After Smith's death he addressed letters to Smith's relatives, and received one answer from a sister of Melissa's mother. Thanking the master, she stated her intention of leaving the Atlantic States for California with her husband in a few months. This was a slight superstructure for the airy castle which the master pictured for Mliss's home, but it was easy to fancy that some loving, sympathetic woman, with the claims of kindred, might better guide her wayward nature. Yet, when the master had read the letter, Mliss listened to it carelessly, received it submissively, and afterward cut figures out of it with her scissors, supposed to represent Clytemnestra, labeled "the white girl," to prevent mistakes, and impaled them upon the outer walls of the schoolhouse.

When the summer was about spent, and the last harvest had been gathered in the valleys, the master bethought him of gathering in a few ripened shoots of the young idea, and of having his Harvest Home, or Examination. So the savants and professionals of Smith's Pocket were gathered to witness that time-honored custom of placing timid children in a constrained positions and bullying them as in a witness box. As usual in such cases, the most audacious and self-possessed were the lucky recipients of the honors. The reader will imagine that in the present instance Mliss and Clytie were preeminent, and divided public attention; Mliss with her clearness of material perception and self-reliance, Clytie with her placid self-esteem and saintlike correctness of deportment. The other little ones were timid and blundering. Mliss's readiness and brilliancy, of course, captivated the greatest number and provoked the greatest applause. Mliss's antecedents had unconsciously awakened the strongest sympathies of a class whose athletic forms were ranged against the walls, or whose handsome bearded faces looked in at the windows. But Mliss's popularity was overthrown by an unexpected circumstance.

McSnagley had invited himself, and had been going through the pleasing entertainment of frightening the more timid pupils by the vaguest and most ambiguous questions delivered in an impressive funereal tone; and Mliss had soared into astronomy, and was tracking the course of our spotted ball through space, and keeping time with the music of the spheres, and defining the tethered orbits of the planets, when McSnagley impressively arose. "Meelissy! ye were speaking of the revolutions of this yere yearth and the move-MENTS of the sun, and I think ye said it had been a doing of it since the creashun, eh?" Mliss nodded a scornful affirmative. "Well, war that the truth?" said McSnagley, folding his arms. "Yes," said Mliss, shutting up her little red lips tightly. The handsome outlines at the windows peered further in the schoolroom, and a saintly Raphael face, with blond beard and soft blue eyes, belonging to the biggest scamp in the diggings, turned toward the child and whispered, "Stick to it, Mliss!" The reverend gentleman heaved a deep sigh, and cast a compassionate glance at the master, then at the children, and then rested his look on Clytie. That young woman softly elevated her round, white arm. Its seductive curves were enhanced by a gorgeous and massive specimen bracelet, the gift of one of her humblest worshipers, worn in honor of the occasion. There was a momentary silence. Clytie's round cheeks were very pink and soft. Clytie's big eyes were very bright and blue. Clytie's low-necked white book muslin rested softly on Clytie's white, plump shoulders. Clytie looked at the master, and the master nodded. Then Clytie spoke softly:

"Joshua commanded the sun to stand still, and it obeyed him!" There was a low hum of applause in the schoolroom, a triumphant expression on McSnagley's face, a grave shadow on the master's, and a comical look of disappointment reflected from the windows. Mliss skimmed rapidly over her astronomy, and then shut the book with a loud snap. A groan burst from McSnagley, an expression of astonishment from the schoolroom, a yell from the windows, as Mliss brought her red fist down on the desk, with the emphatic declaration:

"It's a damn lie. I don't believe it!"

CHAPTER IV

The long wet season had drawn near its close. Signs of spring were visible in the swelling buds and rushing torrents. The pine forests exhaled the fresher spicery. The azaleas were already budding, the ceanothus getting ready its lilac livery for spring. On the green upland which climbed Red Mountain at its southern aspect the long spike of the monkshood shot up from its broad-leaved stool, and once more shook its dark-blue bells. Again the billow above Smith's grave was soft and green, its crest just tossed with the foam of daisies and buttercups. The little graveyard had gathered a few new dwellers in the past year, and the mounds were placed two by two by the little paling until they reached Smith's grave, and there there was but one. General superstition had shunned it, and the plot beside Smith was vacant.

There had been several placards posted about the town, intimating that, at a certain period, a celebrated dramatic company would perform, for a few days, a series of "side-splitting" and "screaming farces"; that, alternating pleasantly with this, there would be some melodrama and a grand divertisement which would include singing, dancing, etc. These announcements occasioned a great fluttering among the little folk, and were the theme of much excitement and great speculation among the master's scholars. The master had promised Mliss, to whom this sort of thing was sacred and rare, that she should go, and on that momentous evening the master and Mliss "assisted."

The performance was the prevalent style of heavy mediocrity; the melodrama was not bad enough to laugh at nor good enough to excite. But the master, turning wearily to the child, was astonished and felt something like self-accusation in noticing the peculiar effect upon her excitable nature. The red blood flushed in her cheeks at each stroke of her panting little heart. Her small passionate lips were slightly parted to give vent to her hurried breath. Her widely opened lids threw up and arched her black eyebrows. She did not laugh at the dismal comicalities of the funny man, for Mliss seldom laughed. Nor was she discreetly affected to the delicate extremes of the corner of a white handkerchief, as was the tender-hearted "Clytie," who was talking with her "feller" and ogling the master at the same moment. But when the performance was over, and the green curtain fell on the little stage, Mliss drew a long deep breath, and turned to the master's grave face with a half-apologetic smile and wearied gesture. Then she said, "Now take me home!" and dropped the lids of her black eyes, as if to dwell once more in fancy on the mimic stage.

On their way to Mrs. Morpher's the master thought proper to ridicule the whole performance. Now he shouldn't wonder if Mliss thought that the young lady who acted so beautifully was really in earnest, and in love with the gentleman who wore such fine clothes. Well, if she were in love with him it was a very unfortunate thing! "Why?" said Mliss, with an upward sweep of the drooping lid. "Oh! well, he couldn't support his wife at his present salary, and pay so much a week for his fine clothes, and then they wouldn't receive as much wages if they were married as if they were merely lovers—that is," added the master, "if they are not already married to somebody else; but I think the husband of the pretty young countess takes the tickets at the door, or pulls up the curtain, or snuffs the candles, or does something equally refined and elegant. As to the young man with nice clothes, which are really nice now, and must cost at least two and a half or three dollars, not to speak of that mantle of red drugget which I happen to know the price of, for I bought some of it for my room once—as to this young man, Lissy, he is a pretty good fellow, and if he does drink occasionally, I don't think people ought to take advantage of it and give him black eyes and throw him in the mud. Do you? I am sure he might owe me two dollars and a half a long time, before I would throw it up in his face, as the fellow did the other night at Wingdam."

Mliss had taken his hand in both of hers and was trying to look in his eyes, which the young man kept as resolutely averted. Mliss had a faint idea of irony, indulging herself sometimes in a species of sardonic humor, which was equally visible in her actions and her speech. But the young man continued in this strain until they had reached Mrs. Morpher's, and he had deposited Mliss in her maternal charge. Waiving the invitation of Mrs. Morpher to refreshment and rest, and shading his eyes with his hand to keep out the blue-eyed Clytemnestra's siren glances, he excused himself, and went home.

For two or three days after the advent of the dramatic company, Mliss was late at school, and the master's usual Friday afternoon ramble was for once omitted, owing to the absence of his trustworthy guide. As he was putting away his books and preparing to leave the schoolhouse, a small voice piped at his side, "Please, sir?" The master turned and there stood Aristides Morpher.

"Well, my little man," said the master, impatiently, "what is it? quick!"

"Please, sir, me and 'Kerg' thinks that Mliss is going to run away again."

"What's that, sir?" said the master, with that unjust testiness with which we always receive disagreeable news.

"Why, sir, she don't stay home any more, and 'Kerg' and me see her talking with one of those actor fellers, and she's with him now; and please, sir, yesterday she told 'Kerg' and me she could make a speech as well as Miss Cellerstina Montmoressy, and she spouted right off by heart," and the little fellow paused in a collapsed condition.

"What actor?" asked the master.

"Him as wears the shiny hat. And hair. And gold pin. And gold chain," said the just Aristides, putting periods for commas to eke out his breath.

The master put on his gloves and hat, feeling an unpleasant tightness in his chest and thorax, and walked out in the road. Aristides trotted along by his side, endeavoring to keep pace with his short legs to the master's strides, when the master stopped suddenly, and Aristides bumped up against him. "Where were they talking?" asked the master, as if continuing the conversation.

"At the Arcade," said Aristides.

When they reached the main street the master paused. "Run down home," said he to the boy. "If Mliss is there, come to the Arcade and tell me. If she isn't there, stay home; run!" And off trotted the short-legged Aristides.

The Arcade was just across the way—a long, rambling building containing a barroom, billiard room, and restaurant. As the young man crossed the plaza he noticed that two or three of the passers-by turned and looked after him. He looked at his clothes, took out his handkerchief, and wiped his face before he entered the barroom. It contained the usual number of loungers, who stared at him as he entered. One of them looked at him so fixedly and with such a strange expression that the master stopped and looked again, and then saw it was only his own reflection in a large mirror. This made the master think that perhaps he was a little excited, and so he took up a copy of the RED MOUNTAIN BANNER from one of the tables, and tried to recover his composure by reading the column of advertisements.

He then walked through the barroom, through the restaurant, and into the billiard room. The child was not there. In the latter apartment a person was standing by one of the tables with a broad-brimmed glazed hat on his head. The master recognized him as the agent of the dramatic company; he had taken a dislike to him at their first meeting, from the peculiar fashion of wearing his beard and hair. Satisfied that the object of his search was not there, he turned to the man with a glazed hat. He had noticed the master, but tried that common trick of unconsciousness in which vulgar natures always fail. Balancing a billiard cue in his hand, he pretended to play with a ball in the center of the table. The master stood opposite to him until he raised his eyes; when their glances met, the master walked up to him.

He had intended to avoid a scene or quarrel, but when he began to speak, something kept rising in his throat and retarded his utterance, and his own voice frightened him, it sounded so distant, low, and resonant. "I understand," he began, "that Melissa Smith, an orphan, and one of my scholars, has talked with you about adopting your profession. Is that so?"

The man with the glazed hat leaned over the table and made an imaginary shot that sent the ball spinning round the cushions. Then, walking round the table, he recovered the ball and placed it upon the spot. This duty discharged, getting ready for another shot, he said:

"S'pose she has?"

The master choked up again, but, squeezing the cushion of the table in his gloved hand, he went on:

"If you are a gentleman, I have only to tell you that I am her guardian, and responsible for her career. You know as well as I do the kind of life you offer her. As you may learn of anyone here, I have already brought her out of an existence worse than death—out of the streets and the contamination of vice. I am trying to do so again. Let us talk like men. She has neither father, mother, sister, or brother. Are you seeking to give her an equivalent for these?"

The man with the glazed hat examined the point of his cue, and then looked around for somebody to enjoy the joke with him.

"I know that she is a strange, willful girl," continued the master, "but she is better than she was. I believe that I have some influence over her still. I beg and hope, therefore, that you will take no further steps in this matter, but as a man, as a gentleman, leave her to me. I am willing—" But here something rose again in the master's throat, and the sentence remained unfinished.

The man with the glazed hat, mistaking the master's silence, raised his head with a coarse, brutal laugh, and said in a loud voice:

"Want her yourself, do you? That cock won't fight here, young man!"

The insult was more in the tone than in the words, more in the glance than tone, and more in the man's instinctive nature than all these. The best appreciable rhetoric to this kind of animal is a blow. The master felt this, and, with his pent-up, nervous energy finding expression in the one act, he struck the brute full in his grinning face. The blow sent the glazed hat one way and the cue another, and tore the glove and skin from the master's hand from knuckle to joint. It opened up the corners of the fellow's mouth, and spoilt the peculiar shape of his beard for some time to come.

There was a shout, an imprecation, a scuffle, and the trampling of many feet. Then the crowd parted right and left, and two sharp quick reports followed each other in rapid succession. Then they closed again about his opponent, and the master was standing alone. He remembered picking bits of burning wadding from his coat sleeve with his left hand. Someone was holding his other hand. Looking at it, he saw it was still bleeding from the blow, but his fingers were clenched around the handle of a glittering knife. He could not remember when or how he got it.

The man who was holding his hand was Mr. Morpher. He hurried the master to the door, but the master held back, and tried to tell him as well as he could with his parched throat about "Mliss." "It's all right, my boy," said Mr. Morpher. "She's home!" And they passed out into the street together. As they walked along Mr. Morpher said that Mliss had come running into the house a few moments before, and had dragged him out, saying that somebody was trying to kill the master at the Arcade. Wishing to be alone, the master promised Mr. Morpher that he would not seek the agent again that night, and parted from him, taking the road toward the schoolhouse. He was surprised in nearing it to find the door open—still more surprised to find Mliss sitting there.

The master's nature, as I have hinted before, had, like most sensitive organizations, a selfish basis. The brutal taunt thrown out by his late adversary still rankled in his heart. It was possible, he thought, that such a construction might be put upon his affection for the child, which at best was foolish and Quixotic. Besides, had she not voluntarily abnegated his authority and affection? And what had everybody else said about her? Why should he alone combat the opinion of all, and be at last obliged tacitly to confess the truth of all they predicted? And he had been a participant in a low barroom fight with a common boor, and risked his life, to prove what? What had he proved? Nothing? What would the people say? What would his friends say? What would McSnagley say?

In his self-accusation the last person he should have wished to meet was Mliss. He entered the door, and going up to his desk, told the child, in a few cold words, that he was busy, and wished to be alone. As she rose he took her vacant seat, and, sitting down, buried his head in his hands. When he looked up again she was still standing there. She was looking at his face with an anxious expression.

"Did you kill him?" she asked.

"No!" said the master.

"That's what I gave you the knife for!" said the child, quickly.

"Gave me the knife?" repeated the master, in bewilderment.

"Yes, gave you the knife. I was there under the bar. Saw you hit him. Saw you both fall. He dropped his old knife. I gave it to you. Why didn't you stick him?" said Mliss rapidly, with an expressive twinkle of the black eyes and a gesture of the little red hand.

The master could only look his astonishment.

"Yes," said Mliss. "If you'd asked me, I'd told you I was off with the play-actors. Why was I off with the play-actors? Because you wouldn't tell me you was going away. I knew it. I heard you tell the Doctor so. I wasn't a goin' to stay here alone with those Morphers. I'd rather die first."

With a dramatic gesture which was perfectly consistent with her character, she drew from her bosom a few limp green leaves, and, holding them out at arm's length, said in her quick vivid way, and in the queer pronunciation of her old life, which she fell into when unduly excited:

"That's the poison plant you said would kill me. I'll go with the play-actors, or I'll eat this and die here. I don't care which. I won't stay here, where they hate and despise me! Neither would you let me, if you didn't hate and despise me too!"

The passionate little breast heaved, and two big tears peeped over the edge of Mliss's eyelids, but she whisked them away with the corner of her apron as if they had been wasps.

"If you lock me up in jail," said Mliss, fiercely, "to keep me from the play-actors, I'll poison myself. Father killed himself—why shouldn't I? You said a mouthful of that root would kill me, and I always carry it here," and she struck her breast with her clenched fist.

The master thought of the vacant plot beside Smith's grave, and of the passionate little figure before him. Seizing her hands in his and looking full into her truthful eyes, he said:

"Lissy, will you go with ME?"

The child put her arms around his neck, and said joyfully, "Yes."

"But now—tonight?"

"Tonight."

And, hand in hand, they passed into the road—the narrow road that had once brought her weary feet to the master's door, and which it seemed she should not tread again alone. The stars glittered brightly above them. For good or ill the lesson had been learned, and behind them the school of Red Mountain closed upon them forever.

* * * * * * * * *

THE RIGHT EYE OF THE COMMANDER

The year of grace 1797 passed away on the coast of California in a southwesterly gale. The little bay of San Carlos, albeit sheltered by the headlands of the blessed Trinity, was rough and turbulent; its foam clung quivering to the seaward wall of the Mission garden; the air was filled with flying sand and spume, and as the Senor Commandante, Hermenegildo Salvatierra, looked from the deep embrasured window of the Presidio guardroom, he felt the salt breath of the distant sea buffet a color into his smoke-dried cheeks.

The Commander, I have said, was gazing thoughtfully from the window of the guardroom. He may have been reviewing the events of the year now about to pass away. But, like the garrison at the Presidio, there was little to review; the year, like its predecessors, had been uneventful—the days had slipped by in a delicious monotony of simple duties, unbroken by incident or interruption. The regularly recurring feasts and saints' days, the half-yearly courier from San Diego, the rare transport ship and rarer foreign vessel, were the mere details of his patriarchal life. If there was no achievement, there was certainly no failure. Abundant harvests and patient industry amply supplied the wants of Presidio and Mission. Isolated from the family of nations, the wars which shook the world concerned them not so much as the last earthquake; the struggle that emancipated their sister colonies on the other side of the continent to them had no suggestiveness. In short, it was that glorious Indian summer of California history around which so much poetical haze still lingers—that bland, indolent autumn of Spanish rule, so soon to be followed by the wintry storms of Mexican independence and the reviving spring of American conquest.

The Commander turned from the window and walked toward the fire that burned brightly on the deep ovenlike hearth. A pile of copybooks, the work of the Presidio school, lay on the table. As he turned over the leaves with a paternal interest, and surveyed the fair round Scripture text— the first pious pothooks of the pupils of San Carlos—an audible commentary fell from his lips: "'Abimelech took her from Abraham'—ah, little one, excellent!—'Jacob sent to see his brother'— body of Christ! that upstroke of thine, Paquita, is marvelous; the Governor shall see it!" A film of honest pride dimmed the Commander's left eye—the right, alas! twenty years before had been sealed by an Indian arrow. He rubbed it softly with the sleeve of his leather jacket, and continued: "The Ishmaelites having arrived—'"

He stopped, for there was a step in the courtyard, a foot upon the threshold, and a stranger entered. With the instinct of an old soldier, the Commander, after one glance at the intruder, turned quickly toward the wall, where his trusty Toledo hung, or should have been hanging. But it was not there, and as he recalled that the last time he had seen that weapon it was being ridden up and down the gallery by Pepito, the infant son of Bautista, the tortilla-maker, he blushed and then contented himself with frowning upon the intruder.

But the stranger's air, though irreverent, was decidedly peaceful. He was unarmed, and wore the ordinary cape of tarpaulin and sea boots of a mariner. Except a villainous smell of codfish, there was little about him that was peculiar.

His name, as he informed the Commander, in Spanish that was more fluent than elegant or precise—his name was Peleg Scudder. He was master of the schooner GENERAL COURT, of the port of Salem in Massachusetts, on a trading voyage to the South Seas, but now driven by stress of weather into the bay of San Carlos. He begged permission to ride out the gale under the headlands of the blessed Trinity, and no more. Water he did not need, having taken in a supply at Bodega. He knew the strict surveillance of the Spanish port regulations in regard to foreign vessels, and would do nothing against the severe discipline and good order of the settlement. There was a slight tinge of sarcasm in his tone as he glanced toward the desolate parade ground of the Presidio and the open unguarded gate. The fact was that the sentry, Felipe Gomez, had discreetly retired to shelter at the beginning of the storm, and was then sound asleep in the corridor.

The Commander hesitated. The port regulations were severe, but he was accustomed to exercise individual authority, and beyond an old order issued ten years before, regarding the American ship COLUMBIA, there was no precedent to guide him. The storm was severe, and a sentiment of humanity urged him to grant the stranger's request. It is but just to the Commander to say that his inability to enforce a refusal did not weigh with his decision. He would have denied with equal disregard of consequences that right to a seventy-four-gun ship which he now yielded so gracefully to this Yankee trading schooner. He stipulated only that there should be no communication between the ship and shore. "For yourself, Senor Captain," he continued, "accept my hospitality. The fort is yours as long as you shall grace it with your distinguished presence"; and with old-fashioned courtesy, he made the semblance of withdrawing from the guardroom.

Master Peleg Scudder smiled as he thought of the half-dismantled fort, the two moldy brass cannon, cast in Manila a century previous, and the shiftless garrison. A wild thought of accepting the Commander's offer literally, conceived in the reckless spirit of a man who never let slip an offer for trade, for a moment filled his brain, but a timely reflection of the commercial unimportance of the transaction checked him. He only took a capacious quid of tobacco as the Commander gravely drew a settle before the fire, and in honor of his guest untied the black-silk handkerchief that bound his grizzled brows.

What passed between Salvatierra and his guest that night it becomes me not, as a grave chronicler of the salient points of history, to relate. I have said that Master Peleg Scudder was a fluent talker, and under the influence of divers strong waters, furnished by his host, he became still more loquacious. And think of a man with a twenty years' budget of gossip! The Commander learned, for the first time, how Great Britain lost her colonies; of the French Revolution; of the great Napoleon, whose achievements, perhaps, Peleg colored more highly than the Commander's superiors would have liked. And when Peleg turned questioner, the Commander was at his mercy. He gradually made himself master of the gossip of the Mission and Presidio, the "small-beer" chronicles of that pastoral age, the conversion of the heathen, the Presidio schools, and even asked the Commander how he had lost his eye! It is said that at this point of the conversation Master Peleg produced from about his person divers small trinkets, kickshaws, and newfangled trifles, and even forced some of them upon his host. It is further alleged that under the malign influence of Peleg and several glasses of aguardiente, the Commander lost somewhat of his decorum, and behaved in a manner unseemly for one in his position, reciting high-flown Spanish poetry, and even piping in a thin, high voice divers madrigals and heathen canzonets of an amorous complexion; chiefly in regard to a "little one" who was his, the Commander's, "soul"! These allegations, perhaps unworthy the notice of a serious chronicler, should be received with great caution, and are introduced here as simple hearsay. That the Commander, however, took a handkerchief and attempted to show his guest the mysteries of the SEMICUACUA, capering in an agile but indecorous manner about the apartment, has been denied. Enough for the purposes of this narrative that at midnight Peleg assisted his host to bed with many protestations of undying friendship, and then, as the gale had abated, took his leave of the Presidio and hurried aboard the GENERAL COURT. When the day broke the ship was gone.

I know not if Peleg kept his word with his host. It is said that the holy fathers at the Mission that night heard a loud chanting in the plaza, as of the heathens singing psalms through their noses; that for many days after an odor of salt codfish prevailed in the settlement; that a dozen hard nutmegs, which were unfit for spice or seed, were found in the possession of the wife of the baker, and that several bushels of shoe pegs, which bore a pleasing resemblance to oats, but were quite inadequate to the purposes of provender, were discovered in the stable of the blacksmith. But when the reader reflects upon the sacredness of a Yankee trader's word, the stringent discipline of the Spanish port regulations, and the proverbial indisposition of my countrymen to impose upon the confidence of a simple people, he will at once reject this part of the story.

A roll of drums, ushering in the year 1798, awoke the Commander. The sun was shining brightly, and the storm had ceased. He sat up in bed, and through the force of habit rubbed his left eye. As the remembrance of the previous night came back to him, he jumped from his couch and ran to the window. There was no ship in the bay. A sudden thought seemed to strike him, and he rubbed both of his eyes. Not content with this, he consulted the metallic mirror which hung beside his crucifix. There was no mistake; the Commander had a visible second eye—a right one—as good, save for the purposes of vision, as the left.

Whatever might have been the true secret of this transformation, but one opinion prevailed at San Carlos. It was one of those rare miracles vouchsafed a pious Catholic community as an evidence to the heathen, through the intercession of the blessed San Carlos himself. That their beloved Commander, the temporal defender of the Faith, should be the recipient of this miraculous manifestation was most fit and seemly. The Commander himself was reticent; he could not tell a falsehood—he dared not tell the truth. After all, if the good folk of San Carlos believed that the powers of his right eye were actually restored, was it wise and discreet for him to undeceive them? For the first time in his life the Commander thought of policy—for the first time he quoted that text which has been the lure of so many well-meaning but easy Christians, of being "all things to all men." Infeliz Hermenegildo Salvatierra!

For by degrees an ominous whisper crept though the little settlement. The Right Eye of the Commander, although miraculous, seemed to exercise a baleful effect upon the beholder. No one could look at it without winking. It was cold, hard, relentless, and unflinching. More than that, it seemed to be endowed with a dreadful prescience—a faculty of seeing through and into the inarticulate thoughts of those it looked upon. The soldiers of the garrison obeyed the eye rather than the voice of their commander, and answered his glance rather than his lips in questioning. The servants could not evade the ever watchful but cold attention that seemed to pursue them. The children of the Presidio school smirched their copybooks under the awful supervision, and poor Paquita, the prize pupil, failed utterly in that marvelous upstroke when her patron stood beside her. Gradually distrust, suspicion, self-accusation, and timidity took the place of trust, confidence, and security throughout San Carlos. Whenever the Right Eye of the Commander fell, a shadow fell with it.

Nor was Salvatierra entirely free from the baleful influence of his miraculous acquisition. Unconscious of its effect upon others, he only saw in their actions evidence of certain things that the crafty Peleg had hinted on that eventful New Year's eve. His most trusty retainers stammered, blushed, and faltered before him. Self-accusations, confessions of minor faults and delinquencies, or extravagant excuses and apologies met his mildest inquiries. The very children that he loved—his pet pupil, Paquita—seemed to be conscious of some hidden sin. The result of this constant irritation showed itself more plainly. For the first half-year the Commander's voice and eye were at variance. He was still kind, tender, and thoughtful in speech. Gradually, however, his voice took upon itself the hardness of his glance and its skeptical, impassive quality, and as the year again neared its close it was plain that the Commander had fitted himself to the eye, and not the eye to the Commander.

It may be surmised that these changes did not escape the watchful solicitude of the Fathers. Indeed, the few who were first to ascribe the right eye of Salvatierra to miraculous origin and the special grace of the blessed San Carlos, now talked openly of witchcraft and the agency of Luzbel, the evil one. It would have fared ill with Hermenegildo Salvatierra had he been aught but Commander or amenable to local authority. But the reverend father, Friar Manuel de Cortes, had no power over the political executive, and all attempts at spiritual advice failed signally. He retired baffled and confused from his first interview with the Commander, who seemed now to take a grim satisfaction in the fateful power of his glance. The holy Father contradicted himself, exposed the fallacies of his own arguments, and even, it is asserted, committed himself to several undoubted heresies. When the Commander stood up at mass, if the officiating priest caught that skeptical and searching eye, the service was inevitably ruined. Even the power of the Holy Church seemed to be lost, and the last hold upon the affections of the people and the good order of the settlement departed from San Carlos.

As the long dry summer passed, the low hills that surrounded the white walls of the Presidio grew more and more to resemble in hue the leathern jacket of the Commander, and Nature herself seemed to have borrowed his dry, hard glare. The earth was cracked and seamed with drought; a blight had fallen upon the orchards and vineyards, and the rain, long-delayed and ardently prayed for, came not. The sky was as tearless as the right eye of the Commander. Murmurs of discontent, insubordination, and plotting among the Indians reached his ears; he only set his teeth the more firmly, tightened the knot of his black-silk handkerchief, and looked up his Toledo.

The last day of the year 1798 found the Commander sitting, at the hour of evening prayers, alone in the guardroom. He no longer attended the services of the Holy Church, but crept away at such times to some solitary spot, where he spent the interval in silent meditation. The firelight played upon the low beams and rafters, but left the bowed figure of Salvatierra in darkness. Sitting thus, he felt a small hand touch his arm, and looking down, saw the figure of Paquita, his little Indian pupil, at his knee. "Ah, littlest of all," said the Commander, with something of his old tenderness, lingering over the endearing diminutives of his native speech—"sweet one, what doest thou here? Art thou not afraid of him whom everyone shuns and fears?"

"No," said the little Indian, readily, "not in the dark. I hear your voice—the old voice; I feel your touch—the old touch; but I see not your eye, Senor Commandante. That only I fear—and that, O senor, O my father," said the child, lifting her little arms towards his—"that I know is not thine own!"

The Commander shuddered and turned away. Then, recovering himself, he kissed Paquita gravely on the forehead and bade her retire. A few hours later, when silence had fallen upon the Presidio, he sought his own couch and slept peacefully.

At about the middle watch of the night a dusky figure crept through the low embrasure of the Commander's apartment. Other figures were flitting through the parade ground, which the Commander might have seen had he not slept so quietly. The intruder stepped noiselessly to the couch and listened to the sleeper's deep-drawn inspiration. Something glittered in the firelight as the savage lifted his arm; another moment and the sore perplexities of Hermenegildo Salvatierra would have been over, when suddenly the savage started and fell back in a paroxysm of terror. The Commander slept peacefully, but his right eye, widely opened, fixed and unaltered, glared coldly on the would-be assassin. The man fell to the earth in a fit, and the noise awoke the sleeper.

To rise to his feet, grasp his sword, and deal blows thick and fast upon the mutinous savages who now thronged the room was the work of a moment. Help opportunely arrived, and the undisciplined Indians were speedily driven beyond the walls, but in the scuffle the Commander received a blow upon his right eye, and, lifting his hand to that mysterious organ, it was gone. Never again was it found, and never again, for bale or bliss, did it adorn the right orbit of the Commander.

With it passed away the spell that had fallen upon San Carlos. The rain returned to invigorate the languid soil, harmony was restored between priest and soldier, the green grass presently waved over the sere hillsides, the children flocked again to the side of their martial preceptor, a TE DEUM was sung in the Mission Church, and pastoral content once more smiled upon the gentle valleys of San Carlos. And far southward crept the GENERAL COURT with its master, Peleg Scudder, trafficking in beads and peltries with the Indians, and offering glass eyes, wooden legs, and other Boston notions to the chiefs.

* * * * * * * * * *

NOTES BY FLOOD AND FIELD

PART I—IN THE FIELD

It was near the close of an October day that I began to be disagreeably conscious of the Sacramento Valley. I had been riding since sunrise, and my course through the depressing monotony of the long level landscape affected me more like a dull dyspeptic dream than a business journey, performed under that sincerest of natural phenomena—a California sky. The recurring stretches of brown and baked fields, the gaping fissures in the dusty trail, the hard outline of the distant hills, and the herds of slowly moving cattle, seemed like features of some glittering stereoscopic picture that never changed. Active exercise might have removed this feeling, but my horse by some subtle instinct had long since given up all ambitious effort, and had lapsed into a dogged trot.

It was autumn, but not the season suggested to the Atlantic reader under that title. The sharply defined boundaries of the wet and dry seasons were prefigured in the clear outlines of the distant hills. In the dry atmosphere the decay of vegetation was too rapid for the slow hectic which overtakes an Eastern landscape, or else Nature was too practical for such thin disguises. She merely turned the Hippocratic face to the spectator, with the old diagnosis of Death in her sharp, contracted features.

In the contemplation of such a prospect there was little to excite any but a morbid fancy. There were no clouds in the flinty blue heavens, and the setting of the sun was accompanied with as little ostentation as was consistent with the dryly practical atmosphere. Darkness soon followed, with a rising wind, which increased as the shadows deepened on the plain. The fringe of alder by the watercourse began to loom up as I urged my horse forward. A half-hour's active spurring brought me to a corral, and a little beyond a house, so low and broad it seemed at first sight to be half-buried in the earth.

My second impression was that it had grown out of the soil, like some monstrous vegetable, its dreary proportions were so in keeping with the vast prospect. There were no recesses along its roughly boarded walls for vagrant and unprofitable shadows to lurk in the daily sunshine. No projection for the wind by night to grow musical over, to wail, whistle, or whisper to; only a long wooden shelf containing a chilly-looking tin basin and a bar of soap. Its uncurtained windows were red with the sinking sun, as though bloodshot and inflamed from a too-long unlidded existence. The tracks of cattle led to its front door, firmly closed against the rattling wind.

To avoid being confounded with this familiar element, I walked to the rear of the house, which was connected with a smaller building by a slight platform. A grizzled, hard-faced old man was standing there, and met my salutation with a look of inquiry, and, without speaking, led the way to the principal room. As I entered, four young men who were reclining by the fire slightly altered their attitudes of perfect repose, but beyond that betrayed neither curiosity nor interest. A hound started from a dark corner with a growl, but was immediately kicked by the old man into obscurity, and silenced again. I can't tell why, but I instantly received the impression that for a long time the group by the fire had not uttered a word or moved a muscle. Taking a seat, I briefly stated my business.

Was a United States surveyor. Had come on account of the Espiritu Santo Rancho. Wanted to correct the exterior boundaries of township lines, so as to connect with the near exteriors of private grants. There had been some intervention to the old survey by a Mr. Tryan who had preempted adjacent—"settled land warrants," interrupted the old man. "Ah, yes! Land warrants—and then this was Mr. Tryan?"

I had spoken mechanically, for I was preoccupied in connecting other public lines with private surveys as I looked in his face. It was certainly a hard face, and reminded me of the singular effect of that mining operation known as "ground sluicing"; the harder lines of underlying character were exposed, and what were once plastic curves and soft outlines were obliterated by some powerful agency.

There was a dryness in his voice not unlike the prevailing atmosphere of the valley, as he launched into an EX PARTE statement of the contest, with a fluency, which, like the wind without, showed frequent and unrestrained expression. He told me—what I had already learned—that the boundary line of the old Spanish grant was a creek, described in the loose phraseology of the DESENO as beginning in the VALDA or skirt of the hill, its precise location long the subject of litigation. I listened and answered with little interest, for my mind was still distracted by the wind which swept violently by the house, as well as by his odd face, which was again reflected in the resemblance that the silent group by the fire bore toward him. He was still talking, and the wind was yet blowing, when my confused attention was aroused by a remark addressed to the recumbent figures.

"Now, then, which on ye'll see the stranger up the creek to Altascar's, tomorrow?"

There was a general movement of opposition in the group, but no decided answer.

"Kin you go, Kerg?"

"Who's to look up stock in Strarberry perar-ie?"

This seemed to imply a negative, and the old man turned to another hopeful, who was pulling the fur from a mangy bearskin on which he was lying, with an expression as though it were somebody's hair.

"Well, Tom, wot's to hinder you from goin'?"

"Mam's goin' to Brown's store at sunup, and I s'pose I've got to pack her and the baby agin."

I think the expression of scorn this unfortunate youth exhibited for the filial duty into which he had been evidently beguiled was one of the finest things I had ever seen.

"Wise?"

Wise deigned no verbal reply, but figuratively thrust a worn and patched boot into the discourse. The old man flushed quickly.

"I told ye to get Brown to give you a pair the last time you war down the river."

"Said he wouldn't without'en order. Said it was like pulling gum teeth to get the money from you even then."

There was a grim smile at this local hit at the old man's parsimony, and Wise, who was clearly the privileged wit of the family, sank back in honorable retirement.

"Well, Joe, ef your boots are new, and you aren't pestered with wimmin and children, p'r'aps you'll go," said Tryan, with a nervous twitching, intended for a smile, about a mouth not remarkably mirthful.

Tom lifted a pair of bushy eyebrows, and said shortly:

"Got no saddle."

"Wot's gone of your saddle?"

"Kerg, there"—indicating his brother with a look such as Cain might have worn at the sacrifice.

"You lie!" returned Kerg, cheerfully.

Tryan sprang to his feet, seizing the chair, flourishing it around his head and gazing furiously in the hard young faces which fearlessly met his own. But it was only for a moment; his arm soon dropped by his side, and a look of hopeless fatality crossed his face. He allowed me to take the chair from his hand, and I was trying to pacify him by the assurance that I required no guide when the irrepressible Wise again lifted his voice:

"Theer's George comin'! why don't ye ask him? He'll go and introduce you to Don Fernandy's darter, too, ef you ain't pertickler."

The laugh which followed this joke, which evidently had some domestic allusion (the general tendency of rural pleasantry), was followed by a light step on the platform, and the young man entered. Seeing a stranger present, he stopped and colored, made a shy salute and colored again, and then, drawing a box from the corner, sat down, his hands clasped lightly together and his very handsome bright blue eyes turned frankly on mine.

Perhaps I was in a condition to receive the romantic impression he made upon me, and I took it upon myself to ask his company as guide, and he cheerfully assented. But some domestic duty called him presently away.

The fire gleamed brightly on the hearth, and, no longer resisting the prevailing influence, I silently watched the spurting flame, listening to the wind which continually shook the tenement. Besides the one chair which had acquired a new importance in my eyes, I presently discovered a crazy table in one corner, with an ink bottle and pen; the latter in that greasy state of decomposition peculiar to country taverns and farmhouses. A goodly array of rifles and double-barreled guns stocked the corner; half a dozen saddles and blankets lay near, with a mild flavor of the horse about them. Some deer and bear skins completed the inventory. As I sat there, with the silent group around me, the shadowy gloom within and the dominant wind without, I found it difficult to believe I had ever known a different existence. My profession had often led me to wilder scenes, but rarely among those whose unrestrained habits and easy unconsciousness made me feel so lonely and uncomfortable I shrank closer to myself, not without grave doubts—which I think occur naturally to people in like situations—that this was the general rule of humanity and I was a solitary and somewhat gratuitous exception. It was a relief when a laconic announcement of supper by a weak-eyed girl caused a general movement in the family. We walked across the dark platform, which led to another low-ceiled room. Its entire length was occupied by a table, at the farther end of which a weak-eyed woman was already taking her repast as she at the same time gave nourishment to a weak-eyed baby. As the formalities of introduction had been dispensed with, and as she took no notice of me, I was enabled to slip into a seat without discomposing or interrupting her. Tryan extemporized a grace, and the attention of the family became absorbed in bacon, potatoes, and dried apples.

The meal was a sincere one. Gentle gurglings at the upper end of the table often betrayed the presence of the "wellspring of pleasure." The conversation generally referred to the labors of the day, and comparing notes as to the whereabouts of missing stock. Yet the supper was such a vast improvement upon the previous intellectual feast that when a chance allusion of mine to the business of my visit brought out the elder Tryan, the interest grew quite exciting. I remember he inveighed bitterly against the system of ranch-holding by the "greasers," as he was pleased to term the native Californians. As the same ideas have been sometimes advanced under more pretentious circumstances they may be worthy of record.

"Look at 'em holdin' the finest grazin' land that ever lay outer doors. Whar's the papers for it? Was it grants? Mighty fine grants—most of 'em made arter the 'Merrikans got possession. More fools the 'Merrikans for lettin' 'em hold 'em. Wat paid for 'em? 'Merrikan and blood money.

"Didn't they oughter have suthin' out of their native country? Wot for? Did they ever improve? Got a lot of yaller-skinned diggers, not so sensible as niggers to look arter stock, and they a sittin' home and smokin'. With their gold and silver candlesticks, and missions, and crucifixens, priests and graven idols, and sich? Them sort things wurent allowed in Mizzoori."

At the mention of improvements, I involuntarily lifted my eyes, and met the half laughing, half embarrassed look of George. The act did not escape detection, and I had at once the satisfaction of seeing that the rest of the family had formed an offensive alliance against us.

"It was agin Nater, and agin God," added Tryan. "God never intended gold in the rocks to be made into heathen candlesticks and crucifixens. That's why he sent 'Merrikans here. Nater never intended such a climate for lazy lopers. She never gin six months' sunshine to be slept and smoked away."

How long he continued and with what further illustration I could not say, for I took an early opportunity to escape to the sitting-room. I was soon followed by George, who called me to an open door leading to a smaller room, and pointed to a bed.

"You'd better sleep there tonight," he said; "you'll be more comfortable, and I'll call you early."

I thanked him, and would have asked him several questions which were then troubling me, but he shyly slipped to the door and vanished.

A shadow seemed to fall on the room when he had gone. The "boys" returned, one by one, and shuffled to their old places. A larger log was thrown on the fire, and the huge chimney glowed like a furnace, but it did not seem to melt or subdue a single line of the hard faces that it lit. In half an hour later, the furs which had served as chairs by day undertook the nightly office of mattresses, and each received its owner's full-length figure. Mr. Tryan had not returned, and I missed George. I sat there until, wakeful and nervous, I saw the fire fall and shadows mount the wall. There was no sound but the rushing of the wind and the snoring of the sleepers. At last, feeling the place insupportable, I seized my hat and opening the door, ran out briskly into the night.

The acceleration of my torpid pulse in the keen fight with the wind, whose violence was almost equal to that of a tornado, and the familiar faces of the bright stars above me, I felt as a blessed relief. I ran not knowing whither, and when I halted, the square outline of the house was lost in the alder bushes. An uninterrupted plain stretched before me, like a vast sea beaten flat by the force of the gale. As I kept on I noticed a slight elevation toward the horizon, and presently my progress was impeded by the ascent of an Indian mound. It struck me forcibly as resembling an island in the sea. Its height gave me a better view of the expanding plain. But even here I found no rest. The ridiculous interpretation Tryan had given the climate was somehow sung in my ears, and echoed in my throbbing pulse as, guided by the star, I sought the house again.

But I felt fresher and more natural as I stepped upon the platform. The door of the lower building was open, and the old man was sitting beside the table, thumbing the leaves of a Bible with a look in his face as though he were hunting up prophecies against the "Greaser." I turned to enter, but my attention was attracted by a blanketed figure lying beside the house, on the platform. The broad chest heaving with healthy slumber, and the open, honest face were familiar. It was George, who had given up his bed to the stranger among his people. I was about to wake him, but he lay so peaceful and quiet, I felt awed and hushed. And I went to bed with a pleasant impression of his handsome face and tranquil figure soothing me to sleep.

I was awakened the next morning from a sense of lulled repose and grateful silence by the cheery voice of George, who stood beside my bed, ostentatiously twirling a riata, as if to recall the duties of the day to my sleep-bewildered eyes. I looked around me. The wind had been magically laid, and the sun shone warmly through the windows. A dash of cold water, with an extra chill on from the tin basin, helped to brighten me. It was still early, but the family had already breakfasted and dispersed, and a wagon winding far in the distance showed that the unfortunate Tom had already "packed" his relatives away. I felt more cheerful—there are few troubles Youth cannot distance with the start of a good night's rest. After a substantial breakfast, prepared by George, in a few moments we were mounted and dashing down the plain.

We followed the line of alder that defined the creek, now dry and baked with summer's heat, but which in winter, George told me, overflowed its banks. I still retain a vivid impression of that morning's ride, the far-off mountains, like silhouettes, against the steel-blue sky, the crisp dry air, and the expanding track before me, animated often by the well-knit figure of George Tryan, musical with jingling spurs and picturesque with flying riata. He rode powerful native roan, wild-eyed, untiring in stride and unbroken in nature. Alas! the curves of beauty were concealed by the cumbrous MACHILLAS of the Spanish saddle, which levels all equine distinctions. The single rein lay loosely on the cruel bit that can gripe, and if need be, crush the jaw it controls.

Again the illimitable freedom of the valley rises before me, as we again bear down into sunlit space. Can this be "Chu Chu," staid and respectable filly of American pedigree—Chu Chu, forgetful of plank roads and cobblestones, wild with excitement, twinkling her small white feet beneath me? George laughs out of a cloud of dust. "Give her her head; don't you see she likes it?" and Chu Chu seems to like it, and whether bitten by native tarantula into native barbarism or emulous of the roan, "blood" asserts itself, and in a moment the peaceful servitude of years is beaten out in the music of her clattering hoofs. The creek widens to a deep gully. We dive into it and up on the opposite side, carrying a moving cloud of impalpable powder with us. Cattle are scattered over the plain, grazing quietly or banded together in vast restless herds. George makes a wide, indefinite sweep with the riata, as if to include them all in his vaquero's loop, and says, "Ours!"

"About how many, George?"

"Don't know."

"How many?"

"'Well, p'r'aps three thousand head," says George, reflecting. "We don't know, takes five men to look 'em up and keep run."

"What are they worth?"

"About thirty dollars a head."

I make a rapid calculation, and look my astonishment at the laughing George. Perhaps a recollection of the domestic economy of the Tryan household is expressed in that look, for George averts his eye and says, apologetically:

"I've tried to get the old man to sell and build, but you know he says it ain't no use to settle down, just yet. We must keep movin'. In fact, he built the shanty for that purpose, lest titles should fall through, and we'd have to get up and move stakes further down."

Suddenly his quick eye detects some unusual sight in a herd we are passing, and with an exclamation he puts his roan into the center of the mass. I follow, or rather Chu Chu darts after the roan, and in a few moments we are in the midst of apparently inextricable horns and hoofs. "TORO!" shouts George, with vaquero enthusiasm, and the band opens a way for the swinging riata. I can feel their steaming breaths, and their spume is cast on Chu Chu's quivering flank.

Wild, devilish-looking beasts are they; not such shapes as Jove might have chosen to woo a goddess, nor such as peacefully range the downs of Devon, but lean and hungry Cassius-like bovines, economically got up to meet the exigencies of a six months' rainless climate, and accustomed to wrestle with the distracting wind and the blinding dust.

"That's not our brand," says George; "they're strange stock," and he points to what my scientific eye recognizes as the astrological sign of Venus deeply seared in the brown flanks of the bull he is chasing. But the herd are closing round us with low mutterings, and George has again recourse to the authoritative "TORO," and with swinging riata divides the "bossy bucklers" on either side. When we are free, and breathing somewhat more easily, I venture to ask George if they ever attack anyone.

"Never horsemen—sometimes footmen. Not through rage, you know, but curiosity. They think a man and his horse are one, and if they meet a chap afoot, they run him down and trample him under hoof, in the pursuit of knowledge. But," adds George, "here's the lower bench of the foothills, and here's Altascar's corral, and that White building you see yonder is the casa."

A whitewashed wall enclosed a court containing another adobe building, baked with the solar beams of many summers. Leaving our horses in the charge of a few peons in the courtyard, who were basking lazily in the sun, we entered a low doorway, where a deep shadow and an agreeable coolness fell upon us, as sudden and grateful as a plunge in cool water, from its contrast with the external glare and heat. In the center of a low-ceiled apartment sat an old man with a black-silk handkerchief tied about his head, the few gray hairs that escaped from its folds relieving his gamboge-colored face. The odor of CIGARRITOS was as incense added to the cathedral gloom of the building.

As Senor Altascar rose with well-bred gravity to receive us, George advanced with such a heightened color, and such a blending of tenderness and respect in his manner, that I was touched to the heart by so much devotion in the careless youth. In fact, my eyes were still dazzled by the effect of the outer sunshine, and at first I did not see the white teeth and black eyes of Pepita, who slipped into the corridor as we entered.

It was no pleasant matter to disclose particulars of business which would deprive the old senor of the greater part of that land we had just ridden over, and I did it with great embarrassment. But he listened calmly—not a muscle of his dark face stirring—and the smoke curling placidly from his lips showed his regular respiration. When I had finished, he offered quietly to accompany us to the line of demarcation. George had meanwhile disappeared, but a suspicious conversation in broken Spanish and English, in the corridor, betrayed his vicinity. When he returned again, a little absent-minded, the old man, by far the coolest and most self-possessed of the party, extinguished his black-silk cap beneath that stiff, uncomely sombrero which all native Californians affect. A serape thrown over his shoulders hinted that he was waiting. Horses are always ready saddled in Spanish ranchos, and in half an hour from the time of our arrival we were again "loping" in the staring sunlight.

But not as cheerfully as before. George and myself were weighed down by restraint, and Altascar was gravely quiet. To break the silence, and by way of a consolatory essay, I hinted to him that there might be further intervention or appeal, but the proffered oil and wine were returned with a careless shrug of the shoulders and a sententious "QUE BUENO?—Your courts are always just."

The Indian mound of the previous night's discovery was a bearing monument of the new line, and there we halted. We were surprised to find the old man Tryan waiting us. For the first time during our interview the old Spaniard seemed moved, and the blood rose in his yellow cheek. I was anxious to close the scene, and pointed out the corner boundaries as clearly as my recollection served.

"The deputies will be here tomorrow to run the lines from this initial point, and there will be no further trouble, I believe, gentlemen."

Senor Altascar had dismounted and was gathering a few tufts of dried grass in his hands. George and I exchanged glances. He presently arose from his stooping posture, and advancing to within a few paces of Joseph Tryan, said, in a voice broken with passion:

"And I, Fernando Jesus Maria Altascar, put you in possession of my land in the fashion of my country."

He threw a sod to each of the cardinal points.

"I don't know your courts, your judges, or your CORREGIDORES. Take the LLANO!—and take this with it. May the drought seize your cattle till their tongues hang down as long as those of your lying lawyers! May it be the curse and torment of your old age, as you and yours have made it of mine!"

We stepped between the principal actors in this scene, which only the passion of Altascar made tragical, but Tryan, with a humility but ill concealing his triumph, interrupted:

"Let him curse on. He'll find 'em coming home to him sooner than the cattle he has lost through his sloth and pride. The Lord is on the side of the just, as well as agin all slanderers and revilers."

Altascar but half guessed the meaning of the Missourian, yet sufficiently to drive from his mind all but the extravagant power of his native invective.

"Stealer of the Sacrament! Open not!—open not, I say, your lying, Judas lips to me! Ah! half-breed, with the soul of a coyote!—car-r-r-ramba!"

With his passion reverberating among the consonants like distant thunder, he laid his hand upon the mane of his horse as though it had been the gray locks of his adversary, swung himself into the saddle and galloped away.

George turned to me:

"Will you go back with us tonight?"

I thought of the cheerless walls, the silent figures by the fire, and the roaring wind, and hesitated.

"Well then, goodby."

"Goodby, George."

Another wring of the hands, and we parted. I had not ridden far when I turned and looked back. The wind had risen early that afternoon, and was already sweeping across the plain. A cloud of dust traveled before it, and a picturesque figure occasionally emerging therefrom was my last indistinct impression of George Tryan.

PART II—IN THE FLOOD

Three months after the survey of the Espiritu Santo Rancho, I was again in the valley of the Sacramento. But a general and terrible visitation had erased the memory of that event as completely as I supposed it had obliterated the boundary monuments I had planted. The great flood of 1861-62 was at its height when, obeying some indefinite yearning, I took my carpetbag and embarked for the inundated valley.

There was nothing to be seen from the bright cabin windows of the GOLDEN CITY but night deepening over the water. The only sound was the pattering rain, and that had grown monotonous for the past two weeks, and did not disturb the national gravity of my countrymen as they silently sat around the cabin stove. Some on errands of relief to friends and relatives wore anxious faces, and conversed soberly on the one absorbing topic. Others, like myself, attracted by curiosity listened eagerly to newer details. But with that human disposition to seize upon any circumstance that might give chance event the exaggerated importance of instinct, I was half-conscious of something more than curiosity as an impelling motive.

The dripping of rain, the low gurgle of water, and a leaden sky greeted us the next morning as we lay beside the half-submerged levee of Sacramento. Here, however, the novelty of boats to convey us to the hotels was an appeal that was irresistible. I resigned myself to a dripping rubber-cased mariner called "Joe," and, wrapping myself in a shining cloak of the like material, about as suggestive of warmth as court plaster might have been, took my seat in the stern sheets of his boat. It was no slight inward struggle to part from the steamer that to most of the passengers was the only visible connecting link between us and the dry and habitable earth, but we pulled away and entered the city, stemming a rapid current as we shot the levee.

We glided up the long level of K Street—once a cheerful, busy thoroughfare, now distressing in its silent desolation. The turbid water which seemed to meet the horizon edge before us flowed at right angles in sluggish rivers through the streets. Nature had revenged herself on the local taste by disarraying the regular rectangles by huddling houses on street corners, where they presented abrupt gables to the current, or by capsizing them in compact ruin. Crafts of all kinds were gliding in and out of low-arched doorways. The water was over the top of the fences surrounding well-kept gardens, in the first stories of hotels and private dwellings, trailing its slime on velvet carpets as well as roughly boarded floors. And a silence quite as suggestive as the visible desolation was in the voiceless streets that no longer echoed to carriage wheel or footfall. The low ripple of water, the occasional splash of oars, or the warning cry of boatmen were the few signs of life and habitation.

With such scenes before my eyes and such sounds in my ears, as I lie lazily in the boat, is mingled the song of my gondolier who sings to the music of his oars. It is not quite as romantic as his brother of the Lido might improvise, but my Yankee "Giuseppe" has the advantage of earnestness and energy, and gives a graphic description of the terrors of the past week and of noble deeds of self-sacrifice and devotion, occasionally pointing out a balcony from which some California Bianca or Laura had been snatched, half-clothed and famished. Giuseppe is otherwise peculiar, and refuses the proffered fare, for—am I not a citizen of San Francisco, which was first to respond to the suffering cry of Sacramento? and is not he, Giuseppe, a member of the Howard Society? No! Giuseppe is poor, but cannot take my money. Still, if I must spend it, there is the Howard Society, and the women and children without food and clothes at the Agricultural Hall.

I thank the generous gondolier, and we go to the Hall—a dismal, bleak place, ghastly with the memories of last year's opulence and plenty, and here Giuseppe's fare is swelled by the stranger's mite. But here Giuseppe tells me of the "Relief Boat" which leaves for the flooded district in the interior, and here, profiting by the lesson he has taught me, I make the resolve to turn my curiosity to the account of others, and am accepted of those who go forth to succor and help the afflicted. Giuseppe takes charge of my carpetbag, and does not part from me until I stand on the slippery deck of "Relief Boat No. 3."

An hour later I am in the pilothouse, looking down upon what was once the channel of a peaceful river. But its banks are only defined by tossing tufts of willow washed by the long swell that breaks over a vast inland sea. Stretches of "tule" land fertilized by its once regular channel and dotted by flourishing ranchos are now cleanly erased. The cultivated profile of the old landscape had faded. Dotted lines in symmetrical perspective mark orchards that are buried and chilled in the turbid flood. The roofs of a few farmhouses are visible, and here and there the smoke curling from chimneys of half-submerged tenements shows an undaunted life within. Cattle and sheep are gathered on Indian mounds waiting the fate of their companions whose carcasses drift by us, or swing in eddies with the wrecks of barns and outhouses. Wagons are stranded everywhere where the tide could carry them. As I wipe the moistened glass, I see nothing but water, pattering on the deck from the lowering clouds, dashing against the window, dripping from the willows, hissing by the wheels, everywhere washing, coiling, sapping, hurrying in rapids, or swelling at last into deeper and vaster lakes, awful in their suggestive quiet and concealment.

As day fades into night the monotony of this strange prospect grows oppressive. I seek the engine room, and in the company of some of the few half-drowned sufferers we have already picked up from temporary rafts, I forget the general aspect of desolation in their individual misery. Later we meet the San Francisco packet, and transfer a number of our passengers. From them we learn how inward-bound vessels report to have struck the well-defined channel of the Sacramento, fifty miles beyond the bar. There is a voluntary contribution taken among the generous travelers for the use of our afflicted, and we part company with a hearty "Godspeed" on either side. But our signal lights are not far distant before a familiar sound comes back to us—an indomitable Yankee cheer—which scatters the gloom.

Our course is altered, and we are steaming over the obliterated banks far in the interior. Once or twice black objects loom up near us—the wrecks of houses floating by. There is a slight rift in the sky toward the north, and a few bearing stars to guide us over the waste. As we penetrate into shallower water, it is deemed advisable to divide our party into smaller boats, and diverge over the submerged prairie. I borrow a peacoat of one of the crew, and in that practical disguise am doubtfully permitted to pass into one of the boats. We give way northerly. It is quite dark yet, although the rift of cloud has widened.

It must have been about three o'clock, and we were lying upon our oars in an eddy formed by a clump of cottonwood, and the light of the steamer is a solitary, bright star in the distance, when the silence is broken by the "bow oar":

"Light ahead."

All eyes are turned in that direction. In a few seconds a twinkling light appears, shines steadily, and again disappears as if by the shifting position of some black object apparently drifting close upon us.

"Stern, all; a steamer!"

"Hold hard there! Steamer be damned!" is the reply of the coxswain. "It's a house, and a big one too."

It is a big one, looming in the starlight like a huge fragment of the darkness. The light comes from a single candle, which shines through a window as the great shape swings by. Some recollection is drifting back to me with it as I listen with beating heart.

"There's someone in it, by heavens! Give way, boys—lay her alongside. Handsomely, now! The door's fastened; try the window; no! here's another!"

In another moment we are trampling in the water which washes the floor to the depth of several inches. It is a large room, at the farther end of which an old man is sitting wrapped in a blanket, holding a candle in one hand, and apparently absorbed in the book he holds with the other. I spring toward him with an exclamation:

"Joseph Tryan!"

He does not move. We gather closer to him, and I lay my hand gently on his shoulder, and say:

"Look up, old man, look up! Your wife and children, where are they? The boys—George! Are they here? are they safe?"

He raises his head slowly, and turns his eyes to mine, and we involuntarily recoil before his look. It is a calm and quiet glance, free from fear, anger, or pain; but it somehow sends the blood curdling through our veins. He bowed his head over his book again, taking no further notice of us. The men look at me compassionately, and hold their peace. I make one more effort:

"Joseph Tryan, don't you know me? the surveyor who surveyed your ranch—the Espiritu Santo? Look up, old man!"

He shuddered and wrapped himself closer in his blanket. Presently he repeated to himself "The surveyor who surveyed your ranch—Espiritu Santo" over and over again, as though it were a lesson he was trying to fix in his memory.

I was turning sadly to the boatmen when he suddenly caught me fearfully by the hand and said:

"Hush!"

We were silent.

"Listen!" He puts his arm around my neck and whispers in my ear, "I'm a MOVING OFF!"

"Moving off?"

"Hush! Don't speak so loud. Moving off. Ah! wot's that? Don't you hear?—there! listen!"

We listen, and hear the water gurgle and click beneath the floor.

"It's them wot he sent!—Old Altascar sent. They've been here all night. I heard 'em first in the creek, when they came to tell the old man to move farther off. They came nearer and nearer. They whispered under the door, and I saw their eyes on the step—their cruel, hard eyes. Ah, why don't they quit?"

I tell the men to search the room and see if they can find any further traces of the family, while Tryan resumes his old attitude. It is so much like the figure I remember on the breezy night that a superstitious feeling is fast overcoming me. When they have returned, I tell them briefly what I know of him, and the old man murmurs again:

"Why don't they quit, then? They have the stock—all gone—gone, gone for the hides and hoofs," and he groans bitterly.

"There are other boats below us. The shanty cannot have drifted far, and perhaps the family are safe by this time," says the coxswain, hopefully.

We lift the old man up, for he is quite helpless, and carry him to the boat. He is still grasping the Bible in his right hand, though its strengthening grace is blank to his vacant eye, and he cowers in the stern as we pull slowly to the steamer while a pale gleam in the sky shows the coming day.

I was weary with excitement, and when we reached the steamer, and I had seen Joseph Tryan comfortably bestowed, I wrapped myself in a blanket near the boiler and presently fell asleep. But even then the figure of the old man often started before me, and a sense of uneasiness about George made a strong undercurrent to my drifting dreams. I was awakened at about eight o'clock in the morning by the engineer, who told me one of the old man's sons had been picked up and was now on board.

"Is it George Tryan?" I ask quickly.

"Don't know; but he's a sweet one, whoever he is," adds the engineer, with a smile at some luscious remembrance. "You'll find him for'ard."

I hurry to the bow of the boat, and find, not George, but the irrepressible Wise, sitting on a coil of rope, a little dirtier and rather more dilapidated than I can remember having seen him.

He is examining, with apparent admiration, some rough, dry clothes that have been put out for his disposal. I cannot help thinking that circumstances have somewhat exalted his usual cheerfulness. He puts me at my ease by at once addressing me:

"These are high old times, ain't they? I say, what do you reckon's become o' them thar bound'ry moniments you stuck? Ah!"

The pause which succeeds this outburst is the effect of a spasm of admiration at a pair of high boots, which, by great exertion, he has at last pulled on his feet.

"So you've picked up the ole man in the shanty, clean crazy? He must have been soft to have stuck there instead o' leavin' with the old woman. Didn't know me from Adam; took me for George!"

At this affecting instance of paternal forgetfulness, Wise was evidently divided between amusement and chagrin. I took advantage of the contending emotions to ask about George.

"Don't know whar he is! If he'd tended stock instead of running about the prairie, packin' off wimmin and children, he might have saved suthin. He lost every hoof and hide, I'll bet a cooky! Say you," to a passing boatman, "when are you goin' to give us some grub? I'm hungry 'nough to skin and eat a hoss. Reckon I'll turn butcher when things is dried up, and save hides, horns, and taller."

I could not but admire this indomitable energy, which under softer climatic influences might have borne such goodly fruit.

"Have you any idea what you'll do, Wise?" I ask.

"Thar ain't much to do now," says the practical young man. "I'll have to lay over a spell, I reckon, till things comes straight. The land ain't worth much now, and won't be, I dessay, for some time. Wonder whar the ole man'll drive stakes next."

"I meant as to your father and George, Wise."

"Oh, the old man and I'll go on to 'Miles's,' whar Tom packed the old woman and babies last week. George'll turn up somewhar atween this and Altascar's ef he ain't thar now."

I ask how the Altascars have suffered.

"Well, I reckon he ain't lost much in stock. I shouldn't wonder if George helped him drive 'em up the foothills. And his casa's built too high. Oh, thar ain't any water thar, you bet. Ah," says Wise, with reflective admiration, "those greasers ain't the darned fools people thinks 'em. I'll bet thar ain't one swamped out in all 'er Californy." But the appearance of "grub" cut this rhapsody short.

"I shall keep on a little farther," I say, "and try to find George."

Wise stared a moment at this eccentricity until a new light dawned upon him.

"I don't think you'll save much. What's the percentage—workin' on shares, eh!"

I answer that I am only curious, which I feel lessens his opinion of me, and with a sadder feeling than his assurance of George's safety might warrant, I walked away.

From others whom we picked up from time to time we heard of George's self-sacrificing devotion, with the praises of the many he had helped and rescued. But I did not feel disposed to return until I had seen him, and soon prepared myself to take a boat to the lower VALDA of the foothills, and visit Altascar. I soon perfected my arrangements, bade farewell to Wise, and took a last look at the old man, who was sitting by the furnace fires quite passive and composed. Then our boat head swung round, pulled by sturdy and willing hands.

It was again raining, and a disagreeable wind had risen. Our course lay nearly west, and we soon knew by the strong current that we were in the creek of the Espiritu Santo. From time to time the wrecks of barns were seen, and we passed many half-submerged willows hung with farming implements.

We emerge at last into a broad silent sea. It is the "LLANO DE ESPIRITU SANTO." As the wind whistles by me, piling the shallower fresh water into mimic waves, I go back, in fancy, to the long ride of October over that boundless plain, and recall the sharp outlines of the distant hills, which are now lost in the lowering clouds. The men are rowing silently, and I find my mind, released from its tension, growing benumbed and depressed as then. The water, too, is getting more shallow as we leave the banks of the creek, and with my hand dipped listlessly over the thwarts, I detect the tops of chimisal, which shows the tide to have somewhat fallen. There is a black mound, bearing to the north of the line of alder, making an adverse current, which, as we sweep to the right to avoid, I recognize. We pull close alongside and I call to the men to stop.

There was a stake driven near its summit with the initials, "L. E. S. I." Tied halfway down was a curiously worked riata. It was George's. It had been cut with some sharp instrument, and the loose gravelly soil of the mound was deeply dented with horses' hoofs. The stake was covered with horsehairs. It was a record, but no clue.

The wind had grown more violent as we still fought our way forward, resting and rowing by turns, and oftener "poling" the shallower surface, but the old VALDA, or bench, is still distant. My recollection of the old survey enables me to guess the relative position of the meanderings of the creek, and an occasional simple professional experiment to determine the distance gives my crew the fullest faith in my ability. Night overtakes us in our impeded progress. Our condition looks more dangerous than it really is, but I urge the men, many of whom are still new in this mode of navigation, to greater exertion by assurance of perfect safety and speedy relief ahead. We go on in this way until about eight o'clock, and ground by the willows. We have a muddy walk for a few hundred yards before we strike a dry trail, and simultaneously the white walls of Altascar's appear like a snowbank before us. Lights are moving in the courtyard; but otherwise the old tomblike repose characterizes the building.

One of the peons recognized me as I entered the court, and Altascar met me on the corridor.

I was too weak to do more than beg his hospitality for the men who had dragged wearily with me. He looked at my hand, which still unconsciously held the broken riata. I began, wearily, to tell him about George and my fears, but with a gentler courtesy than was even his wont, he gravely laid his hand on my shoulder.

"POCO A POCO, senor—not now. You are tired, you have hunger, you have cold. Necessary it is you should have peace."

He took us into a small room and poured out some French cognac, which he gave to the men that had accompanied me. They drank and threw themselves before the fire in the larger room. The repose of the building was intensified that night, and I even fancied that the footsteps on the corridor were lighter and softer. The old Spaniard's habitual gravity was deeper; we might have been shut out from the world as well as the whistling storm, behind those ancient walls with their time-worn inheritor.

Before I could repeat my inquiry he retired. In a few minutes two smoking dishes of CHUPA with coffee were placed before us, and my men ate ravenously. I drank the coffee, but my excitement and weariness kept down the instincts of hunger.

I was sitting sadly by the fire when he reentered.

"You have eat?"

I said, "Yes," to please him.

"BUENO, eat when you can—food and appetite are not always."

He said this with that Sancho-like simplicity with which most of his countrymen utter a proverb, as though it were an experience rather than a legend, and, taking the riata from the floor, held it almost tenderly before him.

"It was made by me, senor."

"I kept it as a clue to him, Don Altascar," I said. "If I could find him—"

"He is here."

"Here! and"—but I could not say "well!" I understood the gravity of the old man's face, the hushed footfalls, the tomblike repose of the building, in an electric flash of consciousness; I held the clue to the broken riata at last. Altascar took my hand, and we crossed the corridor to a somber apartment. A few tall candles were burning in sconces before the window.

In an alcove there was a deep bed with its counterpane, pillows, and sheets heavily edged with lace, in all that splendid luxury which the humblest of these strange people lavish upon this single item of their household. I stepped beside it and saw George lying, as I had seen him once before, peacefully at rest. But a greater sacrifice than that he had known was here, and his generous heart was stilled forever.

"He was honest and brave," said the old man, and turned away. There was another figure in the room; a heavy shawl drawn over her graceful outline, and her long black hair hiding the hands that buried her downcast face. I did not seem to notice her, and, retiring presently, left the loving and loved together.

When we were again beside the crackling fire, in the shifting shadows of the great chamber, Altascar told me how he had that morning met the horse of George Tryan swimming on the prairie; how that, farther on, he found him lying, quite cold and dead, with no marks or bruises on his person; that he had probably become exhausted in fording the creek, and that he had as probably reached the mound only to die for want of that help he had so freely given to others; that, as a last act, he had freed his horse. These incidents were corroborated by many who collected in the great chamber that evening—women and children—most of them succored through the devoted energies of him who lay cold and lifeless above.

He was buried in the Indian mound—the single spot of strange perennial greenness which the poor aborigines had raised above the dusty plain. A little slab of sandstone with the initials "G. T." is his monument, and one of the bearings of the initial corner of the new survey of the "Espiritu Santo Rancho."

* * * * * * * * * *

AN EPISODE OF FIDDLETOWN

In 1858 Fiddletown considered her a very pretty woman. She had a quantity of light chestnut hair, a good figure, a dazzling complexion, and a certain languid grace which passed easily for gentle-womanliness. She always dressed becomingly, and in what Fiddletown accepted as the latest fashion. She had only two blemishes: one of her velvety eyes, when examined closely, had a slight cast; and her left cheek bore a small scar left by a single drop of vitriol—happily the only drop of an entire phial—thrown upon her by one of her own jealous sex, that reached the pretty face it was intended to mar. But when the observer had studied the eyes sufficiently to notice this defect, he was generally incapacitated for criticism; and even the scar on her cheek was thought by some to add piquancy to her smile. The youthful editor of THE FIDDLETOWN AVALANCHE had said privately that it was "an exaggerated dimple." Colonel Starbottle was instantly "reminded of the beautifying patches of the days of Queen Anne, but more particularly, sir, of the blankest beautiful women that, blank you, you ever laid your two blank eyes upon—a Creole woman, sir, in New Orleans. And this woman had a scar—a line extending, blank me, from her eye to her blank chin. And this woman, sir, thrilled you, sir; maddened you, sir; absolutely sent your blank soul to perdition with her blank fascination! And one day I said to her, 'Celeste, how in blank did you come by that beautiful scar, blank you?' And she said to me, 'Star, there isn't another white man that I'd confide in but you; but I made that scar myself, purposely, I did, blank me.' These were her very words, sir, and perhaps you think it a blank lie, sir; but I'll put up any blank sum you can name and prove it, blank me."

Indeed, most of the male population of Fiddletown were or had been in love with her. Of this number, about one-half believed that their love was returned, with the exception, possibly, of her own husband. He alone had been known to express skepticism.

The name of the gentleman who enjoyed this infelicitous distinction was Tretherick. He had been divorced from an excellent wife to marry this Fiddletown enchantress. She, also, had been divorced; but it was hinted that some previous experiences of hers in that legal formality had made it perhaps less novel, and probably less sacrificial. I would not have it inferred from this that she was deficient in sentiment, or devoid of its highest moral expression. Her intimate friend had written (on the occasion of her second divorce), "The cold world does not understand Clara yet"; and Colonel Starbottle had remarked blankly that with the exception of a single woman in Opelousas Parish, La., she had more soul than the whole caboodle of them put together. Few indeed could read those lines entitled "Infelissimus," commencing "Why waves no cypress o'er this brow?" originally published in the AVALANCHE, over the signature of "The Lady Clare," without feeling the tear of sensibility tremble on his eyelids, or the glow of virtuous indignation mantle his cheek, at the low brutality and pitiable jocularity of THE DUTCH FLAT INTELLIGENCER, which the next week had suggested the exotic character of the cypress, and its entire absence from Fiddletown, as a reasonable answer to the query.

Indeed, it was this tendency to elaborate her feelings in a metrical manner, and deliver them to the cold world through the medium of the newspapers, that first attracted the attention of Tretherick. Several poems descriptive of the effects of California scenery upon a too-sensitive soul, and of the vague yearnings for the infinite which an enforced study of the heartlessness of California society produced in the poetic breast, impressed Mr. Tretherick, who was then driving a six-mule freight wagon between Knight's Ferry and Stockton, to seek out the unknown poetess. Mr. Tretherick was himself dimly conscious of a certain hidden sentiment in his own nature; and it is possible that some reflections on the vanity of his pursuit—he supplied several mining camps with whisky and tobacco—in conjunction with the dreariness of the dusty plain on which he habitually drove, may have touched some chord in sympathy with this sensitive woman. Howbeit, after a brief courtship—as brief as was consistent with some previous legal formalities—they were married; and Mr. Tretherick brought his blushing bride to Fiddletown, or "Fideletown," as Mrs. Tretherick preferred to call it in her poems.

The union was not a felicitous one. It was not long before Mr. Tretherick discovered that the sentiment he had fostered while freighting between Stockton and Knight's Ferry was different from that which his wife had evolved from the contemplation of California scenery and her own soul. Being a man of imperfect logic, this caused him to beat her; and she, being equally faulty in deduction, was impelled to a certain degree of unfaithfulness on the same premise. Then Mr. Tretherick began to drink, and Mrs. Tretherick to contribute regularly to the columns of the AVALANCHE. It was at this time that Colonel Starbottle discovered a similarity in Mrs. Tretherick's verse to the genius of Sappho, and pointed it out to the citizens of Fiddletown in a two-columned criticism, signed "A. S.," also published in the AVALANCHE, and supported by extensive quotation. As the AVALANCHE did not possess a font of Greek type, the editor was obliged to reproduce the Leucadian numbers in the ordinary Roman letter, to the intense disgust of Colonel Starbottle, and the vast delight of Fiddletown, who saw fit to accept the text as an excellent imitation of Choctaw—a language with which the colonel, as a whilom resident of the Indian Territories, was supposed to be familiar. Indeed, the next week's INTELLIGENCER contained some vile doggerel supposed to be an answer to Mrs. Tretherick's poem, ostensibly written by the wife of a Digger Indian chief, accompanied by a glowing eulogium signed "A. S. S."

The result of this jocularity was briefly given in a later copy of the AVALANCHE. "An unfortunate rencounter took place on Monday last, between the Hon. Jackson Flash of THE DUTCH FLAT INTELLIGENCER and the well-known Col. Starbottle of this place, in front of the Eureka Saloon. Two shots were fired by the parties without injury to either, although it is said that a passing Chinaman received fifteen buckshot in the calves of his legs from the colonel's double-barreled shotgun, which were not intended for him. John will learn to keep out of the way of Melican man's firearms hereafter. The cause of the affray is not known, although it is hinted that there is a lady in the case. The rumor that points to a well-known and beautiful poetess whose lucubrations have often graced our columns seems to gain credence from those that are posted."

Meanwhile the passiveness displayed by Tretherick under these trying circumstances was fully appreciated in the gulches. "The old man's head is level," said one long-booted philosopher. "Ef the colonel kills Flash, Mrs. Tretherick is avenged: if Flash drops the colonel, Tretherick is all right. Either way, he's got a sure thing." During this delicate condition of affairs, Mrs. Tretherick one day left her husband's home and took refuge at the Fiddletown Hotel, with only the clothes she had on her back. Here she staid for several weeks, during which period it is only justice to say that she bore herself with the strictest propriety.

It was a clear morning in early spring that Mrs. Tretherick, unattended, left the hotel, and walked down the narrow street toward the fringe of dark pines which indicated the extreme limits of Fiddletown. The few loungers at that early hour were preoccupied with the departure of the Wingdown coach at the other extremity of the street; and Mrs. Tretherick reached the suburbs of the settlement without discomposing observation. Here she took a cross street or road, running at right angles with the main thoroughfare of Fiddletown and passing through a belt of woodland. It was evidently the exclusive and aristocratic avenue of the town. The dwellings were few, ambitious, and uninterrupted by shops. And here she was joined by Colonel Starbottle.

The gallant colonel, notwithstanding that he bore the swelling port which usually distinguished him, that his coat was tightly buttoned and his boots tightly fitting, and that his cane, hooked over his arm, swung jauntily, was not entirely at his ease. Mrs. Tretherick, however, vouchsafed him a gracious smile and a glance of her dangerous eyes; and the colonel, with an embarrassed cough and a slight strut, took his place at her side.

"The coast is clear," said the colonel, "and Tretherick is over at Dutch Flat on a spree. There is no one in the house but a Chinaman; and you need fear no trouble from him. I," he continued, with a slight inflation of the chest that imperiled the security of his button, "I will see that you are protected in the removal of your property."

"I'm sure it's very kind of you, and so disinterested!" simpered the lady as they walked along. "It's so pleasant to meet someone who has soul—someone to sympathize with in a community so hardened and heartless as this." And Mrs. Tretherick cast down her eyes, but not until they wrought their perfect and accepted work upon her companion.

"Yes, certainly, of course," said the colonel, glancing nervously up and down the street—"yes, certainly." Perceiving, however, that there was no one in sight or hearing, he proceeded at once to inform Mrs. Tretherick that the great trouble of his life, in fact, had been the possession of too much soul. That many women—as a gentleman she would excuse him, of course, from mentioning names—but many beautiful women had often sought his society, but being deficient, madam, absolutely deficient, in this quality, he could not reciprocate. But when two natures thoroughly in sympathy, despising alike the sordid trammels of a low and vulgar community and the conventional restraints of a hypocritical society—when two souls in perfect accord met and mingled in poetical union, then—but here the colonel's speech, which had been remarkable for a certain whisky-and-watery fluency, grew husky, almost inaudible, and decidedly incoherent. Possibly Mrs. Tretherick may have heard something like it before, and was enabled to fill the hiatus. Nevertheless, the cheek that was on the side of the colonel was quite virginal and bashfully conscious until they reached their destination.

It was a pretty little cottage, quite fresh and warm with paint, very pleasantly relieved against a platoon of pines, some of whose foremost files had been displaced to give freedom to the fenced enclosure in which it sat. In the vivid sunlight and perfect silence, it had a new, uninhabited look, as if the carpenters and painters had just left it. At the farther end of the lot, a Chinaman was stolidly digging; but there was no other sign of occupancy. "The coast," as the colonel had said, was indeed "clear." Mrs. Tretherick paused at the gate. The colonel would have entered with her, but was stopped by a gesture. "Come for me in a couple of hours, and I shall have everything packed," she said, as she smiled, and extended her hand. The colonel seized and pressed it with great fervor. Perhaps the pressure was slightly returned; for the gallant colonel was impelled to inflate his chest, and trip away as smartly as his stubby-toed, high-heeled boots would permit. When he had gone, Mrs. Tretherick opened the door, listened a moment in the deserted hall, and then ran quickly upstairs to what had been her bedroom.

Everything there was unchanged as on the night she left it. On the dressing-table stood her bandbox, as she remembered to have left it when she took out her bonnet. On the mantle lay the other glove she had forgotten in her flight. The two lower drawers of the bureau were half-open (she had forgotten to shut them); and on its marble top lay her shawl pin and a soiled cuff. What other recollections came upon her I know not; but she suddenly grew quite white, shivered, and listened with a beating heart, and her hand upon the door. Then she stepped to the mirror, and half-fearfully, half-curiously, parted with her fingers the braids of her blond hair above her little pink ear, until she came upon an ugly, half-healed scar. She gazed at this, moving her pretty head up and down to get a better light upon it, until the slight cast in her velvety eyes became very strongly marked indeed. Then she turned away with a light, reckless, foolish laugh, and ran to the closet where hung her precious dresses. These she inspected nervously, and missing suddenly a favorite black silk from its accustomed peg, for a moment, thought she should have fainted. But discovering it the next instant lying upon a trunk where she had thrown it, a feeling of thankfulness to a superior Being who protects the friendless for the first time sincerely thrilled her. Then, albeit she was hurried for time, she could not resist trying the effect of a certain lavender neck ribbon upon the dress she was then wearing, before the mirror. And then suddenly she became aware of a child's voice close beside her, and she stopped. And then the child's voice repeated, "Is it Mamma?"

Mrs. Tretherick faced quickly about. Standing in the doorway was a little girl of six or seven. Her dress had been originally fine, but was torn and dirty; and her hair, which was a very violent red, was tumbled seriocomically about her forehead. For all this, she was a picturesque little thing, even through whose childish timidity there was a certain self-sustained air which is apt to come upon children who are left much to themselves. She was holding under her arm a rag doll, apparently of her own workmanship, and nearly as large as herself—a doll with a cylindrical head, and features roughly indicated with charcoal. A long shawl, evidently belonging to a grown person, dropped from her shoulders and swept the floor.

The spectacle did not excite Mrs. Tretherick's delight. Perhaps she had but a small sense of humor. Certainly, when the child, still standing in the doorway, again asked, "Is it Mamma?" she answered sharply, "No, it isn't," and turned a severe look upon the intruder.

The child retreated a step, and then, gaining courage with the distance, said in deliciously imperfect speech:

"Dow 'way then! why don't you dow away?"

But Mrs. Tretherick was eying the shawl. Suddenly she whipped it off the child's shoulders, and said angrily:

"How dared you take my things, you bad child?"

"Is it yours? Then you are my mamma; ain't you? You are Mamma!" she continued gleefully; and before Mrs. Tretherick could avoid her, she had dropped her doll, and, catching the woman's skirts with both hands, was dancing up and down before her.

"What's your name, child?" said Mrs. Tretherick coldly, removing the small and not very white hands from her garments.

"Tarry."

"Tarry?"

"Yeth. Tarry. Tarowline."

"Caroline?"

"Yeth. Tarowline Tretherick."

"Whose child ARE you?" demanded Mrs. Tretherick still more coldly, to keep down a rising fear.

"Why, yours," said the little creature with a laugh. "I'm your little durl. You're my mamma, my new mamma. Don't you know my ol' mamma's dorn away, never to turn back any more? I don't live wid my ol' mamma now. I live wid you and Papa."

"How long have you been here?" asked Mrs. Tretherick snappishly.

"I fink it's free days," said Carry reflectively.

"You think! Don't you know?" sneered Mrs. Tretherick. "Then, where did you come from?"

Carry's lip began to work under this sharp cross-examination. With a great effort and a small gulp, she got the better of it, and answered:

"Papa, Papa fetched me—from Miss Simmons—from Sacramento, last week."

"Last week! You said three days just now," returned Mrs. Tretherick with severe deliberation.

"I mean a monf," said Carry, now utterly adrift in sheer helplessness and confusion.

"Do you know what you are talking about?" demanded Mrs. Tretherick shrilly, restraining an impulse to shake the little figure before her and precipitate the truth by specific gravity.

But the flaming red head here suddenly disappeared in the folds of Mrs. Tretherick's dress, as if it were trying to extinguish itself forever.

"There now—stop that sniffling," said Mrs. Tretherick, extricating her dress from the moist embraces of the child and feeling exceedingly uncomfortable. "Wipe your face now, and run away, and don't bother. Stop," she continued, as Carry moved away. "Where's your papa?"

"He's dorn away too. He's sick. He's been dorn"—she hesitated—"two, free, days."

"Who takes care of you, child?" said Mrs. Tretherick, eying her curiously.

"John, the Chinaman. I tresses myself. John tooks and makes the beds."

"Well, now, run away and behave yourself, and don't bother me any more," said Mrs. Tretherick, remembering the object of her visit. "Stop—where are you going?" she added as the child began to ascend the stairs, dragging the long doll after her by one helpless leg.

"Doin' upstairs to play and be dood, and no bother Mamma."

"I ain't your mamma," shouted Mrs. Tretherick, and then she swiftly re-entered her bedroom and slammed the door.

Once inside, she drew forth a large trunk from the closet and set to work with querulous and fretful haste to pack her wardrobe. She tore her best dress in taking it from the hook on which it hung: she scratched her soft hands twice with an ambushed pin. All the while, she kept up an indignant commentary on the events of the past few moments. She said to herself she saw it all. Tretherick had sent for this child of his first wife—this child of whose existence he had never seemed to care—just to insult her, to fill her place. Doubtless the first wife herself would follow soon, or perhaps there would be a third. Red hair, not auburn, but RED—of course the child, this Caroline, looked like its mother, and, if so, she was anything but pretty. Or the whole thing had been prepared: this red-haired child, the image of its mother, had been kept at a convenient distance at Sacramento, ready to be sent for when needed. She remembered his occasional visits there on—business, as he said. Perhaps the mother already was there; but no, she had gone East. Nevertheless, Mrs. Tretherick, in her then state of mind, preferred to dwell upon the fact that she might be there. She was dimly conscious, also, of a certain satisfaction in exaggerating her feelings. Surely no woman had ever been so shamefully abused. In fancy, she sketched a picture of herself sitting alone and deserted, at sunset, among the fallen columns of a ruined temple, in a melancholy yet graceful attitude, while her husband drove rapidly away in a luxurious coach-and-four, with a red-haired woman at his side. Sitting upon the trunk she had just packed, she partly composed a lugubrious poem describing her sufferings as, wandering alone and poorly clad, she came upon her husband and "another" flaunting in silks and diamonds. She pictured herself dying of consumption, brought on by sorrow—a beautiful wreck, yet still fascinating, gazed upon adoringly by the editor of the AVALANCHE and Colonel Starbottle. And where was Colonel Starbottle all this while? Why didn't he come? He, at least, understood her. He—she laughed the reckless, light laugh of a few moments before; and then her face suddenly grew grave, as it had not a few moments before.

What was that little red-haired imp doing all this time? Why was she so quiet? She opened the door noiselessly, and listened. She fancied that she heard, above the multitudinous small noises and creakings and warpings of the vacant house, a smaller voice singing on the floor above. This, as she remembered, was only an open attic that had been used as a storeroom. With a half-guilty consciousness, she crept softly upstairs and, pushing the door partly open, looked within.

Athwart the long, low-studded attic, a slant sunbeam from a single small window lay, filled with dancing motes, and only half illuminating the barren, dreary apartment. In the ray of this sunbeam she saw the child's glowing hair, as if crowned by a red aureole, as she sat upon the floor with her exaggerated doll between her knees. She appeared to be talking to it; and it was not long before Mrs. Tretherick observed that she was rehearsing the interview of a half-hour before. She catechized the doll severely, cross-examining it in regard to the duration of its stay there, and generally on the measure of time. The imitation of Mrs. Tretherick's manner was exceedingly successful, and the conversation almost a literal reproduction, with a single exception. After she had informed the doll that she was not her mother, at the close of the interview she added pathetically, "that if she was dood, very dood, she might be her mamma, and love her very much."

I have already hinted that Mrs. Tretherick was deficient in a sense of humor. Perhaps it was for this reason that this whole scene affected her most unpleasantly; and the conclusion sent the blood tingling to her cheek. There was something, too, inconceivably lonely in the situation. The unfurnished vacant room, the half-lights, the monstrous doll, whose very size seemed to give a pathetic significance to its speechlessness, the smallness of the one animate, self-centered figure—all these touched more or less deeply the half-poetic sensibilities of the woman. She could not help utilizing the impression as she stood there, and thought what a fine poem might be constructed from this material if the room were a little darker, the child lonelier—say, sitting beside a dead mother's bier, and the wind wailing in the turrets. And then she suddenly heard footsteps at the door below, and recognized the tread of the colonel's cane.

She flew swiftly down the stairs, and encountered the colonel in the hall. Here she poured into his astonished ear a voluble and exaggerated statement of her discovery, and indignant recital of her wrongs. "Don't tell me the whole thing wasn't arranged beforehand; for I know it was!" she almost screamed. "And think," she added, "of the heartlessness of the wretch, leaving his own child alone here in that way."

"It's a blank shame!" stammered the colonel, without the least idea of what he was talking about. In fact, utterly unable as he was to comprehend a reason for the woman's excitement, with his estimate of her character, I fear he showed it more plainly than he intended. He stammered, expanded his chest, looked stern, gallant, tender, but all unintelligently. Mrs. Tretherick, for an instant, experienced a sickening doubt of the existence of natures in perfect affinity.

"It's of no use," said Mrs. Tretherick with sudden vehemence, in answer to some inaudible remark of the colonel's, and withdrawing her hand from the fervent grasp of that ardent and sympathetic man. "It's of no use: my mind is made up. You can send for my trunk as soon as you like; but I shall stay here, and confront that man with the proof of his vileness. I will put him face to face with his infamy."

I do not know whether Colonel Starbottle thoroughly appreciated the convincing proof of Tretherick's unfaithfulness and malignity afforded by the damning evidence of the existence of Tretherick's own child in his own house. He was dimly aware, however, of some unforeseen obstacle to the perfect expression of the infinite longing of his own sentimental nature. But, before he could say anything, Carry appeared on the landing above them, looking timidly, and yet half-critically, at the pair.

"That's her," said Mrs. Tretherick excitedly. In her deepest emotions, in either verse or prose, she rose above a consideration of grammatical construction.

"Ah!" said the colonel, with a sudden assumption of parental affection and jocularity that was glaringly unreal and affected. "Ah! pretty little girl, pretty little girl! How do you do? How are you? You find yourself pretty well, do you, pretty little girl?" The colonel's impulse also was to expand his chest and swing his cane, until it occurred to him that this action might be ineffective with a child of six or seven. Carry, however, took no immediate notice of this advance, but further discomposed the chivalrous colonel by running quickly to Mrs. Tretherick and hiding herself, as if for protection, in the folds of her gown. Nevertheless, the colonel was not vanquished. Falling back into an attitude of respectful admiration, he pointed out a marvelous resemblance to the "Madonna and Child." Mrs. Tretherick simpered, but did not dislodge Carry as before. There was an awkward pause for a moment; and then Mrs. Tretherick, motioning significantly to the child, said in a whisper: "Go now. Don't come here again, but meet me tonight at the hotel." She extended her hand: the colonel bent over it gallantly and, raising his hat, the next moment was gone.

"Do you think," said Mrs. Tretherick with an embarrassed voice and a prodigious blush, looking down, and addressing the fiery curls just visible in the folds of her dress—"do you think you will be 'dood' if I let you stay in here and sit with me?"

"And let me tall you Mamma?" queried Carry, looking up.

"And let you call me Mamma!" assented Mrs. Tretherick with an embarrassed laugh.

"Yeth," said Carry promptly.

They entered the bedroom together. Carry's eye instantly caught sight of the trunk.

"Are you dowin' away adain, Mamma?" she said with a quick nervous look, and a clutch at the woman's dress.

"No-o," said Mrs. Tretherick, looking out of the window.

"Only playing your dowin' away," suggested Carry with a laugh. "Let me play too."

Mrs. Tretherick assented. Carry flew into the next room, and presently reappeared dragging a small trunk, into which she gravely proceeded to pack her clothes. Mrs. Tretherick noticed that they were not many. A question or two regarding them brought out some further replies from the child; and before many minutes had elapsed, Mrs. Tretherick was in possession of all her earlier history. But, to do this, Mrs. Tretherick had been obliged to take Carry upon her lap, pending the most confidential disclosures. They sat thus a long time after Mrs. Tretherick had apparently ceased to be interested in Carry's disclosures; and when lost in thought, she allowed the child to rattle on unheeded, and ran her fingers through the scarlet curls.

"You don't hold me right, Mamma," said Carry at last, after one or two uneasy shiftings of position.

"How should I hold you?" asked Mrs. Tretherick with a half-amused, half-embarrassed laugh.

"Dis way," said Carry, curling up into position, with one arm around Mrs. Tretherick's neck and her cheek resting on her bosom—"dis way—dere." After a little preparatory nestling, not unlike some small animal, she closed her eyes, and went to sleep.

For a few moments the woman sat silent, scarcely daring to breathe in that artificial attitude. And then, whether from some occult sympathy in the touch, or God best knows what, a sudden fancy began to thrill her. She began by remembering an old pain that she had forgotten, an old horror that she had resolutely put away all these years. She recalled days of sickness and distrust—days of an overshadowing fear—days of preparation for something that was to be prevented, that WAS prevented, with mortal agony and fear. She thought of a life that might have been—she dared not say HAD been—and wondered. It was six years ago; if it had lived, it would have been as old as Carry. The arms which were folded loosely around the sleeping child began to tremble, and tighten their clasp. And then the deep potential impulse came, and with a half-sob, half-sigh, she threw her arms out and drew the body of the sleeping child down, down, into her breast, down again and again as if she would hide it in the grave dug there years before. And the gust that shook her passed, and then, ah me! the rain.

A drop or two fell upon the curls of Carry, and she moved uneasily in her sleep. But the woman soothed her again—it was SO easy to do it now—and they sat there quiet and undisturbed, so quiet that they might have seemed incorporate of the lonely silent house, the slowly declining sunbeams, and the general air of desertion and abandonment, yet a desertion that had in it nothing of age, decay, or despair.

Colonel Starbottle waited at the Fiddletown Hotel all that night in vain. And the next morning, when Mr. Tretherick returned to his husks, he found the house vacant and untenanted, except by motes and sunbeams.

When it was fairly known that Mrs. Tretherick had run away, taking Mr. Tretherick's own child with her, there was some excitement and much diversity of opinion, in Fiddletown. THE DUTCH FLAT INTELLIGENCER openly alluded to the "forcible abduction" of the child with the same freedom, and it is to be feared the same prejudice, with which it had criticized the abductor's poetry. All of Mrs. Tretherick's own sex, and perhaps a few of the opposite sex, whose distinctive quality was not, however, very strongly indicated, fully coincided in the views of the

INTELLIGENCER. The majority, however, evaded the moral issue; that Mrs. Tretherick had shaken the red dust of Fiddletown from her dainty slippers was enough for them to know. They mourned the loss of the fair abductor more than her offense. They promptly rejected Tretherick as an injured husband and disconsolate father, and even went so far as to openly cast discredit on the sincerity of his grief. They reserved an ironical condolence for Colonel Starbottle, overbearing that excellent man with untimely and demonstrative sympathy in barrooms, saloons, and other localities not generally deemed favorable to the display of sentiment. "She was alliz a skittish thing, Kernel," said one sympathizer, with a fine affectation of gloomy concern and great readiness of illustration; "and it's kinder nat'ril thet she'd get away someday, and stampede that theer colt: but thet she should shake YOU, Kernel, diet she should jist shake you—is what gits me. And they do say thet you jist hung around thet hotel all night, and payrolled them corriders, and histed yourself up and down them stairs, and meandered in and out o' thet piazzy, and all for nothing?" It was another generous and tenderly commiserating spirit that poured additional oil and wine on the colonel's wounds. "The boys yer let on thet Mrs. Tretherick prevailed on ye to pack her trunk and a baby over from the house to the stage offis, and that the chap ez did go off with her thanked you, and offered you two short bits, and sed ez how he liked your looks, and ud employ you agin—and now you say it ain't so? Well, I'll tell the boys it ain't so, and I'm glad I met you, for stories DO get round."

Happily for Mrs. Tretherick's reputation, however, the Chinaman in Tretherick's employment, who was the only eyewitness of her flight, stated that she was unaccompanied, except by the child. He further deposed that, obeying her orders, he had stopped the Sacramento coach, and secured a passage for herself and child to San Francisco. It was true that Ah Fe's testimony was of no legal value. But nobody doubted it. Even those who were skeptical of the pagan's ability to recognize the sacredness of the truth admitted his passionless, unprejudiced unconcern. But it would appear, from a hitherto unrecorded passage of this veracious chronicle, that herein they were mistaken.

It was about six months after the disappearance of Mrs. Tretherick that Ah Fe, while working in Tretherick's lot, was hailed by two passing Chinamen. They were the ordinary mining coolies, equipped with long poles and baskets for their usual pilgrimages. An animated conversation at once ensued between Ah Fe and his brother Mongolians—a conversation characterized by that usual shrill volubility and apparent animosity which was at once the delight and scorn of the intelligent Caucasian who did not understand a word of it. Such, at least, was the feeling with which Mr. Tretherick on his veranda and Colonel Starbottle, who was passing, regarded their heathenish jargon. The gallant colonel simply kicked them out of his way; the irate Tretherick, with an oath, threw a stone at the group, and dispersed them, but not before one or two slips of yellow rice paper, marked with hieroglyphics, were exchanged, and a small parcel put into Ah Fe's hands. When Ah Fe opened this in the dim solitude of his kitchen, he found a little girl's apron, freshly washed, ironed, and folded. On the corner of the hem were the initials "C. T." Ah

Fe tucked it away in a corner of his blouse, and proceeded to wash his dishes in the sink with a smile of guileless satisfaction.

Two days after this, Ah Fe confronted his master. "Me no likee Fiddletown. Me belly sick. Me go now." Mr. Tretherick violently suggested a profane locality. Ah Fe gazed at him placidly, and withdrew.

Before leaving Fiddletown, however, he accidentally met Colonel Starbottle, and dropped a few incoherent phrases which apparently interested that gentleman. When he concluded, the colonel handed him a letter and a twenty-dollar gold piece. "If you bring me an answer, I'll double that—sabe, John?" Ah Fe nodded. An interview equally accidental, with precisely the same result, took place between Ah Fe and another gentleman, whom I suspect to have been the youthful editor of the AVALANCHE. Yet I regret to state that, after proceeding some distance on his journey, Ah Fe calmly broke the seals of both letters, and after trying to read them upside down and sideways, finally divided them into accurate squares, and in this condition disposed of them to a brother Celestial whom he met on the road, for a trifling gratuity. The agony of Colonel Starbottle on finding his wash bill made out on the unwritten side of one of these squares, and delivered to him with his weekly clean clothes, and the subsequent discovery that the remaining portions of his letter were circulated by the same method from the Chinese laundry of one Fung Ti of Fiddletown, has been described to me as peculiarly affecting. Yet I am satisfied that a higher nature, rising above the levity induced by the mere contemplation of the insignificant details of this breach of trust, would find ample retributive justice in the difficulties that subsequently attended Ah Fe's pilgrimage.

On the road to Sacramento he was twice playfully thrown from the top of the stagecoach by an intelligent but deeply intoxicated Caucasian, whose moral nature was shocked at riding with one addicted to opium-smoking. At Hangtown he was beaten by a passing stranger—purely an act of Christian supererogation. At Dutch Flat he was robbed by well-known hands from unknown motives. At Sacramento he was arrested on suspicion of being something or other, and discharged with a severe reprimand—possibly for not being it, and so delaying the course of justice. At San Francisco he was freely stoned by children of the public schools; but, by carefully avoiding these monuments of enlightened progress, he at last reached, in comparative safety, the Chinese quarters, where his abuse was confined to the police and limited by the strong arm of the law.

The next day he entered the washhouse of Chy Fook as an assistant, and on the following Friday was sent with a basket of clean clothes to Chy Fook's several clients.

It was the usual foggy afternoon as he climbed the long windswept hill of California Street— one of those bleak, gray intervals that made the summer a misnomer to any but the liveliest San Franciscan fancy. There was no warmth or color in earth or sky, no light nor shade within or without, only one monotonous, universal neutral tint over everything. There was a fierce unrest in the wind-whipped streets: there was a dreary vacant quiet in the gray houses. When Ah Fe reached the top of the hill, the Mission Ridge was already hidden, and the chill sea breeze made him shiver. As he put down his basket to rest himself, it is possible that, to his defective intelligence and heathen experience, this "God's own climate," as was called, seemed to possess but scant tenderness, softness, or mercy. But it is possible that Ah Fe illogically confounded this season with his old persecutors, the schoolchildren, who, being released from studious confinement, at this hour were generally most aggressive. So he hastened on, and turning a corner, at last stopped before a small house.

It was the usual San Franciscan urban cottage. There was the little strip of cold green shrubbery before it; the chilly, bare veranda, and above this, again, the grim balcony, on which no one sat. Ah Fe rang the bell. A servant appeared, glanced at his basket, and reluctantly admitted him, as if he were some necessary domestic animal. Ah Fe silently mounted the stairs, and entering the open door of the front chamber, put down the basket and stood passively on the threshold.

A woman, who was sitting in the cold gray light of the window, with a child in her lap, rose listlessly, and came toward him. Ah Fe instantly recognized Mrs. Tretherick; but not a muscle of his immobile face changed, nor did his slant eyes lighten as he met her own placidly. She evidently did not recognize him as she began to count the clothes. But the child, curiously examining him, suddenly uttered a short, glad cry.

"Why, it's John, Mamma! It's our old John what we had in Fiddletown."

For an instant Ah Fe's eyes and teeth electrically lightened. The child clapped her hands, and caught at his blouse. Then he said shortly: "Me John—Ah Fe—allee same. Me know you. How do?"

Mrs. Tretherick dropped the clothes nervously, and looked hard at Ah Fe. Wanting the quick-witted instinct of affection that sharpened Carry's perception, she even then could not distinguish him above his fellows. With a recollection of past pain, and an obscure suspicion of impending danger, she asked him when he had left Fiddletown.

"Longee time. No likee Fiddletown, no likee Tlevelick. Likee San Flisco. Likee washee. Likee Tally."

Ah Fe's laconics pleased Mrs. Tretherick. She did not stop to consider how much an imperfect knowledge of English added to his curt directness and sincerity. But she said, "Don't tell anybody you have seen me," and took out her pocketbook.

Ah Fe, without looking at it, saw that it was nearly empty. Ah Fe, without examining the apartment, saw that it was scantily furnished. Ah Fe, without removing his eyes from blank vacancy, saw that both Mrs. Tretherick and Carry were poorly dressed. Yet it is my duty to state that Ah Fe's long fingers closed promptly and firmly over the half-dollar which Mrs. Tretherick extended to him.

Then he began to fumble in his blouse with a series of extraordinary contortions. After a few moments, he extracted from apparently no particular place a child's apron, which he laid upon the basket with the remark:

"One piecee washman flagittee."

Then he began anew his fumblings and contortions. At last his efforts were rewarded by his producing, apparently from his right ear, a many-folded piece of tissue paper. Unwrapping this carefully, he at last disclosed two twenty-dollar gold pieces, which he handed to Mrs. Tretherick.

"You leavee money topside of blulow, Fiddletown. Me findee money. Me fetchee money to you. All lightee."

"But I left no money on the top of the bureau, John," said Mrs. Tretherick earnestly. "There must be some mistake. It belongs to some other person. Take it back, John."

Ah Fe's brow darkened. He drew away from Mrs. Tretherick's extended hand, and began hastily to gather up his basket.

"Me no takee it back. No, no! Bimeby pleesman he catchee me. He say, 'God damn thief!—catchee flowty dollar: come to jailee.' Me no takee back. You leavee money topside blulow, Fiddletown. Me fetchee money you. Me no takee back."

Mrs. Tretherick hesitated. In the confusion of her flight, she MIGHT have left the money in the manner he had said. In any event, she had no right to jeopardize this honest Chinaman's safety by refusing it. So she said: "Very well, John, I will keep it. But you must come again and see me—" here Mrs. Tretherick hesitated with a new and sudden revelation of the fact that any man could wish to see any other than herself—"and, and—Carry."

Ah Fe's face lightened. He even uttered a short ventriloquistic laugh without moving his mouth. Then, shouldering his basket, he shut the door carefully and slid quietly down stairs. In the lower hall he, however, found an unexpected difficulty in opening the front door, and, after fumbling vainly at the lock for a moment, looked around for some help or instruction. But the Irish handmaid who had let him in was contemptuously oblivious of his needs, and did not appear.

There occurred a mysterious and painful incident, which I shall simply record without attempting to explain. On the hall table a scarf, evidently the property of the servant before alluded to, was lying. As Ah Fe tried the lock with one hand, the other rested lightly on the table. Suddenly, and apparently of its own volition, the scarf began to creep slowly toward Ah Fe's hand; from Ah Fe's hand it began to creep up his sleeve slowly, and with an insinuating, snakelike motion; and then disappeared somewhere in the recesses of his blouse. Without betraying the least interest or concern in this phenomenon, Ah Fe still repeated his experiments upon the lock. A moment later the tablecloth of red damask, moved by apparently the same mysterious impulse, slowly gathered itself under Ah Fe's fingers, and sinuously disappeared by the same hidden channel. What further mystery might have followed, I cannot say; for at this moment Ah Fe discovered the secret of the lock, and was enabled to open the door coincident with the sound of footsteps upon the kitchen stairs. Ah Fe did not hasten his movements, but patiently shouldering his basket, closed the door carefully behind him again, and stepped forth into the thick encompassing fog that now shrouded earth and sky.

From her high casement window, Mrs. Tretherick watched Ah Fe's figure until it disappeared in the gray cloud. In her present loneliness, she felt a keen sense of gratitude toward him, and may have ascribed to the higher emotions and the consciousness of a good deed that certain expansiveness of the chest, and swelling of the bosom, that was really due to the hidden presence of the scarf and tablecloth under his blouse. For Mrs. Tretherick was still poetically sensitive. As the gray fog deepened into night, she drew Carry closer toward her, and, above the prattle of the child, pursued a vein of sentimental and egotistic recollection at once bitter and dangerous. The sudden apparition of Ah Fe linked her again with her past life at Fiddletown. Over the dreary interval between, she was now wandering—a journey so piteous, willful, thorny, and useless that it was no wonder that at last Carry stopped suddenly in the midst of her voluble confidences to throw her small arms around the woman's neck, and bid her not to cry.

Heaven forefend that I should use a pen that should be ever dedicated to an exposition of unalterable moral principle to transcribe Mrs. Tretherick's own theory of this interval and episode, with its feeble palliations, its illogical deductions, its fond excuses, and weak apologies. It would seem, however, that her experience had been hard. Her slender stock of money was soon exhausted. At Sacramento she found that the composition of verse, although appealing to the highest emotions of the human heart, and compelling the editorial breast to the noblest commendation in the editorial pages, was singularly inadequate to defray the expenses of herself and Carry. Then she tried the stage, but failed signally. Possibly her conception of the passions was different from that which obtained with a Sacramento audience; but it was certain that her charming presence, so effective at short range, was not sufficiently pronounced for the footlights. She had admirers enough in the greenroom, but awakened no abiding affection among the audience. In this strait, it occurred to her that she had a voice—a contralto of no very great compass or cultivation, but singularly sweet and touching; and she finally obtained position in a church choir. She held it for three months, greatly to her pecuniary advantage, and, it is said, much to the satisfaction of the gentlemen in the back pews, who faced toward her during the singing of the last hymn.

I remember her quite distinctly at this time. The light that slanted through the oriel of St. Dives's choir was wont to fall very tenderly on her beautiful head with its stacked masses of deerskin-colored hair, on the low black arches of her brows, and to deepen the pretty fringes that shaded her eyes of Genoa velvet. Very pleasant it was to watch the opening and shutting of that small straight mouth, with its quick revelation of little white teeth, and to see the foolish blood faintly deepen her satin cheek as you watched. For Mrs. Tretherick was very sweetly conscious of admiration and, like most pretty women, gathered herself under your eye like a racer under the spur.

And then, of course, there came trouble. I have it from the soprano—a little lady who possessed even more than the usual unprejudiced judgment of her sex—that Mrs. Tretherick's conduct was simply shameful; that her conceit was unbearable; that, if she considered the rest of the choir as slaves, she (the soprano) would like to know it; that her conduct on Easter Sunday with the basso had attracted the attention of the whole congregation; and that she herself had noticed Dr. Cope twice look up during the service; that her (the soprano's) friends had objected to her singing in the choir with a person who had been on the stage, but she had waived this. Yet she had it from the best authority that Mrs. Tretherick had run away from her husband, and that this red-haired child who sometimes came in the choir was not her own. The tenor confided to me behind the organ that Mrs. Tretherick had a way of sustaining a note at the end of a line in order that her voice might linger longer with the congregation—an act that could be attributed only to a defective moral nature; that as a man (he was a very popular dry goods clerk on weekdays, and sang a good deal from apparently behind his eyebrows on the Sabbath)—that as a man, sir, he would put up with it no longer. The basso alone—a short German with a heavy voice, for which he seemed reluctantly responsible, and rather grieved at its possession—stood up for Mrs. Tretherick, and averred that they were jealous of her because she was "bretty." The climax was at last reached in an open quarrel, wherein Mrs. Tretherick used her tongue with such precision of statement and epithet that the soprano burst into hysterical tears, and had to be supported from the choir by her husband and the tenor. This act was marked intentionally to the congregation by the omission of the usual soprano solo. Mrs. Tretherick went home flushed with triumph, but on reaching her room frantically told Carry that they were beggars henceforward; that she—her mother—had just taken the very bread out of her darling's mouth, and ended by bursting into a flood of penitent tears. They did not come so quickly as in her old poetical days; but when they came they stung deeply. She was roused by a formal visit from a vestryman—one of the music committee. Mrs. Tretherick dried her long lashes, put on a new neck ribbon, and went down to the parlor. She staid there two hours—a fact that might have occasioned some remark but that the vestryman was married, and had a family of grownup daughters. When Mrs. Tretherick returned to her room, she sang to herself in the glass and scolded Carry—but she retained her place in the choir.

It was not long, however. In due course of time, her enemies received a powerful addition to their forces in the committeeman's wife. That lady called upon several of the church members and on Dr. Cope's family. The result was that, at a later meeting of the music committee, Mrs. Tretherick's voice was declared inadequate to the size of the building and she was invited to resign. She did so. She had been out of a situation for two months, and her scant means were almost exhausted, when Ah Fe's unexpected treasure was tossed into her lap.

The gray fog deepened into night, and the street lamps started into shivering life as, absorbed in these unprofitable memories, Mrs. Tretherick still sat drearily at her window. Even Carry had slipped away unnoticed; and her abrupt entrance with the damp evening paper in her hand roused Mrs. Tretherick, and brought her back to an active realization of the present. For Mrs. Tretherick was wont to scan the advertisements in the faint hope of finding some avenue of employment— she knew not what—open to her needs; and Carry had noted this habit.

Mrs. Tretherick mechanically closed the shutters, lit the lights, and opened the paper. Her eye fell instinctively on the following paragraph in the telegraphic column:

FIDDLETOWN, 7th.—Mr. James Tretherick, an old resident of this place, died last night of delirium tremens. Mr. Tretherick was addicted to intemperate habits, said to have been induced by domestic trouble.

Mrs. Tretherick did not start. She quietly turned over another page of the paper, and glanced at Carry. The child was absorbed in a book. Mrs. Tretherick uttered no word, but during the remainder of the evening was unusually silent and cold. When Carry was undressed and in bed, Mrs. Tretherick suddenly dropped on her knees beside the bed, and, taking Carry's flaming head between her hands, said:

"Should you like to have another papa, Carry, darling?"

"No," said Carry, after a moment's thought.

"But a papa to help Mamma take care of you, to love you, to give you nice clothes, to make a lady of you when you grow up?"

Carry turned her sleepy eyes toward the questioner. "Should YOU, Mamma?"

Mrs. Tretherick suddenly flushed to the roots of her hair. "Go to sleep," she said sharply, and turned away.

But at midnight the child felt two white arms close tightly around her, and was drawn down into a bosom that heaved, fluttered, and at last was broken up by sobs.

"Don't ky, Mamma," whispered Carry, with a vague retrospect of their recent conversation. "Don't ky. I fink I SHOULD like a new papa, if he loved you very much—very, very much!"

A month afterward, to everybody's astonishment, Mrs. Tretherick was married. The happy bridegroom was one Colonel Starbottle, recently elected to represent Calaveras County in the legislative councils of the State. As I cannot record the event in finer language than that used by the correspondent of THE SACRAMENTO GLOBE, I venture to quote some of his graceful periods. "The relentless shafts of the sly god have been lately busy among our gallant Solons. We quote 'one more unfortunate.' The latest victim is the Hon. C. Starbottle of Calaveras. The fair enchantress in the case is a beautiful widow, a former votary of Thespis, and lately a fascinating St. Cecilia of one of the most fashionable churches of San Francisco, where she commanded a high salary."

THE DUTCH FLAT INTELLIGENCER saw fit, however, to comment upon the fact with that humorous freedom characteristic of an unfettered press. "The new Democratic war horse from Calaveras has lately advented in the legislature with a little bill to change the name of Tretherick to Starbottle. They call it a marriage certificate down there. Mr. Tretherick has been dead just one month; but we presume the gallant colonel is not afraid of ghosts." It is but just to Mrs. Tretherick to state that the colonel's victory was by no means an easy one. To a natural degree of coyness on the part of the lady was added the impediment of a rival—a prosperous undertaker from Sacramento, who had first seen and loved Mrs. Tretherick at the theater and church, his professional habits debarring him from ordinary social intercourse, and indeed any other than the most formal public contact with the sex. As this gentleman had made a snug fortune during the felicitous prevalence of a severe epidemic, the colonel regarded him as a dangerous rival. Fortunately, however, the undertaker was called in professionally to lay out a brother senator, who had unhappily fallen by the colonel's pistol in an affair of honor; and either deterred by physical consideration from rivalry, or wisely concluding that the colonel was professionally valuable, he withdrew from the field.

The honeymoon was brief, and brought to a close by an untoward incident. During their bridal trip, Carry had been placed in the charge of Colonel Starbottle's sister. On their return to the city, immediately on reaching their lodgings, Mrs. Starbottle announced her intention of at once proceeding to Mrs. Culpepper's to bring the child home. Colonel Starbottle, who had been exhibiting for some time a certain uneasiness which he had endeavored to overcome by repeated stimulation, finally buttoned his coat tightly across his breast, and after walking unsteadily once or twice up and down the room, suddenly faced his wife with his most imposing manner.

"I have deferred," said the colonel with an exaggeration of port that increased with his inward fear, and a growing thickness of speech—"I have deferr—I may say poshponed statement o' fack thash my duty ter dishclose ter ye. I did no wish to mar sushine mushal happ'ness, to bligh bud o' promise, to darken conjuglar sky by unpleasht revelashun. Musht be done—by God, m'm, musht do it now. The chile is gone!"

"Gone!" echoed Mrs. Starbottle.

There was something in the tone of her voice, in the sudden drawing-together of the pupils of her eyes, that for a moment nearly sobered the colonel, and partly collapsed his chest.

"I'll splain all in a minit," he said with a deprecating wave of the hand. "Everything shall be splained. The-the-the-melencholly event wish preshipitate our happ'ness—the myster'us prov'nice wish releash you—releash chile! hunerstan?—releash chile. The mom't Tretherick die—all claim you have in chile through him—die too. Thash law. Who's chile b'long to? Tretherick? Tretherick dead. Chile can't b'long dead man. Damn nonshense b'long dead man. I'sh your chile? no! whose chile then? Chile b'long to 'ts mother. Unnerstan?"

"Where is she?" said Mrs. Starbottle, with a very white face and a very low voice.

"I'll splain all. Chile b'long to 'ts mother. Thash law. I'm lawyer, leshlator, and American sis'n. Ish my duty as lawyer, as leshlator, and 'merikan sis'n to reshtore chile to suff'rin mother at any coss—any coss."

"Where is she?" repeated Mrs. Starbottle, with her eyes still fixed on the colonel's face.

"Gone to 'ts m'o'r. Gone East on shteamer, yesserday. Waffed by fav'rin gales to suff'rin p'rent. Thash so!"

Mrs. Starbottle did not move. The colonel felt his chest slowly collapsing, but steadied himself against a chair, and endeavored to beam with chivalrous gallantry not unmixed with magisterial firmness upon her as she sat.

"Your feelin's, m'm, do honor to yer sex, but conshider situashun. Conshider m'or's feelings—conshider MY feelin's." The colonel paused, and flourishing a white handkerchief, placed it negligently in his breast, and then smiled tenderly above it, as over laces and ruffles, on the woman before him. "Why should dark shed-der cass bligh on two sholes with single beat? Chile's fine chile, good chile, but summonelse chile! Chile's gone, Clar'; but all ish'n't gone, Clar'. Conshider dearesht, you all's have me!"

Mrs. Starbottle started to her feet. "YOU!" she cried, bringing out a chest note that made the chandeliers ring—"You that I married to give my darling food and clothes—YOU! a dog that I whistled to my side to keep the men off me—YOU!"

She choked up, and then dashed past him into the inner room, which had been Carry's; then she swept by him again into her own bedroom, and then suddenly reappeared before him, erect, menacing, with a burning fire over her cheekbones, a quick straightening of her arched brows and mouth, a squaring of jaw, and ophidian flattening of the head.

"Listen!" she said in a hoarse, half-grown boy's voice. "Hear me! If you ever expect to set eyes on me again, you must find the child. If you ever expect to speak to me again, to touch me, you must bring her back. For where she goes, I go; you hear me! Where she has gone, look for me."

She struck out past him again with a quick feminine throwing-out of her arms from the elbows down, as if freeing herself from some imaginary bonds, and dashing into her chamber, slammed and locked the door. Colonel Starbottle, although no coward, stood in superstitious fear of an angry woman, and, recoiling as she swept by, lost his unsteady foothold and rolled helplessly on the sofa. Here, after one or two unsuccessful attempts to regain his foothold, he remained, uttering from time to time profane but not entirely coherent or intelligible protests, until at last he succumbed to the exhausting quality of his emotions, and the narcotic quantity of his potations.

Meantime, within, Mrs. Starbottle was excitedly gathering her valuables and packing her trunk, even as she had done once before in the course of this remarkable history. Perhaps some recollection of this was in her mind; for she stopped to lean her burning cheeks upon her hand, as if she saw again the figure of the child standing in the doorway, and heard once more a childish voice asking, "Is it Mamma?" But the epithet now stung her to the quick, and with a quick, passionate gesture she dashed it away with a tear that had gathered in her eye. And then it chanced that, in turning over some clothes, she came upon the child's slipper with a broken sandal string. She uttered a great cry here—the first she had uttered—and caught it to her breast, kissing it passionately again and again, and rocking from side to side with a motion peculiar to her sex. And then she took it to the window, the better to see it through her now streaming eyes. Here she was taken with a sudden fit of coughing that she could not stifle with the handkerchief she put to her feverish lips. And then she suddenly grew very faint. The window seemed to recede before her, the floor to sink beneath her feet; and staggering to the bed, she fell prone upon it with the sandal and handkerchief pressed to her breast. Her face was quite pale, the orbit of her eyes dark; and there was a spot upon her lip, another on her handkerchief, and still another on the white counterpane of the bed.

The wind had risen, rattling the window sashes and swaying the white curtains in a ghostly way. Later, a gray fog stole softly over the roofs, soothing the wind-roughened surfaces, and in-wrapping all things in an uncertain light and a measureless peace. She lay there very quiet—for all her troubles, still a very pretty bride. And on the other side of the bolted door the gallant bridegroom, from his temporary couch, snored peacefully.

A week before Christmas Day, 1870, the little town of Genoa, in the State of New York, exhibited, perhaps more strongly than at any other time, the bitter irony of its founders and sponsors. A driving snowstorm that had whitened every windward hedge, bush, wall, and telegraph pole, played around this soft Italian Capital, whirled in and out of the great staring wooden Doric columns of its post office and hotel, beat upon the cold green shutters of its best houses, and powdered the angular, stiff, dark figures in its streets. From the level of the street, the four principal churches of the town stood out starkly, even while their misshapen spires were kindly hidden in the low, driving storm. Near the railroad station, the new Methodist chapel, whose resemblance to an enormous locomotive was further heightened by the addition of a pyramidal row of front steps, like a cowcatcher, stood as if waiting for a few more houses to be hitched on to proceed to a pleasanter location. But the pride of Genoa—the great Crammer Institute for Young Ladies—stretched its bare brick length and reared its cupola plainly from the bleak Parnassian hill above the principal avenue. There was no evasion in the Crammer Institute of the fact that it was a public institution. A visitor upon its doorsteps, a pretty face at its window, were clearly visible all over the township.

The shriek of the engine of the four-o'clock Northern express brought but few of the usual loungers to the depot. Only a single passenger alighted, and was driven away in the solitary waiting sleigh toward the Genoa Hotel. And then the train sped away again, with that passionless indifference to human sympathies or curiosity peculiar to express trains; the one baggage truck was wheeled into the station again; the station door was locked; and the stationmaster went home.

The locomotive whistle, however, awakened the guilty consciousness of three young ladies of the Crammer Institute, who were even then surreptitiously regaling themselves in the bakeshop and confectionery saloon of Mistress Phillips in a by-lane. For even the admirable regulations of the Institute failed to entirely develop the physical and moral natures of its pupils. They conformed to the excellent dietary rules in public, and in private drew upon the luxurious rations of their village caterer. They attended church with exemplary formality, and flirted informally during service with the village beaux. They received the best and most judicious instruction during school hours, and devoured the trashiest novels during recess. The result of which was an aggregation of quite healthy, quite human, and very charming young creatures that reflected infinite credit on the Institute. Even Mistress Phillips, to whom they owed vast sums, exhilarated by the exuberant spirits and youthful freshness of her guests, declared that the sight of "them young things" did her good, and had even been known to shield them by shameless equivocation.

"Four o'clock, girls! and, if we're not back to prayers by five, we'll be missed," said the tallest of these foolish virgins, with an aquiline nose, and certain quiet elan that bespoke the leader, as she rose from her seat. "Have you got the books, Addy?" Addy displayed three dissipated-looking novels under her waterproof. "And the provisions, Carry?" Carry showed a suspicious parcel filling the pocket of her sack. "All right, then. Come, girls, trudge—Charge it," she added, nodding to her host as they passed toward the door. "I'll pay you when my quarter's allowance comes."

"No, Kate," interposed Carry, producing her purse, "let me pay; it's my turn."

"Never!" said Kate, arching her black brows loftily, "even if you do have rich relatives, and regular remittances from California. Never! Come, girls, forward, march!"

As they opened the door, a gust of wind nearly took them off their feet. Kindhearted Mrs. Phillips was alarmed. "Sakes alive, galls! ye mussn't go out in sich weather. Better let me send word to the Institoot, and make ye up a nice bed tonight in my parlor." But the last sentence was lost in a chorus of half-suppressed shrieks as the girls, hand in hand, ran down the steps into the storm, and were at once whirled away.

The short December day, unlit by any sunset glow, was failing fast. It was quite dark already, and the air was thick with driving snow. For some distance their high spirits, youth, and even inexperience kept them bravely up; but, in ambitiously attempting a short cut from the highroad across an open field, their strength gave out, the laugh grew less frequent, and tears began to stand in Carry's brown eyes. When they reached the road again, they were utterly exhausted. "Let us go back," said Carry.

"We'd never get across that field again," said Addy.

"Let's stop at the first house, then," said Carry.

"The first house," said Addy, peering through the gathering darkness, "is Squire Robinson's." She darted a mischievous glance at Carry that, even in her discomfort and fear, brought the quick blood to her cheek.

"Oh, yes!" said Kate with gloomy irony, "certainly; stop at the squire's by all means, and be invited to tea, and be driven home after by your dear friend Mr. Harry, with a formal apology from Mrs. Robinson, and hopes that the young ladies may be excused this time. No!" continued Kate with sudden energy. "That may suit YOU; but I'm going back as I came—by the window, or not at all" Then she pounced suddenly, like a hawk, on Carry, who was betraying a tendency to sit down on a snowbank and whimper, and shook her briskly. "You'll be going to sleep next. Stay, hold your tongues, all of you—what's that?"

It was the sound of sleigh bells. Coming down toward them out of the darkness was a sleigh with a single occupant. "Hold down your heads, girls: if it's anybody that knows us, we're lost." But it was not, for a voice strange to their ears, but withal very kindly and pleasant, asked if its owner could be of any help to them. As they turned toward him, they saw it was a man wrapped in a handsome sealskin cloak, wearing a sealskin cap; his face, half-concealed by a muffler of the same material, disclosing only a pair of long mustaches, and two keen dark eyes. "It's a son of old Santa Claus!" whispered Addy. The girls tittered audibly as they tumbled into the sleigh; they had regained their former spirits. "Where shall I take you?" said the stranger quietly. There was a hurried whispering; and then Kate said boldly, "To the Institute." They drove silently up the hill, until the long, ascetic building loomed up before them. The stranger reined up suddenly. "You know the way better than I," he said. "Where do you go in?" "Through the back window," said Kate with sudden and appalling frankness. "I see!" responded their strange driver quietly and, alighting quickly, removed the bells from the horses. "We can drive as near as you please now," he added by way of explanation. "He certainly is a son of Santa Claus," whispered Addy. "Hadn't we better ask after his father?" "Hush!" said Kate decidedly. "He is an angel, I dare say." She added with a delicious irrelevance, which was, however, perfectly understood by her feminine auditors, "We are looking like three frights."

Cautiously skirting the fences, they at last pulled up a few feet from a dark wall. The stranger proceeded to assist them to alight. There was still some light from the reflected snow; and as he handed his fair companions to the ground, each was conscious of undergoing an intense though respectful scrutiny. He assisted them gravely to open the window, and then discreetly retired to the sleigh until the difficult and somewhat discomposing ingress was made. He then walked to the window. "Thank you and good night!" whispered three voices. A single figure still lingered. The stranger leaned over the window sill. "Will you permit me to light my cigar here? It might attract attention if I struck a match outside." By the upspringing light he saw the figure of Kate very charmingly framed in by the window. The match burnt slowly out in his fingers. Kate smiled mischievously. The astute young woman had detected the pitiable subterfuge. For what else did she stand at the head of her class, and had doting parents paid three years' tuition?

The storm had passed, and the sun was shining quite cheerily in the eastern recitation room the next morning when Miss Kate, whose seat was nearest the window, placing her hand pathetically upon her heart, affected to fall in bashful and extreme agitation upon the shoulder of Carry, her neighbor. "HE has come," she gasped in a thrilling whisper. "Who?" asked Carry sympathetically, who never clearly understood when Kate was in earnest. "Who?—Why, the man who rescued us last night! I saw him drive to the door this moment. Don't speak; I shall be better in a moment—there!" she said, and the shameless hypocrite passed her hand pathetically across her forehead with a tragic air.

"What can he want?" asked Carry, whose curiosity was excited. "I don't know," said Kate, suddenly relapsing into gloomy cynicism. "Possibly to put his five daughters to school; perhaps to finish his young wife, and warn her against us."

"He didn't look old, and he didn't seem like a married man," rejoined Addy thoughtfully.

"That was his art, you poor creature!" returned Kate scornfully. "You can never tell anything of these men, they are so deceitful. Besides, it's just my fate!"

"Why, Kate," began Carry, in serious concern.

"Hush! Miss Walker is saying something," said Kate, laughing.

"The young ladies will please give attention," said a slow, perfunctory voice. "Miss Carry Tretherick is wanted in the parlor."

Meantime Mr. Jack Prince, the name given on the card, and various letters and credentials submitted to the Rev. Mr. Crammer, paced the somewhat severe apartment known publicly as the "reception parlor" and privately to the pupils as "purgatory." His keen eyes had taken in the various rigid details, from the flat steam "radiator," like an enormous japanned soda cracker, that heated one end of the room to the monumental bust of Dr. Crammer that hopelessly chilled the other; from the Lord's Prayer, executed by a former writing master in such gratuitous variety of elegant calligraphic trifling as to abate considerably the serious value of the composition, to three views of Genoa from the Institute, which nobody ever recognized, taken on the spot by the drawing teacher; from two illuminated texts of Scripture in an English letter, so gratuitously and hideously remote as to chill all human interest, to a large photograph of the senior class, in which the prettiest girls were Ethiopian in complexion, and sat, apparently, on each other's heads and shoulders. His fingers had turned listlessly the leaves of school-catalogues, the SERMONS of Dr. Crammer, the POEMS of Henry Kirke White, the LAYS OF THE SANCTUARY and LIVES OF CELEBRATED WOMEN. His fancy, and it was a nervously active one, had gone over the partings and greetings that must have taken place here, and wondered why the apartment had yet caught so little of the flavor of humanity; indeed, I am afraid he had almost forgotten the object of his visit when the door opened, and Carry Tretherick stood before him.

It was one of those faces he had seen the night before, prettier even than it had seemed then; and yet I think he was conscious of some disappointment, without knowing exactly why. Her abundant waving hair was of a guinea-golden tint, her complexion of a peculiar flowerlike delicacy, her brown eyes of the color of seaweed in deep water. It certainly was not her beauty that disappointed him.

Without possessing his sensitiveness to impression, Carry was, on her part, quite as vaguely ill at ease. She saw before her one of those men whom the sex would vaguely generalize as "nice," that is to say, correct in all the superficial appointments of style, dress, manners, and feature. Yet there was a decidedly unconventional quality about him: he was totally unlike anything or anybody that she could remember; and as the attributes of originality are often as apt to alarm as to attract people, she was not entirely prepossessed in his favor.

"I can hardly hope," he began pleasantly, "that you remember me. It is eleven years ago, and you were a very little girl. I am afraid I cannot even claim to have enjoyed that familiarity that might exist between a child of six and a young man of twenty-one. I don't think I was fond of children. But I knew your mother very well. I was editor of the AVALANCHE in Fiddletown when she took you to San Francisco."

"You mean my stepmother; she wasn't my mother, you know," interposed Carry hastily.

Mr. Prince looked at her curiously. "I mean your stepmother," he said gravely. "I never had the pleasure of meeting your mother."

"No; MOTHER hasn't been in California these twelve years."

There was an intentional emphasizing of the title and of its distinction that began to interest coldly Prince after his first astonishment was past.

"As I come from your stepmother now," he went on with a slight laugh, "I must ask you to go back for a few moments to that point. After your father's death, your mother—I mean your stepmother—recognized the fact that your mother, the first Mrs. Tretherick, was legally and morally your guardian and, although much against her inclination and affections, placed you again in her charge."

"My stepmother married again within a month after father died, and sent me home," said Carry with great directness, and the faintest toss of her head.

Mr. Prince smiled so sweetly, and apparently so sympathetically, that Carry began to like him. With no other notice of the interruption he went on, "After your stepmother had performed this act of simple justice, she entered into an agreement with your mother to defray the expenses of your education until your eighteenth year, when you were to elect and choose which of the two should thereafter be your guardian, and with whom you would make your home. This agreement, I think, you are already aware of, and, I believe, knew at the time."

"I was a mere child then," said Carry.

"Certainly," said Mr. Prince, with the same smile. "Still the conditions, I think, have never been oppressive to you nor your mother; and the only time they are likely to give you the least uneasiness will be when you come to make up your mind in the choice of your guardian. That will be on your eighteenth birthday—the twentieth, I think, of the present month."

Carry was silent.

"Pray do not think that I am here to receive your decision, even if it be already made. I only came to inform you that your stepmother, Mrs. Starbottle, will be in town tomorrow, and will pass a few days at the hotel. If it is your wish to see her before you make up your mind, she will be glad to meet you. She does not, however, wish to do anything to influence your judgment.

"Does Mother know she is coming?" said Carry hastily.

"I do not know," said Prince gravely. "I only know that if you conclude to see Mrs. Starbottle, it will be with your mother's permission. Mrs. Starbottle will keep sacredly this part of the agreement, made ten years ago. But her health is very poor; and the change and country quiet of a few days may benefit her." Mr. Prince bent his keen, bright eyes upon the young girl, and almost held his breath until she spoke again.

"Mother's coming up today or tomorrow," she said, looking up.

"Ah!" said Mr. Prince with a sweet and languid smile.

"Is Colonel Starbottle here too?" asked Carry, after a pause.

"Colonel Starbottle is dead. Your stepmother is again a widow."

"Dead!" repeated Carry.

"Yes," replied Mr. Prince. "Your stepmother has been singularly unfortunate in surviving her affections."

Carry did not know what he meant, and looked so. Mr. Prince smiled reassuringly.

Presently Carry began to whimper.

Mr. Prince softly stepped beside her chair.

"I am afraid," he said with a very peculiar light in his eye, and a singular dropping of the corners of his mustache—"I am afraid you are taking this too deeply. It will be some days before you are called upon to make a decision. Let us talk of something else. I hope you caught no cold last evening."

Carry's face shone out again in dimples.

"You must have thought us so queer! It was too bad to give you so much trouble."

"None whatever, I assure you. My sense of propriety," he added demurely, "which might have been outraged had I been called upon to help three young ladies out of a schoolroom window at night, was deeply gratified at being able to assist them in again." The doorbell rang loudly, and Mr. Prince rose. "Take your own time, and think well before you make your decision." But Carry's ear and attention were given to the sound of voices in the hall. At the same moment, the door was thrown open, and a servant announced, "Mrs. Tretherick and Mr. Robinson."

The afternoon train had just shrieked out its usual indignant protest at stopping at Genoa at all as Mr. Jack Prince entered the outskirts of the town, and drove toward his hotel. He was wearied and cynical. A drive of a dozen miles through unpicturesque outlying villages, past small economic farmhouses, and hideous villas that violated his fastidious taste, had, I fear, left that gentleman in a captious state of mind. He would have even avoided his taciturn landlord as he drove up to the door; but that functionary waylaid him on the steps. "There's a lady in the sittin'-room, waitin' for ye." Mr. Prince hurried upstairs, and entered the room as Mrs. Starbottle flew toward him.

She had changed sadly in the last ten years. Her figure was wasted to half its size. The beautiful curves of her bust and shoulders were broken or inverted. The once full, rounded arm was shrunken in its sleeve; and the golden hoops that encircled her wan wrists almost slipped from her hands as her long, scant fingers closed convulsively around Jack's. Her cheekbones were painted that afternoon with the hectic of fever: somewhere in the hollows of those cheeks were buried the dimples of long ago, but their graves were forgotten. Her lustrous eyes were still beautiful, though the orbits were deeper than before. Her mouth was still sweet, although the lips parted more easily over the little teeth, even in breathing, and showed more of them than she was wont to do before. The glory of her blond hair was still left: it was finer, more silken and ethereal, yet it failed even in its plenitude to cover the hollows of the blue-veined temples.

"Clara!" said Jack reproachfully.

"Oh, forgive me, Jack!" she said, falling into a chair, but still clinging to his hand—"forgive me, dear; but I could not wait longer. I should have died, Jack—died before another night. Bear with me a little longer (it will not be long), but let me stay. I may not see her, I know; I shall not speak to her: but it's so sweet to feel that I am at last near her, that I breathe the same air with my darling. I am better already, Jack, I am indeed. And you have seen her today? How did she look? What did she say? Tell me all, everything, Jack. Was she beautiful? They say she is. Has she grown? Would you have known her again? Will she come, Jack? Perhaps she has been here already; perhaps"—she had risen with tremulous excitement, and was glancing at the door—"perhaps she is here now. Why don't you speak, Jack? Tell me all."

The keen eyes that looked down into hers were glistening with an infinite tenderness that none, perhaps, but she would have deemed them capable of. "Clara," he said gently and cheerily, "try and compose yourself. You are trembling now with the fatigue and excitement of your journey. I have seen Carry; she is well and beautiful. Let that suffice you now."

His gentle firmness composed and calmed her now, as it had often done before. Stroking her thin hand, he said, after a pause, "Did Carry ever write to you?"

"Twice, thanking me for some presents. They were only schoolgirl letters," she added, nervously answering the interrogation of his eyes.

"Did she ever know of your own troubles? of your poverty, of the sacrifices you made to pay her bills, of your pawning your clothes and jewels, of your—"

"No, no!" interrupted the woman quickly: "no! How could she? I have no enemy cruel enough to tell her that."

"But if she—or if Mrs. Tretherick—had heard of it? If Carry thought you were poor, and unable to support her properly, it might influence her decision. Young girls are fond of the position that wealth can give. She may have rich friends, maybe a lover."

Mrs. Starbottle winced at the last sentence. "But," she said eagerly, grasping Jack's hand, "when you found me sick and helpless at Sacramento, when you—God bless you for it, Jack!— offered to help me to the East, you said you knew of something, you had some plan, that would make me and Carry independent."

"Yes," said Jack hastily; "but I want you to get strong and well first. And, now that you are calmer, you shall listen to my visit to the school."

It was then that Mr. Jack Prince proceeded to describe the interview already recorded, with a singular felicity and discretion that shames my own account of that proceeding. Without suppressing a single fact, without omitting a word or detail, he yet managed to throw a poetic veil over that prosaic episode, to invest the heroine with a romantic roseate atmosphere, which, though not perhaps entirely imaginary, still, I fear, exhibited that genius which ten years ago had made the columns of THE FIDDLETOWN AVALANCHE at once fascinating and instructive. It was not until he saw the heightening color, and heard the quick breathing, of his eager listener, that he felt a pang of self-reproach. "God help her and forgive me!" he muttered between his clinched teeth; "but how can I tell her ALL now!"

That night, when Mrs. Starbottle laid her weary head upon her pillow, she tried to picture to herself Carry at the same moment sleeping peacefully in the great schoolhouse on the hill; and it was a rare comfort to this yearning, foolish woman to know that she was so near. But at this moment Carry was sitting on the edge of her bed, half-undressed, pouting her pretty lips and twisting her long, leonine locks between her fingers as Miss Kate Van Corlear—dramatically wrapped in a long white counterpane, her black eyes sparkling, and her thoroughbred nose thrown high in air—stood over her like a wrathful and indignant ghost; for Carry had that evening imparted her woes and her history to Miss Kate, and that young lady had "proved herself no friend" by falling into a state of fiery indignation over Carry's "ingratitude," and openly and shamelessly espousing the claims of Mrs. Starbottle. "Why, if the half you tell me is true, your mother and those Robinsons are making of you not only a little coward, but a little snob, miss. Respectability, forsooth! Look you, my family are centuries before the Tredericks; but if my family had ever treated me in this way, and then asked me to turn my back on my best friend, I'd whistle them down the wind;" and here Kate snapped her fingers, bent her black brows, and glared around the room as if in search of a recreant Van Corlear.

"You just talk this way because you have taken a fancy to that Mr. Prince," said Carry.

In the debasing slang of the period, that had even found its way into the virgin cloisters of the Crammer Institute, Miss Kate, as she afterward expressed it, instantly "went for her."

First, with a shake of her head, she threw her long black hair over one shoulder, then, dropping one end of the counterpane from the other like a vestal tunic, she stepped before Carry with a purposely exaggerated classic stride. "And what if I have, miss! What if I happen to know a gentleman when I see him! What if I happen to know that among a thousand such traditional, conventional, feeble editions of their grandfathers as Mr. Harry Robinson, you cannot find one original, independent, individualized gentleman like your Prince! Go to bed, miss, and pray to Heaven that he may be YOUR Prince indeed. Ask to have a contrite and grateful heart, and thank the Lord in particular for having sent you such a friend as Kate Van Corlear." Yet, after an imposing dramatic exit, she reappeared the next moment as a straight white flash, kissed Carry between the brows, and was gone.

The next day was a weary one to Jack Prince. He was convinced in his mind that Carry would not come; yet to keep this consciousness from Mrs. Starbottle, to meet her simple hopefulness with an equal degree of apparent faith, was a hard and difficult task. He would have tried to divert her mind by taking her on a long drive; but she was fearful that Carry might come during her absence; and her strength, he was obliged to admit, had failed greatly. As he looked into her large and awe-inspiring clear eyes, a something he tried to keep from his mind—to put off day by day from contemplation—kept asserting itself directly to his inner consciousness. He began to doubt the expediency and wisdom of his management. He recalled every incident of his interview with Carry, and half-believed that its failure was due to himself. Yet Mrs. Starbottle was very patient and confident; her very confidence shook his faith in his own judgment. When her strength was equal to the exertion, she was propped up in her chair by the window, where she could see the school and the entrance to the hotel. In the intervals she would elaborate pleasant plans for the future, and would sketch a country home. She had taken a strange fancy, as it seemed to Prince, to the present location; but it was notable that the future, always thus outlined, was one of quiet and repose. She believed she would get well soon; in fact, she thought she was now much better than she had been, but it might be long before she should be quite strong again. She would whisper on in this way until Jack would dash madly down into the barroom, order liquors that he did not drink, light cigars that he did not smoke, talk with men that he did not listen to, and behave generally as our stronger sex is apt to do in periods of delicate trials and perplexity.

The day closed with a clouded sky and a bitter, searching wind. With the night fell a few wandering flakes of snow. She was still content and hopeful; and, as Jack wheeled her from the window to the fire, she explained to him how that, as the school term was drawing near its close, Carry was probably kept closely at her lessons during the day, and could only leave the school at night. So she sat up the greater part of the evening, and combed her silken hair, and as far as her strength would allow, made an undress toilet to receive her guest. "We must not frighten the child, Jack," she said apologetically, and with something of her old coquetry.

It was with a feeling of relief that, at ten o'clock, Jack received a message from the landlord, saying that the doctor would like to see him for a moment downstairs. As Jack entered the grim, dimly lighted parlor, he observed the hooded figure of a woman near the fire. He was about to withdraw again when a voice that he remembered very pleasantly said:

"Oh, it's all right! I'm the doctor."

The hood was thrown back, and Prince saw the shining black hair and black, audacious eyes of Kate Van Corlear.

"Don't ask any questions. I'm the doctor, and there's my prescription," and she pointed to the half-frightened, half-sobbing Carry in the corner—"to be taken at once."

"Then Mrs. Tretherick has given her permission?"

"Not much, if I know the sentiments of that lady," replied Kate saucily.

"Then how did you get away?" asked Prince gravely.

"BY THE WINDOW."

When Mr. Prince had left Carry in the arms of her stepmother, he returned to the parlor.

"Well?" demanded Kate.

"She will stay—YOU will, I hope, also—tonight."

"As I shall not be eighteen, and my own mistress on the twentieth, and as I haven't a sick stepmother, I won't."

"Then you will give me the pleasure of seeing you safely through the window again?"

When Mr. Prince returned an hour later, he found Carry sitting on a low stool at Mrs. Starbottle's feet. Her head was in her stepmother's lap, and she had sobbed herself to sleep. Mrs. Starbottle put her finger to her lip. "I told you she would come. God bless you, Jack! and good night."

The next morning Mrs. Tretherick, indignant, the Rev. Asa Crammer, principal, injured, and Mr. Joel Robinson, Sr., complacently respectable, called upon Mr. Prince. There was a stormy meeting, ending in a demand for Carry. "We certainly cannot admit of this interference," said Mrs. Tretherick, a fashionably dressed, indistinctive-looking woman. "It is several days before the expiration of our agreement; and we do not feel, under the circumstances, justified in releasing Mrs. Starbottle from its conditions." "Until the expiration of the school term, we must consider Miss Tretherick as complying entirely with its rules and discipline," imposed Dr. Crammer. "The whole proceeding is calculated to injure the prospects, and compromise the position, of Miss Tretherick in society," suggested Mr. Robinson.

In vain Mr. Prince urged the failing condition of Mrs. Starbottle, her absolute freedom from complicity with Carry's flight, the pardonable and natural instincts of the girl, and his own assurance that they were willing to abide by her decision. And then, with a rising color in his cheek, a dangerous look in his eye, but a singular calmness in his speech, he added:

"One word more. It becomes my duty to inform you of a circumstance which would certainly justify me, as an executor of the late Mr. Tretherick, in fully resisting your demands. A few months after Mr. Tretherick's death, through the agency of a Chinaman in his employment, it was discovered that he had made a will, which was subsequently found among his papers. The insignificant value of his bequest—mostly land, then quite valueless—prevented his executors from carrying out his wishes, or from even proving the will, or making it otherwise publicly known, until within the last two or three years, when the property had enormously increased in value. The provisions of that bequest are simple, but unmistakable. The property is divided between Carry and her stepmother, with the explicit condition that Mrs. Starbottle shall become her legal guardian, provide for her education, and in all details stand to her IN LOCO PARENTIS."

"What is the value of this bequest?" asked Mr. Robinson. "I cannot tell exactly, but not far from half a million, I should say," returned Prince. "Certainly, with this knowledge, as a friend of Miss Tretherick I must say that her conduct is as judicious as it is honorable to her," responded Mr. Robinson. "I shall not presume to question the wishes, or throw any obstacles in the way of carrying out the intentions, of my dead husband," added Mrs. Tretherick; and the interview was closed.

When its result was made known to Mrs. Starbottle, she raised Jack's hand to her feverish lips. "It cannot add to MY happiness now, Jack; but tell me, why did you keep it from her?" Jack smiled, but did not reply.

Within the next week the necessary legal formalities were concluded, and Carry was restored to her stepmother. At Mrs. Starbottle's request, a small house in the outskirts of the town was procured; and thither they removed to wait the spring, and Mrs. Starbottle's convalescence. Both came tardily that year.

Yet she was happy and patient. She was fond of watching the budding of the trees beyond her window—a novel sight to her Californian experience—and of asking Carry their names and seasons. Even at this time she projected for that summer, which seemed to her so mysteriously withheld, long walks with Carry through the leafy woods, whose gray, misty ranks she could see along the hilltop. She even thought she could write poetry about them, and recalled the fact as evidence of her gaining strength; and there is, I believe, still treasured by one of the members of this little household a little carol so joyous, so simple, and so innocent that it might have been an echo of the robin that called to her from the window, as perhaps it was.

And then, without warning, there dropped from Heaven a day so tender, so mystically soft, so dreamily beautiful, so throbbing and alive with the fluttering of invisible wings, so replete and bounteously overflowing with an awakening and joyous resurrection not taught by man or limited by creed, that they thought it fit to bring her out and lay her in that glorious sunshine that sprinkled like the droppings of a bridal torch the happy lintels and doors. And there she lay beatified and calm.

Wearied by watching, Carry had fallen asleep by her side; and Mrs. Starbottle's thin fingers lay like a benediction on her head. Presently she called Jack to her side.

"Who was that," she whispered, "who just came in?"

"Miss Van Corlear," said Jack, answering the look in her great hollow eyes.

"Jack," she said, after a moment's silence, "sit by me a moment; dear Jack: I've something I must say. If I ever seemed hard, or cold, or coquettish to you in the old days, it was because I loved you, Jack, too well to mar your future by linking it with my own. I always loved you, dear Jack, even when I seemed least worthy of you. That is gone now. But I had a dream lately, Jack, a foolish woman's dream—that you might find what I lacked in HER," and she glanced lovingly at the sleeping girl at her side; "that you might love her as you have loved me. But even that is not to be, Jack, is it?" and she glanced wistfully in his face. Jack pressed her hand, but did not speak. After a few moments' silence, she again said: "Perhaps you are right in your choice. She is a goodhearted girl, Jack—but a little bold."

And with this last flicker of foolish, weak humanity in her struggling spirit, she spoke no more. When they came to her a moment later, a tiny bird that had lit upon her breast flew away; and the hand that they lifted from Carry's head fell lifeless at her side.

* * * * * * * * *

BARKER'S LUCK

A bird twittered! The morning sun shining through the open window was apparently more potent than the cool mountain air, which had only caused the sleeper to curl a little more tightly in his blankets. Barker's eyes opened instantly upon the light and the bird on the window ledge. Like all healthy young animals he would have tried to sleep again, but with his momentary consciousness came the recollection that it was his turn to cook the breakfast that morning, and he regretfully rolled out of his bunk to the floor. Without stopping to dress, he opened the door and stepped outside, secure in the knowledge that he was overlooked only by the Sierras, and plunged his head and shoulders in the bucket of cold water that stood by the door. Then he began to clothe himself, partly in the cabin and partly in the open air, with a lapse between the putting on of his trousers and coat which he employed in bringing in wood. Raking together the few embers on the adobe hearth, not without a prudent regard to the rattlesnake which had once been detected in haunting the warm ashes, he began to prepare breakfast. By this time the other sleepers, his partners Stacy and Demorest, young men of about his own age, were awake, alert, and lazily critical of his progress.

"I don't care about my quail on toast being underdone for breakfast," said Stacy, with a yawn; "and you needn't serve with red wine. I'm not feeling very peckish this morning."

"And I reckon you can knock off the fried oysters after the Spanish mackerel for ME," said Demorest gravely. "The fact is, that last bottle of Veuve Clicquot we had for supper wasn't as dry as I am this morning."

Accustomed to these regular Barmecide suggestions, Barker made no direct reply. Presently, looking up from the fire, he said, "There's no more saleratus, so you mustn't blame me if the biscuit is extra heavy. I told you we had none when you went to the grocery yesterday."

"And I told you we hadn't a red cent to buy any with," said Stacy, who was also treasurer. "Put these two negatives together and you make the affirmative—saleratus. Mix freely and bake in a hot oven."

Nevertheless, after a toilet as primitive as Barker's they sat down to what he had prepared with the keen appetite begotten of the mountain air and the regretful fastidiousness born of the recollection of better things. Jerked beef, frizzled with salt pork in a frying-pan, boiled potatoes, biscuit, and coffee composed the repast. The biscuits, however, proving remarkably heavy after the first mouthful, were used as missiles, thrown through the open door at an empty bottle which had previously served as a mark for revolver practice, and a few moments later pipes were lit to counteract the effects of the meal and take the taste out of their mouths. Suddenly they heard the sound of horses' hoofs, saw the quick passage of a rider in the open space before the cabin, and felt the smart impact upon the table of some small object thrown by him. It was the regular morning delivery of the county newspaper!

"He's getting to be a mighty sure shot," said Demorest approvingly, looking at his upset can of coffee as he picked up the paper, rolled into a cylindrical wad as tightly as a cartridge, and began to straighten it out. This was no easy matter, as the sheet had evidently been rolled while yet damp from the press; but Demorest eventually opened it and ensconced himself behind it.

"Nary news?" asked Stacy.

"No. There never is any," said Demorest scornfully. "We ought to stop the paper."

"You mean the paper man ought to. WE don't pay him," said Barker gently.

"Well, that's the same thing, smarty. No news, no pay. Hallo!" he continued, his eyes suddenly riveted on the paper. Then, after the fashion of ordinary humanity, he stopped short and read the interesting item to himself. When he had finished he brought his fist and the paper, together, violently down upon the table. "Now look at this! Talk of luck, will you? Just think of it. Here are WE—hard-working men with lots of sabe, too—grubbin' away on this hillside like niggers, glad to get enough at the end of the day to pay for our soggy biscuits and horse-bean coffee, and just look what falls into the lap of some lazy sneakin' greenhorn who never did a stoke of work in his life! Here are WE, with no foolishness, no airs nor graces, and yet men who would do credit to twice that amount of luck—and seem born to it, too—and we're set aside for some long, lank, pen-wiping scrub who just knows enough to sit down on his office stool and hold on to a bit of paper."

"What's up now?" asked Stacy, with the carelessness begotten of familiarity with his partner's extravagance.

"Listen," said Demorest, reading. "Another unprecedented rise has taken place in the shares of the 'Yellow Hammer First Extension Mine' since the sinking of the new shaft. It was quoted yesterday at ten thousand dollars a foot. When it is remembered that scarcely two years ago the original shares, issued at fifty dollars per share, had dropped to only fifty cents a share, it will be seen that those who were able to hold on have got a good thing."

"What mine did you say?" asked Barker, looking up meditatively from the dishes he was already washing.

"The Yellow Hammer First Extension," returned Demorest shortly.

"I used to have some shares in that, and I think I have them still," said Barker musingly.

"Yes," said Demorest promptly; "the paper speaks of it here. 'We understand,'" he continued, reading aloud, "'that our eminent fellow citizen, George Barker, otherwise known as "Get Left Barker" and "Chucklehead," is one of these fortunate individuals.'"

"No," said Barker, with a slight flush of innocent pleasure, "it can't say that. How could it know?"

Stacy laughed, but Demorest coolly continued: "You didn't hear all. Listen! 'We say WAS one of them; but having already sold his apparently useless certificates to our popular druggist, Jones, for corn plasters, at a reduced rate, he is unable to realize.'"

"You may laugh, boys," said Barker, with simple seriousness; "but I really believe I have got 'em yet. Just wait. I'll see!" He rose and began to drag out a well-worn valise from under his bunk. "You see," he continued, "they were given to me by an old chap in return—"

"For saving his life by delaying the Stockton boat that afterward blew up," returned Demorest briefly. "We know it all! His hair was white, and his hand trembled slightly as he laid these shares in yours, saying, and you never forgot the words, 'Take 'em, young man—and'—"

"For lending him two thousand dollars, then," continued Barker with a simple ignoring of the interruption, as he quietly brought out the valise.

"TWO THOUSAND DOLLARS!" repeated Stacy. "When did YOU have two thousand dollars?"

"When I first left Sacramento—three years ago," said Barker, unstrapping the valise.

"How long did you have it?" said Demorest incredulously.

"At least two days, I think," returned Barker quietly. "Then I met that man. He was hard-up, and I lent him my pile and took those shares. He died afterward."

"Of course he did," said Demorest severely. "They always do. Nothing kills a man more quickly than an action of that kind." Nevertheless the two partners regarded Barker rummaging among some loose clothes and papers with a kind of paternal toleration. "If you can't find them, bring out your government bonds," suggested Stacy. But the next moment, flushed and triumphant, Barker rose from his knees, and came toward them carrying some papers in his hands. Demorest seized them from him, opened them, spread them on the table, examined hurriedly the date, signatures, and transfers, glanced again quickly at the newspaper paragraph, looked wildly at Stacy and then at Barker, and gasped:

"By the living hookey! it is SO!"

"B'gosh! he HAS got 'em!" echoed Stacy.

"Twenty shares," continued Demorest breathlessly, "at ten thousand dollars a share—even if it's only a foot—is two hundred thousand dollars! Jerusalem!"

"Tell me, fair sir," said Stacy, with sparkling eyes, "hast still left in yonder casket any rare jewels, rubies, sarcenet, or links of fine gold? Peradventure a pearl or two may have been overlooked!"

"No—that's all," returned Barker simply.

"You hear him! Rothschild says 'that's all.' Prince Esterhazy says he hasn't another red cent—only two hundred thousand dollars."

"What ought I to do, boys?" asked Barker, timidly glancing from one to the other. Yet he remembered with delight all that day, and for many a year afterward, that he saw in their faces only unselfish joy and affection at that supreme moment.

"Do?" said Demorest promptly. "Stand on your head and yell! No! stop! Come here!" He seized both Barker and Stacy by the hand, and ran out into the open air. Here they danced violently with clasped hands around a small buckeye, in perfect silence, and then returned to the cabin, grave but perspiring.

"Of course," said Barker, wiping his forehead, "we'll just get some money on these certificates and buy up that next claim which belongs to old Carter—where you know we thought we saw the indication."

"We'll do nothing of the kind," said Demorest decidedly. "WE ain't in it. That money is yours, old chap—every cent of it—property acquired before marriage, you know; and the only thing we'll do is to be damned before we'll see you drop a dime of it into this Godforsaken hole. No!"

"But we're partners," gasped Barker.

"Not in THIS! The utmost we can do for you, opulent sir—though it ill becomes us horny-handed sons of toil to rub shoulders with Dives—is perchance to dine with you, to take a pasty and a glass of Malvoisie, at some restaurant in Sacramento—when you've got things fixed, in honor of your return to affluence. But more would ill become us!"

"But what are YOU going to do?" said Barker, with a half-hysteric, half-frightened smile.

"We have not yet looked through our luggage," said Demorest with invincible gravity, "and there's a secret recess—a double FOND—to my portmanteau, known only to a trusty page, which has not been disturbed since I left my ancestral home in Faginia. There may be a few First Debentures of Erie or what not still there."

"I felt some strange, disklike protuberances in my dress suit the other day, but belike they are but poker chips," said Stacy thoughtfully.

An uneasy feeling crept over Barker. The color which had left his fresh cheek returned to it quickly, and he turned his eyes away. Yet he had seen nothing in his companions' eyes but affection—with even a certain kind of tender commiseration that deepened his uneasiness. "I suppose," he said desperately, after a pause, "I ought to go over to Boomville and make some inquiries."

"At the bank, old chap; at the bank!" said Demorest emphatically. "Take my advice and don't go ANYWHERE ELSE. Don't breathe a word of your luck to anybody. And don't, whatever you do, be tempted to sell just now; you don't know how high that stock's going to jump yet."

"I thought," stammered Barker, "that you boys might like to go over with me."

"We can't afford to take another holiday on grub wages, and we're only two to work today," said Demorest, with a slight increase of color and the faintest tremor in his voice. "And it won't do, old chap, for us to be seen bumming round with you on the heels of your good fortune. For everybody knows we're poor, and sooner or later everybody'll know you WERE rich even when you first came to us."

"Nonsense!" said Barker indignantly.

"Gospel, my boy!" said Demorest shortly.

"The frozen truth, old man!" said Stacy.

Barker took up his hat with some stiffness and moved toward the door. Here he stopped irresolutely, an irresolution that seemed to communicate itself to his partners. There was a moment's awkward silence. Then Demorest suddenly seized him by the shoulders with a grip that was half a caress, and walked him rapidly to the door. "And now don't stand foolin' with us, Barker boy; but just trot off like a little man, and get your grip on that fortune; and when you've got your hooks in it hang on like grim death. You'll"—he hesitated for an instant only, possibly to find the laugh that should have accompanied his speech—"you're sure to find US here when you get back."

Hurt to the quick, but restraining his feelings, Barker clapped his hat on his head and walked quickly away. The two partners stood watching him in silence until his figure was lost in the underbrush. Then they spoke.

"Like him—wasn't it?" said Demorest.

"Just him all over," said Stacy.

"Think of him having that stock stowed away all these years and never even bothering his dear old head about it!"

"And think of his wanting to put the whole thing into this rotten hillside with us!"

"And he'd have done it, by gosh! and never thought of it again. That's Barker."

"Dear old man!"

"Good old chap!"

"I've been wondering if one of us oughtn't to have gone with him? He's just as likely to pour his money into the first lap that opens for it," said Stacy.

"The more reason why we shouldn't prevent him, or seem to prevent him," said Demorest almost fiercely. "There will be knaves and fools enough who will try and put the idea of our using him into his simple heart without that. No! Let him do as he likes with it—but let him be himself. I'd rather have him come back to us even after he's lost the money—his old self and empty-handed—than try to change the stuff God put into him and make him more like others."

The tone and manner were so different from Demorest's usual levity that Stacy was silent. After a pause he said: "Well! we shall miss him on the hillside—won't we?"

Demorest did not reply. Reaching out his hand abstractedly, he wrenched off a small slip from a sapling near him, and began slowly to pull the leaves off, one by one, until they were all gone. Then he switched it in the air, struck his bootleg smartly with it, said roughly: "Come, let's get to work!" and strode away.

Meantime Barker on his way to Boomville was no less singular in his manner. He kept up his slightly affected attitude until he had lost sight of the cabin. But, being of a simple nature, his emotions were less complex. If he had not seen the undoubted look of affection in the eyes of his partners he would have imagined that they were jealous of his good fortune. Yet why had they refused his offer to share it with him? Why had they so strangely assumed that their partnership with him had closed? Why had they declined to go with him? Why had this money—of which he had thought so little, and for which he had cared so little—changed them toward him? It had not changed HIM—HE was the same! He remembered how they had often talked and laughed over a prospective "strike" in mining and speculated what THEY would do together with the money! And now that "luck" had occurred to one of them, individually, the effect was only to alienate them! He could not make it out. He was hurt, wounded—yet oddly enough he was conscious now of a certain power within him to hurt and wound in retribution. He was rich: he would let them see HE could do without them. He was quite free now to think only of himself and Kitty.

For it must be recorded that with all this young gentleman's simplicity and unselfishness, with all his loyal attitude to his partners, his FIRST thought at the moment he grasped the fact of his wealth was of a young lady. It was Kitty Carter, the daughter of the hotelkeeper at Boomville, who owned the claim that the partners had mutually coveted. That a pretty girl's face should flash upon him with his conviction that he was now a rich man meant perhaps no disloyalty to his partners, whom he would still have helped. But it occurred to him now, in his half-hurt, half-vengeful state, that they had often joked him about Kitty, and perhaps further confidence with them was debarred. And it was only due to his dignity that he should now see Kitty at once.

This was easy enough, for in the naive simplicity of Boomville and the economic arrangements of her father, she occasionally waited upon the hotel table. Half the town was always actively in love with her; the other half HAD BEEN, and was silent, cynical, but hopeless in defeat. For Kitty was one of those singularly pretty girls occasionally met with in Southwestern frontier civilization whose distinct and original refinement of face and figure were so remarkable and original as to cast a doubt on the sagacity and prescience of one parent and the morality of the other, yet no doubt with equal injustice. But the fact remained that she was slight, graceful, and self-contained, and moved beside her stumpy, commonplace father, and her faded, commonplace mother in the dining-room of the Boomville Hotel like some distinguished alien. The three partners, by virtue, perhaps, of their college education and refined manners, had been exceptionally noticed by Kitty. And for some occult reason—the more serious, perhaps, because it had no obvious or logical presumption to the world generally—Barker was particularly favored.

He quickened his pace, and as the flagstaff of the Boomville Hotel rose before him in the little hollow, he seriously debated whether he had not better go to the bank first, deposit his shares, and get a small advance on them to buy a new necktie or a "boiled shirt" in which to present himself to Miss Kitty; but, remembering that he had partly given his word to Demorest that he would keep his shares intact for the present, he abandoned this project, probably from the fact that his projected confidence with Kitty was already a violation of Demorest's injunctions of secrecy, and his conscience was sufficiently burdened with that breach of faith.

But when he reached the hotel, a strange trepidation overcame him. The dining-room was at its slack water, between the ebb of breakfast and before the flow of the preparation for the midday meal. He could not have his interview with Kitty in that dreary waste of reversed chairs and bare trestlelike tables, and she was possibly engaged in her household duties. But Miss Kitty had already seen him cross the road, and had lounged into the dining-room with an artfully simulated air of casually examining it. At the unexpected vision of his hopes, arrayed in the sweetest and freshest of rosebud-sprigged print, his heart faltered. Then, partly with the desperation of a timid man, and partly through the working of a half-formed resolution, he met her bright smile with a simple inquiry for her father. Miss Kitty bit her pretty lip, smiled slightly, and preceded him with great formality to the office. Opening the door, without raising her lashes to either her father or the visitor, she said, with a mischievous accenting of the professional manner, "Mr. Barker to see you on business," and tripped sweetly away.

And this slight incident precipitated the crisis. For Barker instantly made up his mind that he must purchase the next claim for his partners of this man Carter, and that he would be obliged to confide to him the details of his good fortune, and as a proof of his sincerity and his ability to pay for it, he did so bluntly. Carter was a shrewd business man, and the well-known simplicity of Barker was a proof of his truthfulness, to say nothing of the shares that were shown to him. His selling price for his claim had been two hundred dollars, but here was a rich customer who, from a mere foolish sentiment, would be no doubt willing to pay more. He hesitated with a bland but superior smile. "Ah, that was my price at my last offer, Mr. Barker," he said suavely; "but, you see, things are going up since then."

The keenest duplicity is apt to fail before absolute simplicity. Barker, thoroughly believing him, and already a little frightened at his own presumption—not for the amount of the money involved, but from the possibility of his partners refusing his gift utterly—quickly took advantage of this LOCUS PENITENTIAE. "No matter, then," he said hurriedly; "perhaps I had better consult my partners first; in fact," he added, with a gratuitous truthfulness all his own, "I hardly know whether they will take it of me, so I think I'll wait."

Carter was staggered; this would clearly not do! He recovered himself with an insinuating smile. "You pulled me up too short, Mr. Barker; I'm a business man, but hang it all! what's that among friends? If you reckoned I GAVE MY WORD at two hundred—why, I'm there! Say no more about it—the claim's yours. I'll make you out a bill of sale at once."

"But," hesitated Barker, "you see I haven't got the money yet, and—"

"Money!" echoed Carter bluntly, "what's that among friends? Gimme your note at thirty days—that's good enough for ME. An' we'll settle the whole thing now—nothing like finishing a job while you're about it." And before the bewildered and doubtful visitor could protest, he had filled up a promissory note for Barker's signature and himself signed a bill of sale for the property. "And I reckon, Mr. Barker, you'd like to take your partners by surprise about this little gift of yours," he added smilingly. "Well, my messenger is starting for the Gulch in five minutes; he's going by your cabin, and he can just drop this bill o' sale, as a kind o' settled fact, on 'em afore they can say anything, see! There's nothing like actin' on the spot in these sort of things. And don't you hurry 'bout them either! You see, you sorter owe us a friendly call—havin' always dropped inter the hotel only as a customer—so ye'll stop here over luncheon, and I reckon, as the old woman is busy, why Kitty will try to make the time pass till then by playin' for you on her new pianner."

Delighted, yet bewildered by the unexpected invitation and opportunity, Barker mechanically signed the promissory note, and as mechanically addressed the envelope of the bill of sale to Demorest, which Carter gave to the messenger. Then he followed his host across the hall to the apartment known as "Miss Kitty's parlor." He had often heard of it as a sanctum impervious to the ordinary guest. Whatever functions the young girl assumed at the hotel and among her father's boarders, it was vaguely understood that she dropped them on crossing that sacred threshold, and became "MISS Carter." The county judge had been entertained there, and the wife of the bank manager. Barker's admission there was consequently an unprecedented honor.

He cast his eyes timidly round the room, redolent and suggestive in various charming little ways of the young girl's presence. There was the cottage piano which had been brought up in sections on the backs of mules from the foot of the mountain; there was a crayon head of Minerva done by the fair occupant at the age of twelve; there was a profile of herself done by a traveling artist; there were pretty little china ornaments and many flowers, notably a faded but still scented woodland shrub which Barker had presented to her two weeks ago, and over which Miss Kitty had discreetly thrown her white handkerchief as he entered. A wave of hope passed over him at the act, but it was quickly spent as Mr. Carter's roughly playful voice introduced him:

"Ye kin give Mr. Barker a tune or two to pass time afore lunch, Kitty. You kin let him see what you're doing in that line. But you'll have to sit up now, for this young man's come inter some property, and will be sasheying round in 'Frisco afore long with a biled shirt and a stovepipe, and be givin' the go-by to Boomville. Well! you young folks will excuse me for a while, as I reckon I'll just toddle over and get the recorder to put that bill o' sale on record. Nothin' like squaring things to onct, Mr. Barker."

As he slipped away, Barker felt his heart sink. Carter had not only bluntly forestalled him with the news and taken away his excuse for a confidential interview, but had put an ostentatious construction on his visit. What could she think of him now? He stood ashamed and embarrassed before her.

But Miss Kitty, far from noticing his embarrassment in a sudden concern regarding the "horrid" untidiness of the room, which made her cheeks quite pink in one spot and obliged her to take up and set down in exactly the same place several articles, was exceedingly delighted. In fact, she did not remember ever having been so pleased before in her life! These things were always so unexpected! Just like the weather, for instance. It was quite cool last night—and now it was just stifling. And so dusty! Had Mr. Barker noticed the heat coming from the Gulch? Or perhaps, being a rich man, he—with a dazzling smile—was above walking now. It was so kind of him to come here first and tell her father.

"I really wanted to tell only—YOU, Miss Carter," stammered Barker. "You see—" he hesitated. But Miss Kitty saw perfectly. He wanted to tell HER, and, seeing her, he asked for HER FATHER! Not that it made the slightest difference to her, for her father would have been sure to have told her. It was also kind of her father to invite him to luncheon. Otherwise she might not have seen him before he left Boomville.

But this was more than Barker could stand. With the same desperate directness and simplicity with which he had approached her father, he now blurted out his whole heart to her. He told her how he had loved her hopelessly from the first time that they had spoken together at the church picnic. Did she remember it? How he had sat and worshiped her, and nothing else, at church! How her voice in the church choir had sounded like an angel's; how his poverty and his uncertain future had kept him from seeing her often, lest he should be tempted to betray his hopeless passion. How as soon as he realized that he had a position, that his love for her need not make her ridiculous to the world's eyes, he came to tell her ALL. He did not even dare to hope! But she would HEAR him at least, would she not?

Indeed, there was no getting away from his boyish, simple, outspoken declaration. In vain Kitty smiled, frowned, glanced at her pink cheeks in the glass, and stopped to look out of the window. The room was filled with his love—it was encompassing her—and, despite his shy attitude, seemed to be almost embracing her. But she managed at last to turn upon him a face that was now as white and grave as his own was eager and glowing.

"Sit down," she said gently.

He did so obediently, but wonderingly. She then opened the piano and took a seat upon the music stool before it, placed some loose sheets of music in the rack, and ran her fingers lightly over the keys. Thus intrenched, she let her hands fall idly in her lap, and for the first time raised her eyes to his.

"Now listen to me—be good and don't interrupt! There!—not so near; you can hear what I have to say well enough where you are. That will do."

Barker had halted with the chair he was dragging toward her and sat down.

"Now," said Miss Kitty, withdrawing her eyes and looking straight before her, "I believe everything you say; perhaps I oughtn't to—or at least SAY it—but I do. There! But because I do believe you—it seems to me all wrong! For the very reasons that you give for not having spoken to me BEFORE, if you really felt as you say you did, are the same reasons why you should not speak to me now. You see, all this time you have let nobody but yourself know how you felt toward me. In everybody's eyes YOU and your partners have been only the three stuck-up, exclusive, college-bred men who mined a poor claim in the Gulch, and occasionally came here to this hotel as customers. In everybody's eyes I have been only the rich hotel-keeper's popular daughter who sometimes waited upon you—but nothing more. But at least we were then pretty much alike, and as good as each other. And now, as soon as you have become suddenly rich, and, of course, the SUPERIOR, you rush down here to ask me to acknowledge it by accepting you!"

"You know I never meant that, Miss Kitty," burst out Barker vehemently, but his protest was drowned in a rapid roulade from the young lady's fingers on the keys. He sank back in his chair.

"Of course you never MEANT it," she said with an odd laugh; "but everybody will take it in that way, and you cannot go round to everybody in Boomville and make the pretty declaration you have just made to me. Everybody will say I accepted you for your money; everybody will say it was a put-up job of my father's. Everybody will say that you threw yourself away on me. And I don't know but that they would be right. Sit down, please! or I shall play again.

"You see," she went on, without looking at him, "just now you like to remember that you fell in love with me first as a pretty waiter girl, but if I became your wife it's just what you would like to FORGET. And I shouldn't, for I should always like to think of the time when you came here, whenever you could afford it and sometimes when you couldn't, just to see me; and how we used to make excuses to speak with each other over the dishes. You don't know what these things mean to a woman who"—she hesitated a moment, and then added abruptly, "but what does that matter? You would not care to be reminded of it. So," she said, rising up with a grave smile and grasping her hands tightly behind her, "it's a good deal better that you should begin to forget it now. Be a good boy and take my advice. Go to San Francisco. You will meet some girl there in a way you will not afterward regret. You are young, and your riches, to say nothing," she added in a faltering voice that was somewhat inconsistent with the mischievous smile that played upon her lips, "of your kind and simple heart, will secure that which the world would call unselfish affection from one more equal to you, but would always believe was only BOUGHT if it came from me."

"I suppose you are right," he said simply.

She glanced quickly at him, and her eyebrows straightened. He had risen, his face white and his gray eyes widely opened. "I suppose you are right," he went on, "because you are saying to me what my partners said to me this morning, when I offered to share my wealth with them, God knows as honestly as I offered to share my heart with you. I suppose that you are both right; that there must be some curse of pride or selfishness upon the money that I have got; but I have not felt it yet, and the fault does not lie with me."

She gave her shoulders a slight shrug, and turned impatiently toward the window. When she turned back again he was gone. The room around her was empty; this room, which a moment before had seemed to be pulsating with his boyish passion, was now empty, and empty of HIM. She bit her lips, rose, and ran eagerly to the window. She saw his straw hat and brown curls as he crossed the road. She drew her handkerchief sharply away from the withered shrub over which she had thrown it, and cast the once treasured remains in the hearth. Then, possibly because she had it ready in her hand, she clapped the handkerchief to her eyes, and sinking sideways upon the chair he had risen from, put her elbows on its back, and buried her face in her hands.

It is the characteristic and perhaps cruelty of a simple nature to make no allowance for complex motives, or to even understand them! So it seemed to Barker that his simplicity had been met with equal directness. It was the possession of this wealth that had in some way hopelessly changed his relations with the world. He did not love Kitty any the less; he did not even think she had wronged him; they, his partners and his sweetheart, were cleverer than he; there must be some occult quality in this wealth that he would understand when he possessed it, and perhaps it might even make him ashamed of his generosity; not in the way they had said, but in his tempting them so audaciously to assume a wrong position. It behoved him to take possession of it at once, and to take also upon himself alone the knowledge, the trials, and responsibilities it would incur. His cheeks flushed again as he thought he had tried to tempt an innocent girl with it, and he was keenly hurt that he had not seen in Kitty's eyes the tenderness that had softened his partners' refusal. He resolved to wait no longer, but sell his dreadful stock at once. He walked directly to the bank.

The manager, a shrewd but kindly man, to whom Barker was known already, received him graciously in recognition of his well-known simple honesty, and respectfully as a representative of the equally well-known poor but "superior" partnership of the Gulch. He listened with marked attention to Barker's hesitating but brief story, only remarking at its close:

"You mean, of course, the 'SECOND Extension' when you say 'First'?"

"No," said Barker; "I mean the 'First'—and it said First in the Boomville paper."

"Yes, yes!—I saw it—it was a printer's error. The stock of the 'First' was called in two years ago. No! You mean the 'Second,' for, of course, you've followed the quotations, and are likely to know what stock you're holding shares of. When you go back, take a look at them, and you'll see I am right."

"But I brought them with me," said Barker, with a slight flushing as he felt in his pocket, "and I am quite sure they are the 'First'." He brought them out and laid them on the desk before the manager.

The words "First Extension" were plainly visible. The manager glanced curiously at Barker, and his brow darkened.

"Did anybody put this up on you?" he said sternly. "Did your partners send you here with this stuff?"

"No! no!" said Barker eagerly. "No one! It's all MY mistake. I see it now. I trusted to the newspaper."

"And you mean to say you never examined the stock or the quotations, nor followed it in any way, since you had it?"

"Never!" said Barker. "Never thought about IT AT ALL till I saw the newspaper. So it's not worth anything?" And, to the infinite surprise of the manager, there was a slight smile on his boyish face.

"I am afraid it is not worth the paper it's written on," said the manager gently.

The smile on Barker's face increased to a little laugh, in which his wondering companion could not help joining. "Thank you," said Barker suddenly, and rushed away.

"He beats everything!" said the manager, gazing after him. "Damned if he didn't seem even PLEASED."

He WAS pleased. The burden of wealth had fallen from his shoulders; the dreadful incubus that had weighed him down and parted his friends from him was gone! And he had not got rid of it by spending it foolishly. It had not ruined anybody yet; it had not altered anybody in HIS eyes. It was gone; and he was a free and happy man once more. He would go directly back to his partners; they would laugh at him, of course, but they could not look at him now with the same sad, commiserating eyes. Perhaps even Kitty—but here a sudden chill struck him. He had forgotten the bill of sale! He had forgotten the dreadful promissory note given to her father in the rash presumption of his wealth! How could it ever be paid? And more than that, it had been given in a fraud. He had no money when he gave it, and no prospect of any but what he was to get from those worthless shares. Would anybody believe him that it was only a stupid blunder of his own? Yes, his partners might believe him; but, horrible thought, he had already implicated THEM in his fraud! Even now, while he was standing there hesitatingly in the road, they were entering upon the new claim he had NOT PAID FOR—COULD NOT PAY FOR—and in the guise of a benefactor he was dishonoring them. Yet it was Carter he must meet first; he must confess all to him. He must go back to the hotel—that hotel where he had indignantly left her, and tell the father he was a fraud. It was terrible to think of; perhaps it was part of that money curse that he could not get rid of, and was now realizing; but it MUST be done. He was simple, but his very simplicity had that unhesitating directness of conclusion which is the main factor of what men call "pluck."

He turned back to the hotel and entered the office. But Mr. Carter had not yet returned. What was to be done? He could not wait there; there was no time to be lost; there was only one other person who knew his expectations, and to whom he could confide his failure—it was Kitty. It was to taste the dregs of his humiliation, but it must be done. He ran up the staircase and knocked timidly at the sitting-room door. There was a momentary pause, and a weak voice said "Come in." Barker opened the door; saw the vision of a handkerchief thrown away, of a pair of tearful eyes that suddenly changed to stony indifference, and a graceful but stiffening figure. But he was past all insult now.

"I would not intrude," he said simply, "but I came only to see your father. I have made an awful blunder—more than a blunder, I think—a FRAUD. Believing that I was rich, I purchased your father's claim for my partners, and gave him my promissory note. I came here to give him back his claim—for that note can NEVER be paid! I have just been to the bank; I find I have made a stupid mistake in the name of the shares upon which I based my belief in my wealth. The ones I own are worthless—am as poor as ever—I am even poorer, for I owe your father money I can never pay!"

To his amazement he saw a look of pain and scorn come into her troubled eyes which he had never seen before. "This is a feeble trick," she said bitterly; "it is unlike you—it is unworthy of you!"

"Good God! You must believe me. Listen! it was all a mistake—a printer's error. I read in the paper that the stock for the First Extension mine had gone up, when it should have been the Second. I had some old stock of the First, which I had kept for years, and only thought of when I read the announcement in the paper this morning. I swear to you—"

But it was unnecessary. There was no doubting the truth of that voice—that manner. The scorn fled from Miss Kitty's eyes to give place to a stare, and then suddenly changed to two bubbling blue wells of laughter. She went to the window and laughed. She sat down to the piano and laughed. She caught up the handkerchief, and hiding half her rosy face in it, laughed. She finally collapsed into an easy chair, and, burying her brown head in its cushions, laughed long and confidentially until she brought up suddenly against a sob. And then was still.

Barker was dreadfully alarmed. He had heard of hysterics before. He felt he ought to do something. He moved toward her timidly, and gently drew away her handkerchief. Alas! the blue wells were running over now. He took her cold hands in his; he knelt beside her and passed his arm around her waist. He drew her head upon his shoulder. He was not sure that any of these things were effective until she suddenly lifted her eyes to his with the last ray of mirth in them vanishing in a big teardrop, put her arms round his neck, and sobbed:

"Oh, George! You blessed innocent!"

An eloquent silence was broken by a remorseful start from Barker.

"But I must go and warn my poor partners, dearest; there yet may be time; perhaps they have not yet taken possession of your father's claim."

"Yes, George dear," said the young girl, with sparkling eyes; "and tell them to do so AT ONCE!"

"What?" gasped Barker.

"At once—do you hear?—or it may be too late! Go quick."

"But your father—Oh, I see, dearest, you will tell him all yourself, and spare me."

"I shall do nothing so foolish, Georgey. Nor shall you! Don't you see the note isn't due for a month? Stop! Have you told anybody but Paw and me?"

"Only the bank manager."

She ran out of the room and returned in a minute tying the most enchanting of hats by a ribbon under her oval chin. "I'll run over and fix him," she said.

"Fix him?" returned Barker, aghast.

"Yes, I'll say your wicked partners have been playing a practical joke on you, and he mustn't give you away. He'll do anything for me."

"But my partners didn't! On the contrary—"

"Don't tell me, George," said Miss Kitty severely. "THEY ought never to have let you come here with that stuff. But come! You must go at once. You must not meet Paw; you'll blurt out everything to him; I know you! I'll tell him you could not stay to luncheon. Quick, now; go. What? Well—there!"

Whatever it represented, the exclamation was apparently so protracted that Miss Kitty was obliged to push her lover to the front landing before she could disappear by the back stairs. But once in the street, Barker no longer lingered. It was a good three miles back to the Gulch; he might still reach it by the time his partners were taking their noonday rest, and he resolved that although the messenger had preceded him, they would not enter upon the new claim until the afternoon. For Barker, in spite of his mistress's injunction, had no idea of taking what he couldn't pay for; he would keep the claim intact until something could be settled. For the rest, he walked on air! Kitty loved him! The accursed wealth no longer stood between them. They were both poor now—everything was possible.

The sun was beginning to send dwarf shadows toward the east when he reached the Gulch. Here a new trepidation seized him. How would his partners receive the news of his utter failure? HE was happy, for he had gained Kitty through it. But they? For a moment it seemed to him that he had purchased his happiness through their loss. He stopped, took off his hat, and ran his fingers remorsefully through his damp curls.

Another thing troubled him. He had reached the crest of the Gulch, where their old working ground was spread before him like a map. They were not there; neither were they lying under the four pines on the ridge where they were wont to rest at midday. He turned with some alarm to the new claim adjoining theirs, but there was no sign of them there either. A sudden fear that they had, after parting from him, given up the claim in a fit of disgust and depression, and departed, now overcame him. He clapped his hand on his head and ran in the direction of the cabin.

He had nearly reached it when the rough challenge of "Who's there?" from the bushes halted him, and Demorest suddenly swung into the trail. But the singular look of sternness and impatience which he was wearing vanished as he saw Barker, and with a loud shout of "All right, it's only Barker! Hooray!" he ran toward him. In an instant he was joined by Stacy from the cabin, and the two men, catching hold of their returning partner, waltzed him joyfully and breathlessly into the cabin. But the quick-eyed Demorest suddenly let go his hold and stared at Barker's face. "Why, Barker, old boy, what's up?"

"Everything's up," gasped the breathless Barker. "It's all up about these stocks. It's all a mistake; all an infernal lie of that newspaper. I never had the right kind of shares. The ones I have are worthless rags"; and the next instant he had blurted out his whole interview with the bank manager.

The two partners looked at each other, and then, to Barker's infinite perplexity, the same extraordinary convulsion that had seized Miss Kitty fell upon them. They laughed, holding on each other's shoulders; they laughed, clinging to Barker's struggling figure; they went out and laughed with their backs against a tree. They laughed separately and in different corners. And then they came up to Barker with tears in their eyes, dropped their heads on his shoulder, and murmured exhaustedly:

"You blessed ass!"

"But," said Stacy suddenly, "how did you manage to buy the claim?"

"Ah! that's the most awful thing, boys. I've NEVER PAID FOR IT," groaned Barker.

"But Carter sent us the bill of sale," persisted Demorest, "or we shouldn't have taken it."

"I gave my promissory note at thirty days," said Barker desperately, "and where's the money to come from now? But," he added wildly, as the men glanced at each other—"you said 'taken it.' Good heavens! you don't mean to say that I'm TOO late—that you've—you've touched it?"

"I reckon that's pretty much what we HAVE been doing," drawled Demorest.

"It looks uncommonly like it," drawled Stacy.

Barker glanced blankly from the one to the other. "Shall we pass our young friend in to see the show?" said Demorest to Stacy.

"Yes, if he'll be perfectly quiet and not breathe on the glasses," returned Stacy.

They each gravely took one of Barker's hands and led him to the corner of the cabin. There, on an old flour barrel, stood a large tin prospecting pan, in which the partners also occasionally used to knead their bread. A dirty towel covered it. Demorest whisked it dexterously aside, and disclosed three large fragments of decomposed gold and quartz. Barker started back.

"Heft it!" said Demorest grimly.

Barker could scarcely lift the pan!

"Four thousand dollars' weight if a penny!" said Stacy, in short staccato sentences. "In a pocket! Brought it out the second stroke of the pick! We'd been awfully blue after you left. Awfully blue, too, when that bill of sale came, for we thought you'd been wasting your money on US. Reckoned we oughtn't to take it, but send it straight back to you. Messenger gone! Then Demorest reckoned as it was done it couldn't be undone, and we ought to make just one 'prospect' on the claim, and strike a single stroke for you. And there it is. And there's more on the hillside."

"But it isn't MINE! It isn't YOURS! It's Carter's. I never had the money to pay for it—and I haven't got it now."

"But you gave the note—and it is not due for thirty days."

A recollection flashed upon Barker. "Yes," he said with thoughtful simplicity, "that's what Kitty said."

"Oh, Kitty said so," said both partners, gravely.

"Yes," stammered Barker, turning away with a heightened color, "and, as I didn't stay there to luncheon, I think I'd better be getting it ready." He picked up the coffeepot and turned to the hearth as his two partners stepped beyond the door.

"Wasn't it exactly like him?" said Demorest.

"Him all over," said Stacy.

"And his worry over that note?" said Demorest.

"And 'what Kitty said,'" said Stacy.

"Look here! I reckon that wasn't ALL that Kitty said."

"Of course not."

"What luck!"

* * * * * * * * * *

A YELLOW DOG

I never knew why in the Western States of America a yellow dog should be proverbially considered the acme of canine degradation and incompetency, nor why the possession of one should seriously affect the social standing of its possessor. But the fact being established, I think we accepted it at Rattlers Ridge without question. The matter of ownership was more difficult to settle; and although the dog I have in my mind at the present writing attached himself impartially and equally to everyone in camp, no one ventured to exclusively claim him; while, after the perpetration of any canine atrocity, everybody repudiated him with indecent haste.

"Well, I can swear he hasn't been near our shanty for weeks," or the retort, "He was last seen comin' out of YOUR cabin," expressed the eagerness with which Rattlers Ridge washed its hands of any responsibility. Yet he was by no means a common dog, nor even an unhandsome dog; and it was a singular fact that his severest critics vied with each other in narrating instances of his sagacity, insight, and agility which they themselves had witnessed.

He had been seen crossing the "flume" that spanned Grizzly Canyon at a height of nine hundred feet, on a plank six inches wide. He had tumbled down the "shoot" to the South Fork, a thousand feet below, and was found sitting on the riverbank "without a scratch, 'cept that he was lazily givin' himself with his off hind paw." He had been forgotten in a snowdrift on a Sierran shelf, and had come home in the early spring with the conceited complacency of an Alpine traveler and a plumpness alleged to have been the result of an exclusive diet of buried mail bags and their contents. He was generally believed to read the advance election posters, and disappear a day or two before the candidates and the brass band—which he hated—came to the Ridge. He was suspected of having overlooked Colonel Johnson's hand at poker, and of having conveyed to the Colonel's adversary, by a succession of barks, the danger of betting against four kings.

While these statements were supplied by wholly unsupported witnesses, it was a very human weakness of Rattlers Ridge that the responsibility of corroboration was passed to the dog himself, and HE was looked upon as a consummate liar.

"Snoopin' round yere, and CALLIN' yourself a poker sharp, are ye! Scoot, you yaller pizin!" was a common adjuration whenever the unfortunate animal intruded upon a card party. "Ef thar was a spark, an ATOM of truth in THAT DOG, I'd believe my own eyes that I saw him sittin' up and trying to magnetize a jay bird off a tree. But wot are ye goin' to do with a yaller equivocator like that?"

I have said that he was yellow—or, to use the ordinary expression, "yaller." Indeed, I am inclined to believe that much of the ignominy attached to the epithet lay in this favorite pronunciation. Men who habitually spoke of a "YELLOW bird," a "YELLOW-hammer," a "YELLOW leaf," always alluded to him as a "YALLER dog."

He certainly WAS yellow. After a bath—usually compulsory—he presented a decided gamboge streak down his back, from the top of his forehead to the stump of his tail, fading in his sides and flank to a delicate straw color. His breast, legs, and feet—when not reddened by "slumgullion," in which he was fond of wading—were white. A few attempts at ornamental decoration from the India-ink pot of the storekeeper failed, partly through the yellow dog's excessive agility, which would never give the paint time to dry on him, and partly through his success in transferring his markings to the trousers and blankets of the camp.

The size and shape of his tail—which had been cut off before his introduction to Rattlers Ridge—were favorite sources of speculation to the miners, as determining both his breed and his moral responsibility in coming into camp in that defective condition. There was a general opinion that he couldn't have looked worse with a tail, and its removal was therefore a gratuitous effrontery.

His best feature was his eyes, which were a lustrous Vandyke brown, and sparkling with intelligence; but here again he suffered from evolution through environment, and their original trustful openness was marred by the experience of watching for flying stones, sods, and passing kicks from the rear, so that the pupils were continually reverting to the outer angle of the eyelid.

Nevertheless, none of these characteristics decided the vexed question of his BREED. His speed and scent pointed to a "hound," and it is related that on one occasion he was laid on the trail of a wildcat with such success that he followed it apparently out of the State, returning at the end of two weeks footsore, but blandly contented.

Attaching himself to a prospecting party, he was sent under the same belief, "into the brush" to drive off a bear, who was supposed to be haunting the campfire. He returned in a few minutes WITH the bear, DRIVING IT INTO the unarmed circle and scattering the whole party. After this the theory of his being a hunting dog was abandoned. Yet it was said—on the usual uncorroborated evidence—that he had "put up" a quail; and his qualities as a retriever were for a long time accepted, until, during a shooting expedition for wild ducks, it was discovered that the one he had brought back had never been shot, and the party were obliged to compound damages with an adjacent settler.

His fondness for paddling in the ditches and "slumgullion" at one time suggested a water spaniel. He could swim, and would occasionally bring out of the river sticks and pieces of bark that had been thrown in; but as HE always had to be thrown in with them, and was a good-sized dog, his aquatic reputation faded also. He remained simply "a yaller dog." What more could be said? His actual name was "Bones"—given to him, no doubt, through the provincial custom of confounding the occupation of the individual with his quality, for which it was pointed out precedent could be found in some old English family names.

But if Bones generally exhibited no preference for any particular individual in camp, he always made an exception in favor of drunkards. Even an ordinary roistering bacchanalian party brought him out from under a tree or a shed in the keenest satisfaction. He would accompany them through the long straggling street of the settlement, barking his delight at every step or misstep of the revelers, and exhibiting none of that mistrust of eye which marked his attendance upon the sane and the respectable. He accepted even their uncouth play without a snarl or a yelp, hypocritically pretending even to like it; and I conscientiously believe would have allowed a tin can to be attached to his tail if the hand that tied it on were only unsteady, and the voice that bade him "lie still" were husky with liquor. He would "see" the party cheerfully into a saloon, wait outside the door—his tongue fairly lolling from his mouth in enjoyment—until they reappeared, permit them even to tumble over him with pleasure, and then gambol away before them, heedless of awkwardly projected stones and epithets. He would afterward accompany them separately home, or lie with them at crossroads until they were assisted to their cabins. Then he would trot rakishly to his own haunt by the saloon stove, with the slightly conscious air of having been a bad dog, yet of having had a good time.

We never could satisfy ourselves whether his enjoyment arose from some merely selfish conviction that he was more SECURE with the physically and mentally incompetent, from some active sympathy with active wickedness, or from a grim sense of his own mental superiority at such moments. But the general belief leant toward his kindred sympathy as a "yaller dog" with all that was disreputable. And this was supported by another very singular canine manifestation—the "sincere flattery" of simulation or imitation.

"Uncle Billy" Riley for a short time enjoyed the position of being the camp drunkard, and at once became an object of Bones' greatest solicitude. He not only accompanied him everywhere, curled at his feet or head according to Uncle Billy's attitude at the moment, but, it was noticed, began presently to undergo a singular alteration in his own habits and appearance. From being an active, tireless scout and forager, a bold and unovertakable marauder, he became lazy and apathetic; allowed gophers to burrow under him without endeavoring to undermine the settlement in his frantic endeavors to dig them out, permitted squirrels to flash their tails at him a hundred yards away, forgot his usual caches, and left his favorite bones unburied and bleaching in the sun. His eyes grew dull, his coat lusterless, in proportion as his companion became bleareyed and ragged; in running, his usual arrowlike directness began to deviate, and it was not unusual to meet the pair together, zigzagging up the hill. Indeed, Uncle Billy's condition could be predetermined by Bones' appearance at times when his temporary master was invisible. "The old man must have an awful jag on today," was casually remarked when an extra fluffiness and imbecility was noticeable in the passing Bones. At first it was believed that he drank also, but when careful investigation proved this hypothesis untenable, he was freely called a "derned timeservin', yaller hypocrite." Not a few advanced the opinion that if Bones did not actually lead Uncle Billy astray, he at least "slavered him over and coddled him until the old man got conceited in his wickedness." This undoubtedly led to a compulsory divorce between them, and Uncle Billy was happily dispatched to a neighboring town and a doctor.

Bones seemed to miss him greatly, ran away for two days, and was supposed to have visited him, to have been shocked at his convalescence, and to have been "cut" by Uncle Billy in his reformed character; and he returned to his old active life again, and buried his past with his forgotten bones. It was said that he was afterward detected in trying to lead an intoxicated tramp into camp after the methods employed by a blind man's dog, but was discovered in time by the— of course—uncorroborated narrator.

I should be tempted to leave him thus in his original and picturesque sin, but the same veracity which compelled me to transcribe his faults and iniquities obliges me to describe his ultimate and somewhat monotonous reformation, which came from no fault of his own.

It was a joyous day at Rattlers Ridge that was equally the advent of his change of heart and the first stagecoach that had been induced to diverge from the highroad and stop regularly at our settlement. Flags were flying from the post office and Polka saloon, and Bones was flying before the brass band that he detested, when the sweetest girl in the county—Pinkey Preston—daughter of the county judge and hopelessly beloved by all Rattlers Ridge, stepped from the coach which she had glorified by occupying as an invited guest.

"What makes him run away?" she asked quickly, opening her lovely eyes in a possibly innocent wonder that anything could be found to run away from her.

"He don't like the brass band," we explained eagerly.

"How funny," murmured the girl; "is it as out of tune as all that?"

This irresistible witticism alone would have been enough to satisfy us—we did nothing but repeat it to each other all the next day—but we were positively transported when we saw her suddenly gather her dainty skirts in one hand and trip off through the red dust toward Bones, who, with his eyes over his yellow shoulder, had halted in the road, and half-turned in mingled disgust and rage at the spectacle of the descending trombone. We held our breath as she approached him. Would Bones evade her as he did us at such moments, or would he save our reputation, and consent, for the moment, to accept her as a new kind of inebriate? She came nearer; he saw her; he began to slowly quiver with excitement—his stump of a tail vibrating with such rapidity that the loss of the missing portion was scarcely noticeable. Suddenly she stopped before him, took his yellow head between her little hands, lifted it, and looked down in his handsome brown eyes with her two lovely blue ones. What passed between them in that magnetic glance no one ever knew. She returned with him; said to him casually: "We're not afraid of brass bands, are we?" to which he apparently acquiesced, at least stifling his disgust of them while he was near her—which was nearly all the time.

During the speechmaking her gloved hand and his yellow head were always near together, and at the crowning ceremony—her public checking of Yuba Bill's "waybill" on behalf of the township, with a gold pencil presented to her by the Stage Company—Bones' joy, far from knowing no bounds, seemed to know nothing but them, and he witnessed it apparently in the air. No one dared to interfere. For the first time a local pride in Bones sprang up in our hearts—and we lied to each other in his praises openly and shamelessly.

Then the time came for parting. We were standing by the door of the coach, hats in hand, as Miss Pinkey was about to step into it; Bones was waiting by her side, confidently looking into the interior, and apparently selecting his own seat on the lap of Judge Preston in the corner, when Miss Pinkey held up the sweetest of admonitory fingers. Then, taking his head between her two hands, she again looked into his brimming eyes, and said, simply, "GOOD dog," with the gentlest of emphasis on the adjective, and popped into the coach.

The six bay horses started as one, the gorgeous green and gold vehicle bounded forward, the red dust rose behind, and the yellow dog danced in and out of it to the very outskirts of the settlement. And then he soberly returned.

A day or two later he was missed—but the fact was afterward known that he was at Spring Valley, the county town where Miss Preston lived, and he was forgiven. A week afterward he was missed again, but this time for a longer period, and then a pathetic letter arrived from Sacramento for the storekeeper's wife.

"Would you mind," wrote Miss Pinkey Preston, "asking some of your boys to come over here to Sacramento and bring back Bones? I don't mind having the dear dog walk out with me at Spring Valley, where everyone knows me; but here he DOES make one so noticeable, on account of HIS COLOR. I've got scarcely a frock that he agrees with. He don't go with my pink muslin, and that lovely buff tint he makes three shades lighter. You know yellow is SO trying."

A consultation was quickly held by the whole settlement, and a deputation sent to Sacramento to relieve the unfortunate girl. We were all quite indignant with Bones—but, oddly enough, I think it was greatly tempered with our new pride in him. While he was with us alone, his peculiarities had been scarcely appreciated, but the recurrent phrase "that yellow dog that they keep at the Rattlers" gave us a mysterious importance along the countryside, as if we had secured a "mascot" in some zoological curiosity.

This was further indicated by a singular occurrence. A new church had been built at the crossroads, and an eminent divine had come from San Francisco to preach the opening sermon. After a careful examination of the camp's wardrobe, and some felicitous exchange of apparel, a few of us were deputed to represent "Rattlers" at the Sunday service. In our white ducks, straw hats, and flannel blouses, we were sufficiently picturesque and distinctive as "honest miners" to be shown off in one of the front pews.

Seated near the prettiest girls, who offered us their hymn books—in the cleanly odor of fresh pine shavings, and ironed muslin, and blown over by the spices of our own woods through the open windows, a deep sense of the abiding peace of Christian communion settled upon us. At this supreme moment someone murmured in an awe-stricken whisper:

"WILL you look at Bones?"

We looked. Bones had entered the church and gone up in the gallery through a pardonable ignorance and modesty; but, perceiving his mistake, was now calmly walking along the gallery rail before the astounded worshipers. Reaching the end, he paused for a moment, and carelessly looked down. It was about fifteen feet to the floor below—the simplest jump in the world for the mountain-bred Bones. Daintily, gingerly, lazily, and yet with a conceited airiness of manner, as if, humanly speaking, he had one leg in his pocket and were doing it on three, he cleared the distance, dropping just in front of the chancel, without a sound, turned himself around three times, and then lay comfortably down.

Three deacons were instantly in the aisle, coming up before the eminent divine, who, we fancied, wore a restrained smile. We heard the hurried whispers: "Belongs to them." "Quite a local institution here, you know." "Don't like to offend sensibilities;" and the minister's prompt "By no means," as he went on with his service.

A short month ago we would have repudiated Bones; today we sat there in slightly supercilious attitudes, as if to indicate that any affront offered to Bones would be an insult to ourselves, and followed by our instantaneous withdrawal in a body.

All went well, however, until the minister, lifting the large Bible from the communion table and holding it in both hands before him, walked toward a reading stand by the altar rails. Bones uttered a distinct growl. The minister stopped.

We, and we alone, comprehended in a flash the whole situation. The Bible was nearly the size and shape of one of those soft clods of sod which we were in the playful habit of launching at Bones when he lay half-asleep in the sun, in order to see him cleverly evade it.

We held our breath. What was to be done? But the opportunity belonged to our leader, Jeff Briggs—a confoundedly good-looking fellow, with the golden mustache of a northern viking and the curls of an Apollo. Secure in his beauty and bland in his self-conceit, he rose from the pew, and stepped before the chancel rails.

"I would wait a moment, if I were you, sir," he said, respectfully, "and you will see that he will go out quietly."

"What is wrong?" whispered the minister in some concern.

"He thinks you are going to heave that book at him, sir, without giving him a fair show, as we do."

The minister looked perplexed, but remained motionless, with the book in his hands. Bones arose, walked halfway down the aisle, and vanished like a yellow flash!

With this justification of his reputation, Bones disappeared for a week. At the end of that time we received a polite note from Judge Preston, saying that the dog had become quite domiciled in their house, and begged that the camp, without yielding up their valuable PROPERTY in him, would allow him to remain at Spring Valley for an indefinite time; that both the judge and his daughter—with whom Bones was already an old friend—would be glad if the members of the camp would visit their old favorite whenever they desired, to assure themselves that he was well cared for.

I am afraid that the bait thus ingenuously thrown out had a good deal to do with our ultimate yielding. However, the reports of those who visited Bones were wonderful and marvelous. He was residing there in state, lying on rugs in the drawing-room, coiled up under the judicial desk in the judge's study, sleeping regularly on the mat outside Miss Pinkey's bedroom door, or lazily snapping at flies on the judge's lawn.

"He's as yaller as ever," said one of our informants, "but it don't somehow seem to be the same back that we used to break clods over in the old time, just to see him scoot out of the dust."

And now I must record a fact which I am aware all lovers of dogs will indignantly deny, and which will be furiously bayed at by every faithful hound since the days of Ulysses. Bones not only FORGOT, but absolutely CUT US! Those who called upon the judge in "store clothes" he would perhaps casually notice, but he would sniff at them as if detecting and resenting them under their superficial exterior. The rest he simply paid no attention to. The more familiar term of "Bonesy"—formerly applied to him, as in our rare moments of endearment—produced no response. This pained, I think, some of the more youthful of us; but, through some strange human weakness, it also increased the camp's respect for him. Nevertheless, we spoke of him familiarly to strangers at the very moment he ignored us. I am afraid that we also took some pains to point out that he was getting fat and unwieldy, and losing his elasticity, implying covertly that his choice was a mistake and his life a failure.

A year after, he died, in the odor of sanctity and respectability, being found one morning coiled up and stiff on the mat outside Miss Pinkey's door. When the news was conveyed to us, we asked permission, the camp being in a prosperous condition, to erect a stone over his grave. But when it came to the inscription we could only think of the two words murmured to him by Miss Pinkey, which we always believe effected his conversion:

"GOOD Dog!"

* * * * * * * * *

A MOTHER OF FIVE

She was a mother—and a rather exemplary one—of five children, although her own age was barely nine. Two of these children were twins, and she generally alluded to them as "Mr. Amplach's children," referring to an exceedingly respectable gentleman in the next settlement who, I have reason to believe, had never set eyes on her or them. The twins were quite naturally alike—having been in a previous state of existence two ninepins—and were still somewhat vague and inchoate below their low shoulders in their long clothes, but were also firm and globular about the head, and there were not wanting those who professed to see in this an unmistakable resemblance to their reputed father. The other children were dolls of different ages, sex, and condition, but the twins may be said to have been distinctly her own conception. Yet such was her admirable and impartial maternity that she never made any difference between them. "The Amplach's children" was a description rather than a distinction.

She was herself the motherless child of Robert Foulkes, a hardworking but somewhat improvident teamster on the Express Route between Big Bend and Reno. His daily avocation, when she was not actually with him in the wagon, led to an occasional dispersion of herself and her progeny along the road and at wayside stations between those places. But the family was generally collected together by rough but kindly hands already familiar with the handling of her children. I have a very vivid recollection of Jim Carter trampling into a saloon, after a five-mile walk through a snowdrift, with an Amplach twin in his pocket. "Suthin' ought to be done," he growled, "to make Meary a little more careful o' them Amplach children; I picked up one outer the snow a mile beyond Big Bend." "God bless my soul!" said a casual passenger, looking up hastily; "I didn't know Mr. Amplach was married." Jim winked diabolically at us over his glass. "No more did I," he responded gloomily, "but you can't tell anything about the ways o' them respectable, psalm-singing jay birds." Having thus disposed of Amplach's character, later on, when he was alone with Mary, or "Meary," as she chose to pronounce it, the rascal worked upon her feelings with an account of the infant Amplach's sufferings in the snowdrift and its agonized whisperings for "Meary! Meary!" until real tears stood in Mary's blue eyes. "Let this be a lesson to you," he concluded, drawing the ninepin dexterously from his pocket, "for it took nigh a quart of the best forty-rod whisky to bring that child to." Not only did Mary firmly believe him, but for weeks afterwards "Julian Amplach"—this unhappy twin—was kept in a somnolent attitude in the cart, and was believed to have contracted dissipated habits from the effects of his heroic treatment.

Her numerous family was achieved in only two years, and succeeded her first child, which was brought from Sacramento at considerable expense by a Mr. William Dodd, also a teamster, on her seventh birthday. This, by one of those rare inventions known only to a child's vocabulary, she at once called "Misery"—probably a combination of "Missy," as she herself was formerly termed by strangers, and "Missouri," her native State. It was an excessively large doll at first—

Mr. Dodd wishing to get the worth of his money—but time, and perhaps an excess of maternal care, remedied the defect, and it lost flesh and certain unemployed parts of its limbs very rapidly. It was further reduced in bulk by falling under the wagon and having the whole train pass over it, but singularly enough its greatest attenuation was in the head and shoulders—the complexion peeling off as a solid layer, followed by the disappearance of distinct strata of its extraordinary composition. This continued until the head and shoulders were much too small for even its reduced frame, and all the devices of childish millinery—a shawl secured with tacks and well hammered in, and a hat which tilted backward and forward and never appeared at the same angle—failed to restore symmetry. Until one dreadful morning, after an imprudent bath, the whole upper structure disappeared, leaving two hideous iron prongs standing erect from the spinal column. Even an imaginative child like Mary could not accept this sort of thing as a head. Later in the day Jack Roper, the blacksmith at the "Crossing," was concerned at the plaintive appearance before his forge of a little girl clad in a bright-blue pinafore of the same color as her eyes, carrying her monstrous offspring in her arms. Jack recognized her and instantly divined the situation. "You haven't," he suggested kindly, "got another head at home—suthin' left over," Mary shook her head sadly; even her prolific maternity was not equal to the creation of children in detail. "Nor anythin' like a head?" he persisted sympathetically. Mary's loving eyes filled with tears. "No, nuffen!" "You couldn't," he continued thoughtfully, "use her the other side up?—we might get a fine pair o' legs outer them irons," he added, touching the two prongs with artistic suggestion. "Now look here"—he was about to tilt the doll over when a small cry of feminine distress and a swift movement of a matronly little arm arrested the evident indiscretion. "I see," he said gravely. "Well, you come here tomorrow, and we'll fix up suthin' to work her." Jack was thoughtful the rest of the day, more than usually impatient with certain stubborn mules to be shod, and even knocked off work an hour earlier to walk to Big Bend and a rival shop. But the next morning when the trustful and anxious mother appeared at the forge she uttered a scream of delight. Jack had neatly joined a hollow iron globe, taken from the newel post of some old iron staircase railing, to the two prongs, and covered it with a coat of red fireproof paint. It was true that its complexion was rather high, that it was inclined to be top-heavy, and that in the long run the other dolls suffered considerably by enforced association with this unyielding and implacable head and shoulders, but this did not diminish Mary's joy over her restored first-born. Even its utter absence of features was no defect in a family where features were as evanescent as in hers, and the most ordinary student of evolution could see that the "Amplach" ninepins were in legitimate succession to the globular-headed "Misery." For a time I think that Mary even preferred her to the others. Howbeit it was a pretty sight to see her on a summer afternoon sitting upon a wayside stump, her other children dutifully ranged around her, and the hard, unfeeling head of Misery pressed deep down into her loving little heart as she swayed from side to side, crooning her plaintive lullaby. Small wonder that the bees took up the song and droned a slumberous accompaniment, or that high above her head the enormous pines, stirred through their depths by the soft Sierran air—or Heaven knows what—let slip flickering lights and shadows to play over that cast-iron face, until the child, looking down upon it with the quick, transforming power of love, thought that it smiled.

The two remaining members of the family were less distinctive. "Gloriana"—pronounced as two words: "Glory Anna"—being the work of her father, who also named it, was simply a cylindrical roll of canvas wagon-covering, girt so as to define a neck and waist, with a rudely inked face—altogether a weak, pitiable, manlike invention; and "Johnny Dear," alleged to be the representative of John Doremus, a young storekeeper who occasionally supplied Mary with gratuitous sweets. Mary never admitted this, and as we were all gentlemen along that road, we were blind to the suggestion. "Johnny Dear" was originally a small plaster phrenological cast of a head and bust, begged from some shop window in the county town, with a body clearly constructed by Mary herself. It was an ominous fact that it was always dressed as a BOY, and was distinctly the most HUMAN-looking of all her progeny. Indeed, in spite of the faculties that were legibly printed all over its smooth, white, hairless head, it was appallingly lifelike. Left sometimes by Mary astride of the branch of a wayside tree, horsemen had been known to dismount hurriedly and examine it, returning with a mystified smile, and it was on record that Yuba Bill had once pulled up the Pioneer Coach at the request of curious and imploring passengers, and then grimly installed "Johnny Dear" beside him on the box seat, publicly delivering him to Mary at Big Bend, to her wide-eyed confusion and the first blush we had ever seen on her round, chubby, sunburnt cheeks. It may seem strange that with her great popularity and her well-known maternal instincts, she had not been kept fully supplied with proper and more conventional dolls; but it was soon recognized that she did not care for them—left their waxen faces, rolling eyes, and abundant hair in ditches, or stripped them to help clothe the more extravagant creatures of her fancy. So it came that "Johnny Dear's" strictly classical profile looked out from under a girl's fashionable straw sailor hat, to the utter obliteration of his prominent intellectual faculties; the Amplach twins wore bonnets on their ninepins heads, and even an attempt was made to fit a flaxen scalp on the iron-headed Misery. But her dolls were always a creation of her own—her affection for them increasing with the demand upon her imagination. This may seem somewhat inconsistent with her habit of occasionally abandoning them in the woods or in the ditches. But she had an unbounded confidence in the kindly maternity of Nature, and trusted her children to the breast of the Great Mother as freely as she did herself in her own motherlessness. And this confidence was rarely betrayed. Rats, mice, snails, wildcats, panther, and bear never touched her lost waifs. Even the elements were kindly; an Amplach twin buried under a snowdrift in high altitudes reappeared smilingly in the spring in all its wooden and painted integrity. We were all Pantheists then—and believed this implicitly. It was only when exposed to the milder forces of civilization that Mary had anything to fear. Yet even then, when Patsy O'Connor's domestic goat had once tried to "sample" the lost Misery, he had retreated with the loss of three front teeth, and Thompson's mule came out of an encounter with that iron-headed prodigy with a sprained hind leg and a cut and swollen pastern.

But these were the simple Arcadian days of the road between Big Bend and Reno, and progress and prosperity, alas! brought changes in their wake. It was already whispered that Mary ought to be going to school, and Mr. Amplach—still happily oblivious of the liberties taken with his name—as trustee of the public school at Duckville, had intimated that Mary's bohemian wanderings were a scandal to the county. She was growing up in ignorance, a dreadful ignorance of everything but the chivalry, the deep tenderness, the delicacy and unselfishness of the rude men around her, and obliviousness of faith in anything but the immeasurable bounty of Nature toward her and her children. Of course there was a fierce discussion between "the boys" of the road and the few married families of the settlement on this point, but, of course, progress and "snivelization"—as the boys chose to call it—triumphed. The projection of a railroad settled it; Robert Foulkes, promoted to a foremanship of a division of the line, was made to understand that his daughter must be educated. But the terrible question of Mary's family remained. No school would open its doors to that heterogeneous collection, and Mary's little heart would have broken over the rude dispersal or heroic burning of her children. The ingenuity of Jack Roper suggested a compromise. She was allowed to select one to take to school with her; the others were ADOPTED by certain of her friends, and she was to be permitted to visit them every Saturday afternoon. The selection was a cruel trial, so cruel that, knowing her undoubted preference for her firstborn, Misery, we would not have interfered for worlds, but in her unexpected choice of "Johnny Dear" the most unworldly of us knew that it was the first glimmering of feminine tact— her first submission to the world of propriety that she was now entering. "Johnny Dear" was undoubtedly the most presentable; even more, there was an educational suggestion in its prominent, mapped-out phrenological organs. The adopted fathers were loyal to their trust. Indeed, for years afterward the blacksmith kept the iron-headed Misery on a rude shelf, like a shrine, near his bunk; nobody but himself and Mary ever knew the secret, stolen, and thrilling interviews that took place during the first days of their separation. Certain facts, however, transpired concerning Mary's equal faithfulness to another of her children. It is said that one Saturday afternoon, when the road manager of the new line was seated in his office at Reno in private business discussion with two directors, a gentle tap was heard at the door. It was opened to an eager little face, a pair of blue eyes, and a blue pinafore. To the astonishment of the directors, a change came over the face of the manager. Taking the child gently by the hand, he walked to his desk, on which the papers of the new line were scattered, and drew open a drawer from which he took a large ninepin extraordinarily dressed as a doll. The astonishment of the two gentlemen was increased at the following quaint colloquy between the manager and the child.

"She's doing remarkably well in spite of the trying weather, but I have had to keep her very quiet," said the manager, regarding the ninepin critically.

"Ess," said Mary quickly, "It's just the same with Johnny Dear; his cough is fightful at nights. But Misery's all right. I've just been to see her."

"There's a good deal of scarlet fever around," continued the manager with quiet concern, "and we can't be too careful. But I shall take her for a little run down the line tomorrow."

The eyes of Mary sparkled and overflowed like blue water. Then there was a kiss, a little laugh, a shy glance at the two curious strangers, the blue pinafore fluttered away, and the colloquy ended. She was equally attentive in her care of the others, but the rag baby "Gloriana," who had found a home in Jim Carter's cabin at the Ridge, living too far for daily visits, was brought down regularly on Saturday afternoon to Mary's house by Jim, tucked in asleep in his saddle bags or riding gallantly before him on the horn of his saddle. On Sunday there was a dress parade of all the dolls, which kept Mary in heart for the next week's desolation.

But there came one Saturday and Sunday when Mary did not appear, and it was known along the road that she had been called to San Francisco to meet an aunt who had just arrived from "the States." It was a vacant Sunday to "the boys," a very hollow, unsanctified Sunday, somehow, without that little figure. But the next, Sunday, and the next, were still worse, and then it was known that the dreadful aunt was making much of Mary, and was sending her to a grand school—a convent at Santa Clara—where it was rumored girls were turned out so accomplished that their own parents did not know them. But WE knew that was impossible to our Mary; and a letter which came from her at the end of the month, and before the convent had closed upon the blue pinafore, satisfied us, and was balm to our anxious hearts. It was characteristic of Mary; it was addressed to nobody in particular, and would—but for the prudence of the aunt—have been entrusted to the post office open and undirected. It was a single sheet, handed to us without a word by her father; but as we passed it from hand to hand, we understood it as if we had heard our lost playfellow's voice.

"Ther's more houses in 'Frisco than you kin shake a stick at and wimmens till you kant rest, but mules and jakasses ain't got no sho, nor blacksmiffs shops, wich is not to be seen no wear. Rapits and Skwirls also bares and panfers is on-noun and unforgotten on account of the streets and Sunday skoles. Jim Roper you orter be very good to Mizzery on a kount of my not bein' here, and not harten your hart to her bekos she is top heavy—which is ontroo and simply an imptient lie—like you allus make. I have a kinary bird wot sings deliteful—but isn't a yellerhamer sutch as I know, as you'd think. Dear Mister Montgommery, don't keep Gulan Amplak to mutch shet up in office drors; it isn't good for his lungs and chest. And don't you ink his head—nother! youre as bad as the rest. Johnny Dear, you must be very kind to your attopted father, and you, Glory Anna, must lov your kind Jimmy Carter verry mutch for taking you hossback so offen. I has been buggy ridin' with an orficer who has killed injuns real! I am comin' back soon with grate affeckshun, so luke out and mind."

But it was three years before she returned, and this was her last and only letter. The "adopted fathers" of her children were faithful, however, and when the new line was opened, and it was understood that she was to be present with her father at the ceremony, they came, with a common understanding, to the station to meet their old playmate. They were ranged along the platform—poor Jack Roper a little overweighted with a bundle he was carrying on his left arm. And then a young girl in the freshness of her teens and the spotless purity of a muslin frock that although brief in skirt was perfect in fit, faultlessly booted and gloved, tripped from the train, and offered a delicate hand in turn to each of her old friends. Nothing could be prettier than the smile on the cheeks that were no longer sunburnt; nothing could be clearer than the blue eyes lifted frankly to theirs. And yet, as she gracefully turned away with her father, the faces of the four adopted parents were found to be as red and embarrassed as her own on the day that Yuba Bill drove up publicly with "Johnny Dear" on the box seat.

"You weren't such a fool," said Jack Montgomery to Roper, "as to bring Misery here with you?"

"I was," said Roper with a constrained laugh—"and you?" He had just caught sight of the head of a ninepin peeping from the manager's pocket. The man laughed, and then the four turned silently away.

"Mary" had indeed come back to them; but not "The Mother of Five!"

* * * * * * * * * *

BULGER'S REPUTATION

We all remembered very distinctly Bulger's advent in Rattlesnake Camp. It was during the rainy season—a season singularly inducive to settled reflective impressions as we sat and smoked around the stove in Mosby's grocery. Like older and more civilized communities, we had our periodic waves of sentiment and opinion, with the exception that they were more evanescent with us, and as we had just passed through a fortnight of dissipation and extravagance, owing to a visit from some gamblers and speculators, we were now undergoing a severe moral revulsion, partly induced by reduced finances and partly by the arrival of two families with grownup daughters on the hill. It was raining, with occasional warm breaths, through the open window, of the southwest trades, redolent of the saturated spices of the woods and springing grasses, which perhaps were slightly inconsistent with the hot stove around which we had congregated. But the stove was only an excuse for our listless, gregarious gathering; warmth and idleness went well together, and it was currently accepted that we had caught from the particular reptile which gave its name to our camp much of its pathetic, lifelong search for warmth, and its habit of indolently basking in it.

A few of us still went through the affectation of attempting to dry our damp clothes by the stove, and sizzling our wet boots against it; but as the same individuals calmly permitted the rain to drive in upon them through the open window without moving, and seemed to take infinite delight in the amount of steam they generated, even that pretense dropped. Crotalus himself, with his tail in a muddy ditch, and the sun striking cold fire from his slit eyes as he basked his head on a warm stone beside it, could not have typified us better.

Percy Briggs took his pipe from his mouth at last and said, with reflective severity:

"Well, gentlemen, if we can't get the wagon road over here, and if we're going to be left out by the stagecoach company, we can at least straighten up the camp, and not have it look like a cross between a tenement alley and a broken-down circus. I declare, I was just sick when these two Baker girls started to make a short cut through the camp. Darned if they didn't turn round and take to the woods and the rattlers again afore they got halfway. And that benighted idiot, Tom Rollins, standin' there in the ditch, spattered all over with slumgullion 'til he looked like a spotted tarrypin, wavin' his fins and sashaying backwards and forrards and sayin', 'This way, ladies; this way!'"

"I didn't," returned Tom Rollins, quite casually, without looking up from his steaming boots; "I didn't start in night afore last to dance 'The Green Corn Dance' outer 'Hiawatha,' with feathers in my hair and a red blanket on my shoulders, round that family's new potato patch, in order that it might 'increase and multiply.' I didn't sing 'Sabbath Morning Bells' with an anvil accompaniment until twelve o'clock at night over at the Crossing, so that they might dream of their Happy

Childhood's Home. It seems to me that it wasn't me did it. I might be mistaken—it was late—but I have the impression that it wasn't me."

From the silence that followed, this would seem to have been clearly a recent performance of the previous speaker, who, however, responded quite cheerfully:

"An evenin' o' simple, childish gaiety don't count. We've got to start in again FAIR. What we want here is to clear up and encourage decent immigration, and get rid o' gamblers and blatherskites that are makin' this yer camp their happy hunting-ground. We don't want any more permiskus shootin'. We don't want any more paintin' the town red. We don't want any more swaggerin' galoots ridin' up to this grocery and emptyin' their six-shooters in the air afore they 'light. We want to put a stop to it peacefully and without a row—and we kin. We ain't got no bullies of our own to fight back, and they know it, so they know they won't get no credit bullyin' us; they'll leave, if we're only firm. It's all along of our cussed fool good-nature; they see it amuses us, and they'll keep it up as long as the whisky's free. What we want to do is, when the next man comes waltzin' along—"

A distant clatter from the rocky hillside here mingled with the puff of damp air through the window.

"Looks as ef we might hev a show even now," said Tom Rollins, removing his feet from the stove as we all instinctively faced toward the window.

"I reckon you're in with us in this, Mosby?" said Briggs, turning toward the proprietor of the grocery, who had been leaning listlessly against the wall behind his bar.

"Arter the man's had a fair show," said Mosby, cautiously. He deprecated the prevailing condition of things, but it was still an open question whether the families would prove as valuable customers as his present clients. "Everything in moderation, gentlemen."

The sound of galloping hoofs came nearer, now swishing in the soft mud of the highway, until the unseen rider pulled up before the door. There was no shouting, however, nor did he announce himself with the usual salvo of firearms. But when, after a singularly heavy tread and the jingle of spurs on the platform, the door flew open to the newcomer, he seemed a realization of our worst expectations. Tall, broad, and muscular, he carried in one hand a shotgun, while from his hip dangled a heavy navy revolver. His long hair, unkempt but oiled, swept a greasy circle around his shoulders; his enormous mustache, dripping with wet, completely concealed his mouth. His costume of fringed buckskin was wild and outre even for our frontier camp. But what was more confirmative of our suspicions was that he was evidently in the habit of making an impression, and after a distinct pause at the doorway, with only a side glance at us, he strode toward the bar.

"As there don't seem to be no hotel hereabouts, I reckon I kin put up my mustang here and have a shakedown somewhere behind that counter," he said. His voice seemed to have added to its natural depth the hoarseness of frequent overstraining.

"Ye ain't got no bunk to spare, you boys, hev ye?" asked Mosby, evasively, glancing at Percy Briggs without looking at the stranger. We all looked at Briggs also; it was HIS affair after all— HE had originated this opposition. To our surprise he said nothing.

The stranger leaned heavily on the counter.

"I was speaking to YOU," he said, with his eyes on Mosby, and slightly accenting the pronoun with a tap of his revolver butt on the bar. "Ye don't seem to catch on."

Mosby smiled feebly, and again cast an imploring glance at Briggs. To our greater astonishment, Briggs said, quietly: "Why don't you answer the stranger, Mosby?"

"Yes, yes," said Mosby, suavely, to the newcomer, while an angry flush crossed his check as he recognized the position in which Briggs had placed him. "Of course, you're welcome to what doings I hev here, but I reckoned these gentlemen over there," with a vicious glance at Briggs, "might fix ye up suthin' better; they're so pow'ful kind to your sort."

The stranger threw down a gold piece on the counter and said: "Fork out your whisky, then," waited until his glass was filled, took it in his hand, and then, drawing an empty chair to the stove, sat down beside Briggs. "Seein' as you're that kind," he said, placing his heavy hand on Briggs's knee, "mebbe ye kin tell me ef thar's a shanty or a cabin at Rattlesnake that I kin get for a couple o' weeks. I saw an empty one at the head o' the hill. You see, gennelmen," he added confidentially as he swept the drops of whisky from his long mustache with his fingers and glanced around our group, "I've got some business over at Bigwood," our nearest town, "but ez a place to stay AT it ain't my style."

"What's the matter with Bigwood?" said Briggs, abruptly.

"It's too howlin', too festive, too rough; thar's too much yellin' and shootin' goin' day and night. Thar's too many card sharps and gay gamboliers cavortin' about the town to please me. Too much permiskus soakin' at the bar and free jimjams. What I want is a quiet place what a man kin give his mind and elbow a rest from betwixt grippin' his shootin' irons and crookin' in his whisky. A sort o' slow, quiet, easy place LIKE THIS."

We all stared at him, Percy Briggs as fixedly as any. But there was not the slightest trace of irony, sarcasm, or peculiar significance in his manner. He went on slowly:

"When I struck this yer camp a minit ago; when I seed that thar ditch meanderin' peaceful like through the street, without a hotel or free saloon or express office on either side; with the smoke just a curlin' over the chimbley of that log shanty, and the bresh just set fire to and a smolderin' in that potato patch with a kind o' old-time stingin' in your eyes and nose, and a few women's duds just a flutterin' on a line by the fence, I says to myself: 'Bulger—this is peace! This is wot you're lookin' for, Bulger—this is wot you're wantin'—this is wot YOU'LL HEV!'"

"You say you've business over at Bigwood. What business?" said Briggs.

"It's a peculiar business, young fellow," returned the stranger, gravely. "Thar's different men ez has different opinions about it. Some allows it's an easy business, some allows it's a rough business; some says it's a sad business, others says it's gay and festive. Some wonders ez how I've got into it, and others wonder how I'll ever get out of it. It's a payin' business—it's a peaceful sort o' business when left to itself. It's a peculiar business—a business that sort o' b'longs to me, though I ain't got no patent from Washington for it. It's MY OWN business." He paused, rose, and saying, "Let's meander over and take a look at that empty cabin, and ef she suits me, why, I'll plank down a slug for her on the spot, and move in tomorrow," walked towards the door. "I'll pick up suthin' in the way o' boxes and blankets from the grocery," he added, looking at Mosby, "and ef thar's a corner whar I kin stand my gun and a nail to hang up my revolver—why, I'm all thar!"

By this time we were no longer astonished when Briggs rose also, and not only accompanied the sinister-looking stranger to the empty cabin, but assisted him in negotiating with its owner for a fortnight's occupancy. Nevertheless, we eagerly assailed Briggs on his return for some explanation of this singular change in his attitude toward the stranger. He coolly reminded us, however, that while his intention of excluding ruffianly adventurers from the camp remained the same, he had no right to go back on the stranger's sentiments, which were evidently in accord with our own, and although Mr. Bulger's appearance was inconsistent with them, that was only an additional reason why we should substitute a mild firmness for that violence which we all deprecated, but which might attend his abrupt dismissal. We were all satisfied except Mosby, who had not yet recovered from Briggs's change of front, which he was pleased to call "craw-fishing." "Seemed to me his account of his business was extraordinary satisfactory! Sorter filled the bill all round—no mistake thar," he suggested, with a malicious irony. "I like a man that's outspoken."

"I understood him very well," said Briggs, quietly.

"In course you did. Only when you've settled in your MIND whether he was describing horse-stealing or tract-distributing, mebbe you'll let ME know."

It would seem, however, that Briggs did not interrogate the stranger again regarding it, nor did we, who were quite content to leave matters in Briggs's hands. Enough that Mr. Bulger moved into the empty cabin the next day, and, with the aid of a few old boxes from the grocery, which he quickly extemporized into tables and chairs, and the purchase of some necessary cooking utensils, soon made himself at home. The rest of the camp, now thoroughly aroused, made a point of leaving their work in the ditches, whenever they could, to stroll carelessly around Bulger's tenement in the vague hope of satisfying a curiosity that had become tormenting. But they could not find that he was doing anything of a suspicious character—except, perhaps, from the fact that it was not OUTWARDLY suspicious, which I grieve to say did not lull them to security. He seemed to be either fixing up his cabin or smoking in his doorway. On the second day he checked this itinerant curiosity by taking the initiative himself, and quietly walking from claim to claim and from cabin to cabin with a pacific but by no means a satisfying interest. The shadow of his tall figure carrying his inseparable gun, which had not yet apparently "stood in the corner," falling upon an excavated bank beside the delving miners, gave them a sense of uneasiness they could not explain; a few characteristic yells of boisterous hilarity from their noontide gathering under a cottonwood somehow ceased when Mr. Bulger was seen gravely approaching, and his casual stopping before a poker party in the gulch actually caused one of the most reckless gamblers to weakly recede from "a bluff" and allow his adversary to sweep the board. After this it was felt that matters were becoming serious. There was no subsequent patrolling of the camp before the stranger's cabin. Their curiosity was singularly abated. A general feeling of repulsion, kept within bounds partly by the absence of any overt act from Bulger, and partly by an inconsistent over-consciousness of his shotgun, took its place. But an unexpected occurrence revived it.

One evening, as the usual social circle were drawn around Mosby's stove, the lazy silence was broken by the familiar sounds of pistol shots and a series of more familiar shrieks and yells from the rocky hill road. The circle quickly recognized the voices of their old friends the roisterers and gamblers from Sawyer's Dam; they as quickly recognized the returning shouts here and there from a few companions who were welcoming them. I grieve to say that in spite of their previous attitude of reformation a smile of gratified expectancy lit up the faces of the younger members, and even the older ones glanced dubiously at Briggs. Mosby made no attempt to conceal a sigh of relief as he carefully laid out an extra supply of glasses in his bar. Suddenly the oncoming yells ceased, the wild gallop of hoofs slackened into a trot, and finally halted, and even the responsive shouts of the camp stopped also. We all looked vacantly at each other; Mosby leaped over his counter and went to the door; Briggs followed with the rest of us. The night was dark, and it was a few minutes before we could distinguish a straggling, vague, but silent procession moving through the moist, heavy air on the hill. But, to our surprise, it was moving away from us—absolutely LEAVING the camp! We were still staring in expectancy when out of the darkness slowly emerged a figure which we recognized at once as Captain Jim, one of the most reckless members of our camp. Pushing us back into the grocery he entered without a word, closed the door behind him, and threw himself vacantly into a chair. We at once pressed around him. He looked up at us dazedly, drew a long breath, and said slowly:

"It's no use, gentlemen! Suthin's GOT to be done with that Bulger; and mighty quick."

"What's the matter?" we asked eagerly.

"Matter!" he repeated, passing his hand across his forehead. "Matter! Look yere! Ye all of you heard them boys from Sawyer's Dam coming over the hill? Ye heard their music—mebbe ye heard US join in the chorus? Well, on they came waltzing down the hill, like old times, and we waitin' for 'em. Then, jest as they passed the old cabin, who do you think they ran right into—shooting iron, long hair and mustache, and all that—standing there plump in the road? why, Bulger!"

"Well?"

"Well!—Whatever it was—don't ask ME—but, dern my skin, ef after a word or two from HIM—them boys just stopped yellin', turned round like lambs, and rode away, peaceful-like, along with him. We ran after them a spell, still yellin', when that thar Bulger faced around, said to us that he'd 'come down here for quiet,' and ef he couldn't hev it he'd have to leave with those gentlemen WHO WANTED IT too! And I'm gosh darned ef those GENTLEMEN—you know 'em all—Patsey Carpenter, Snapshot Harry, and the others—ever said a darned word, but kinder nodded 'So long' and went away!"

Our astonishment and mystification were complete; and I regret to say, the indignation of Captain Jim and Mosby equally so. "If we're going to be bossed by the first newcomer," said the former, gloomily, "I reckon we might as well take our chances with the Sawyer's Dam boys, whom we know."

"Ef we are going to hev the legitimate trade of Rattlesnake interfered with by the cranks of some hidin' horse thief or retired road agent," said Mosby, "we might as well invite the hull of Joaquin Murietta's gang here at once! But I suppose this is part o' Bulger's particular 'business,'" he added, with a withering glance at Briggs.

"I understand it all," said Briggs, quietly. "You know I told you that bullies couldn't live in the same camp together. That's human nature—and that's how plain men like you and me manage to scud along without getting plugged. You see, Bulger wasn't going to hev any of his own kind jumpin' his claim here. And I reckon he was pow'ful enough to back down Sawyer's Dam. Anyhow, the bluff told—and here we are in peace and quietness."

"Until he lets us know what is his little game," sneered Mosby.

Nevertheless, such is the force of mysterious power that although it was exercised against what we firmly believed was the independence of the camp, it extorted a certain respect from us. A few thought it was not a bad thing to have a professional bully, and even took care to relate the discomfiture of the wicked youth of Sawyer's Dam for the benefit of a certain adjacent and powerful camp who had looked down upon us. He himself, returning the same evening from his self-imposed escort, vouchsafed no other reason than the one he had already given. Preposterous as it seemed, we were obliged to accept it, and the still more preposterous inference that he had sought Rattlesnake Camp solely for the purpose of acquiring and securing its peace and quietness. Certainly he had no other occupation; the little work he did upon the tailings of the abandoned claim which went with his little cabin was scarcely a pretense. He rode over on certain days to Bigwood on account of his business, but no one had ever seen him there, nor could the description of his manner and appearance evoke any information from the Bigwoodians. It remained a mystery.

It had also been feared that the advent of Bulger would intensify that fear and dislike of riotous Rattlesnake which the two families had shown, and which was the origin of Briggs's futile attempt at reformation. But it was discovered that since his arrival the young girls had shown less timidity in entering the camp, and had even exchanged some polite conversation and good-humoured badinage with its younger and more impressible members. Perhaps this tended to make these youths more observant, for a few days later, when the vexed question of Bulger's business was again under discussion, one of them remarked, gloomily:

"I reckon there ain't no doubt WHAT he's here for!"

The youthful prophet was instantly sat upon after the fashion of all elderly critics since Job's. Nevertheless, after a pause he was permitted to explain.

"Only this morning, when Lance Forester and me were chirping with them gals out on the hill, who should we see hanging around in the bush but that cussed Bulger! We allowed at first that it might be only a new style of his interferin', so we took no notice, except to pass a few remarks about listeners and that sort o' thing, and perhaps to bedevil the girls a little more than we'd hev done if we'd been alone. Well, they laughed, and we laughed—and that was the end of it. But this afternoon, as Lance and me were meandering down by their cabin, we sorter turned into the woods to wait till they'd come out. Then all of a sudden Lance stopped as rigid as a pointer that's flushed somethin', and says, 'B'gosh!' And thar, under a big redwood, sat that slimy hypocrite Bulger, twisting his long mustaches and smiling like clockwork alongside o' little Meely Baker—you know her, the pootiest of the two sisters—and she smilin' back on him. Think of it! that unknown, unwashed, longhaired tramp and bully, who must be forty if a day, and that innocent gal of sixteen. It was simply disgustin'!"

I need not say that the older cynics and critics already alluded to at once improved the occasion. 'What more could be expected? Women, the world over, were noted for this sort of thing! This long-haired, swaggering bully, with his air of mystery, had captivated them, as he always had done since the days of Homer. Simple merit, which sat lowly in barrooms, and conceived projects for the public good around the humble, unostentatious stove, was nowhere! Youth could not too soon learn this bitter lesson. And in this case youth too, perhaps, was right in its conjectures, for this WAS, no doubt, the little game of the perfidious Bulger. We recalled the fact that his unhallowed appearance in camp was almost coincident with the arrival of the two families. We glanced at Briggs; to our amazement, for the first time he looked seriously concerned. But Mosby in the meantime leaned his elbows lazily over the counter and, in a slow voice, added fuel to the flame.

"I wouldn't hev spoken of it before," he said, with a sidelong glance at Briggs, "for it might be all in the line o' Bulger's 'business,' but suthin' happened the other night that, for a minit, got me! I was passin' the Bakers' shanty, and I heard one of them gals a singing a camp-meeting hymn. I don't calkilate to run agin you young fellers in any sparkin' or canoodlin' that's goin' on, but her voice sounded so pow'ful soothin' and pretty thet I jest stood there and listened. Then the old woman—old Mother Baker—SHE joined in, and I listened too. And then—dern my skin!—but a man's voice joined in—jest belching outer that cabin!—and I sorter lifted myself up and kem away.

"That voice, gentlemen," said Mosby, lingering artistically as he took up a glass and professionally eyed it before wiping it with his towel, "that voice, cumf'bly fixed thar in thet cabin among them wimen folks, was Bulger's!"

Briggs got up, with his eyes looking the darker for his flushed face. "Gentlemen," he said huskily, "thar's only one thing to be done. A lot of us have got to ride over to Sawyer's Dam tomorrow morning and pick up as many square men as we can muster; there's a big camp meeting goin' on there, and there won't be no difficulty in that. When we've got a big enough crowd to show we mean business, we must march back here and ride Bulger out of this camp! I don't hanker arter Vigilance Committees, as a rule—it's a rough remedy—it's like drinkin' a quart o' whisky agin rattlesnake poison but it's got to be done! We don't mind being sold ourselves but when it comes to our standin' by and seein' the only innocent people in Rattlesnake given away—we kick! Bulger's got to be fired outer this camp! And he will be!"

But he was not.

For when, the next morning, a determined and thoughtful procession of the best and most characteristic citizens of Rattlesnake Camp filed into Sawyer's Dam, they found that their mysterious friends had disappeared, although they met with a fraternal but subdued welcome from the general camp. But any approach to the subject of their visit, however, was received with a chilling dissapproval. Did they not know that lawlessness of any kind, even under the rude mantle of frontier justice, was to be deprecated and scouted when a "means of salvation, a power of regeneration," such as was now sweeping over Sawyer's Dam, was at hand? Could they not induce this man who was to be violently deported to accompany them willingly to Sawyer's Dam and subject himself to the powerful influence of the "revival" then in full swing?

The Rattlesnake boys laughed bitterly, and described the man of whom they talked so lightly; but in vain. "It's no use, gentlemen," said a more worldly bystander, in a lower voice, "the camp meetin's got a strong grip here, and betwixt you and me there ain't no wonder. For the man that runs it—the big preacher—has got new ways and methods that fetches the boys every time. He don't preach no cut-and-dried gospel; he don't carry around no slop-shop robes and clap 'em on you whether they fit or not; but he samples and measures the camp afore he wades into it. He scouts and examines; he ain't no mere Sunday preacher with a comfortable house and once-a-week church, but he gives up his days and nights to it, and makes his family work with him, and even sends 'em forward to explore the field. And he ain't no white-choker shadbelly either, but fits himself, like his gospel, to the men he works among. Ye ought to hear him afore you go. His tent is just out your way. I'll go with you."

Too dejected to offer any opposition, and perhaps a little curious to see this man who had unwittingly frustrated their design of lynching Bulger, they halted at the outer fringe of worshipers who packed the huge inclosure. They had not time to indulge their cynicisms over this swaying mass of emotional, half-thinking, and almost irresponsible beings, nor to detect any similarity between THEIR extreme methods and the scheme of redemption they themselves were seeking, for in a few moments, apparently lifted to his feet on a wave of religious exultation, the famous preacher arose. The men of Rattlesnake gasped for breath.

It was Bulger!

But Briggs quickly recovered himself. "By what name," said he, turning passionately towards his guide, "does this man—this impostor—call himself here?"

"Baker."

"Baker?" echoed the Rattlesnake contingent.

"Baker?" repeated Lance Forester, with a ghastly smile.

"Yes," returned their guide. "You oughter know it too! For he sent his wife and daughters over, after his usual style, to sample your camp, a week ago! Come, now, what are you givin' us?"

* * * * * * * * *

IN THE TULES

He had never seen a steamboat in his life. Born and reared in one of the Western Territories, far from a navigable river, he had only known the "dugout" or canoe as a means of conveyance across the scant streams whose fordable waters made even those scarcely a necessity. The long, narrow, hooded wagon, drawn by swaying oxen, known familiarly as a "prairie schooner," in which he journeyed across the plains to California in '53, did not help his conception by that nautical figure. And when at last he dropped upon the land of promise through one of the Southern mountain passes he halted all unconsciously upon the low banks of a great yellow river amidst a tangled brake of strange, reed-like grasses that were unknown to him. The river, broadening as it debouched through many channels into a lordly bay, seemed to him the ULTIMA THULE of his journeyings. Unyoking his oxen on the edge of the luxuriant meadows which blended with scarcely any line of demarcation into the great stream itself, he found the prospect "good" according to his lights and prairial experiences, and, converting his halted wagon into a temporary cabin, he resolved to rest here and "settle."

There was little difficulty in so doing. The cultivated clearings he had passed were few and far between; the land would be his by discovery and occupation; his habits of loneliness and self-reliance made him independent of neighbors. He took his first meal in his new solitude under a spreading willow, but so near his natural boundary that the waters gurgled and oozed in the reeds but a few feet from him. The sun sank, deepening the gold of the river until it might have been the stream of Pactolus itself. But Martin Morse had no imagination; he was not even a gold-seeker; he had simply obeyed the roving instincts of the frontiersman in coming hither. The land was virgin and unoccupied; it was his; he was alone. These questions settled, he smoked his pipe with less concern over his three thousand miles' transference of habitation than the man of cities who had moved into a next street. When the sun sank, he rolled himself in his blankets in the wagon bed and went quietly to sleep.

But he was presently awakened by something which at first he could not determine to be a noise or an intangible sensation. It was a deep throbbing through the silence of the night—a pulsation that seemed even to be communicated to the rude bed whereon he lay. As it came nearer it separated itself into a labored, monotonous panting, continuous, but distinct from an equally monotonous but fainter beating of the waters, as if the whole track of the river were being coursed and trodden by a multitude of swiftly trampling feet. A strange feeling took possession of him—half of fear, half of curious expectation. It was coming nearer. He rose, leaped hurriedly from the wagon, and ran to the bank. The night was dark; at first he saw nothing before him but the steel-black sky pierced with far-spaced, irregularly scattered stars. Then there seemed to be approaching him, from the left, another and more symmetrical constellation—a few red and blue stars high above the river, with three compact lines of larger planetary lights flashing towards him and apparently on his own level. It was almost upon him; he involuntarily drew back as the strange phenomenon swept abreast of where he stood, and resolved itself into a dark yet airy bulk, whose vagueness, topped by enormous towers, was yet illuminated by those open squares of light that he had taken for stars, but which he saw now were brilliantly lit windows.

Their vivid rays shot through the reeds and sent broad bands across the meadow, the stationary wagon, and the slumbering oxen. But all this was nothing to the inner life they disclosed through lifted curtains and open blinds, which was the crowning revelation of this strange and wonderful spectacle. Elegantly dressed men and women moved through brilliantly lit and elaborately gilt saloons; in one a banquet seemed to be spread, served by white-jacketed servants; in another were men playing cards around marble-topped tables; in another the light flashed back again from the mirrors and glistening glasses and decanters of a gorgeous refreshment saloon; in smaller openings there was the shy disclosure of dainty white curtains and velvet lounges of more intimate apartments.

Martin Morse stood enthralled and mystified. It was as if some invisible Asmodeus had revealed to this simple frontiersman a world of which he had never dreamed. It was THE world—a world of which he knew nothing in his simple, rustic habits and profound Western isolation—sweeping by him with the rush of an unknown planet. In another moment it was gone; a shower of sparks shot up from one of the towers and fell all around him, and then vanished, even as he remembered the set piece of "Fourth of July" fireworks had vanished in his own rural town when he was a boy. The darkness fell with it too. But such was his utter absorption and breathless preoccupation that only a cold chill recalled him to himself, and he found he was standing mid-leg deep in the surge cast over the low banks by this passage of the first steamboat he had ever seen!

He waited for it the next night, when it appeared a little later from the opposite direction on its return trip. He watched it the next night and the next. Hereafter he never missed it, coming or going—whatever the hard and weary preoccupations of his new and lonely life. He felt he could not have slept without seeing it go by. Oddly enough, his interest and desire did not go further. Even had he the time and money to spend in a passage on the boat, and thus actively realize the great world of which he had only these rare glimpses, a certain proud, rustic shyness kept him from it. It was not HIS world; he could not affront the snubs that his ignorance and inexperience would have provoked, and he was dimly conscious, as so many of us are in our ignorance, that in mingling with it he would simply lose the easy privileges of alien criticism. For there was much that he did not understand, and some things that grated upon his lonely independence.

One night, a lighter one than those previous, he lingered a little longer in the moonlight to watch the phosphorescent wake of the retreating boat. Suddenly it struck him that there was a certain irregular splashing in the water, quite different from the regular, diagonally crossing surges that the boat swept upon the bank. Looking at it more intently, he saw a black object turning in the water like a porpoise, and then the unmistakable uplifting of a black arm in an unskillful swimmer's overhand stroke. It was a struggling man. But it was quickly evident that the current was too strong and the turbulence of the shallow water too great for his efforts. Without a moment's hesitation, clad as he was in only his shirt and trousers, Morse strode into the reeds, and the next moment, with a call of warning, was swimming toward the now wildly struggling figure. But, from some unknown reason, as Morse approached him nearer the man uttered some incoherent protest and desperately turned away, throwing off Morse's extended arm.

Attributing this only to the vague convulsions of a drowning man, Morse, a skilled swimmer, managed to clutch his shoulder, and propelled him at arm's length, still struggling, apparently with as much reluctance as incapacity, toward the bank. As their feet touched the reeds and slimy bottom the man's resistance ceased, and he lapsed quite listlessly in Morse's arms. Half lifting, half dragging his burden, he succeeded at last in gaining the strip of meadow, and deposited the unconscious man beneath the willow tree. Then he ran to his wagon for whisky.

But, to his surprise, on his return the man was already sitting up and wringing the water from his clothes. He then saw for the first time, by the clear moonlight, that the stranger was elegantly dressed and of striking appearance, and was clearly a part of that bright and fascinating world which Morse had been contemplating in his solitude. He eagerly took the proffered tin cup and drank the whisky. Then he rose to his feet, staggered a few steps forward, and glanced curiously around him at the still motionless wagon, the few felled trees and evidence of "clearing," and even at the rude cabin of logs and canvas just beginning to rise from the ground a few paces distant, and said, impatiently:

"Where the devil am I?"

Morse hesitated. He was unable to name the locality of his dwelling-place. He answered briefly:

"On the right bank of the Sacramento."

The stranger turned upon him a look of suspicion not unmingled with resentment. "Oh!" he said, with ironical gravity, "and I suppose that this water you picked me out of was the Sacramento River. Thank you!"

Morse, with slow Western patience, explained that he had only settled there three weeks ago, and the place had no name.

"What's your nearest town, then?"

"Thar ain't any. Thar's a blacksmith's shop and grocery at the crossroads, twenty miles further on, but it's got no name as I've heard on."

The stranger's look of suspicion passed. "Well," he said, in an imperative fashion, which, however, seemed as much the result of habit as the occasion, "I want a horse, and mighty quick, too."

"H'ain't got any."

"No horse? How did you get to this place?"

Morse pointed to the slumbering oxen.

The stranger again stared curiously at him. After a pause he said, with a half-pitying, half-humorous smile: "Pike—aren't you?"

Whether Morse did or did not know that this current California slang for a denizen of the bucolic West implied a certain contempt, he replied simply:

"I'm from Pike County, Mizzouri."

"Well," said the stranger, resuming his impatient manner, "you must beg or steal a horse from your neighbors."

"Thar ain't any neighbor nearer than fifteen miles."

"Then send fifteen miles! Stop." He opened his still clinging shirt and drew out a belt pouch, which he threw to Morse. "There! there's two hundred and fifty dollars in that. Now, I want a horse. Sabe?"

"Thar ain't anyone to send," said Morse, quietly.

"Do you mean to say you are all alone here?"

"Yes.

"And you fished me out—all by yourself?"

"Yes."

The stranger again examined him curiously. Then he suddenly stretched out his hand and grasped his companion's.

"All right; if you can't send, I reckon I can manage to walk over there tomorrow."

"I was goin' on to say," said Morse, simply, "that if you'll lie by tonight, I'll start over sunup, after puttin' out the cattle, and fetch you back a horse afore noon."

"That's enough." He, however, remained looking curiously at Morse. "Did you never hear," he said, with a singular smile, "that it was about the meanest kind of luck that could happen to you to save a drowning man?"

"No," said Morse, simply. "I reckon it orter be the meanest if you DIDN'T."

"That depends upon the man you save," said the stranger, with the same ambiguous smile, "and whether the SAVING him is only putting things off. Look here," he added, with an abrupt return to his imperative style, "can't you give me some dry clothes?"

Morse brought him a pair of overalls and a "hickory shirt," well worn, but smelling strongly of a recent wash with coarse soap. The stranger put them on while his companion busied himself in collecting a pile of sticks and dry leaves.

"What's that for?" said the stranger, suddenly.

"A fire to dry your clothes."

The stranger calmly kicked the pile aside.

"Not any fire tonight if I know it," he said, brusquely. Before Morse could resent his quickly changing moods he continued, in another tone, dropping to an easy reclining position beneath the tree, "Now, tell me all about yourself, and what you are doing here."

Thus commanded, Morse patiently repeated his story from the time he had left his backwoods cabin to his selection of the river bank for a "location." He pointed out the rich quality of this alluvial bottom and its adaptability for the raising of stock, which he hoped soon to acquire. The stranger smiled grimly, raised himself to a sitting position, and, taking a penknife from his damp clothes, began to clean his nails in the bright moonlight—an occupation which made the simple Morse wander vaguely in his narration.

"And you don't know that this hole will give you chills and fever till you'll shake yourself out of your boots?"

Morse had lived before in aguish districts, and had no fear.

"And you never heard that some night the whole river will rise up and walk over you and your cabin and your stock?"

"No. For I reckon to move my shanty farther back."

The man shut up his penknife with a click and rose.   ·

"If you've got to get up at sunrise, we'd better be turning in. I suppose you can give me a pair of blankets?"

Morse pointed to the wagon. "Thar's a shakedown in the wagon bed; you kin lie there." Nevertheless he hesitated, and, with the inconsequence and abruptness of a shy man, continued the previous conversation.

"I shouldn't like to move far away, for them steamboats is pow'ful kempany o' nights. I never seed one afore I kem here," and then, with the inconsistency of a reserved man, and without a word of further preliminary, he launched into a confidential disclosure of his late experiences. The stranger listened with a singular interest and a quietly searching eye.

"Then you were watching the boat very closely just now when you saw me. What else did you see? Anything before that—before you saw me in the water?"

"No—the boat had got well off before I saw you at all."

"Ah," said the stranger. "Well, I'm going to turn in." He walked to the wagon, mounted it, and by the time that Morse had reached it with his wet clothes he was already wrapped in the blankets. A moment later he seemed to be in a profound slumber.

It was only then, when his guest was lying helplessly at his mercy, that he began to realize his strange experiences. The domination of this man had been so complete that Morse, although by nature independent and self-reliant, had not permitted himself to question his right or to resent his rudeness. He had accepted his guest's careless or premeditated silence regarding the particulars of his accident as a matter of course, and had never dreamed of questioning him. That it was a natural accident of that great world so apart from his own experiences he did not doubt, and thought no more about it. The advent of the man himself was greater to him than the causes which brought him there. He was as yet quite unconscious of the complete fascination this mysterious stranger held over him, but he found himself shyly pleased with even the slight interest he had displayed in his affairs, and his hand felt yet warm and tingling from his sudden soft but expressive grasp, as if it had been a woman's. There is a simple intuition of friendship in some lonely, self-abstracted natures that is nearly akin to love at first sight. Even the audacities and insolence of this stranger affected Morse as he might have been touched and captivated by the coquetries or imperiousness of some bucolic virgin. And this reserved and shy frontiersman found himself that night sleepless, and hovering with an abashed timidity and consciousness around the wagon that sheltered his guest, as if he had been a very Corydon watching the moonlit couch of some slumbering Amaryllis.

He was off by daylight—after having placed a rude breakfast by the side of the still sleeping guest—and before midday he had returned with a horse. When he handed the stranger his pouch, less the amount he had paid for the horse, the man said curtly:

"What's that for?"

"Your change. I paid only fifty dollars for the horse."

The stranger regarded him with his peculiar smile. Then, replacing the pouch in his belt, he shook Morse's hand again and mounted the horse.

"So your name's Martin Morse! Well—goodby, Morsey!"

Morse hesitated. A blush rose to his dark check. "You didn't tell me your name," he said. "In case—"

"In case I'm WANTED? Well, you can call me Captain Jack." He smiled, and, nodding his head, put spurs to his mustang and cantered away.

Morse did not do much work that day, falling into abstracted moods and living over his experiences of the previous night, until he fancied he could almost see his strange guest again. The narrow strip of meadow was haunted by him. There was the tree under which he had first placed him, and that was where he had seen him sitting up in his dripping but well-fitting clothes. In the rough garments he had worn and returned lingered a new scent of some delicate soap, overpowering the strong alkali flavor of his own. He was early by the river side, having a vague hope, he knew not why, that he should again see him and recognize him among the passengers. He was wading out among the reeds, in the faint light of the rising moon, recalling the exact spot where he had first seen the stranger, when he was suddenly startled by the rolling over in the water of some black object that had caught against the bank, but had been dislodged by his movements. To his horror it bore a faint resemblance to his first vision of the preceding night. But a second glance at the helplessly floating hair and bloated outline showed him that it was a DEAD man, and of a type and build far different from his former companion. There was a bruise upon his matted forehead and an enormous wound in his throat already washed bloodless, white, and waxen. An inexplicable fear came upon him, not at the sight of the corpse, for he had been in Indian massacres and had rescued bodies mutilated beyond recognition; but from some moral dread that, strangely enough, quickened and deepened with the far-off pant of the advancing steamboat. Scarcely knowing why, he dragged the body hurriedly ashore, concealing it in the reeds, as if he were disposing of the evidence of his own crime. Then, to his preposterous terror, he noticed that the panting of the steamboat and the beat of its paddles were "slowing" as the vague bulk came in sight, until a huge wave from the suddenly arrested wheels sent a surge like an enormous heartbeat pulsating through the sedge that half submerged him. The flashing of three or four lanterns on deck and the motionless line of lights abreast of him dazzled his eyes, but he knew that the low fringe of willows hid his house and wagon completely from view. A vague murmur of voices from the deck was suddenly overridden by a sharp order, and to his relief the slowly revolving wheels again sent a pulsation through the water, and the great fabric moved solemnly away. A sense of relief came over him, he knew not why, and he was conscious that for the first time he had not cared to look at the boat.

When the moon arose he again examined the body, and took from its clothing a few articles of identification and some papers of formality and precision, which he vaguely conjectured to be some law papers from their resemblance to the phrasing of sheriffs' and electors' notices which he had seen in the papers. He then buried the corpse in a shallow trench, which he dug by the light of the moon. He had no question of responsibility; his pioneer training had not included coroners' inquests in its experience; in giving the body a speedy and secure burial from predatory animals he did what one frontiersman would do for another—what he hoped might be done for him. If his previous unaccountable feelings returned occasionally, it was not from that; but rather from some uneasiness in regard to his late guest's possible feelings, and a regret that he had not been here at the finding of the body. That it would in some way have explained his own accident he did not doubt.

The boat did not "slow up" the next night, but passed as usual; yet three or four days elapsed before he could look forward to its coming with his old extravagant and half-exalted curiosity—which was his nearest approach to imagination. He was then able to examine it more closely, for the appearance of the stranger whom he now began to call "his friend" in his verbal communings with himself—but whom he did not seem destined to again discover; until one day, to his astonishment, a couple of fine horses were brought to his clearing by a stock-drover. They had been "ordered" to be left there. In vain Morse expostulated and questioned.

"Your name's Martin Morse, ain't it?" said the drover, with business brusqueness; "and I reckon there ain't no other man o' that name around here?"

"No," said Morse.

"Well, then, they're YOURS."

"But who sent them?" insisted Morse. "What was his name, and where does he live?"

"I didn't know ez I was called upon to give the pedigree o' buyers," said the drover dryly; "but the horses is 'Morgan,' you can bet your life." He grinned as he rode away.

That Captain Jack sent them, and that it was a natural prelude to his again visiting him, Morse did not doubt, and for a few days he lived in that dream. But Captain Jack did not come. The animals were of great service to him in "rounding up" the stock he now easily took in for pasturage, and saved him the necessity of having a partner or a hired man. The idea that this superior gentleman in fine clothes might ever appear to him in the former capacity had even flitted through his brain, but he had rejected it with a sigh. But the thought that, with luck and industry, he himself might, in course of time, approximate to Captain Jack's evident station, DID occur to him, and was an incentive to energy. Yet it was quite distinct from the ordinary working man's ambition of wealth and state. It was only that it might make him more worthy of his friend. The great world was still as it had appeared to him in the passing boat—a thing to wonder at—to be above—and to criticize.

For all that, he prospered in his occupation. But one day he woke with listless limbs and feet that scarcely carried him through his daily labors. At night his listlessness changed to active pain and a feverishness that seemed to impel him toward the fateful river, as if his one aim in life was to drink up its waters and bathe in its yellow stream. But whenever he seemed to attempt it, strange dreams assailed him of dead bodies arising with swollen and distorted lips to touch his own as he strove to drink, or of his mysterious guest battling with him in its current, and driving him ashore. Again, when he essayed to bathe his parched and crackling limbs in its flood, he would be confronted with the dazzling lights of the motionless steamboat and the glare of stony eyes—until he fled in aimless terror. How long this lasted he knew not, until one morning he awoke in his new cabin with a strange man sitting by his bed and a Negress in the doorway.

"You've had a sharp attack of 'tule fever,'" said the stranger, dropping Morse's listless wrist and answering his questioning eyes, "but you're all right now, and will pull through."

"Who are you?" stammered Morse feebly.

"Dr. Duchesne, of Sacramento."

"How did you come here?"

"I was ordered to come to you and bring a nurse, as you were alone. There she is." He pointed to the smiling Negress.

"WHO ordered you?"

The doctor smiled with professional tolerance. "One of your friends, of course."

"But what was his name?"

"Really, I don't remember. But don't distress yourself. He has settled for everything right royally. You have only to get strong now. My duty is ended, and I can safely leave you with the nurse. Only when you are strong again, I say—and HE says—keep back farther from the river."

And that was all he knew. For even the nurse who attended him through the first days of his brief convalescence would tell him nothing more. He quickly got rid of her and resumed his work, for a new and strange phase of his simple, childish affection for his benefactor, partly superinduced by his illness, was affecting him. He was beginning to feel the pain of an unequal friendship; he was dimly conscious that his mysterious guest was only coldly returning his hospitality and benefits, while holding aloof from any association with him—and indicating the immeasurable distance that separated their future intercourse. He had withheld any kind message or sympathetic greeting; he had kept back even his NAME. The shy, proud, ignorant heart of the frontiersman swelled beneath the fancied slight, which left him helpless alike of reproach or resentment. He could not return the horses, although in a fit of childish indignation he had resolved not to use them; he could not reimburse him for the doctor's bill, although he had sent away the nurse.

He took a foolish satisfaction in not moving back from the river, with a faint hope that his ignoring of Captain Jack's advice might mysteriously be conveyed to him. He even thought of selling out his location and abandoning it, that he might escape the cold surveillance of his heartless friend. All this was undoubtedly childish—but there is an irrepressible simplicity of youth in all deep feeling, and the worldly inexperience of the frontiersman left him as innocent as a child. In this phase of his unrequited affection he even went so far as to seek some news of Captain Jack at Sacramento, and, following out his foolish quest, even to take the steamboat from thence to Stockton.

What happened to him then was perhaps the common experience of such natures. Once upon the boat the illusion of the great world it contained for him utterly vanished. He found it noisy, formal, insincere, and—had he ever understood or used the word in his limited vocabulary— VULGAR. Rather, perhaps, it seemed to him that the prevailing sentiment and action of those who frequented it—and for whom it was built—were of a lower grade than his own. And, strangely enough, this gave him none of his former sense of critical superiority, but only of his own utter and complete isolation. He wandered in his rough frontiersman's clothes from deck to cabin, from airy galleries to long saloons, alone, unchallenged, unrecognized, as if he were again haunting it only in spirit, as he had so often done in his dreams.

His presence on the fringe of some voluble crowd caused no interruption; to him their speech was almost foreign in its allusions to things he did not understand, or, worse, seemed inconsistent with their eagerness and excitement. How different from all this were his old recollections of slowly oncoming teams, uplifted above the level horizon of the plains in his former wanderings; the few sauntering figures that met him as man to man, and exchanged the chronicle of the road; the record of Indian tracks; the finding of a spring; the discovery of pasturage, with the lazy, restful hospitality of the night! And how fierce here this continual struggle for dominance and existence, even in this lull of passage. For above all and through all he was conscious of the feverish haste of speed and exertion.

The boat trembled, vibrated, and shook with every stroke of the ponderous piston. The laughter of the crowd, the exchange of gossip and news, the banquet at the long table, the newspapers and books in the reading-room, even the luxurious couches in the staterooms, were all dominated, thrilled, and pulsating with the perpetual throb of the demon of hurry and unrest. And when at last a horrible fascination dragged him into the engine room, and he saw the cruel relentless machinery at work, he seemed to recognize and understand some intelligent but pitiless Moloch, who was dragging this feverish world at its heels.

Later he was seated in a corner of the hurricane deck, whence he could view the monotonous banks of the river; yet, perhaps by certain signs unobservable to others, he knew he was approaching his own locality. He knew that his cabin and clearing would be undiscernible behind the fringe of willows on the bank, but he already distinguished the points where a few cottonwoods struggled into a promontory of lighter foliage beyond them. Here voices fell upon his ear, and he was suddenly aware that two men had lazily crossed over from the other side of the boat, and were standing before him looking upon the bank.

"It was about here, I reckon," said one, listlessly, as if continuing a previous lagging conversation, "that it must have happened. For it was after we were making for the bend we've just passed that the deputy, goin' to the stateroom below us, found the door locked and the window open. But both men—Jack Despard and Seth Hall, the sheriff—weren't to be found. Not a trace of 'em. The boat was searched, but all for nothing. The idea is that the sheriff, arter getting his prisoner comf'ble in the stateroom, took off Jack's handcuffs and locked the door; that Jack, who was mighty desp'rate, bolted through the window into the river, and the sheriff, who was no slouch, arter him. Others allow—for the chairs and things was all tossed about in the stateroom—that the two men clinched THAR, and Jack choked Hall and chucked him out, and then slipped cl'ar into the water himself, for the stateroom window was just ahead of the paddle box, and the cap'n allows that no man or men could fall afore the paddles and live. Anyhow, that was all they ever knew of it."

"And there wasn't no trace of them found?" said the second man, after a long pause.

"No. Cap'n says them paddles would hev' just snatched 'em and slung 'em round and round and buried 'em way down in the ooze of the river bed, with all the silt of the current atop of 'em, and they mightn't come up for ages; or else the wheels might have waltzed 'em way up to Sacramento until there wasn't enough left of 'em to float, and dropped 'em when the boat stopped."

"It was a mighty fool risk for a man like Despard to take," resumed the second speaker as he turned away with a slight yawn.

"Bet your life! but he was desp'rate, and the sheriff had got him sure! And they DO say that he was superstitious, like all them gamblers, and allowed that a man who was fixed to die by a rope or a pistol wasn't to be washed out of life by water."

The two figures drifted lazily away, but Morse sat rigid and motionless. Yet, strange to say, only one idea came to him clearly out of this awful revelation—the thought that his friend was still true to him—and that his strange absence and mysterious silence were fully accounted for and explained. And with it came the more thrilling fancy that this man was alive now to HIM alone.

HE was the sole custodian of his secret. The morality of the question, while it profoundly disturbed him, was rather in reference to its effect upon the chances of Captain Jack and the power it gave his enemies than his own conscience. He would rather that his friend should have proven the proscribed outlaw who retained an unselfish interest in him than the superior gentleman who was coldly wiping out his gratitude. He thought he understood now the reason of his visitor's strange and varying moods—even his bitter superstitious warning in regard to the probable curse entailed upon one who should save a drowning man. Of this he recked little; enough that he fancied that Captain Jack's concern in his illness was heightened by that fear, and this assurance of his protecting friendship thrilled him with pleasure.

There was no reason now why he should not at once go back to his farm, where, at least, Captain Jack would always find him; and he did so, returning on the same boat. He was now fully recovered from his illness, and calmer in mind; he redoubled his labors to put himself in a position to help the mysterious fugitive when the time should come. The remote farm should always be a haven of refuge for him, and in this hope he forbore to take any outside help, remaining solitary and alone, that Captain Jack's retreat should be inviolate. And so the long, dry season passed, the hay was gathered, the pasturing herds sent home, and the first rains, dimpling like shot the broadening surface of the river, were all that broke his unending solitude. In this enforced attitude of waiting and expectancy he was exalted and strengthened by a new idea. He was not a religious man, but, dimly remembering the exhortations of some camp meeting of his boyhood, he conceived the idea that he might have been selected to work out the regeneration of Captain Jack. What might not come of this meeting and communing together in this lonely spot? That anything was due to the memory of the murdered sheriff, whose bones were rotting in the trench that he daily but unconcernedly passed, did not occur to him. Perhaps his mind was not large enough for the double consideration. Friendship and love—and, for the matter of that, religion—are eminently one-ideaed.

But one night he awakened with a start. His hand, which was hanging out of his bunk, was dabbling idly in water. He had barely time to spring to his middle in what seemed to be a slowly filling tank before the door fell out as from that inward pressure, and his whole shanty collapsed like a pack of cards. But it fell outwards, the roof sliding from over his head like a withdrawn canopy; and he was swept from his feet against it, and thence out into what might have been another world! For the rain had ceased, and the full moon revealed only one vast, illimitable expanse of water! It was not an overflow, but the whole rushing river magnified and repeated a thousand times, which, even as he gasped for breath and clung to the roof, was bearing him away he knew not whither. But it was bearing him away upon its center, for as he cast one swift glance toward his meadows he saw they were covered by the same sweeping torrent, dotted with his sailing hayricks and reaching to the wooded foothills. It was the great flood of '54. In its awe-inspiring completeness it might have seemed to him the primeval Deluge.

As his frail raft swept under a cottonwood he caught at one of the overhanging limbs, and, working his way desperately along the bough, at last reached a secure position in the fork of the tree. Here he was for the moment safe. But the devastation viewed from this height was only the more appalling. Every sign of his clearing, all evidence of his past year's industry, had disappeared. He was now conscious for the first time of the lowing of the few cattle he had kept as, huddled together on a slight eminence, they one by one slipped over struggling into the flood. The shining bodies of his dead horses rolled by him as he gazed. The lower-lying limbs of the sycamore near him were bending with the burden of the lighter articles from his overturned wagon and cabin which they had caught and retained, and a rake was securely lodged in a bough. The habitual solitude of his locality was now strangely invaded by drifting sheds, agricultural implements, and fence rails from unknown and remote neighbors, and he could faintly hear the far-off calling of some unhappy farmer adrift upon a spar of his wrecked and shattered house. When day broke he was cold and hungry.

Hours passed in hopeless monotony, with no slackening or diminution of the waters. Even the drifts became less, and a vacant sea at last spread before him on which nothing moved. An awful silence impressed him. In the afternoon rain again began to fall on this gray, nebulous expanse, until the whole world seemed made of aqueous vapor. He had but one idea now—the coming of the evening boat, and he would reserve his strength to swim to it. He did not know until later that it could no longer follow the old channel of the river, and passed far beyond his sight and hearing. With his disappointment and exposure that night came a return of his old fever. His limbs were alternately racked with pain or benumbed and lifeless. He could scarcely retain his position—at times he scarcely cared to—and speculated upon ending his sufferings by a quick plunge downward. In other moments of lucid misery he was conscious of having wandered in his mind; of having seen the dead face of the murdered sheriff, washed out of his shallow grave by the flood, staring at him from the water; to this was added the hallucination of noises. He heard voices, his own name called by a voice he knew—Captain Jack's!

Suddenly he started, but in that fatal movement lost his balance and plunged downward. But before the water closed above his head he had had a cruel glimpse of help near him; of a flashing light—of the black hull of a tug not many yards away—of moving figures—the sensation of a sudden plunge following his own, the grip of a strong hand upon his collar, and—unconsciousness!

When he came to he was being lifted in a boat from the tug and rowed through the deserted streets of a large city, until he was taken in through the second-story window of a half-submerged hotel and cared for. But all his questions yielded only the information that the tug—a privately procured one, not belonging to the Public Relief Association—had been dispatched for him with special directions, by a man who acted as one of the crew, and who was the one who had plunged in for him at the last moment. The man had left the boat at Stockton. There was nothing more? Yes!—he had left a letter. Morse seized it feverishly. It contained only a few lines:

We are quits now. You are all right. I have saved YOU from drowning, and shifted the curse to my own shoulders. Good-by.

CAPTAIN JACK.

The astounded man attempted to rise—to utter an exclamation—but fell back, unconscious.

Weeks passed before he was able to leave his bed—and then only as an impoverished and physically shattered man. He had no means to restock the farm left bare by the subsiding water. A kindly train-packer offered him a situation as muleteer in a pack train going to the mountains—for he knew tracks and passes and could ride. The mountains gave him back a little of the vigor he had lost in the river valley, but none of its dreams and ambitions. One day, while tracking a lost mule, he stopped to slake his thirst in a waterhole—all that the summer had left of a lonely mountain torrent. Enlarging the hole to give drink to his beast also, he was obliged to dislodge and throw out with the red soil some bits of honeycomb rock, which were so queer-looking and so heavy as to attract his attention. Two of the largest he took back to camp with him. They were gold! From the locality he took out a fortune. Nobody wondered. To the Californian's superstition it was perfectly natural. It was "nigger luck"—the luck of the stupid, the ignorant, the inexperienced, the nonseeker—the irony of the gods!

But the simple, bucolic nature that had sustained itself against temptation with patient industry and lonely self-concentration succumbed to rapidly acquired wealth. So it chanced that one day, with a crowd of excitement-loving spendthrifts and companions, he found himself on the outskirts of a lawless mountain town. An eager, frantic crowd had already assembled there—a desperado was to be lynched! Pushing his way through the crowd for a nearer view of the exciting spectacle, the changed and reckless Morse was stopped by armed men only at the foot of a cart, which upheld a quiet, determined man, who, with a rope around his neck, was scornfully surveying the mob, that held the other end of the rope drawn across the limb of a tree above him. The eyes of the doomed man caught those of Morse—his expression changed—a kindly smile lit his face—he bowed his proud head for the first time, with an easy gesture of farewell.

And then, with a cry, Morse threw himself upon the nearest armed guard, and a fierce struggle began. He had overpowered one adversary and seized another in his hopeless fight toward the cart when the half-astonished crowd felt that something must be done. It was done with a sharp report, the upward curl of smoke and the falling back of the guard as Morse staggered forward FREE—with a bullet in his heart. Yet even then he did not fall until he reached the cart, when he lapsed forward, dead, with his arms outstretched and his head at the doomed man's feet.

There was something so supreme and all-powerful in this hopeless act of devotion that the heart of the multitude thrilled and then recoiled aghast at its work, and a single word or a gesture from the doomed man himself would have set him free. But they say—and it is credibly recorded—that as Captain Jack Despard looked down upon the hopeless sacrifice at his feet his eyes blazed, and he flung upon the crowd a curse so awful and sweeping that, hardened as they were, their blood ran cold, and then leaped furiously to their cheeks.

"And now," he said, coolly tightening the rope around his neck with a jerk of his head—"Go on, and be damned to you! I'm ready."

They did not hesitate this time. And Martin Morse and Captain Jack Despard were buried in the same grave.

* * * * * * * * *

A CONVERT OF THE MISSION

The largest tent of the Tasajara camp meeting was crowded to its utmost extent. The excitement of that dense mass was at its highest pitch. The Reverend Stephen Masterton, the single erect, passionate figure of that confused medley of kneeling worshipers, had reached the culminating pitch of his irresistible exhortatory power. Sighs and groans were beginning to respond to his appeals, when the reverend brother was seen to lurch heavily forward and fall to the ground.

At first the effect was that of a part of his performance; the groans redoubled, and twenty or thirty brethren threw themselves prostrate in humble imitation of the preacher. But Sister Deborah Stokes, perhaps through some special revelation of feminine intuition, grasped the fallen man, tore loose his black silk necktie, and dragged him free of the struggling, frantic crowd whose paroxysms he had just evoked. Howbeit he was pale and unconscious, and unable to continue the service. Even the next day, when he had slightly recovered, it was found that any attempt to renew his fervid exhortations produced the same disastrous result.

A council was hurriedly held by the elders. In spite of the energetic protests of Sister Stokes, it was held that the Lord "was wrestlin' with his sperrit," and he was subjected to the same extraordinary treatment from the whole congregation that he himself had applied to THEM. Propped up pale and trembling in the "Mourners' Bench" by two brethren, he was "striven with," exhorted, prayed over, and admonished, until insensibility mercifully succeeded convulsions. Spiritual therapeutics having failed, he was turned over to the weak and carnal nursing of "womenfolk." But after a month of incapacity he was obliged to yield to "the flesh," and, in the local dialect, "to use a doctor."

It so chanced that the medical practitioner of the district was a man of large experience, of military training, and plain speech. When, therefore, he one day found in his surgery a man of rude Western type, strong-limbed and sunburned, but trembling, hesitating and neurotic in movement, after listening to his symptoms gravely, he asked, abruptly: "And how much are you drinking now?"

"I am a lifelong abstainer," stammered his patient in quivering indignation. But this was followed by another question so frankly appalling to the hearer that he staggered to his feet.

"I'm Stephen Masterton—known of men as a circuit preacher, of the Northern California district," he thundered—"and an enemy of the flesh in all its forms."

"I beg your pardon," responded Dr. Duchesne, grimly, "but as you are suffering from excessive and repeated excitation of the nervous system, and the depression following prolonged artificial exaltation—it makes little difference whether the cause be spiritual, as long as there is a certain physical effect upon your BODY—which I believe you have brought to me to cure. Now—as to diet? you look all wrong there.

"My food is of the simplest—I have no hankering for fleshpots," responded the patient.

"I suppose you call saleratus bread and salt pork and flapjacks SIMPLE?" said the doctor, coolly; "they are COMMON enough, and if you were working with your muscles instead of your nerves in that frame of yours they might not hurt you; but you are suffering as much from eating more than you can digest as the veriest gourmand. You must stop all that. Go down to a quiet watering-place for two months." . . .

"I go to a watering-place?" interrupted Masterton; "to the haunt of the idle, the frivolous and wanton—never!"

"Well, I'm not particular about a 'watering-place,'" said the doctor, with a shrug, "although a little idleness and frivolity with different food wouldn't hurt you—but you must go somewhere and change your habits and mode of life COMPLETELY. I will find you some sleepy old Spanish town in the southern country where you can rest and diet. If this is distasteful to you," he continued, grimly, "you can always call it 'a trial.'"

Stephen Masterton may have thought it so when, a week later, he found himself issuing from a rocky gorge into a rough, badly paved, hilly street, which seemed to be only a continuation of the mountain road itself. It broadened suddenly into a square or plaza, flanked on each side by an irregular row of yellowing adobe houses, with the inevitable verandaed tienda in each corner, and the solitary, galleried fonda, with a half-Moorish archway leading into an inner patio or courtyard in the center.

The whole street stopped as usual at the very door of the Mission church, a few hundred yards farther on, and under the shadow of the two belfry towers at each angle of the facade, as if this were the ultima thule of every traveler. But all that the eye rested on was ruined, worn, and crumbling. The adobe houses were cracked by the incessant sunshine of the half-year-long summer, or the more intermittent earthquake shock; the paved courtyard of the fonda was so uneven and sunken in the center that the lumbering wagon and faded diligencia stood on an incline, and the mules with difficulty kept their footing while being unladen; the whitened plaster had fallen from the feet of the two pillars that flanked the Mission doorway, like bandages from a gouty limb, leaving the reddish core of adobe visible; there were apparently as many broken tiles in the streets and alleys as there were on the heavy red roofs that everywhere asserted themselves—and even seemed to slide down the crumbling walls to the ground. There were hopeless gaps in grille and grating of doorways and windows, where the iron bars had dropped helplessly out, or were bent at different angles. The walls of the peaceful Mission garden and the warlike presidio were alike lost in the escalading vines or leveled by the pushing boughs of gnarled pear and olive trees that now surmounted them. The dust lay thick and impalpable in hollow and gutter, and rose in little vapory clouds with a soft detonation at every stroke of his horse's hoofs. Over all this dust and ruin, idleness seemed to reign supreme. From the velvet-jacketed figures lounging motionless in the shadows of the open doorways—so motionless that only the lazy drift of cigarette smoke betokened their breathing—to the reclining peons in the shade of a catalpa, or the squatting Indians in the arroyo—all was sloth and dirt.

The Rev. Stephen Masterton felt his throat swell with his old exhortative indignation. A gaudy yellow fan waved languidly in front of a black rose-crested head at a white-curtained window. He knew he was stifling with righteous wrath, and clapped his spurs to his horse.

Nevertheless, in a few days, by the aid of a letter to the innkeeper, he was installed in a dilapidated adobe house, not unlike those he had seen, but situated in the outskirts and overlooking the garden and part of the refectory of the old Mission. It had even a small garden of its own—if a strip of hot wall, overburdened with yellow and white roses, a dozen straggling callas, a bank of heliotrope, and an almond tree could be called a garden. It had an open doorway, but so heavily recessed in the thick walls that it preserved seclusion, a sitting-room, and an alcoved bedroom with deep embrasured windows that however excluded the unwinking sunlight and kept an even monotone of shade.

Strange to say, he found it cool, restful, and, in spite of the dust, absolutely clean, and, but for the scent of heliotrope, entirely inodorous. The dry air seemed to dissipate all noxious emanations and decay—the very dust itself in its fine impalpability was volatile with a spicelike piquancy, and left no stain.

A wrinkled Indian woman, brown and veined like a tobacco leaf, ministered to his simple wants. But these wants had also been regulated by Dr. Duchesne. He found himself, with some grave doubts of his effeminacy, breakfasting on a single cup of chocolate instead of his usual bowl of molasses-sweetened coffee; crumbling a crisp tortilla instead of the heavy saleratus bread, greasy flapjack, or the lard-fried steak, and, more wonderful still, completing his repast with purple grapes from the Mission wall. He could not deny that it was simple—that it was even refreshing and consistent with the climate and his surroundings. On the other hand, it was the frugal diet of the commonest peasant—and were not those peons slothful idolaters?

At the end of the week—his correspondence being also restricted by his doctor to a few lines to himself regarding his progress—he wrote to that adviser:

"The trembling and unquiet has almost ceased; I have less nightly turmoil and visions; my carnal appetite seems to be amply mollified and soothed by these viands, whatever may be their ultimate effect upon the weakness of our common sinful nature. But I should not be truthful to you if I did not warn you that I am viewing with the deepest spiritual concern a decided tendency toward sloth, and a folding of the hands over matters that often, I fear, are spiritual as well as temporal. I would ask you to consider, in a spirit of love, if it be not wise to rouse my apathetic flesh, so as to strive, even with the feeblest exhortations, against this sloth in others—if only to keep one's self from falling into the pit of easy indulgence."

What answer he received is not known, but it is to be presumed that he kept loyal faith with his physician, and gave himself up to simple walks and rides and occasional meditation. His solitude was not broken in upon; curiosity was too active a vice, and induced too much exertion for his indolent neighbors, and the Americano's basking seclusion, though unlike the habits of his countrymen, did not affect them. The shopkeeper and innkeeper saluted him always with a profound courtesy which awakened his slight resentment, partly because he was conscious that it was grateful to him, and partly that he felt he ought to have provoked in them a less satisfied condition.

Once, when he had unwittingly passed the confines of his own garden, through a gap in the Mission orchard, a lissome, black-coated shadow slipped past him with an obeisance so profound and gentle that he was startled at first into an awkward imitation of it himself, and then into an angry self-examination. He knew that he loathed that long-skirted, womanlike garment, that dangling, ostentatious symbol, that air of secrecy and mystery, and he inflated his chest above his loosely tied cravat and unbuttoned waistcoat with a contrasted sense of freedom. But he was conscious the next day of weakly avoiding a recurrence of this meeting, and in his self-examination put it down to his self-disciplined observance of his doctor's orders. But when he was strong again, and fitted for his Master's work, how strenuously he should improve the occasion this gave him of attacking the Scarlet Woman among her slaves and worshipers!

His afternoon meditations and the perusal of his only book—the Bible—were regularly broken in upon at about sunset by two or three strokes from the cracked bell that hung in the open belfry which reared itself beyond the gnarled pear tees. He could not say that it was aggressive or persistent, like his own church bells, nor that it even expressed to him any religious sentiment. Moreover, it was not a "Sabbath" bell, but a DAILY one, and even then seemed to be only a signal to ears easily responsive, rather than a stern reminder. And the hour was always a singularly witching one.

It was when the sun had slipped from the glaring red roofs, and the yellowing adobe of the Mission walls and the tall ranks of wild oats on the hillside were all of the one color of old gold. It was when the quivering heat of the arroyo and dusty expanse of plaza was blending with the soft breath of the sea fog that crept through the clefts of the coast range, until a refreshing balm seemed to fall like a benediction on all nature. It was when the trade-wind-swept and irritated surfaces of the rocky gorge beyond were soothed with clinging vapors; when the pines above no longer rocked monotonously, and the great undulating sea of the wild-oat plains had gone down and was at rest. It was at this hour, one afternoon, that, with the released scents of the garden, there came to him a strange and subtle perfume that was new to his senses. He laid aside his book, went into the garden, and, half-unconscious of his trespass, passed through the Mission orchard and thence into the little churchyard beside the church.

Looking at the strange inscriptions in an unfamiliar tongue, he was singularly touched with the few cheap memorials lying upon the graves—like childish toys—and for the moment overlooked the papistic emblems that accompanied them. It struck him vaguely that Death, the common leveler, had made even the symbols of a faith eternal inferior to those simple records of undying memory and affection, and he was for a moment startled into doubt.

He walked to the door of the church; to his surprise it was open. Standing upon the threshold, he glanced inside, and stood for a moment utterly bewildered. In a man of refined taste and education that bizarre and highly colored interior would have only provoked a smile or shrug; to Stephen Masterton's highly emotional nature, but artistic inexperience, strangely enough it was profoundly impressive. The heavily timbered, roughly hewn roof, barred with alternate bands of blue and Indian red, the crimson hangings, the gold and black draperies, affected this religious backwoodsman exactly as they were designed to affect the heathen and acolytes for whose conversion the temple had been reared. He could scarcely take his eyes from the tinsel-crowned Mother of Heaven, resplendent in white and gold and glittering with jewels; the radiant shield before the Host, illuminated by tall spectral candles in the mysterious obscurity of the altar, dazzled him like the rayed disk of the setting sun.

A gentle murmur, as of the distant sea, came from the altar. In his naive bewilderment he had not seen the few kneeling figures in the shadow of column and aisle; it was not until a man, whom he recognized as a muleteer he had seen that afternoon gambling and drinking in the fonda, slipped by him like a shadow and sank upon his knees in the center of the aisle that he realized the overpowering truth.

HE, Stephen Masterton, was looking upon some rite of Popish idolatry! He was turning quickly away when the keeper of the tienda—a man of sloth and sin—gently approached him from the shadow of a column with a mute gesture, which he took to be one of invitation. A fierce protest of scorn and indignation swelled to his throat, but died upon his lips. Yet he had strength enough to erect his gaunt emaciated figure, throwing out his long arms and extended palms in the attitude of defiant exorcism, and then rush swiftly from the church. As he did so he thought he saw a faint smile cross the shopkeeper's face, and a whispered exchange of words with a neighboring worshiper of more exalted appearance came to his ears. But it was not intelligible to his comprehension.

The next day he wrote to his doctor in that quaint grandiloquence of written speech with which the half-educated man balances the slips of his colloquial phrasing:

Do not let the purgation of my flesh be unduly protracted. What with the sloth and idolatries of Baal and Ashteroth, which I see daily around me, I feel that without a protest not only the flesh but the spirit is mortified. But my bodily strength is mercifully returning, and I found myself yesterday able to take a long ride at that hour which they here keep sacred for an idolatrous rite, under the beautiful name of "The Angelus." Thus do they bear false witness to Him! Can you tell me the meaning of the Spanish words "Don Keyhotter"? I am ignorant of these sensuous Southern languages, and am aware that this is not the correct spelling, but I have striven to give the phonetic equivalent. It was used, I am inclined to think, in reference to MYSELF, by an idolater.

P.S.—You need not trouble yourself. I have just ascertained that the words in question were simply the title of an idle novel, and, of course, could not possibly refer to ME.

Howbeit it was as "Don Quixote"—that is, the common Spaniard's conception of the Knight of La Mancha, merely the simple fanatic and madman—that Mr. Stephen Masterton ever after rode all unconsciously through the streets of the Mission, amid the half-pitying, half-smiling glances of the people.

In spite of his meditations, his single volume, and his habit of retiring early, he found his evenings were growing lonely and tedious. He missed the prayer meeting, and, above all, the hymns. He had a fine baritone voice, sympathetic, as may be imagined, but not cultivated. One night, in the seclusion of his garden, and secure in his distance from other dwellings, he raised his voice in a familiar camp-meeting hymn with a strong Covenanter's ring in the chorus. Growing bolder as he went on, he at last filled the quiet night with the strenuous sweep of his chant. Surprised at his own fervor, he paused for a moment, listening, half frightened, half ashamed of his outbreak. But there was only the trilling of the night wind in the leaves, or the far-off yelp of a coyote.

For a moment he thought he heard the metallic twang of a stringed instrument in the Mission garden beyond his own, and remembered his contiguity to the church with a stir of defiance. But he was relieved, nevertheless. His pent-up emotion had found vent, and without the nervous excitement that had followed his old exaltation. That night he slept better. He had found the Lord again—with Psalmody!

The next evening he chanced upon a softer hymn of the same simplicity, but with a vein of human tenderness in its aspirations, which his more hopeful mood gently rendered. At the conclusion of the first verse he was, however, distinctly conscious of being followed by the same twanging sound he had heard on the previous night, and which even his untutored ear could recognize as an attempt to accompany him. But before he had finished the second verse the unknown player, after an ingenious but ineffectual essay to grasp the right chord, abandoned it with an impatient and almost pettish flourish, and a loud bang upon the sounding-board of the unseen instrument. Masterton finished it alone.

With his curiosity excited, however, he tried to discover the locality of the hidden player. The sound evidently came from the Mission garden; but in his ignorance of the language he could not even interrogate his Indian housekeeper. On the third night, however, his hymn was uninterrupted by any sound from the former musician. A sense of disappointment, he knew not why, came over him. The kindly overture of the unseen player had been a relief to his loneliness. Yet he had barely concluded the hymn when the familiar sound again struck his ears. But this time the musician played boldly, confidently, and with a singular skill on the instrument.

The brilliant prelude over, to his entire surprise and some confusion, a soprano voice, high, childish, but infinitely quaint and fascinating, was mischievously uplifted. But alas! even to his ears, ignorant of the language, it was very clearly a song of levity and wantonness, of freedom and license, of coquetry and incitement! Yet such was its fascination that he fancied it was reclaimed by the delightful childlike and innocent expression of the singer.

Enough that this tall, gaunt, broad-shouldered man arose and, overcome by a curiosity almost as childlike, slipped into the garden and glided with an Indian softness of tread toward the voice. The moon shone full upon the ruined Mission wall tipped with clusters of dark foliage. Half hiding, half mingling with one of them—an indistinct bulk of light-colored huddled fleeces like an extravagant bird's nest—hung the unknown musician. So intent was the performer's preoccupation that Masterton actually reached the base of the wall immediately below the figure without attracting its attention. But his foot slipped on the crumbling debris with a snapping of dry twigs. There was a quick little cry from above. He had barely time to recover his position before the singer, impulsively leaning over the parapet, had lost hers, and fell outward. But Masterton was tall, alert, and self-possessed, and threw out his long arms. The next moment they were full of soft flounces, a struggling figure was against his breast, and a woman's frightened little hands around his neck. But he had broken her fall, and almost instantly, yet with infinite gentleness, he released her unharmed, with hardly her crisp flounces crumpled, in an upright position against the wall. Even her guitar, still hanging from her shoulder by a yellow ribbon, had bounded elastic and resounding against the wall, but lay intact at her satin-slippered feet. She caught it up with another quick little cry, but this time more of sauciness than fear, and drew her little hand across its strings, half defiantly.

"I hope you are not hurt?" said the circuit preacher, gravely.

She broke into a laugh so silvery that he thought it no extravagance to liken it to the moonbeams that played over her made audible. She was lithe, yet plump; barred with black and yellow and small-waisted like a pretty wasp. Her complexion in that light was a sheen of pearl satin that made her eyes blacker and her little mouth redder than any other color could. She was small, but, remembering the fourteen-year-old wife of the shopkeeper, he felt that, for all her childish voice and features, she was a grown woman, and a sudden shyness took hold of him.

But she looked pertly in his face, stood her guitar upright before her, and put her hands behind her back as she leaned saucily against the wall and shrugged her shoulders.

"It was the fault of you," she said, in a broken English that seemed as much infantine as foreign. "What for you not remain to yourself in your own CASA? So it come. You creep so—in the dark—and shake my wall, and I fall. And she," pointing to the guitar, "is a'most broke! And for all thees I have only make to you a serenade. Ingrate!"

"I beg your pardon," said Masterton quickly, "but I was curious. I thought I might help you, and—"

"Make yourself another cat on the wall, eh? No; one is enough, thank you!"

A frown lowered on Masterton's brow. "You don't understand me," he said, bluntly. "I did not know WHO was here."

"Ah, BUENO! Then it is Pepita Ramirez, you see," she said, tapping her bodice with one little finger, "all the same; the niece from Manuel Garcia, who keeps the Mission garden and lif there. And you?"

"My name is Masterton."

"How mooch?"

"Masterton," he repeated.

She tried to pronounce it once or twice desperately, and then shook her little head so violently that a yellow rose fastened over her ear fell to the ground. But she did not heed it, nor the fact that Masterton had picked it up.

"Ah, I cannot!" she said, poutingly. "It is as deefeecult to make go as my guitar with your serenade."

"Can you not say 'Stephen Masterton'?" he asked, more gently, with a returning and forgiving sense of her childishness.

"Es-stefen? Ah, ESTEBAN! Yes; Don Esteban! BUENO! Then, Don Esteban, what for you sink so melank-olly one night, and one night so fierce? The melank-olly, he ees not so bad; but the fierce—ah! he is weeked! Ess it how the Americano make always his serenade?"

Masterton's brow again darkened. And his hymn of exultation had been mistaken by these people—by this—this wanton child!

"It was no serenade," he replied, curtly; "it was in the praise of the Lord!"

"Of how mooch?"

"Of the Lord of Hosts—of the Almighty in Heaven." He lifted his long arms reverently on high.

"Oh!" she said, with a frightened look, slightly edging away from the wall. At a secure distance she stopped. "Then you are a soldier, Don Esteban?"

"No!"

"Then what for you sink 'I am a soldier of the Lord,' and you will make die 'in His army'? Oh, yes; you have said." She gathered up her guitar tightly under her arm, shook her small finger at him gravely, and said, "You are a hoombog, Don Esteban; good a' night," and began to glide away.

"One moment, Miss—Miss Ramirez," called Masterton. "I—that is you—you have—forgotten your rose," he added, feebly, holding up the flower. She halted.

"Ah, yes; he have drop, you have pick him up, he is yours. I have drop, you have pick ME up, but I am NOT yours. Good a' night, COMANDANTE Don Esteban!"

With a light laugh she ran along beside the wall for a little distance, suddenly leaped up and disappeared in one of the largest gaps in its ruined and helpless structure. Stephen Masterton gazed after her stupidly, still holding the rose in his hand. Then he threw it away and re-entered his home.

Lighting his candle, he undressed himself, prayed fervently—so fervently that all remembrance of the idle, foolish incident was wiped from his mind, and went to bed. He slept well and dreamlessly. The next morning, when his thoughts recurred to the previous night, this seemed to him a token that he had not deviated from his spiritual integrity; it did not occur to him that the thought itself was a tacit suspicion.

So his feet quite easily sought the garden again in the early sunshine, even to the wall where she had stood. But he had not taken into account the vivifying freshness of the morning, the renewed promise of life and resurrection in the pulsing air and potent sunlight, and as he stood there he seemed to see the figure of the young girl again leaning against the wall in all the charm of her irrepressible and innocent youth. More than that, he found the whole scene re-enacting itself before him; the nebulous drapery half hidden in the foliage, the cry and the fall; the momentary soft contact of the girl's figure against his own, the clinging arms around his neck, the brush and fragrance of her flounces—all this came back to him with a strength he had NOT felt when it occurred.

He was turning hurriedly away when his eyes fell upon the yellow rose still lying in the debris where he had thrown it—but still pure, fresh, and unfaded. He picked it up again, with a singular fancy that it was the girl herself, and carried it into the house.

As he placed it half shyly in a glass on his table a wonderful thought occurred to him. Was not the episode of last night a special providence? Was not that young girl, wayward and childlike, a mere neophyte in her idolatrous religion, as yet unsteeped in sloth and ignorance, presented to him as a brand to be snatched from the burning? Was not this the opportunity of conversion he had longed for—this the chance of exercising his gifts of exhortation that he had been hiding in the napkin of solitude and seclusion? Nay, was not all this PREDESTINED? His illness, his consequent exile to this land of false gods—this contiguity to the Mission—was not all this part of a supremely ordered plan for the girl's salvation—and was HE not elected and ordained for that service? Nay, more, was not the girl herself a mere unconscious instrument in the hands of a higher power; was not her voluntary attempt to accompany him in his devotional exercise a vague stirring of that predestined force within her? Was not even that wantonness and frivolity contrasted with her childishness—which he had at first misunderstood—the stirrings of the flesh and the spirit, and was he to abandon her in that struggle of good and evil?

He lifted his bowed head, that had been resting on his arm before the little flower on the table—as if it were a shrine—with a flash of resolve in his blue eyes. The wrinkled Concepcion coming to her duties in the morning scarcely recognized her gloomily abstracted master in this transfigured man. He looked ten years younger.

She met his greeting, and the few direct inquiries that his new resolve enabled him to make more freely, with some information—which a later talk with the shopkeeper, who had a fuller English vocabulary, confirmed in detail.

"YES! truly this was a niece of the Mission gardener, who lived with her uncle in the ruined wing of the presidio. She had taken her first communion four years ago. Ah, yes, she was a great musician, and could play on the organ. And the guitar, ah, yes—of a certainty. She was gay, and flirted with the caballeros, young and old, but she cared not for any."

Whatever satisfaction this latter statement gave Masterton, he believed it was because the absence of any disturbing worldly affection would make her an easier convert.

But how continue this chance acquaintance and effect her conversion? For the first time Masterton realized the value of expediency; while his whole nature impelled him to seek her society frankly and publicly and exhort her openly, he knew that this was impossible; still more, he remembered her unmistakable fright at his first expression of faith; he must "be wise as the serpent and harmless as the dove." He must work upon her soul alone, and secretly. He, who would have shrunk from any clandestine association with a girl from mere human affection, saw no wrong in a covert intimacy for the purpose of religious salvation. Ignorant as he was of the ways of the world, and inexperienced in the usages of society, he began to plan methods of secretly meeting her with all the intrigue of a gallant. The perspicacity as well as the intuition of a true lover had descended upon him in this effort of mere spiritual conquest.

Armed with his information and a few Spanish words, he took the yellow Concepcion aside and gravely suborned her to carry a note to be delivered secretly to Miss Ramirez. To his great relief and some surprise the old woman grinned with intelligence, and her withered hand closed with a certain familiar dexterity over the epistle and the accompanying gratuity. To a man less naively one-ideaed it might have awakened some suspicion; but to the more sanguine hopefulness of Masterton it only suggested the fancy that Concepcion herself might prove to be open to conversion, and that he should in due season attempt HER salvation also. But that would be later. For Concepcion was always with him and accessible; the girl was not.

The note, which had cost him some labor of composition, simple and almost businesslike as was the result, ran as follows:

"I wish to see you upon some matter of grave concern to yourself. Will you oblige me by coming again to the wall of the Mission tonight at early candlelight? It would avert worldly suspicion if you brought also your guitar."

The afternoon dragged slowly on; Concepcion returned; she had, with great difficulty, managed to see the senorita, but not alone; she had, however, slipped the note into her hand, not daring to wait for an answer.

In his first hopefulness Masterton did not doubt what the answer would be, but as evening approached he grew concerned as to the girl's opportunities of coming, and regretted that he had not given her a choice of time.

Before his evening meal was finished he began to fear for her willingness, and doubt the potency of his note. He was accustomed to exhort ORALLY—perhaps he ought to have waited for the chance of SPEAKING to her directly without writing.

When the moon rose he was already in the garden. Lingering at first in the shadow of an olive tree, he waited until the moonbeams fell on the wall and its crests of foliage. But nothing moved among that ebony tracery; his ear was strained for the familiar tinkle of the guitar—all was silent. As the moon rose higher he at last boldly walked to the wall, and listened for any movement on the other side of it. But nothing stirred. She was evidently NOT coming—his note had failed.

He was turning away sadly, but as he faced his home again he heard a light laugh beside him. He stopped. A black shadow stepped out from beneath his own almond tree. He started when, with a gesture that seemed familiar to him, the upper part of the shadow seemed to fall away with a long black mantilla and the face of the young girl was revealed.

He could see now that she was clad in black lace from head to foot. She looked taller, older, and he fancied even prettier than before. A sudden doubt of his ability to impress her, a swift realization of all the difficulties of the attempt, and, for the first time perhaps, a dim perception of the incongruity of the situation came over him.

"I was looking for you on the wall," he stammered.

"MADRE DE DIOS!" she retorted, with a laugh and her old audacity, "you would that I shall ALWAYS hang there, and drop upon you like a pear when you shake the tree? No!"

"You haven't brought your guitar," he continued, still more awkwardly, as he noticed that she held only a long black fan in her hand.

"For why? You would that I PLAY it, and when my uncle say 'Where go Pepita? She is loss,' someone shall say, 'Oh! I have hear her tink-a-tink in the garden of the Americano, who lif alone.' And then—it ess finish!"

Masterton began to feel exceedingly uncomfortable. There was something in this situation that he had not dreamed of. But with the persistency of an awkward man he went on.

"But you played on the wall the other night, and tried to accompany me."

"But that was lass night and on the wall. I had not speak to you, you had not speak to me. You had not sent me the leetle note by your peon." She stopped, and suddenly opening her fan before her face, so that only her mischievous eyes were visible, added: "You had not asked me then to come to hear you make lof to me, Don Esteban. That is the difference."

The circuit preacher felt the blood rush to his face. Anger, shame, mortification, remorse, and fear alternately strove with him, but above all and through all he was conscious of a sharp, exquisite pleasure—that frightened him still more. Yet he managed to exclaim:

"No! no! You cannot think me capable of such a cowardly trick?"

The girl started, more at the unmistakable sincerity of his utterance than at the words, whose full meaning she may have only imperfectly caught.

"A treek? A treek?" she slowly and wonderingly repeated. Then suddenly, as if comprehending him, she turned her round black eyes full upon him and dropped her fan from her face.

"And WHAT for you ask me to come here then?"

"I wanted to talk with you," he began, "on far more serious matters. I wished to—" but he stopped. He could not address this quaint child-woman staring at him in black-eyed wonder, in either the measured or the impetuous terms with which he would have exhorted a maturer responsible being. He made a step toward her; she drew back, striking at his extended hand half impatiently, half mischievously with her fan.

He flushed—and then burst out bluntly, "I want to talk with you about your soul."

"My what?"

"Your immortal soul, unhappy girl."

"What have you to make with that? Are you a devil?" Her eyes grew rounder, though she faced him boldly.

"I am a Minister of the Gospel," he said, in hurried entreaty. "You must hear me for a moment. I would save your soul."

"My immortal soul lif with the Padre at the Mission—you moost seek her there! My mortal BODY," she added, with a mischievous smile, "say to you, 'good a' night, Don Esteban.'" She dropped him a little curtsy and—ran away.

"One moment, Miss Ramirez," said Masterton, eagerly; but she had already slipped beyond his reach. He saw her little black figure passing swiftly beside the moonlit wall, saw it suddenly slide into a shadowy fissure, and vanish.

In his blank disappointment he could not bear to re-enter the house he had left so sanguinely a few moments before, but walked moodily in the garden. His discomfiture was the more complete since he felt that his defeat was owing to some mistake in his methods, and not the incorrigibility of his subject.

Was it not a spiritual weakness in him to have resented so sharply the girl's imputation that he wished to make love to her? He should have borne it as Christians had even before now borne slander and false testimony for their faith! He might even have ACCEPTED it, and let the triumph of her conversion in the end prove his innocence. Or was his purpose incompatible with that sisterly affection he had so often preached to the women of his flock? He might have taken her hand, and called her "Sister Pepita," even as he had called Deborah "Sister." He recalled the fact that he had for an instant held her struggling in his arms: he remembered the thrill that the recollection had caused him, and somehow it now sent a burning blush across his face. He hurried back into the house.

The next day a thousand wild ideas took the place of his former settled resolution. He would seek the Padre, this custodian of the young girl's soul; he would convince HIM of his error, or beseech him to give him an equal access to her spirit! He would seek the uncle of the girl, and work upon his feelings.

Then for three or four days he resolved to put the young girl from his mind, trusting after the fashion of his kind for some special revelation from a supreme source as an indication for his conduct. This revelation presently occurred, as it is apt to occur when wanted.

One evening his heart leaped at the familiar sound of Pepita's guitar in the distance. Whatever his ultimate intention now, he hurriedly ran into the garden. The sound came from the former direction, but as he unhesitatingly approached the Mission wall, he could see that she was not upon it, and as the notes of her guitar were struck again, he knew that they came from the other side. But the chords were a prelude to one of his own hymns, and he stood entranced as her sweet, childlike voice rose with the very words that he had sung. The few defects were those of purely oral imitation, the accents, even the slight reiteration of the "s," were Pepita's own:

```
Cheeldren oof the Heavenly King,
As ye journey essweetly ssing;
Essing your great Redeemer's praise,
Glorioos in Hees works and ways.
```

He was astounded. Her recollection of the air and words was the more wonderful, for he remembered now that he had only sung that particular hymn once. But to his still greater delight and surprise, her voice rose again in the second verse, with a touch of plaintiveness that swelled his throat:

```
We are traveling home to God,
In the way our farzers trod,
They are happy now, and we
Soon their happiness shall see.
```

The simple, almost childish words—so childish that they might have been the fitting creation of her own childish lips—here died away with a sweep and crash of the whole strings. Breathless silence followed, in which Stephen Masterton could feel the beatings of his own heart.

"Miss Ramirez," he called, in a voice that scarcely seemed his own. There was no reply. "Pepita!" he repeated; it was strangely like the accent of a lover, but he no longer cared. Still the singer's voice was silent.

Then he ran swiftly beside the wall, as he had seen her run, until he came to the fissure. It was overgrown with vines and brambles almost as impenetrable as an abatis, but if she had pierced it in her delicate crape dress, so could he! He brushed roughly through, and found himself in a glimmering aisle of pear trees close by the white wall of the Mission church.

For a moment in that intricate tracing of ebony and ivory made by the rising moon, he was dazzled, but evidently his irruption into the orchard had not been as lithe and silent as her own, for a figure in a parti-colored dress suddenly started into activity, and running from the wall, began to course through the trees until it became apparently a part of that involved pattern. Nothing daunted, however, Stephen Masterton pursued, his speed increased as he recognized the flounces of Pepita's barred dress, but the young girl had the advantage of knowing the locality, and could evade her pursuer by unsuspected turns and doubles.

For some moments this fanciful sylvan chase was kept up in perfect silence; it might have been a woodland nymph pursued by a wandering shepherd. Masterton presently saw that she was making toward a tiled roof that was now visible as projecting over the presidio wall, and was evidently her goal of refuge. He redoubled his speed; with skillful audacity and sheer strength of his broad shoulders he broke through a dense ceanothus hedge which Pepita was swiftly skirting, and suddenly appeared between her and her house.

With her first cry, the young girl turned and tried to bury herself in the hedge; but in another stride the circuit preacher was at her side, and caught her panting figure in his arms.

While he had been running he had swiftly formulated what he should do and what he should say to her. To his simple appeal for her companionship and willing ear he would add a brotherly tenderness, that should invite her trustfulness in him; he would confess his wrong and ask her forgiveness of his abrupt solicitations; he would propose to teach her more hymns, they would practice psalmody together; even this priest, the custodian of her soul, could not object to that; but chiefly he would thank her: he would tell her how she had pleased him, and this would lead to more serious and thoughtful converse. All this was in his mind while he ran, was upon his lips as he caught her and for an instant she lapsed, exhausted, in his arms. But, alas! even in that moment he suddenly drew her toward him, and kissed her as only a lover could!

The wire grass was already yellowing on the Tasajara plains with the dusty decay of the long, dry summer when Dr. Duchesne returned to Tasajara. He came to see the wife of Deacon Sanderson, who, having for the twelfth time added to the population of the settlement, was not "doing as well" as everybody—except, possibly, Dr. Duchesne—expected. After he had made this hollow-eyed, over-burdened, undernourished woman as comfortable as he could in her rude, neglected surroundings, to change the dreary chronicle of suffering, he turned to the husband, and said, "And what has become of Mr. Masterton, who used to be in your—vocation?" A long groan came from the deacon.

"Hallo! I hope he has not had a relapse," said the doctor, earnestly. "I thought I'd knocked all that nonsense out of him—I beg your pardon—I mean," he added, hurriedly, "he wrote to me only a few weeks ago that he was picking up his strength again and doing well!"

"In his weak, gross, sinful flesh—yes, no doubt," returned the Deacon, scornfully, "and, perhaps, even in a worldly sense, for those who value the vanities of life; but he is lost to us, for all time, and lost to eternal life forever. Not," he continued in sanctimonious vindictiveness, "but that I often had my doubts of Brother Masterton's steadfastness. He was too much given to imagery and song."

"But what has he done?" persisted Dr. Duchesne.

"Done! He has embraced the Scarlet Woman!"

"Dear me!" said the doctor, "so soon? Is it anybody you knew here?—not anybody's wife? Eh?"

"He has entered the Church of Rome," said the Deacon, indignantly, "he has forsaken the God of his fathers for the tents of the idolaters; he is the consort of Papists and the slave of the Pope!"

"But are you SURE?" said Dr. Duchesne, with perhaps less concern than before.

"Sure," returned the Deacon angrily, "didn't Brother Bulkley, on account of warning reports made by a God-fearing and soul-seeking teamster, make a special pilgrimage to this land of Sodom to inquire and spy out its wickedness? Didn't he find Stephen Masterton steeped in the iniquity of practicing on an organ—he that scorned even a violin or harmonium in the tents of the Lord—in an idolatrous chapel, with a foreign female Papist for a teacher? Didn't he find him a guest at the board of a Jesuit priest, visiting the schools of the Mission where this young Jezebel of a singer teaches the children to chant in unknown tongues? Didn't he find him living with a wrinkled Indian witch who called him 'Padrone'—and speaking her gibberish? Didn't he find him, who left here a man mortified in flesh and spirit and pale with striving with sinners, fat and rosy from native wines and fleshpots, and even vain and gaudy in colored apparel? And last of all, didn't Brother Bulkley hear that a rumor was spread far and wide that this miserable backslider was to take to himself a wife—in one of these strange women—that very Jezebel who seduced him? What do you call that?"

"It looks a good deal like human nature," said the doctor, musingly, "but I call it a cure!"

* * * * * * * * * *

THE INDISCRETION OF ELSBETH

The American paused. He had evidently lost his way. For the last half hour he had been wandering in a medieval town, in a profound medieval dream. Only a few days had elapsed since he had left the steamship that carried him hither; and the accents of his own tongue, the idioms of his own people, and the sympathetic community of New World tastes and expressions still filled his mind until he woke up, or rather, as it seemed to him, was falling asleep in the past of this Old World town which had once held his ancestors. Although a republican, he had liked to think of them in quaint distinctive garb, representing state and importance—perhaps even aristocratic pre-eminence—content to let the responsibility of such "bad eminence" rest with them entirely, but a habit of conscientiousness and love for historic truth eventually led him also to regard an honest BAUER standing beside his cattle in the quaint market place, or a kindly-faced black-eyed DIENSTMADCHEN in a doorway, with a timid, respectful interest, as a possible type of his progenitors. For, unlike some of his traveling countrymen in Europe, he was not a snob, and it struck him—as an American—that it was, perhaps, better to think of his race as having improved than as having degenerated. In these ingenuous meditations he had passed the long rows of quaint, high houses, whose sagging roofs and unpatched dilapidations were yet far removed from squalor, until he had reached the road bordered by poplars, all so unlike his own country's waysides—and knew that he had wandered far from his hotel.

He did not care, however, to retrace his steps and return by the way he had come. There was, he reasoned, some other street or turning that would eventually bring him to the market place and his hotel, and yet extend his experience of the town. He turned at right angles into a narrow grass lane, which was, however, as neatly kept and apparently as public as the highway. A few moments' walking convinced him that it was not a thoroughfare and that it led to the open gates of a park. This had something of a public look, which suggested that his intrusion might be at least a pardonable trespass, and he relied, like most strangers, on the exonerating quality of a stranger's ignorance. The park lay in the direction he wished to go, and yet it struck him as singular that a park of such extent should be still allowed to occupy such valuable urban space. Indeed, its length seemed to be illimitable as he wandered on, until he became conscious that he must have again lost his way, and he diverged toward the only boundary, a high, thickset hedge to the right, whose line he had been following.

As he neared it he heard the sound of voices on the other side, speaking in German, with which he was unfamiliar. Having, as yet, met no one, and being now impressed with the fact that for a public place the park was singularly deserted, he was conscious that his position was getting serious, and he determined to take this only chance of inquiring his way. The hedge was thinner in some places than in others, and at times he could see not only the light through it but even the moving figures of the speakers, and the occasional white flash of a summer gown. At last he determined to penetrate it, and with little difficulty emerged on the other side. But here he paused motionless. He found himself behind a somewhat formal and symmetrical group of figures with their backs toward him, but all stiffened into attitudes as motionless as his own, and all gazing with a monotonous intensity in the direction of a handsome building, which had been invisible above the hedge but which now seemed to arise suddenly before him. Some of the figures were in uniform. Immediately before him, but so slightly separated from the others that he was enabled to see the house between her and her companions, he was confronted by the pretty back, shoulders, and blond braids of a young girl of twenty. Convinced that he had unwittingly intruded upon some august ceremonial, he instantly slipped back into the hedge, but so silently that his momentary presence was evidently undetected. When he regained the park side he glanced back through the interstices; there was no movement of the figures nor break in the silence to indicate that his intrusion had been observed. With a long breath of relief he hurried from the park.

It was late when he finally got back to his hotel. But his little modern adventure had, I fear, quite outrun his previous medieval reflections, and almost his first inquiry of the silver-chained porter in the courtyard was in regard to the park. There was no public park in Alstadt! The Herr possibly alluded to the Hof Gardens—the Schloss, which was in the direction he indicated. The Schloss was the residency of the hereditary Grand Duke. JA WOHL! He was stopping there with several Hoheiten. There was naturally a party there—a family reunion. But it was a private enclosure. At times, when the Grand Duke was "not in residence," it was open to the public. In point of fact, at such times tickets of admission were to be had at the hotel for fifty pfennige each. There was not, of truth, much to see except a model farm and dairy—the pretty toy of a previous Grand Duchess.

But he seemed destined to come into closer collision with the modern life of Alstadt. On entering the hotel, wearied by his long walk, he passed the landlord and a man in half-military uniform on the landing near his room. As he entered his apartment he had a vague impression, without exactly knowing why, that the landlord and the military stranger had just left it. This feeling was deepened by the evident disarrangement of certain articles in his unlocked portmanteau and the disorganization of his writing case. A wave of indignation passed over him. It was followed by a knock at the door, and the landlord blandly appeared with the stranger.

"A thousand pardons," said the former, smilingly, "but Herr Sanderman, the Ober-Inspector of Police, wishes to speak with you. I hope we are not intruding?"

"Not NOW," said the American, dryly.

The two exchanged a vacant and deprecating smile.

"I have to ask only a few formal questions," said the Ober-Inspector in excellent but somewhat precise English, "to supplement the report which, as a stranger, you may not know is required by the police from the landlord in regard to the names and quality of his guests who are foreign to the town. You have a passport?"

"I have," said the American still more dryly. "But I do not keep it in an unlocked portmanteau or an open writing case."

"An admirable precaution," said Sanderman, with unmoved politeness. "May I see it? Thanks," he added, glancing over the document which the American produced from his pocket. "I see that you are a born American citizen—and an earlier knowledge of that fact would have prevented this little contretemps. You are aware, Mr. Hoffman, that your name is German?"

"It was borne by my ancestors, who came from this country two centuries ago," said Hoffman, curtly.

"We are indeed honored by your return to it," returned Sanderman suavely, "but it was the circumstance of your name being a local one, and the possibility of your still being a German citizen liable to unperformed military duty, which has caused the trouble." His manner was clearly civil and courteous, but Hoffman felt that all the time his own face and features were undergoing a profound scrutiny from the speaker.

"And you are making sure that you will know me again?" said Hoffman, with a smile.

"I trust, indeed, both," returned Sanderman, with a bow, "although you will permit me to say that your description here," pointing to the passport, "scarcely does you justice. ACH GOTT! it is the same in all countries; the official eye is not that of the young DAMEN."

Hoffman, though not conceited, had not lived twenty years without knowing that he was very good-looking, yet there was something in the remark that caused him to color with a new uneasiness.

The Ober-Inspector rose with another bow, and moved toward the door. "I hope you will let me make amends for this intrusion by doing anything I can to render your visit here a pleasant one. Perhaps," he added, "it is not for long."

But Hoffman evaded the evident question, as he resented what he imagined was a possible sneer.

"I have not yet determined my movements," he said.

The Ober-Inspector brought his heels together in a somewhat stiffer military salute and departed.

Nothing, however, could have exceeded the later almost servile urbanity of the landlord, who seemed to have been proud of the official visit to his guest. He was profuse in his attentions, and even introduced him to a singularly artistic-looking man of middle age, wearing an order in his buttonhole, whom he met casually in the hall.

"Our Court photographer," explained the landlord with some fervor, "at whose studio, only a few houses distant, most of the Hoheiten and Prinzessinen of Germany have sat for their likenesses."

"I should feel honored if the distinguished American Herr would give me a visit," said the stranger gravely, as he gazed at Hoffman with an intensity which recalled the previous scrutiny of the Police Inspector, "and I would be charmed if he would avail himself of my poor skill to transmit his picturesque features to my unique collection."

Hoffman returned a polite evasion to this invitation, although he was conscious of being struck with this second examination of his face, and the allusion to his personality.

The next morning the porter met him with a mysterious air. The Herr would still like to see the Schloss? Hoffman, who had quite forgotten his adventure in the park, looked vacant. JA WOHL—the Hof authorities had no doubt heard of his visit and had intimated to the hotel proprietor that he might have permission to visit the model farm and dairy. As the American still looked indifferent the porter pointed out with some importance that it was a Ducal courtesy not to be lightly treated; that few, indeed, of the burghers themselves had ever been admitted to this eccentric whim of the late Grand Duchess. He would, of course, be silent about it; the Court would not like it known that they had made an exception to their rules in favor of a foreigner; he would enter quickly and boldly alone. There would be a housekeeper or a dairymaid to show him over the place.

More amused at this important mystery over what he, as an American, was inclined to classify as a "free pass" to a somewhat heavy "side show," he gravely accepted the permission, and the next morning after breakfast set out to visit the model farm and dairy. Dismissing his driver, as he had been instructed, Hoffman entered the gateway with a mingling of expectancy and a certain amusement over the "boldness" which the porter had suggested should characterize his entrance. Before him was a beautifully kept lane bordered by arbored and trellised roses, which seemed to sink into the distance. He was instinctively following it when he became aware that he was mysteriously accompanied by a man in the livery of a chasseur, who was walking among the trees almost abreast of him, keeping pace with his step, and after the first introductory military salute preserving a ceremonious silence. There was something so ludicrous in this solemn procession toward a peaceful, rural industry that by the time they had reached the bottom of the lane the American had quite recovered his good humor. But here a new astonishment awaited him. Nestling before him in a green amphitheater lay a little wooden farm-yard and outbuildings, which irresistibly suggested that it had been recently unpacked and set up from a box of Nuremberg toys. The symmetrical trees, the galleried houses with preternaturally glazed windows, even the spotty, disproportionately sized cows in the white-fenced barnyards were all unreal, wooden and toylike.

Crossing a miniature bridge over a little stream, from which he was quite prepared to hook metallic fish with a magnet their own size, he looked about him for some real being to dispel the illusion. The mysterious chasseur had disappeared. But under the arch of an arbor, which seemed to be composed of silk ribbons, green glass, and pink tissue paper, stood a quaint but delightful figure.

At first it seemed as if he had only dispelled one illusion for another. For the figure before him might have been made of Dresden china—so daintily delicate and unique it was in color and arrangement. It was that of a young girl dressed in some forgotten medieval peasant garb of velvet braids, silver-staylaced corsage, lace sleeves, and helmeted metallic comb. But, after the Dresden method, the pale yellow of her hair was repeated in her bodice, the pink of her cheeks was in the roses of her chintz overskirt. The blue of her eyes was the blue of her petticoat; the dazzling whiteness of her neck shone again in the sleeves and stockings. Nevertheless she was real and human, for the pink deepened in her cheeks as Hoffman's hat flew from his head, and she recognized the civility with a grave little curtsy.

"You have come to see the dairy," she said in quaintly accurate English; "I will show you the way."

"If you please," said Hoffman, gaily, "but—"

"But what?" she said, facing him suddenly with absolutely astonished eyes.

Hoffman looked into them so long that their frank wonder presently contracted into an ominous mingling of restraint and resentment. Nothing daunted, however, he went on:

"Couldn't we shake all that?"

The look of wonder returned. "Shake all that?" she repeated. "I do not understand."

"Well! I'm not positively aching to see cows, and you must be sick of showing them. I think, too, I've about sized the whole show. Wouldn't it be better if we sat down in that arbor—supposing it won't fall down—and you told me all about the lot? It would save you a heap of trouble and keep your pretty frock cleaner than trapesing round. Of course," he said, with a quick transition to the gentlest courtesy, "if you're conscientious about this thing we'll go on and not spare a cow. Consider me in it with you for the whole morning."

She looked at him again, and then suddenly broke into a charming laugh. It revealed a set of strong white teeth, as well as a certain barbaric trace in its cadence which civilized restraint had not entirely overlaid.

"I suppose she really is a peasant, in spite of that pretty frock," he said to himself as he laughed too.

But her face presently took a shade of reserve, and with a gentle but singular significance she said:

"I think you must see the dairy."

Hoffman's hat was in his hand with a vivacity that tumbled the brown curls on his forehead. "By all means," he said instantly, and began walking by her side in modest but easy silence. Now that he thought her a conscientious peasant he was quiet and respectful.

Presently she lifted her eyes, which, despite her gravity, had not entirely lost their previous mirthfulness, and said:

"But you Americans—in your rich and prosperous country, with your large lands and your great harvests—you must know all about farming."

"Never was in a dairy in my life," said Hoffman gravely. "I'm from the city of New York, where the cows give swill milk, and are kept in cellars."

Her eyebrows contracted prettily in an effort to understand. Then she apparently gave it up, and said with a slanting glint of mischief in her eyes:

"Then you come here like the other Americans in hope to see the Grand Duke and Duchess and the Princesses?"

"No. The fact is I almost tumbled into a lot of 'em—standing like wax figures—the other side of the park lodge, the other day—and got away as soon as I could. I think I prefer the cows."

Her head was slightly turned away. He had to content himself with looking down upon the strong feet in their serviceable but smartly buckled shoes that uplifted her upright figure as she moved beside him.

"Of course," he added with boyish but unmistakable courtesy, "if it's part of your show to trot out the family, why I'm in that, too. I dare say you could make them interesting."

"But why," she said with her head still slightly turned away toward a figure—a sturdy-looking woman, which, for the first time, Hoffman perceived was walking in a line with them as the chasseur had done—"why did you come here at all?"

"The first time was a fool accident," he returned frankly. "I was making a short cut through what I thought was a public park. The second time was because I had been rude to a Police Inspector whom I found going through my things, but who apologized—as I suppose—by getting me an invitation from the Grand Duke to come here, and I thought it only the square thing to both of 'em to accept it. But I'm mighty glad I came; I wouldn't have missed YOU for a thousand dollars. You see I haven't struck anyone I cared to talk to since." Here he suddenly remarked that she hadn't looked at him, and that the delicate whiteness of her neck was quite suffused with pink, and stopped instantly. Presently he said quite easily:

"Who's the chorus?"

"The lady?"

"Yes. She's watching us as if she didn't quite approve, you know—just as if she didn't catch on."

"She's the head housekeeper of the farm. Perhaps you would prefer to have her show you the dairy; shall I call her?"

The figure in question was very short and stout, with voluminous petticoats.

"Please don't; I'll stay without your setting that paperweight on me. But here's the dairy. Don't let her come inside among those pans of fresh milk with that smile, or there'll be trouble."

The young girl paused too, made a slight gesture with her hand, and the figure passed on as they entered the dairy. It was beautifully clean and fresh. With a persistence that he quickly recognized as mischievous and ironical, and with his characteristic adaptability accepted with even greater gravity and assumption of interest, she showed him all the details. From thence they passed to the farmyard, where he hung with breathless attention over the names of the cows and made her repeat them. Although she was evidently familiar with the subject, he could see that her zeal was fitful and impatient.

"Suppose we sit down," he said, pointing to an ostentatious rustic seat in the center of the green.

"Sir down?" she repeated wonderingly. "What for?"

"To talk. We'll knock off and call it half a day."

"But if you are not looking at the farm you are, of course, going," she said quickly.

"Am I? I don't think these particulars were in my invitation."

She again broke into a fit of laughter, and at the same time cast a bright eye around the field.

"Come," he said gently, "there are no other sightseers waiting, and your conscience is clear," and he moved toward the rustic seat.

"Certainly not—there," she added in a low voice.

They moved on slowly together to a copse of willows which overhung the miniature stream.

"You are not staying long in Alstadt?" she said.

"No; I only came to see the old town that my ancestors came from."

They were walking so close together that her skirt brushed his trousers, but she suddenly drew away from him, and looking him fixedly in the eye said:

"Ah, you have relations here?"

"Yes, but they are dead two hundred years."

She laughed again with a slight expression of relief. They had entered the copse and were walking in dense shadow when she suddenly stopped and sat down upon a rustic bench. To his surprise he found that they were quite alone.

"Tell me about these relatives," she said, slightly drawing aside her skirt to make room for him on the seat.

He did not require a second invitation. He not only told her all about his ancestral progenitors, but, I fear, even about those more recent and more nearly related to him; about his own life, his vocation—he was a clever newspaper correspondent with a roving commission—his ambitions, his beliefs and his romance.

"And then, perhaps, of this visit—you will also make 'copy'?"

He smiled at her quick adaptation of his professional slang, but shook his head.

"No," he said gravely. "No—this is YOU. The CHICAGO INTERVIEWER is big pay and is rich, but it hasn't capital enough to buy you from me."

He gently slid his hand toward hers and slipped his fingers softly around it. She made a slight movement of withdrawal, but even then—as if in forgetfulness or indifference—permitted her hand to rest unresponsively in his. It was scarcely an encouragement to gallantry, neither was it a rejection of an unconscious familiarity.

"But you haven't told me about yourself," he said.

"Oh, I," she returned, with her first approach to coquetry in a laugh and a sidelong glance, "of what importance is that to you? It is the Grand Duchess and Her Highness the Princess that you Americans seek to know. I am—what I am—as you see."

"You bet," said Hoffman with charming decision.

"I WHAT?"

"You ARE, you know, and that's good enough for me, but I don't even know your name."

She laughed again, and after a pause, said: "Elsbeth."

"But I couldn't call you by your first name on our first meeting, you know."

"Then you Americans are really so very formal—eh?" she said slyly, looking at her imprisoned hand.

"Well, yes," returned Hoffman, disengaging it. "I suppose we are respectful, or mean to be. But whom am I to inquire for? To write to?"

"You are neither to write nor inquire."

"What?" She had moved in her seat so as to half-face him with eyes in which curiosity, mischief, and a certain seriousness alternated, but for the first time seemed conscious of his hand, and accented her words with a slight pressure.

"You are to return to your hotel presently, and say to your landlord: 'Pack up my luggage. I have finished with this old town and my ancestors, and the Grand Duke, whom I do not care to see, and I shall leave Alstadt tomorrow!'"

"Thank you! I don't catch on."

"Of what necessity should you? I have said it. That should be enough for a chivalrous American like you." She again significantly looked down at her hand.

"If you mean that you know the extent of the favor you ask of me, I can say no more," he said seriously; "but give me some reason for it."

"Ah so!" she said, with a slight shrug of her shoulders. "Then I must tell you. You say you do not know the Grand Duke and Duchess. Well! THEY KNOW YOU. The day before yesterday you were wandering in the park, as you admit. You say, also, you got through the hedge and interrupted some ceremony. That ceremony was not a Court function, Mr. Hoffman, but something equally sacred—the photographing of the Ducal family before the Schloss. You say that you instantly withdrew. But after the photograph was taken the plate revealed a stranger standing actually by the side of the Princess Alexandrine, and even taking the PAS of the Grand Duke himself. That stranger was you!"

"And the picture was spoiled," said the American, with a quiet laugh.

"I should not say that," returned the lady, with a demure glance at her companion's handsome face, "and I do not believe that the Princess—who first saw the photograph—thought so either. But she is very young and willful, and has the reputation of being very indiscreet, and unfortunately she begged the photographer not to destroy the plate, but to give it to her, and to say nothing about it, except that the plate was defective, and to take another. Still it would have ended there if her curiosity had not led her to confide a description of the stranger to the Police Inspector, with the result you know."

"Then I am expected to leave town because I accidentally stumbled into a family group that was being photographed?"

"Because a certain Princess was indiscreet enough to show her curiosity about you," corrected the fair stranger.

"But look here! I'll apologize to the Princess, and offer to pay for the plate."

"Then you do want to see the Princess?" said the young girl smiling; "you are like the others."

"Bother the Princess! I want to see YOU. And I don't see how they can prevent it if I choose to remain."

"Very easily. You will find that there is something wrong with your passport, and you will be sent on to Pumpernickel for examination. You will unwittingly transgress some of the laws of the town and be ordered to leave it. You will be shadowed by the police until you quarrel with them—like a free American—and you are conducted to the frontier. Perhaps you will strike an officer who has insulted you, and then you are finished on the spot."

The American's crest rose palpably until it cocked his straw hat over his curls.

"Suppose I am content to risk it—having first laid the whole matter and its trivial cause before the American Minister, so that he could make it hot for this whole caboodle of a country if they happened to 'down me.' By Jove! I shouldn't mind being the martyr of an international episode if they'd spare me long enough to let me get the first 'copy' over to the other side." His eyes sparkled.

"You could expose them, but they would then deny the whole story, and you have no evidence. They would demand to know your informant, and I should be disgraced, and the Princess, who is already talked about, made a subject of scandal. But no matter! It is right that an American's independence shall not be interfered with."

She raised the hem of her handkerchief to her blue eyes and slightly turned her head aside. Hoffman gently drew the handkerchief away, and in so doing possessed himself of her other hand.

"Look here, Miss—Miss—Elsbeth. You know I wouldn't give you away, whatever happened. But couldn't I get hold of that photographer—I saw him, he wanted me to sit to him—and make him tell me?"

"He wanted you to sit to him," she said hurriedly, "and did you?"

"No," he replied. "He was a little too fresh and previous, though I thought he fancied some resemblance in me to somebody else."

"Ah!" She said something to herself in German which he did not understand, and then added aloud:

"You did well; he is a bad man, this photographer. Promise me you shall not sit for him."

"How can I if I'm fired out of the place like this?" He added ruefully, "But I'd like to make him give himself away to me somehow."

"He will not, and if he did he would deny it afterward. Do not go near him nor see him. Be careful that he does not photograph you with his instantaneous instrument when you are passing. Now you must go. I must see the Princess."

"Let me go, too. I will explain it to her," said Hoffman.

She stopped, looked at him keenly, and attempted to withdraw her hands. "Ah, then it IS so. It is the Princess you wish to see. You are curious—you, too; you wish to see this lady who is interested in you. I ought to have known it. You are all alike."

He met her gaze with laughing frankness, accepting her outburst as a charming feminine weakness, half jealousy, half coquetry—but retained her hands.

"Nonsense," he said. "I wish to see her that I may have the right to see you—that you shall not lose your place here through me; that I may come again."

"You must never come here again."

"Then you must come where I am. We will meet somewhere when you have an afternoon off. You shall show me the town—the houses of my ancestors—their tombs; possibly—if the Grand Duke rampages—the probable site of my own."

She looked into his laughing eyes with her clear, stedfast, gravely questioning blue ones. "Do not you Americans know that it is not the fashion here, in Germany, for the young men and the young women to walk together—unless they are VERLOBT?"

"VER—which?"

"Engaged." She nodded her head thrice: viciously, decidedly, mischievously.

"So much the better."

"ACH GOTT!" She made a gesture of hopelessness at his incorrigibility, and again attempted to withdraw her hands.

"I must go now."

"Well then, good-by."

It was easy to draw her closer by simply lowering her still captive hands. Then he suddenly kissed her coldly startled lips, and instantly released her. She as instantly vanished.

"Elsbeth," he called quickly. "Elsbeth!"

Her now really frightened face reappeared with a heightened color from the dense foliage—quite to his astonishment.

"Hush," she said, with her finger on her lips. "Are you mad?"

"I only wanted to remind you to square me with the Princess," he laughed as her head disappeared.

He strolled back toward the gate. Scarcely had he quitted the shrubbery before the same chasseur made his appearance with precisely the same salute; and, keeping exactly the same distance, accompanied him to the gate. At the corner of the street he hailed a droshky and was driven to his hotel.

The landlord came up smiling. He trusted that the Herr had greatly enjoyed himself at the Schloss. It was a distinguished honor—in fact, quite unprecedented. Hoffman, while he determined not to commit himself, nor his late fair companion, was nevertheless anxious to learn something more of her relations to the Schloss. So pretty, so characteristic, and marked a figure must be well known to sightseers. Indeed, once or twice the idea had crossed his mind with a slightly jealous twinge that left him more conscious of the impression she had made on him than he had deemed possible. He asked if the model farm and dairy were always shown by the same attendants.

"ACH GOTT! no doubt, yes; His Royal Highness had quite a retinue when he was in residence."

"And were these attendants in costume?"

"There was undoubtedly a livery for the servants."

Hoffman felt a slight republican irritation at the epithet—he knew not why. But this costume was rather a historical one; surely it was not entrusted to everyday menials—and he briefly described it.

His host's blank curiosity suddenly changed to a look of mysterious and arch intelligence.

"ACH GOTT! yes!" He remembered now (with his finger on his nose) that when there was a fest at the Schloss the farm and dairy were filled with shepherdesses, in quaint costume worn by the ladies of the Grand Duke's own theatrical company, who assumed the characters with great vivacity. Surely it was the same, and the Grand Duke had treated the Herr to this special courtesy. Yes—there was one pretty, blonde young lady—the Fraulein Wimpfenbuttel, a most popular soubrette, who would play it to the life! And the description fitted her to a hair! Ah, there was no doubt of it; many persons, indeed, had been so deceived.

But happily, now that he had given him the wink, the Herr could corroborate it himself by going to the theater tonight. Ah, it would be a great joke—quite colossal! if he took a front seat where she could see him. And the good man rubbed his hands in gleeful anticipation.

Hoffman had listened to him with a slow repugnance that was only equal to his gradual conviction that the explanation was a true one, and that he himself had been ridiculously deceived. The mystery of his fair companion's costume, which he had accepted as part of the "show"; the inconsistency of her manner and her evident occupation; her undeniable wish to terminate the whole episode with that single interview; her mingling of worldly aplomb and rustic innocence; her perfect self-control and experienced acceptance of his gallantry under the simulated attitude of simplicity—all now struck him as perfectly comprehensible. He recalled the actress's inimitable touch in certain picturesque realistic details in the dairy—which she had not spared him; he recognized it now even in their bowered confidences (how like a pretty ballet scene their whole interview on the rustic bench was!), and it breathed through their entire conversation—to their theatrical parting at the close! And the whole story of the photograph was, no doubt, as pure a dramatic invention as the rest! The Princess's romantic interest in him—that Princess who had never appeared (why had he not detected the old, well-worn, sentimental situation here?)—was all a part of it. The dark, mysterious hint of his persecution by the police was a necessary culmination to the little farce. Thank Heaven! he had not "risen" at the Princess, even if he had given himself away to the clever actress in her own humble role. Then the humor of the whole situation predominated and he laughed until the tears came to his eyes, and his forgotten ancestors might have turned over in their graves without his heeding them. And with this humanizing influence upon him he went to the theater.

It was capacious even for the town, and although the performance was a special one he had no difficulty in getting a whole box to himself. He tried to avoid this public isolation by sitting close to the next box, where there was a solitary occupant—an officer—apparently as lonely as himself. He had made up his mind that when his fair deceiver appeared he would let her see by his significant applause that he recognized her, but bore no malice for the trick she had played on him. After all, he had kissed her—he had no right to complain. If she should recognize him, and this recognition led to a withdrawal of her prohibition, and their better acquaintance, he would be a fool to cavil at her pleasant artifice. Her vocation was certainly a more independent and original one than that he had supposed; for its social quality and inequality he cared nothing. He found himself longing for the glance of her calm blue eyes, for the pleasant smile that broke the seriousness of her sweetly restrained lips. There was no doubt that he should know her even as the heroine of DER CZAR UND DER ZIMMERMANN on the bill before him. He was becoming impatient. And the performance evidently was waiting. A stir in the outer gallery, the clatter of sabers, the filing of uniforms into the royal box, and a triumphant burst from the orchestra showed the cause. As a few ladies and gentlemen in full evening dress emerged from the background of uniforms and took their places in the front of the box, Hoffman looked with some interest for the romantic Princess. Suddenly he saw a face and shoulders in a glitter of diamonds that startled him, and then a glance that transfixed him.

He leaned over to his neighbor. "Who is the young lady in the box?"

"The Princess Alexandrine."

"I mean the young lady in blue with blond hair and blue eyes."

"It is the Princess Alexandrine Elsbeth Marie Stephanie, the daughter of the Grand Duke—there is none other there."

"Thank you."

He sat silently looking at the rising curtain and the stage. Then he rose quietly, gathered his hat and coat, and left the box. When he reached the gallery he turned instinctively and looked back at the royal box. Her eyes had followed him, and as he remained a moment motionless in the doorway her lips parted in a grateful smile, and she waved her fan with a faint but unmistakable gesture of farewell.

The next morning he left Alstadt. There was some little delay at the Zoll on the frontier, and when Hoffman received back his trunk it was accompanied by a little sealed packet which was handed to him by the Customhouse Inspector. Hoffman did not open it until he was alone.

There hangs upon the wall of his modest apartment in New York a narrow, irregular photograph ingeniously framed, of himself standing side by side with a young German girl, who, in the estimation of his compatriots, is by no means stylish and only passably good-looking. When he is joked by his friends about the post of honor given to this production, and questioned as to the lady, he remains silent. The Princess Alexandrine Elsbeth Marie Stephanie von Westphalen-Alstadt, among her other royal qualities, knew whom to trust.

* * * * * * * * * *

THE DEVOTION OF ENRIQUEZ

In another chronicle which dealt with the exploits of "Chu Chu," a Californian mustang, I gave some space to the accomplishments of Enriquez Saltillo, who assisted me in training her, and who was also brother to Consuelo Saitillo, the young lady to whom I had freely given both the mustang and my youthful affections. I consider it a proof of the superiority of masculine friendship that neither the subsequent desertion of the mustang nor that of the young lady ever made the slightest difference to Enriquez or me in our exalted amity. To a wondering doubt as to what I ever could possibly have seen in his sister to admire he joined a tolerant skepticism of the whole sex. This he was wont to express in that marvelous combination of Spanish precision and California slang for which he was justly famous. "As to thees women and their little game," he would say, "believe me, my friend, your old Oncle 'Enry is not in it. No; he will ever take a back seat when lofe is around. For why? Regard me here! If she is a horse, you shall say, 'She will buck-jump,' 'She will ess-shy,' 'She will not arrive,' or 'She will arrive too quick.' But if it is thees women, where are you? For when you shall say, 'She will ess-shy,' look you, she will walk straight; or she will remain tranquil when you think she buck-jump; or else she will arrive and, look you, you will not. You shall get left. It is ever so. My father and the brother of my father have both make court to my mother when she was but a senorita. My father think she have lofe his brother more. So he say to her: 'It is enofe; tranquillize yourself. I will go. I will efface myself. Adios! Shake hands! Ta-ta! So long! See you again in the fall.' And what make my mother? Regard me! She marry my father—on the instant! Of thees women, believe me, Pancho, you shall know nothing. Not even if they shall make you the son of your father or his nephew."

I have recalled this characteristic speech to show the general tendency of Enriquez' convictions at the opening of this little story. It is only fair to say, however, that his usual attitude toward the sex he so cheerfully maligned exhibited little apprehension or caution in dealing with them. Among the frivolous and light-minded intermixture of his race he moved with great freedom and popularity. He danced well; when we went to fandangos together his agility and the audacity of his figures always procured him the prettiest partners, his professed sentiments, I presume, shielding him from subsequent jealousies, heartburnings, or envy. I have a vivid recollection of him in the mysteries of the SEMICUACUA, a somewhat corybantic dance which left much to the invention of the performers, and very little to the imagination of the spectator. In one of the figures a gaudy handkerchief, waved more or less gracefully by dancer and danseuse before the dazzled eyes of each other, acted as love's signal, and was used to express alternate admiration and indifference, shyness and audacity, fear and transport, coyness and coquetry, as the dance proceeded. I need not say that Enriquez' pantomimic illustration of these emotions was peculiarly extravagant; but it was always performed and accepted with a gravity that was an essential feature of the dance. At such times sighs would escape him which were supposed to portray the incipient stages of passion; snorts of jealousy burst from him at the suggestion of a rival; he was overtaken by a sort of St. Vitus's dance that expressed his timidity in making the first advances of affection; the scorn of his ladylove struck him with something like a dumb ague; and a single gesture of invitation from her produced marked delirium. All this was very like Enriquez; but on the particular occasion to which I refer, I think no one was prepared to see him begin the figure with the waving of FOUR handkerchiefs! Yet this he did, pirouetting, capering, brandishing his silken signals like a ballerina's scarf in the languishment or fire of passion, until, in a final figure, where the conquered and submitting fair one usually sinks into the arms of her partner, need it be said that the ingenious Enriquez was found in the center of the floor supporting four of the dancers! Yet he was by no means unduly excited either by the plaudits of the crowd or by his evident success with the fair. "Ah, believe me, it is nothing," he said quietly, rolling a fresh cigarette as he leaned against the doorway. "Possibly, I shall have to offer the chocolate or the wine to thees girls, or make to them a promenade in the moonlight on the veranda. It is ever so. Unless, my friend," he said, suddenly turning toward me in an excess of chivalrous self-abnegation, "unless you shall yourself take my place. Behold, I gif them to you! I vamos! I vanish! I make track! I skedaddle!" I think he would have carried his extravagance to the point of summoning his four gypsy witches of partners, and committing them to my care, if the crowd had not at that moment parted before the remaining dancers, and left one of the onlookers, a tall, slender girl, calmly surveying them through gold-rimmed eyeglasses in complete critical absorption. I stared in amazement and consternation; for I recognized in the fair stranger Miss Urania Mannersley, the Congregational minister's niece!

Everybody knew Rainie Mannersley throughout the length and breadth of the Encinal. She was at once the envy and the goad of the daughters of those Southwestern and Eastern immigrants who had settled in the valley. She was correct, she was critical, she was faultless and observant. She was proper, yet independent; she was highly educated; she was suspected of knowing Latin and Greek; she even spelled correctly! She could wither the plainest field nosegay in the hands of other girls by giving the flowers their botanical names. She never said "Ain't you?" but "Aren't you?" She looked upon "Did I which?" as an incomplete and imperfect form of "What did I do?" She quoted from Browning and Tennyson, and was believed to have read them. She was from Boston. What could she possibly be doing at a free-and-easy fandango?

Even if these facts were not already familiar to everyone there, her outward appearance would have attracted attention. Contrasted with the gorgeous red, black, and yellow skirts of the dancers, her plain, tightly fitting gown and hat, all of one delicate gray, were sufficiently notable in themselves, even had they not seemed, like the girl herself, a kind of quiet protest to the glaring flounces before her. Her small, straight waist and flat back brought into greater relief the corsetless, waistless, swaying figures of the Mexican girls, and her long, slim, well-booted feet, peeping from the stiff, white edges of her short skirt, made their broad, low-quartered slippers, held on by the big toe, appear more preposterous than ever. Suddenly she seemed to realize that she was standing there alone, but without fear or embarrassment. She drew back a little, glancing carelessly behind her as if missing some previous companion, and then her eyes fell upon mine. She smiled an easy recognition; then a moment later, her glance rested more curiously upon

Enriquez, who was still by my side. I disengaged myself and instantly joined her, particularly as I noticed that a few of the other bystanders were beginning to stare at her with little reserve.

"Isn't it the most extraordinary thing you ever saw?" she said quietly. Then, presently noticing the look of embarrassment on my face, she went on, more by way of conversation than of explanation:

"I just left uncle making a call on a parishioner next door, and was going home with Jocasta (a peon servant of her uncle's), when I heard the music, and dropped in. I don't know what has become of her," she added, glancing round the room again; "she seemed perfectly wild when she saw that creature over there bounding about with his handkerchiefs. You were speaking to him just now. Do tell me—is he real?"

"I should think there was little doubt of that," I said with a vague laugh.

"You know what I mean," she said simply. "Is he quite sane? Does he do that because he likes it, or is he paid for it?"

This was too much. I pointed out somewhat hurriedly that he was a scion of one of the oldest Castilian families, that the performance was a national gypsy dance which he had joined in as a patriot and a patron, and that he was my dearest friend. At the same time I was conscious that I wished she hadn't seen his last performance.

"You don't mean to say that all that he did was in the dance?" she said. "I don't believe it. It was only like him." As I hesitated over this palpable truth, she went on: "I do wish he'd do it again. Don't you think you could make him?"

"Perhaps he might if YOU asked him," I said a little maliciously.

"Of course I shouldn't do that," she returned quietly. "All the same, I do believe he is really going to do it—or something else. Do look!"

I looked, and to my horror saw that Enriquez, possibly incited by the delicate gold eyeglasses of Miss Mannersley, had divested himself of his coat, and was winding the four handkerchiefs, tied together, picturesquely around his waist, preparatory to some new performance. I tried furtively to give him a warning look, but in vain.

"Isn't he really too absurd for anything?" said Miss Mannersley, yet with a certain comfortable anticipation in her voice. "You know, I never saw anything like this before. I wouldn't have believed such a creature could have existed."

Even had I succeeded in warning him, I doubt if it would have been of any avail. For, seizing a guitar from one of the musicians, he struck a few chords, and suddenly began to zigzag into the center of the floor, swaying his body languishingly from side to side in time with the music and the pitch of a thin Spanish tenor. It was a gypsy love song. Possibly Miss Mannersley's lingual accomplishments did not include a knowledge of Castilian, but she could not fail to see that the gestures and illustrative pantomime were addressed to her. Passionately assuring her that she was the most favored daughter of the Virgin, that her eyes were like votive tapers, and yet in the same breath accusing her of being a "brigand" and "assassin" in her attitude toward "his heart," he balanced with quivering timidity toward her, threw an imaginary cloak in front of her neat boots as a carpet for her to tread on, and with a final astonishing pirouette and a languishing twang of his guitar, sank on one knee, and blew, with a rose, a kiss at her feet.

If I had been seriously angry with him before for his grotesque extravagance, I could have pitied him now for the young girl's absolute unconsciousness of anything but his utter ludicrousness. The applause of dancers and bystanders was instantaneous and hearty; her only contribution to it was a slight parting of her thin red lips in a half-incredulous smile. In the silence that followed the applause, as Enriquez walked pantingly away, I heard her saying, half to herself, "Certainly a most extraordinary creature!" In my indignation I could not help turning suddenly upon her and looking straight into her eyes. They were brown, with that peculiar velvet opacity common to the pupils of nearsighted persons, and seemed to defy internal scrutiny. She only repeated carelessly, "Isn't he?" and added: "Please see if you can find Jocasta. I suppose we ought to be going now; and I dare say he won't be doing it again. Ah! there she is. Good gracious, child! what have you got there?"

It was Enriquez' rose which Jocasta had picked up, and was timidly holding out toward her mistress.

"Heavens! I don't want it. Keep it yourself."

I walked with them to the door, as I did not fancy a certain glitter in the black eyes of the Senoritas Manuela and Pepita, who were watching her curiously. But I think she was as oblivious of this as she was of Enriquez' particular attentions. As we reached the street I felt that I ought to say something more.

"You know," I began casually, "that although those poor people meet here in this public way, their gathering is really quite a homely pastoral and a national custom; and these girls are all honest, hardworking peons or servants enjoying themselves in quite the old idyllic fashion."

"Certainly," said the young girl, half-abstractedly. "Of course it's a Moorish dance, originally brought over, I suppose, by those old Andalusian immigrants two hundred years ago. It's quite Arabic in its suggestions. I have got something like it in an old CANCIONERO I picked up at a bookstall in Boston. But," she added, with a gasp of reminiscent satisfaction, "that's not like HIM! Oh, no! HE is decidedly original. Heavens! yes."

I turned away in some discomfiture to join Enriquez, who was calmly awaiting me, with a cigarette in his mouth, outside the sala. Yet he looked so unconscious of any previous absurdity that I hesitated in what I thought was a necessary warning. He, however, quickly precipitated it. Glancing after the retreating figures of the two women, he said: "Thees mees from Boston is return to her house. You do not accompany her? I shall. Behold me—I am there." But I linked my arm firmly in his. Then I pointed out, first, that she was already accompanied by a servant; secondly, that if I, who knew her, had hesitated to offer myself as an escort, it was hardly proper for him, a perfect stranger, to take that liberty; that Miss Mannersley was very punctilious of etiquette, which he, as a Castilian gentleman, ought to appreciate.

"But will she not regard lofe—the admiration excessif?" he said, twirling his thin little mustache meditatively.

"No; she will not," I returned sharply; "and you ought to understand that she is on a different level from your Manuelas and Carmens."

"Pardon, my friend," he said gravely; "thees women are ever the same. There is a proverb in my language. Listen: 'Whether the sharp blade of the Toledo pierce the satin or the goatskin, it shall find behind it ever the same heart to wound.' I am that Toledo blade—possibly it is you, my friend. Wherefore, let us together pursue this girl of Boston on the instant."

But I kept my grasp on Enriquez' arm, and succeeded in restraining his mercurial impulses for the moment. He halted, and puffed vigorously at his cigarette; but the next instant he started forward again. "Let us, however, follow with discretion in the rear; we shall pass her house; we shall gaze at it; it shall touch her heart."

Ridiculous as was this following of the young girl we had only just parted from, I nevertheless knew that Enriquez was quite capable of attempting it alone, and I thought it better to humor him by consenting to walk with him in that direction; but I felt it necessary to say:

"I ought to warn you that Miss Mannersley already looks upon your performances at the sala as something outre and peculiar, and if I were you I shouldn't do anything to deepen that impression."

"You are saying she ees shock?" said Enriquez, gravely.

I felt I could not conscientiously say that she was shocked, and he saw my hesitation. "Then she have jealousy of the senoritas," he observed, with insufferable complacency. "You observe! I have already said. It is ever so."

I could stand it no longer. "Look here, Harry," I said, "if you must know it, she looks upon you as an acrobat—a paid performer."

"Ah!"—his black eyes sparkled—"the torero, the man who fights the bull, he is also an acrobat."

"Yes; but she thinks you a clown!—a GRACIOSO DE TEATRO—there!"

"Then I have make her laugh?" he said coolly.

I don't think he had; but I shrugged my shoulders.

"BUENO!" he said cheerfully. "Lofe, he begin with a laugh, he make feenish with a sigh."

I turned to look at him in the moonlight. His face presented its habitual Spanish gravity—a gravity that was almost ironical. His small black eyes had their characteristic irresponsible audacity—the irresponsibility of the vivacious young animal. It could not be possible that he was really touched with the placid frigidities of Miss Mannersley. I remembered his equally elastic gallantries with Miss Pinkey Smith, a blonde Western belle, from which both had harmlessly rebounded. As we walked on slowly I continued more persuasively: "Of course this is only your nonsense; but don't you see, Miss Mannersley thinks it all in earnest and really your nature?" I hesitated, for it suddenly struck me that it WAS really his nature. "And—hang it all!—you don't want her to believe you a common buffoon., or some intoxicated muchacho."

"Intoxicated?" repeated Enriquez, with exasperating languishment. "Yes; that is the word that shall express itself. My friend, you have made a shot in the center—you have ring the bell every time! It is intoxication—but not of aguardiente. Look! I have long time an ancestor of whom is a pretty story. One day in church he have seen a young girl—a mere peasant girl—pass to the confessional. He look her in her eye, he stagger"—here Enriquez wobbled pantomimically into the road—"he fall!"—he would have suited the action to the word if I had not firmly held him up. "They have taken him home, where he have remain without his clothes, and have dance and sing. But it was the drunkenness of lofe. And, look you, thees village girl was a nothing, not even pretty. The name of my ancestor was—"

"Don Quixote de La Mancha," I suggested maliciously. "I suspected as much. Come along. That will do."

"My ancestor's name," continued Enriquez, gravely, "was Antonio Hermenegildo de Salvatierra, which is not the same. Thees Don Quixote of whom you speak exist not at all."

"Never mind. Only, for heaven's sake, as we are nearing the house, don't make a fool of yourself again."

It was a wonderful moonlight night. The deep redwood porch of the Mannersley parsonage, under the shadow of a great oak—the largest in the Encinal—was diapered in black and silver. As the women stepped upon the porch their shadows were silhouetted against the door. Miss Mannersley paused for an instant, and turned to give a last look at the beauty of the night as Jocasta entered. Her glance fell upon us as we passed. She nodded carelessly and unaffectedly to me, but as she recognized Enriquez she looked a little longer at him with her previous cold and invincible curiosity. To my horror Enriquez began instantly to affect a slight tremulousness of gait and a difficulty of breathing; but I gripped his arm savagely, and managed to get him past the house as the door closed finally on the young lady.

"You do not comprehend, friend Pancho," he said gravely, "but those eyes in their glass are as the ESPEJO USTORIO, the burning mirror. They burn, they consume me here like paper. Let us affix to ourselves thees tree. She will, without doubt, appear at her window. We shall salute her for good night."

"We will do nothing of the kind," I said sharply. Finding that I was determined, he permitted me to lead him away. I was delighted to notice, however, that he had indicated the window which I knew was the minister's study, and that as the bedrooms were in the rear of the house, this later incident was probably not overseen by the young lady or the servant. But I did not part from Enriquez until I saw him safely back to the sala, where I left him sipping chocolate, his arm alternating around the waists of his two previous partners in a delightful Arcadian and childlike simplicity, and an apparent utter forgetfulness of Miss Mannersley.

The fandangos were usually held on Saturday night, and the next day, being Sunday, I missed Enriquez; but as he was a devout Catholic I remembered that he was at mass in the morning, and possibly at the bullfight at San Antonio in the afternoon. But I was somewhat surprised on the Monday morning following, as I was crossing the plaza, to have my arm taken by the Rev. Mr. Mannersley in the nearest approach to familiarity that was consistent with the reserve of this eminent divine. I looked at him inquiringly. Although scrupulously correct in attire, his features always had a singular resemblance to the national caricature known as "Uncle Sam," but with the humorous expression left out. Softly stroking his goatee with three fingers, he began condescendingly: "You are, I think, more or less familiar with the characteristics and customs of the Spanish as exhibited by the settlers here." A thrill of apprehension went through me. Had he heard of Enriquez' proceedings? Had Miss Mannersley cruelly betrayed him to her uncle? "I have not given that attention myself to their language and social peculiarities," he continued, with a large wave of the hand, "being much occupied with a study of their religious beliefs and superstitions"—it struck me that this was apt to be a common fault of people of the Mannersley type—"but I have refrained from a personal discussion of them; on the contrary, I have held somewhat broad views on the subject of their remarkable missionary work, and have suggested a scheme of co-operation with them, quite independent of doctrinal teaching, to my brethren of other Protestant Christian sects. These views I first incorporated in a sermon last Sunday week, which I am told has created considerable attention." He stopped and coughed slightly. "I have not yet heard from any of the Roman clergy, but I am led to believe that my remarks were not ungrateful to Catholics generally."

I was relieved, although still in some wonder why he should address me on this topic. I had a vague remembrance of having heard that he had said something on Sunday which had offended some Puritans of his flock, but nothing more. He continued: "I have just said that I was unacquainted with the characteristics of the Spanish-American race. I presume, however, they have the impulsiveness of their Latin origin. They gesticulate—eh? They express their gratitude, their joy, their affection, their emotions generally, by spasmodic movements? They naturally dance—sing—eh?" A horrible suspicion crossed my mind; I could only stare helplessly at him. "I see," he said graciously; "perhaps it is a somewhat general question. I will explain myself. A rather singular occurrence happened to me the other night. I had returned from visiting a parishioner, and was alone in my study reviewing my sermon for the next day. It must have been quite late before I concluded, for I distinctly remember my niece had returned with her servant fully an hour before. Presently I heard the sounds of a musical instrument in the road, with the accents of someone singing or rehearsing some metrical composition in words that, although couched in a language foreign to me, in expression and modulation gave me the impression of being distinctly adulatory. For some little time, in the greater preoccupation of my task, I paid little attention to the performance; but its persistency at length drew me in no mere idle curiosity to the window. From thence, standing in my dressing-gown, and believing myself unperceived, I noticed under the large oak in the roadside the figure of a young man who, by the imperfect light, appeared to be of Spanish extraction. But I evidently miscalculated my own invisibility; for he moved rapidly forward as I came to the window, and in a series of the most extraordinary pantomimic gestures saluted me. Beyond my experience of a few Greek plays in earlier days, I confess I am not an adept in the understanding of gesticulation; but it struck me that the various phases of gratitude, fervor, reverence, and exaltation were successively portrayed. He placed his hands upon his head, his heart, and even clasped them together in this manner." To my consternation the reverend gentleman here imitated Enriquez' most extravagant pantomime. "I am willing to confess," he continued, "that I was singularly moved by them, as well as by the highly creditable and Christian interest that evidently produced them. At last I opened the window. Leaning out, I told him that I regretted that the lateness of the hour prevented any further response from me than a grateful though hurried acknowledgment of his praiseworthy emotion, but that I should be glad to see him for a few moments in the vestry before service the next day, or at early candlelight, before the meeting of the Bible class. I told him that as my sole purpose had been the creation of an evangelical brotherhood and the exclusion of merely doctrinal views, nothing could be more gratifying to me than his spontaneous and unsolicited testimony to my motives. He appeared for an instant to be deeply affected, and, indeed, quite overcome with emotion, and then gracefully retired, with some agility and a slight saltatory movement."

He paused. A sudden and overwhelming idea took possession of me, and I looked impulsively into his face. Was it possible that for once Enriquez' ironical extravagance had been understood, met, and vanquished by a master hand? But the Rev. Mr. Mannersley's self-satisfied face betrayed no ambiguity or lurking humor. He was evidently in earnest; he had complacently accepted for himself the abandoned Enriquez' serenade to his niece. I felt a hysterical desire to laugh, but it was checked by my companion's next words.

"I informed my niece of the occurrence in the morning at breakfast. She had not heard anything of the strange performance, but she agreed with me as to its undoubted origin in a grateful recognition of my liberal efforts toward his coreligionists. It was she, in fact, who suggested that your knowledge of these people might corroborate my impressions."

I was dumfounded. Had Miss Mannersley, who must have recognized Enriquez' hand in this, concealed the fact in a desire to shield him? But this was so inconsistent with her utter indifference to him, except as a grotesque study, that she would have been more likely to tell her uncle all about his previous performance. Nor could it be that she wished to conceal her visit to the fandango. She was far too independent for that, and it was even possible that the reverend gentleman, in his desire to know more of Enriquez' compatriots, would not have objected. In my confusion I meekly added my conviction to hers, congratulated him upon his evident success, and slipped away. But I was burning with a desire to see Enriquez and know all. He was imaginative but not untruthful. Unfortunately, I learned that he was just then following one of his erratic impulses, and had gone to a rodeo at his cousin's, in the foothills, where he was alternately exercising his horsemanship in catching and breaking wild cattle and delighting his relatives with his incomparable grasp of the American language and customs, and of the airs of a young man of fashion. Then my thoughts recurred to Miss Mannersley. Had she really been oblivious that night to Enriquez' serenade? I resolved to find out, if I could, without betraying Enriquez. Indeed, it was possible, after all, that it might not have been he.

Chance favored me. The next evening I was at a party where Miss Mannersley, by reason of her position and quality, was a distinguished—I had almost written a popular—guest. But, as I have formerly stated, although the youthful fair of the Encinal were flattered by her casual attentions, and secretly admired her superior style and aristocratic calm, they were more or less uneasy under the dominance of her intelligence and education, and were afraid to attempt either confidence or familiarity. They were also singularly jealous of her, for although the average young man was equally afraid of her cleverness and her candor, he was not above paying a tremulous and timid court to her for its effect upon her humbler sisters. This evening she was surrounded by her usual satellites, including, of course, the local notables and special guests of distinction. She had been discussing, I think, the existence of glaciers on Mount Shasta with a spectacled geologist, and had participated with charming frankness in a conversation on anatomy with the local doctor and a learned professor, when she was asked to take a seat at the piano. She played with remarkable skill and wonderful precision, but coldly and brilliantly. As she sat there in her subdued but perfectly fitting evening dress, her regular profile and short but slender neck firmly set upon her high shoulders, exhaling an atmosphere of refined puritanism and provocative intelligence, the utter incongruity of Enriquez' extravagant attentions if ironical, and their equal hopelessness if not, seemed to me plainer than ever. What had this well-poised, coldly observant spinster to do with that quaintly ironic ruffler, that romantic cynic, that rowdy Don Quixote, that impossible Enriquez? Presently she ceased playing. Her slim, narrow slipper, revealing her thin ankle, remained upon the pedal; her delicate fingers were resting idly on the keys; her head was slightly thrown back, and her narrow eyebrows prettily knit toward the ceiling in an effort of memory.

"Something of Chopin's," suggested the geologist, ardently.

"That exquisite sonata!" pleaded the doctor.

"Suthin' of Rubinstein. Heard him once," said a gentleman of Siskiyou. "He just made that pianner get up and howl. Play Rube."

She shook her head with parted lips and a slight touch of girlish coquetry in her manner. Then her fingers suddenly dropped upon the keys with a glassy tinkle; there were a few quick pizzicato chords, down went the low pedal with a monotonous strumming, and she presently began to hum to herself. I started—as well I might—for I recognized one of Enriquez' favorite and most extravagant guitar solos. It was audacious; it was barbaric; it was, I fear, vulgar. As I remembered it—as he sang it—it recounted the adventures of one Don Francisco, a provincial gallant and roisterer of the most objectionable type. It had one hundred and four verses, which Enriquez never spared me. I shuddered as in a pleasant, quiet voice the correct Miss Mannersley warbled in musical praise of the PELLEJO, or wineskin, and a eulogy of the dicebox came caressingly from her thin red lips. But the company was far differently affected: the strange, wild air and wilder accompaniment were evidently catching; people moved toward the piano; somebody whistled the air from a distant corner; even the faces of the geologist and doctor brightened.

"A tarantella, I presume?" blandly suggested the doctor.

Miss Mannersley stopped, and rose carelessly from the piano. "It is a Moorish gypsy song of the fifteenth century," she said dryly.

"It seemed sorter familiar, too," hesitated one of the young men, timidly, "like as if—don't you know?—you had without knowing it, don't you know?"—he blushed slightly—"sorter picked it up somewhere."

"I 'picked it up,' as you call it, in the collection of medieval manuscripts of the Harvard Library, and copied it," returned Miss Mannersley coldly as she turned away.

But I was not inclined to let her off so easily. I presently made my way to her side. "Your uncle was complimentary enough to consult me as to the meaning of the appearance of a certain exuberant Spanish visitor at his house the other night." I looked into her brown eyes, but my own slipped off her velvety pupils without retaining anything. Then she reinforced her gaze with a pince-nez, and said carelessly:

"Oh, it's you? How are you? Well, could you give him any information?"

"Only generally," I returned, still looking into her eyes. "These people are impulsive. The Spanish blood is a mixture of gold and quicksilver."

She smiled slightly. "That reminds me of your volatile friend. He was mercurial enough, certainly. Is he still dancing?"

"And singing sometimes," I responded pointedly. But she only added casually, "A singular creature," without exhibiting the least consciousness, and drifted away, leaving me none the wiser. I felt that Enriquez alone could enlighten me. I must see him.

I did, but not in the way I expected. There was a bullfight at San Antonio the next Saturday afternoon, the usual Sunday performance being changed in deference to the Sabbatical habits of the Americans. An additional attraction was offered in the shape of a bull-and-bear fight, also a concession to American taste, which had voted the bullfight "slow," and had averred that the bull "did not get a fair show." I am glad that I am able to spare the reader the usual realistic horrors, for in the Californian performances there was very little of the brutality that distinguished this function in the mother country. The horses were not miserable, worn-out hacks, but young and alert mustangs; and the display of horsemanship by the picadors was not only wonderful, but secured an almost absolute safety to horse and rider. I never saw a horse gored; although unskillful riders were sometimes thrown in wheeling quickly to avoid the bull's charge, they generally regained their animals without injury.

The Plaza de Toros was reached through the decayed and tile-strewn outskirts of an old Spanish village. It was a rudely built oval amphitheater, with crumbling, whitewashed adobe walls, and roofed only over portions of the gallery reserved for the provincial "notables," but now occupied by a few shopkeepers and their wives, with a sprinkling of American travelers and ranchmen. The impalpable adobe dust of the arena was being whirled into the air by the strong onset of the afternoon trade winds, which happily, however, helped also to dissipate a reek of garlic, and the acrid fumes of cheap tobacco rolled in cornhusk cigarettes. I was leaning over the second barrier, waiting for the meager and circuslike procession to enter with the keys of the bull pen, when my attention was attracted to a movement in the reserved gallery. A lady and gentleman of a quality that was evidently unfamiliar to the rest of the audience were picking their way along the rickety benches to a front seat. I recognized the geologist with some surprise, and the lady he was leading with still greater astonishment. For it was Miss Mannersley, in her precise, well-fitting walking-costume—a monotone of sober color among the parti-colored audience.

However, I was perhaps less surprised than the audience, for I was not only becoming as accustomed to the young girl's vagaries as I had been to Enriquez' extravagance, but I was also satisfied that her uncle might have given her permission to come, as a recognition of the Sunday concession of the management, as well as to conciliate his supposed Catholic friends. I watched her sitting there until the first bull had entered, and, after a rather brief play with the picadors and banderilleros, was dispatched. At the moment when the matador approached the bull with his lethal weapon I was not sorry for an excuse to glance at Miss Mannersley. Her hands were in her lap, her head slightly bent forward over her knees. I fancied that she, too, had dropped her eyes before the brutal situation; to my horror, I saw that she had a drawing-book in her hand and was actually sketching it. I turned my eyes in preference to the dying bull.

The second animal led out for this ingenious slaughter was, however, more sullen, uncertain, and discomposing to his butchers. He accepted the irony of a trial with gloomy, suspicious eyes, and he declined the challenge of whirling and insulting picadors. He bristled with banderillas like a hedgehog, but remained with his haunches backed against the barrier, at times almost hidden in the fine dust raised by the monotonous stroke of his sullenly pawing hoof—his one dull, heavy protest. A vague uneasiness had infected his adversaries; the picadors held aloof, the banderilleros skirmished at a safe distance. The audience resented only the indecision of the bull. Galling epithets were flung at him, followed by cries of "ESPADA!" and, curving his elbow under his short cloak, the matador, with his flashing blade in hand, advanced and—stopped. The bull remained motionless.

For at that moment a heavier gust of wind than usual swept down upon the arena, lifted a suffocating cloud of dust, and whirled it around the tiers of benches and the balcony, and for a moment seemed to stop the performance. I heard an exclamation from the geologist, who had risen to his feet. I fancied I heard even a faint cry from Miss Mannersley; but the next moment, as the dust was slowly settling, we saw a sheet of paper in the air, that had been caught up in this brief cyclone, dropping, dipping from side to side on uncertain wings, until it slowly descended in the very middle of the arena. It was a leaf from Miss Mannersley's sketchbook, the one on which she had been sketching.

In the pause that followed it seemed to be the one object that at last excited the bull's growing but tardy ire. He glanced at it with murky, distended eyes; he snorted at it with vague yet troubled fury. Whether he detected his own presentment in Miss Mannersley's sketch, or whether he recognized it as an unknown and unfamiliar treachery in his surroundings, I could not conjecture; for the next moment the matador, taking advantage of the bull's concentration, with a complacent leer at the audience, advanced toward the paper. But at that instant a young man cleared the barrier into the arena with a single bound, shoved the matador to one side, caught up the paper, turned toward the balcony and Miss Mannersley with a gesture of apology, dropped gaily before the bull, knelt down before him with an exaggerated humility, and held up the drawing as if for his inspection. A roar of applause broke from the audience, a cry of warning and exasperation from the attendants, as the goaded bull suddenly charged the stranger. But he sprang to one side with great dexterity, made a courteous gesture to the matador as if passing the bull over to him, and still holding the paper in his hand, re-leaped the barrier, and rejoined the audience in safety. I did not wait to see the deadly, dominant thrust with which the matador received the charging bull; my eyes were following the figure now bounding up the steps to the balcony, where with an exaggerated salutation he laid the drawing in Miss Mannersley's lap and vanished. There was no mistaking that thin lithe form, the narrow black mustache, and gravely dancing eyes. The audacity of conception, the extravagance of execution, the quaint irony of the sequel, could belong to no one but Enriquez.

I hurried up to her as the six yoked mules dragged the carcass of the bull away. She was placidly putting up her book, the unmoved focus of a hundred eager and curious eyes. She smiled slightly as she saw me. "I was just telling Mr. Briggs what an extraordinary creature it was, and how you knew him. He must have had great experience to do that sort of thing so cleverly and safely. Does he do it often? Of course, not just that. But does he pick up cigars and things that I see they throw to the matador? Does he belong to the management? Mr. Briggs thinks the whole thing was a feint to distract the bull," she added, with a wicked glance at the geologist, who, I fancied, looked disturbed.

"I am afraid," I said dryly, "that his act was as unpremeditated and genuine as it was unusual."

"Why afraid?"

It was a matter-of-fact question, but I instantly saw my mistake. What right had I to assume that Enriquez' attentions were any more genuine than her own easy indifference; and if I suspected that they were, was it fair in me to give my friend away to this heartless coquette? "You are not very gallant," she said, with a slight laugh, as I was hesitating, and turned away with her escort before I could frame a reply. But at least Enriquez was now accessible, and I should gain some information from him. I knew where to find him, unless he were still lounging about the building, intent upon more extravagance; but I waited until I saw Miss Mannersley and Briggs depart without further interruption.

The hacienda of Ramon Saltillo, Enriquez' cousin, was on the outskirts of the village. When I arrived there I found Enriquez' pinto mustang steaming in the corral, and although I was momentarily delayed by the servants at the gateway, I was surprised to find Enriquez himself lying languidly on his back in a hammock in the patio. His arms were hanging down listlessly on each side as if in the greatest prostration, yet I could not resist the impression that the rascal had only just got into the hammock when he heard of my arrival.

"You have arrived, friend Pancho, in time," he said, in accents of exaggerated weakness. "I am absolutely exhaust. I am bursted, caved in, kerflummoxed. I have behold you, my friend, at the barrier. I speak not, I make no sign at the first, because I was on fire; I speak not at the feenish—for I am exhaust."

"I see; the bull made it lively for you."

He instantly bounded up in the hammock. "The bull! Caramba! Not a thousand bulls! And thees one, look you, was a craven. I snap my fingers over his horn; I roll my cigarette under his nose."

"Well, then—what was it?"

He instantly lay down again, pulling up the sides of the hammock. Presently his voice came from its depths, appealing in hollow tones to the sky. "He asks me—thees friend of my soul, thees brother of my life, thees Pancho that I lofe—what it was? He would that I should tell him why I am game in the legs, why I shake in the hand, crack in the voice, and am generally wipe out! And yet he, my pardner—thees Francisco—know that I have seen the mees from Boston! That I have gaze into the eye, touch the hand, and for the instant possess the picture that hand have drawn! It was a sublime picture, Pancho," he said, sitting up again suddenly, "and have kill the bull before our friend Pepe's sword have touch even the bone of hees back and make feenish of him."

"Look here, Enriquez," I said bluntly, "have you been serenading that girl?"

He shrugged his shoulders without the least embarrassment, and said: "Ah, yes. What would you? It is of a necessity."

"Well," I retorted, "then you ought to know that her uncle took it all to himself—thought you some grateful Catholic pleased with his religious tolerance."

He did not even smile. "BUENO," he said gravely. "That make something, too. In thees affair it is well to begin with the duenna. He is the duenna."

"And," I went on relentlessly, "her escort told her just now that your exploit in the bull ring was only a trick to divert the bull, suggested by the management."

"Bah! her escort is a geologian. Naturally, she is to him as a stone."

I would have continued, but a peon interrupted us at this moment with a sign to Enriquez, who leaped briskly from the hammock, bidding me wait his return from a messenger in the gateway.

Still unsatisfied of mind, I waited, and sat down in the hammock that Enriquez had quitted. A scrap of paper was lying in its meshes, which at first appeared to be of the kind from which Enriquez rolled his cigarettes; but as I picked it up to throw it away, I found it was of much firmer and stouter material. Looking at it more closely, I was surprised to recognize it as a piece of the tinted drawing-paper torn off the "block" that Miss Mannersley had used. It had been deeply creased at right angles as if it had been folded; it looked as if it might have been the outer half of a sheet used for a note.

It might have been a trifling circumstance, but it greatly excited my curiosity. I knew that he had returned the sketch to Miss Mannersley, for I had seen it in her hand. Had she given him another? And if so, why had it been folded to the destruction of the drawing? Or was it part of a note which he had destroyed? In the first impulse of discovery I walked quickly with it toward the gateway where Enriquez had disappeared, intending to restore it to him. He was just outside talking with a young girl. I started, for it was Jocasta—Miss Mannersley's maid.

With this added discovery came that sense of uneasiness and indignation with which we illogically are apt to resent the withholding of a friend's confidence, even in matters concerning only himself. It was no use for me to reason that it was no business of mine, that he was right in keeping a secret that concerned another—and a lady; but I was afraid I was even more meanly resentful because the discovery quite upset my theory of his conduct and of Miss Mannersley's attitude toward him. I continued to walk on to the gateway, where I bade Enriquez a hurried good-by, alleging the sudden remembrance of another engagement, but without appearing to recognize the girl, who was moving away when, to my further discomfiture, the rascal stopped me with an appealing wink, threw his arms around my neck, whispered hoarsely in my ear, "Ah! you see—you comprehend—but you are the mirror of discretion!" and returned to Jocasta. But whether this meant that he had received a message from Miss Mannersley, or that he was trying to suborn her maid to carry one, was still uncertain. He was capable of either. During the next two or three weeks I saw him frequently; but as I had resolved to try the effect of ignoring Miss Mannersley in our conversation, I gathered little further of their relations, and, to my surprise, after one or two characteristic extravagances of allusion, Enriquez dropped the subject, too. Only one afternoon, as we were parting, he said carelessly: "My friend, you are going to the casa of Mannersley tonight. I too have the honor of the invitation. But you will be my Mercury—my Leporello—you will take of me a message to thees Mees Boston, that I am crushed, desolated, prostrate, and flabbergasted—that I cannot arrive, for I have of that night to sit up with the grand-aunt of my brother-in-law, who has a quinsy to the death. It is sad."

This was the first indication I had received of Miss Mannersley's advances. I was equally surprised at Enriquez' refusal.

"Nonsense!" I said bluntly. "Nothing keeps you from going."

"My friend," returned Enriquez, with a sudden lapse into languishment that seemed to make him absolutely infirm, "it is everything that shall restrain me. I am not strong. I shall become weak of the knee and tremble under the eye of Mees Boston. I shall precipitate myself to the geologian by the throat. Ask me another conundrum that shall be easy."

He seemed idiotically inflexible, and did not go. But I did. I found Miss Mannersley exquisitely dressed and looking singularly animated and pretty. The lambent glow of her inscrutable eye as she turned toward me might have been flattering but for my uneasiness in regard to Enriquez. I delivered his excuses as naturally as I could. She stiffened for an instant, and seemed an inch higher. "I am so sorry," she said at last in a level voice. "I thought he would have been so amusing. Indeed, I had hoped we might try an old Moorish dance together which I have found and was practicing."

"He would have been delighted, I know. It's a great pity he didn't come with me," I said quickly; "but," I could not help adding, with emphasis on her words, "he is such an 'extraordinary creature,' you know."

"I see nothing extraordinary in his devotion to an aged relative," returned Miss Mannersley quietly as she turned away, "except that it justifies my respect for his character."

I do not know why I did not relate this to him. Possibly I had given up trying to understand them; perhaps I was beginning to have an idea that he could take care of himself. But I was somewhat surprised a few days later when, after asking me to go with him to a rodeo at his uncle's he added composedly, "You will meet Mees Boston."

I stared, and but for his manner would have thought it part of his extravagance. For the rodeo—a yearly chase of wild cattle for the purpose of lassoing and branding them—was a rather brutal affair, and purely a man's function; it was also a family affair—a property stock-taking of the great Spanish cattle-owners—and strangers, particularly Americans, found it difficult to gain access to its mysteries and the fiesta that followed.

"But how did she get an invitation?" I asked. "You did not dare to ask—" I began.

"My friend," said Enriquez, with a singular deliberation, "the great and respectable Boston herself, and her serene, venerable oncle, and other Boston magnificos, have of a truth done me the inexpressible honor to solicit of my degraded, papistical oncle that she shall come—that she shall of her own superior eye behold the barbaric customs of our race."

His tone and manner were so peculiar that I stepped quickly before him, laid my hands on his shoulders, and looked down into his face. But the actual devil which I now for the first time saw in his eyes went out of them suddenly, and he relapsed again in affected languishment in his chair. "I shall be there, friend Pancho," he said, with a preposterous gasp. "I shall nerve my arm to lasso the bull, and tumble him before her at her feet. I shall throw the 'buck-jump' mustang at the same sacred spot. I shall pluck for her the buried chicken at full speed from the ground, and present it to her. You shall see it, friend Pancho. I shall be there."

He was as good as his word. When Don Pedro Amador, his uncle, installed Miss Mannersley, with Spanish courtesy, on a raised platform in the long valley where the rodeo took place, the gallant Enriquez selected a bull from the frightened and galloping herd, and, cleverly isolating him from the band, lassoed his hind legs, and threw him exactly before the platform where Miss Mannersley was seated. It was Enriquez who caught the unbroken mustang, sprang from his own saddle to the bare back of his captive, and with the lasso for a bridle, halted him on rigid haunches at Miss Mannersley's feet. It was Enriquez who, in the sports that followed, leaned from his saddle at full speed, caught up the chicken buried to its head in the sand, without wringing its neck, and tossed it unharmed and fluttering toward his mistress. As for her, she wore the same look of animation that I had seen in her face at our previous meeting. Although she did not bring her sketchbook with her, as at the bullfight, she did not shrink from the branding of the cattle, which took place under her very eyes.

Yet I had never seen her and Enriquez together; they had never, to my actual knowledge, even exchanged words. And now, although she was the guest of his uncle, his duties seemed to keep him in the field, and apart from her. Nor, as far as I could detect, did either apparently make any effort to have it otherwise. The peculiar circumstance seemed to attract no attention from anyone else. But for what I alone knew—or thought I knew—of their actual relations, I should have thought them strangers.

But I felt certain that the fiesta which took place in the broad patio of Don Pedro's casa would bring them together. And later in the evening, as we were all sitting on the veranda watching the dancing of the Mexican women, whose white-flounced sayas were monotonously rising and falling to the strains of two melancholy harps, Miss Mannersley rejoined us from the house. She seemed to be utterly absorbed and abstracted in the barbaric dances, and scarcely moved as she leaned over the railing with her cheek resting on her hand. Suddenly she arose with a little cry.

"What is it?" asked two or three.

"Nothing—only I have lost my fan." She had risen, and was looking abstractedly on the floor.

Half a dozen men jumped to their feet. "Let me fetch it," they said.

"No, thank you. I think I know where it is, and will go for it myself." She was moving away.

But Don Pedro interposed with Spanish gravity. Such a thing was not to be heard of in his casa. If the senorita would not permit HIM—an old man—to go for it, it must be brought by Enriquez, her cavalier of the day.

But Enriquez was not to be found. I glanced at Miss Mannersley's somewhat disturbed face, and begged her to let me fetch it. I thought I saw a flush of relief come into her pale cheek as she said, in a lower voice, "On the stone seat in the garden."

I hurried away, leaving Don Pedro still protesting. I knew the gardens, and the stone seat at an angle of the wall, not a dozen yards from the casa. The moon shone full upon it. There, indeed, lay the little gray-feathered fan. But beside it, also, lay the crumpled black gold-embroidered riding-gauntlet that Enriquez had worn at the rodeo.

I thrust it hurriedly into my pocket, and ran back. As I passed through the gateway I asked a peon to send Enriquez to me. The man stared. Did I not know that Don Enriquez had ridden away two minutes ago?

When I reached the veranda, I handed the fan to Miss Mannersley without a word. "BUENO," said Don Pedro, gravely; "it is as well. There shall be no bones broken over the getting of it, for Enriquez, I hear, has had to return to the Encinal this very evening."

Miss Mannersley retired early. I did not inform her of my discovery, nor did I seek in any way to penetrate her secret. There was no doubt that she and Enriquez had been together, perhaps not for the first time; but what was the result of their interview? From the young girl's demeanor and Enriquez' hurried departure, I could only fear the worst for him. Had he been tempted into some further extravagance and been angrily rebuked, or had he avowed a real passion concealed under his exaggerated mask and been deliberately rejected? I tossed uneasily half the night, following in my dreams my poor friend's hurrying hoofbeats, and ever starting from my sleep at what I thought was the sound of galloping hoofs.

I rose early, and lounged into the patio; but others were there before me, and a small group of Don Pedro's family were excitedly discussing something, and I fancied they turned away awkwardly and consciously as I approached. There was an air of indefinite uneasiness everywhere. A strange fear came over me with the chill of the early morning air. Had anything happened to Enriquez? I had always looked upon his extravagance as part of his playful humor. Could it be possible that under the sting of rejection he had made his grotesque threat of languishing effacement real? Surely Miss Mannersley would know or suspect something, if it were the case.

I approached one of the Mexican women and asked if the senorita had risen. The woman started, and looked covertly round before she replied. Did not Don Pancho know that Miss Mannersley and her maid had not slept in their beds that night, but had gone, none knew where?

For an instant I felt an appalling sense of my own responsibility in this suddenly serious situation, and hurried after the retreating family group. But as I entered the corridor a vaquero touched me on the shoulder. He had evidently just dismounted, and was covered with the dust of the road. He handed me a note written in pencil on a leaf from Miss Mannersley's sketchbook. It was in Enriquez' hand, and his signature was followed by his most extravagant rubric.

Friend Pancho: When you read this line you shall of a possibility think I am no more. That is where you shall slip up, my little brother! I am much more—I am two times as much, for I have marry Miss Boston. At the Mission Church, at five of the morning, sharp! No cards shall be left! I kiss the hand of my venerable uncle-in-law. You shall say to him that we fly to the South wilderness as the combined evangelical missionary to the heathen! Miss Boston herself say this. Ta-ta! How are you now?

Your own Enriquez.

* * * * * * * * *

Made in the USA
Coppell, TX
27 November 2019